HUNGER
IN HIS
BLOOD

<u>Warriors of Luxiria</u>

The Alien's Prize

The Alien's Mate

The Alien's Lover

The Alien's Touch

The Alien's Dream

The Alien's Obsession

The Alien's Seduction

The Alien's Claim

<u>Horde Kings of Dakkar</u>

Captive of the Horde King

Claimed by the Horde King

Madness of the Horde King

Broken by the Horde King

Taken by the Horde King

Throne of the Horde King

<u>Brides of the Kylorr</u>

Desire in His Blood

Craving in His Blood

Hunger in His Blood

<u>Hordes of the Elthika</u>

The Horde King of Shadow

<u>Standalones</u>

Rescued by the Luxirian

The Midnight Arrow

<u>Warrior of Rozun</u>

Wicked Captor

Wicked Mate

<u>The Krave of Everton</u>

Kraving Khiva

Prince of Firestones

Kraving Dravka

Kraving Tavak

HUNGER IN HIS BLOOD

ZOEY DRAVEN

HUNGER IN HIS BLOOD

An unrequited love. A broken heart. A stolen secret.

I've loved Kaldur of House Kaalium since the first moment I laid eyes on him. He's a sinfully charming, *lore*-smoking playboy with a smile that makes me see stars. As the High Lord of Vyaan, his vast power and wealth extends throughout the entirety of our nation—and he's as untouchable as he is devastatingly handsome.

Me? I'm a lowly human keeper on his grand estate. An orphan with no family. A dreamer, who lives in the adventure of my own fictional stories. I couldn't be more beneath his notice or unlike the plethora of pretty, clever socialites who warm his bed.

For two years, he has no idea I even exist…until one afternoon, a tiny cut on my palm changes everything. He discovers that I'm his *kyrana*, his blood mate. The one female that will sate his vampiric hunger and calm the berserker rages of his race. I thought every dream I'd had was finally coming true—my winged prince finally come.

Until Kaldur breaks my heart so callously, reinforcing every pain and insecurity I'd ever had.

And when he realizes his mistake and sets his mind to winning me back? He'll have the fight of his life if he thinks I'll *ever* give him my heart again.

Hunger in His Blood contains some themes and depictions that might be sensitive to certain readers. Please go to the book's page on my website (zoeydraven.com/books/hunger-in-his-blood), or scan the QR code below, for a full list of content considerations.

CHAPTER 1

ERINA

There was a hallway within the High Lord of Vyaan's keep that seemed as if it was painted in starlight.

The narrow hallway was located in the North Wing of the grand ancestral home, tucked away in a quiet section that led to a private sitting room, one that I regularly dusted and scrubbed.

The mysterious hallway presented an array of different-sized windows, and no two were the same. One was circular, another was arched. One was rectangular with silver metal panes running through it, another oval shaped. One appeared faceted like a gem, another had sharp, angular lines that comprised into the shape of a diamond.

The only thing all these windows had in common was the glass. Stained the darkest shades of blue, with navy and indigo, the glass was cut and assembled within each window until they made a stunning display of patchwork colors. Imbedded within the blue glass were silvery star-shaped gems.

This hallway was a stained-glass kaleidoscope of a starry night, as if it was perpetually bathed in moonlight. Even on the sunniest of days, this part of the keep felt like the calmest of nights.

That day, there was pelting rain pattering outside on the glass as my feet dipped into the blue pools of light, the silvery shafts of the stars stretching toward me.

Heaving out a long breath and sweating as I moved to the next window, I lugged my heavy stepladder to reposition it. I climbed back up, balancing on my tiptoes to reach the highest point of a crescent moon–shaped pane. *If only I had wings like the Kylorr, then this would be easy,* I thought.

Washing windows was one of my least favorite tasks, but I never minded in this part of the house. It was quiet, if a little drafty, and I could hum to myself without Maudoric shooting me a sharp look in disapproval, though I was somewhat convinced that was just how she always looked. I'd never seen her mouth not pinched down into a severe line.

As I polished the glass, my mind drifted. I thought of Kavelyn and her adventures, of the story I was currently working on. I thought of sparkling crystalline caves, deep in the wild night jungle, and I wondered how she would feel, surrounded by shimmering gems that shone like the stars in this hallway. Would she be tempted to take them? To bring them back to her poor village, even if theft was against Noxillian law, punishable by death? I wondered what I could call the gems in the cave. Or were they crystals? Were gems and crystals the same thing? Could they be considered as such in the kingdom of Noxily? They *could* be the same, I supposed.

That was the beauty of stories—I could make anything possible in them.

I frowned. How would the cave light be captured in my illustrations? What expression would be on Kavelyn's face? One of awe? Or one of sadness? Her heart had just been broken, of course. Most terribly.

I sighed. I draped the window rag over my shoulder and dug my hands into the deep pockets of my apron. Velle never understood why I wore such a "bulky, ugly thing" as I cleaned. But it was because the ordinary keeper's uniforms didn't have pockets at all, only a belt, and I could hardly keep my notebook and my pencils secured there. Maudoric had called my apron "sensible," especially when I'd told her it was to help carry cleaning supplies and spare cloths. And so the Head Keeper had given me leave to wear it.

I pulled out my notebook and unwound the leather cord. The material was so worn that it felt supple and smooth beneath my fingertips. I flipped to one of the back pages—for this notebook was nearly filled up—and under my existing list titled *Things to Ask Syndras* I wrote: *Are crystals and gems the same thing?*

I stared down at the growing list. Then, after a small moment of deliberation, I added another: *What does heartbreak feel like?*

Syndras would know that. Surely. She was nearly eighty. And if she didn't…then perhaps more research in the library was due.

I flipped the page, glancing over a sketch I had done that morning, as dawn had broken over the territory of Vyaan, creeping its fingers beneath my frayed window curtain.

It was a messy sketch, half-drawn in desperation as I'd chased a dream. But I could see him in the smudged lines of it. His proud nose and cheekbones like daggers. The softened shadowed divots beneath them that made them all the deadlier. His curving, thick horns like black steel. The rugged scar that ran from the middle of his outer cheek down to his mouth. The charming smirk of his full lips, his sharp fangs poking into the bottom one.

I bit my own, feeling a pulse of longing, and sighed again. Pulled into the vision of him, I sat down on the top step of the ladder, plucking out a pencil from my pocket before absentmindedly shading in the outline of his black wings behind him—something I hadn't been able to finish this morning before breakfast had been called. I'd only drawn him from the waist up, since the small pages of my notebook wouldn't have been able to do the rest of him justice.

He might not have been in color, only a charcoal sketch with my pencils, but his eyes, shaded with a light hand, were relatively close to the real thing. Eyes like silver pools. Eyes like *zylarrs*, which restless souls could feed from. Only, whenever I spied his eyes, it felt like *they* were feeding from *me*. Taking a bit of my soul, a bit of my heart, every last time—though it was in my imaginings only.

Kaldur of House Kaalium. The High Lord of Vyaan.

The Kylorr male that I was in love with. A foolish, silly, hopeful kind of love, one that had struck me at first sight two years ago. On a rainy day—much like this one—when I'd come to work in his keep.

I darkened the outline of his irises, lingering on them before I forced myself to look away.

I flipped back to the last page, to my list for Syndras, my eyes running over the last question I'd jotted down.

What *did* heartbreak feel like when the male you loved didn't even know you existed?

"What are you doing, Erina?" came the soft hiss. I jerked my head up, snapping my notebook closed out of reflex, already wrapping the cord tight as I regarded Velle. "You were meant to help me in the west library, remember?"

"Oh!" I said. "I'm sorry—I thought that was after lunch."

"It *is* after lunch. You missed it."

I blinked, noticing that my stomach *was* rumbling now that I focused on it. Another thing about being in this hallway was that it made time seem to slow. I strongly suspected there were many souls in this part of the keep, that the placement of a *zylarr*, even within this hallway, would be beneficial.

"I lost track of time," I said simply, maneuvering off the stepladder until I was on my feet as Velle approached. I shoved my notebook into my apron, watching her eyes narrow on the movement.

Her dark blue hair was pulled back into a loose braid. My

fellow keeper and friend was a hybrid—her father was half-Kylorr but her mother was fully human. The beautiful color of her hair was the only thing she took from her father. Velle had no wings, her eyes were a human brown like mine, and her horns had budded when she'd been an infant but had never grown. I knew that she was self-conscious of the still-present bumps, which she tried to hide with a fabric scarf she used as a headband.

"And you haven't even finished with the windows," Velle grumbled, inspecting the glass like how I imagined Maudoric might: with discerning displeasure. "You're going to get in trouble if you don't focus."

This was about the dinner party next week, I knew. Nobles of Vyaan, close family friends, and a few chosen guests came nearly every month to dine with Kaldur of House Kaalium. Maudoric always handpicked the keepers to help with these events, and Velle always made it her mission to be chosen. Because she would be seen...by some of the wealthiest and most influential individuals within Vyaan.

We both had aspirations for love, I supposed.

Just a vastly different kind, I thought, staring at the hybrid beauty.

"I'm sorry about the library," I said, feeling the heavy weight of my notebook within my apron. "I'll finish here and then come find you."

"Don't bother," Velle said, the words barbed. "But I'm not covering for you again with Maudoric."

A soft sigh escaped me after I watched her turn on her heel and retreat as swiftly as she'd appeared. I *did* feel bad. My distracted daydreaming often got me into trouble. Luc, my dearest friend, had always joked that I should endeavor to keep my feet firmly planted to the earth or else I might float away into the unforgiving atmosphere of Krynn. He would tell me to wave at the stars as I drifted past.

A smile tugged at my lips, though it was coupled with a dull tinge of melancholy, of missing Luc, as far away as he was.

I glanced down the starlight hallway, glad to see I was nearly done. If I hurried to finish, perhaps I could help Velle with whatever tasks she had left for the day. Maybe then she would forgive me for breaking my promise.

Determination pushed my shoulders back, and I lugged the stepladder over to the next window. Just as I got it into place, however, I heard something shatter.

The unmistakable sound of glass shooting across the floor came from the direction of the private sitting room. I frowned, my heart giving a lurch, because no one was ever in this part of the keep at this time of day.

Maybe a draft knocked something over, I thought next, already cataloguing all the items in that room as I strode toward it, hoping it wasn't the forest-green vase with hand-painted flowers and vines I often admired as I cleaned. Dismay that it could be made my steps quicken, and when I reached the closed black door, I didn't hesitate to push it open.

I was so preoccupied scouring the floor for broken shards of pottery along the opposite wall that I didn't realize my grave error before it was too late. My eyes went wide on a fully intact green vase, still perched on its round table, the moment I heard a breathy moan, followed by a throaty laugh.

I swung around, an apology already perched on my lips. But it died in my throat as my tongue went bone dry.

I met silver eyes.

A flash of a moment passed as I took in the scene.

Her name was Lydrasa. The eldest Kylorr daughter of House Azola, one of the old legacy families in this region. She was strikingly beautiful with pin-straight black hair, dark gray skin, and luminous blue eyes. Her lips were painted a dark indigo to complement her complexion, and it was those same lips that curved into an amused smile now as we watched one another.

Behind her was Kaldur of House Kaalium, High Lord of Vyaan. His pants were shoved down below his hips. Lydrasa was bent over the back of the velvety black chaise lounge, Kaldur's fingers digging into her hips from behind, her dress bunched just below her wings.

A shattered decorative glass orb was beside them on the floor, an unlucky victim to their hurried and eager activity.

I felt the burn start in the middle of my chest, and I blinked rapidly, feeling my heart restart, throbbing at a thunderous pace. My tongue felt twisted in my mouth, and I was desperately trying not to cry.

Kaldur's silver eyes were on me. I couldn't read his expression. Gone was his usual disarming charm, a mask he seemed to wear at all hours of the day. He was neither smirking—like Lydrasa was at being caught—nor did it seem like he particularly cared.

And why would he? I was only a lowly keeper, one who cleaned his floors and windows and did everything she could to stay out of sight.

Lydrasa's hands moved. She gripped one of Kaldur's large palms and moved it to one of her exposed breasts. Another moan tumbled from her throat as she pinched his fingers around her nipple, and she bucked her hips back.

"I doubt she's ever seen this before, the little thing," Lydrasa purred, her eyes still on me. "Shall we give her a show?"

"Get out," Kaldur's roughened voice commanded me, thick with his desire.

Then his eyes left me, and I realized I was already forgotten to him. He lowered himself over Lydrasa's back, resting his forehead above her wings. A strong surge of his hips followed, the guttural catch in his throat making my eyes sting.

"*Raazos*, her perfume is strong," Lydrasa laughed, followed by a breathless moan.

I fled.

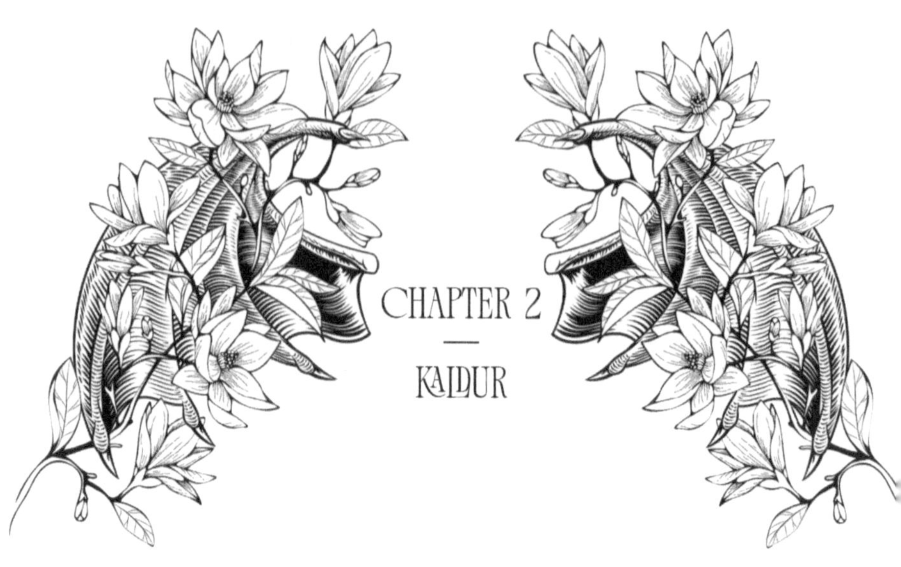

CHAPTER 2
—
KALDUR

*L*ydrasa clicked her tongue at me when she flitted over the shards of glass littering the floor. I shot her an edged smirk as I tucked my softening cock back into my trews, tying up the corded black laces. *Tight*, so my amorous lover wouldn't try to tempt me for a second round.

"So destructive," she scolded softly, a coy smile playing over her darkly painted lips. "But I do so love the sound of shattering glass. There's a musicality to it, especially when it's accompanied with sharp, impatient moans."

I ignored the words. My mind was already sliding to the meeting I had with my brothers in a short while. Now that the buzzing under my skin had dulled, chased away by an orgasm, I could focus. Azur, my eldest brother, would likely want an update on the South Road—one of the largest infrastructure projects House Kaalium had worked on in the last four decades. The road was nearing completion and—

Something fell and shattered. Not into hundreds of shards like the glass orb, but I saw large jagged pieces of what looked like an embellished green vase.

Lydrasa was not one to be ignored. She stood next to the

round table the vase had been placed on, her finger skimming over the now empty surface.

"Beautiful," she commented, but her blue eyes were narrowed on me. "Like a symphony."

My sharpened smile belied the jolt of irritation I felt burst in my chest. The perfume that the human keeper had been wearing still made my nose twitch, adding to my ire. My voice was a purr when I chided, "Enough, Lydrasa. My keepers have enough to do besides cleaning up your messes."

"Have Velle do it," she suggested, quirking a brow.

"Who's Velle?" I grumbled, running a hand over my horn before I gestured to the door. "I'll see you out. I have a meeting soon so unfortunately, *zendra*, you will need to leave."

Zendra, a common sweet name that meant *flower bloom*, was meant to soften the words. Lydrasa both pouted and preened, but I knew it was all for show. She was eight years older than me, had been nearly married thrice, and knew almost everyone of importance in Vyaan and Krynn's capital of Laras. Everything she did was for show…or because she was bored.

But she made a decent ally—and a more than adventurous lover.

A flash of the human keeper's shocked face when she'd discovered us flitted into my mind. Now that the tight squeeze of lust and desire had eased its fist around me, I felt a prick of discomforting guilt. I was certain my proclivities were well discussed among my keepers…but that didn't mean I wanted one of them to be witness to it. The human keeper was under my employ, and I should've been more careful, more discreet.

I could just hear Kythel, one of my brothers, say in his disapproving way, *You fuck like a* lyvin *in heat. Have more control. Your keep is not your brothel.*

I chuffed out a sharp breath and then went to take Lydrasa's arm. Her left wing brushed my side as I led her from the room.

"Aren't you happy I came?" she asked, a demure smirk appearing on her lips at the double meaning.

"Your company is always a pleasure, *zendra*," I replied smoothly. "I'm only sorry I can't entertain you longer."

Luckily I spotted Maudoric just down the dark hallway of stained-glass windows. She was speaking to the human keeper who'd interrupted us—the one with thick, dark red hair and whose cheeks were always flushed pink. Even from here, I swore I could smell her perfume, so I stayed back, catching Maudoric's attention with a small snap of my wing. The girl had her head hung, likely having received a scolding from my Head Keeper, but for what I didn't know. I watched as Maudoric dismissed the girl, who went scurrying down the hallway. Our eyes met briefly when she looked back—sad brown eyes that glimmered in the darkness—and that familiar wiggling of guilt returned to me. I rubbed at my chest, briefly, frowning.

Then the hallway swallowed her up and she was gone.

When my uncle had been in charge of Vyaan, before this territory had become mine to oversee and protect, I'd come to visit the keep to learn from him. From the time I'd been a young boy with soft horns, every season I'd come here. And every season I'd avoided this hallway. I'd never once walked down it, preferring to take the long way round. Too many lost souls here. Ancient souls.

When Maudoric stepped up to the both of us, I released Lydrasa. To my Head Keeper, I said, "Please see Lady Lydrasa home. I'll be in my study if you need me."

"Gladly," Maudoric replied, her smile polite but tight on the daughter of House Azola.

Maudoric was as shrewd and disapproving as Kythel was, and that was why I'd hired her. It brought me joy to watch the lines around her mouth deepen, even when I knew that she would do anything for me. I loved her like I would an aunt—and I certainly tested her like she was. She'd been one of the cooks under my uncle's rule, and she'd run her kitchen like she now ran my keep: efficiently and without mercy. The only exception was for me. Not even my brothers escaped her ire sometimes.

Though she *had* taken a liking to Millie, Kythel's wife and blood mate, when they'd come to visit during the last moon winds. But Millie's father had been a renowned chef, and they'd bonded over their love of food. I knew they sent letters back and forth to one another, usually sharing recipes, and I also knew that Maudoric, who I would've never described as sentimental, kept the letters pressed into one of her favorite books to keep them flat and protected.

While Maudoric and Lydrasa went down the dark hallway, I went down the other, my thoughts already turning to my meeting with my brothers.

When I arrived to my study, I immediately patched in the Com call on my Halo orb, knowing I was already late. I didn't sit at my desk. Instead, I stood, pacing, already feeling the buzzing begin beneath my skin. Frustration pricked, but I tried to ignore it. I didn't know what else to do. It had started nearly two years ago and made me feel constantly on edge. I'd consulted healers and mystics. I'd tried to fuck it out of my system—which helped briefly. I'd tried a variety of different blood from blood givers—which didn't help, even when I gorged myself. I'd tried herbal blends smuggled in from the Kaazor to the north. I'd tried smoking copious amounts of *lore*, drinking the strongest of Southern brews. Nothing helped calm it except for sex…and even then it was mere moments of relief.

When it had first begun happening, I'd thought it might be blood sickness—the disease my mother had died from. I'd been tested in private, but the results had been negative, mercifully.

In the last year, I'd given up. I took my release wherever and whenever I could because sex was the only thing that helped. And if Kythel wanted to be disapproving about my choices, then I would ignore it. He could never understand what this felt like.

Speaking of, I thought, seeing his form project into my study. The rest of my brothers flickered in after him until it felt like we were all together once more. Azur, the eldest—though he was only the eldest by a few moments over Kythel. Thaine—the sibling I was closest to, though we couldn't be more opposite. And Lucen, the youngest of the brothers, though I always considered him the best of us all.

"You're late," Kythel said with a sigh.

I smiled, though it was edged. "I was otherwise engaged. My apologies."

Kythel snorted. He knew what "otherwise engaged" meant.

I ignored him as I scanned the projections of my brothers. "Where's Kalia?"

Our only sister.

"Away," Azur replied with an unreadable expression.

I frowned. "Again?" I turned to Lucen. "Where does she keep sneaking off to?"

Lucen and Kalia were closest—though Kalia had chosen to live in the capital of Laras in Azur's keep.

"She's been going to Grandfather's island. Across the Silver Sea," Lucen told me. "At least that's what she's been telling me."

"Why?"

He shrugged. "She said she feels connected to Mother there. To our ancestors. She's been working on the garden, planting more starwood blooms because she said they've died back."

That buzzing grew with my anger, though I kept it locked tight.

I looked at Thaine, who met my eyes. We shared the same thought, and he interjected by saying, "I don't think it's wise to let her so far from the keep, Azur. Especially after the threat with Zyre. We all know what he wants. *Her.* She's vulnerable away from our borders. I don't trust the Kaazor, but with war looming...we should keep her close."

"Try telling that to *your* sister," Azur said. His tone matched

Thaine's—reasonable and patient—though I saw the underlying bite in Azur's expression. "She doesn't like to be told what to do. How do you think she'd react if I told her she needed to stay in the keep? With guards? She'd go mad."

"If we told her about what Zyre threatened, she would understand," Lucen reasoned. "But we've kept her in the dark, which I, again, did *not* agree with. You think I like lying to my sister?"

"You think *we* do?" Kythel asked. "But this goes beyond Kalia. This involves the entire Kaalium, *all* our citizens."

"And you insult Kalia in thinking she wouldn't understand that. She would marry Zyre tomorrow if it meant helping the Kaalium," Lucen argued.

"Which is what we are trying to prevent," Azur drawled. "You think any of us want to see our only sister married off to a mad Kaazor who *killed* his own father?"

We'd uncovered a plot of war among our enemies across the sea—the Thryki and the Dyaar were joining forces to plan an attack on the Kaalium, our beloved homeland. The Kaazor to the north might've been our only allies, and Zyre was their king. We'd met with him over a month ago and he'd made an offering of a war bond—but we all knew that war bonds were typically sealed in blood *and* marriage. With the Kaazor at our side—and their dragon-like beasts, the *kyriv*—the Thryki and the Dyaar would fall.

We could end a war swiftly—or perhaps even prevent one entirely. How many lives would that save?

But it would come at the cost of Kalia.

"Enough," Thaine interjected, his wings flaring and his voice cutting through the rising tension between us. We all loved one another—of course we did—and I would die right here in this study for any of them. I knew they would do the same for me. But these meetings often ended in arguments and barbs. Thaine —or even myself—tried to keep the peace, perhaps one of the only things we had in common.

But family was family. Family was *everything*. Our mother had taught us that.

I dug my claws into my palm, feeling my skin hum. I wondered if Lydrasa was still in the keep or if she'd managed to charm her way into the kitchens with Maudoric so she could stay longer. There might still be time to catch her.

I caught Kythel's glacially blue eyes. *The ice to Azur's fire.* That was what our mother always said about Kythel. She'd meant it as compliment. She'd always believed in balance. Balance was beautiful, and her beloved twins were as balanced as they could possibly be. Kythel kept Azur in check—like he did with all of us —and Azur reminded Kythel…well, not to be such an unfeeling, cold prick all the time.

Looking into Kythel's eyes, my sudden smile felt more like a grimace.

Have more control, he would say.

Perhaps, for once, I should listen to him.

———

THE MOMENT THE MEETING ENDED WITH MY BROTHERS—WE'D managed to stay on topic concerning the South Road construction after our hundredth discussion about Kalia—I went to look for Lydrasa. But instead I found Maudoric in the kitchens, alone, sipping on tea as she watched a keeper scrub the dishes from the afternoon meal.

"Not so hard, Velle," Maudoric chided. "Be careful of the silver around the edges."

I remembered Lydrasa mentioning a Velle. I looked at the woman—a hybrid female with deep blue hair—whose eyes widened when she saw me enter, her wet hands coming to her hair to smooth it back. She was pretty, but…I remembered her now. She had hungry eyes, and so I'd stayed far away, recognizing the signs of a female whose sole ambition was status and wealth.

A *Kyzaire* could give her both, and I wasn't foolish enough to fall into the trappings of a pretty keeper. My uncle had, and it had cost him *everything*. I remembered that lesson well.

Lydrasa was gone. But then I remembered the keeper. Remembered that I needed to do something first, something which might be unpleasant enough to distract me. *Apologize.*

"*Vaan*," I cursed under my breath. "Maudoric, where is that keeper you spoke to earlier? The one in the hallway?"

Maudoric disapproved that I didn't know the names of the keepers in my employ. In my defense, there were too many and they did their jobs so well that I rarely saw or interacted with a single one outside of my Head Keeper and Leeta, who served me most of my meals.

"*Erina*," Maudoric began, "is cleaning up broken glass in the private sitting room you and the Lady of House Azola were occupied in."

That burn of discomfort returned.

I grinned at Maudoric, stooping down to press my lips against her cheek. She didn't react, though I swore I caught the stray edge of a smile. "Thank you for reminding me. What would I ever do without you?"

"Perish," she drawled. It was her version of a tease though her expression remained stoic.

I chuckled and then turned out of the kitchens, avoiding the main stairwell that would lead to the North Wing. Instead, I went around from the East Wing. When I came to a stop in front of the familiar door, my nose burned from perfume—something spiced and yet strongly floral.

The keeper—*Erina,* I reminded myself—was inside. Good.

Now I didn't have to track her down.

CHAPTER 3

KALDUR

hen I stepped inside the room, I heard a sharp sniffle though I didn't see her.

"Erina," I called out, my eyes zeroed in the high-backed chair that was hiding her from view.

I heard the catch in her throat and what sounded like her patting her cheeks. I frowned.

A crown of dark red hair popped out behind the chair, plaited into a messy braid that hung over her shoulder, though it couldn't contain a few wild, wavy tendrils that had escaped it. Her eyes—glassy brown now—were wide with disbelief and her face was a bright pink, mottled with splotches across her round cheeks and down her neck.

She'd been...*crying*. I rubbed at my chest again, my wings going a little restless behind me with that knowledge.

"Kaldur," she greeted breathlessly, though she seemed too shocked to stand from her kneeling position. I paused, the sound of my name jarring and surprising falling from her lips. Her face flamed a deeper red, and she quickly corrected, "*Kyzaire*. My—my apologies. I—I didn't mean..."

Kyzaire was a word in the Krynn language meaning "High

Lord." A respectful term that I heard more than I heard my own true name.

Truthfully, I preferred hearing the shock of my own name from her. It was refreshing. Something I didn't expect. Something that wasn't quite forbidden but that toed the line of it…and that piqued my interest.

Yet I couldn't quite ignore the way my nostrils burned as I drew nearer.

"May I ask you something?" I asked.

She nodded, though she didn't seem like she was quite *present*. Like she couldn't understand how I could suddenly appear in this room or how we could be in this room together.

"Why do you wear that awful perfume, Erina?" I asked, flashing her a small smile to take the sting out of my words.

She blinked her glassy eyes. She really was quite pretty, I realized with a start, in that innocent kind of way, which had never been my type. And her being a keeper most certainly made her off limits, despite what my brothers believed I did with *their* keepers when I visited the different provinces.

It was a High Lord's responsibility to care for the people under their employ. I would never involve myself with a keeper—at my own home or at my brothers'—for that reason alone. Though I had certainly fucked my way through some of the noble Houses in the last couple years and had my fair share of dalliances in different provinces, they'd always been outside my own keep.

"My…my perfume?" she repeated, slowly seeming like she was returning to herself. "It was a gift. One I promised to wear every day. I didn't realize it was so…so overwhelming to the Kylorr. I should have known better—you have much better senses than we do. It's just cheap, you see. He couldn't afford anything else. And I never minded it."

Ah. A lover of her own, then.

"And the smell, it reminds me of what I imagine the garden forests of Noxily would smell like."

My brow furrowed as I watched her. Noxily? Was that off planet? I'd never heard of it, and I'd heard of a lot of places, had studied a lot of places.

"Noxily?"

The keeper's face went brighter, and I got the sense that she hadn't meant to say that. "Noxily is, um, a world of mine."

My brows rose, and I slid my arms across my chest, a flicker of amusement building in my chest. "A world of yours? Do you have many?"

"No, I write stories. Illustrated stories. With my own drawings. I've done it since I was a child. Noxily is a world I created. Me and Luc did actually. We would dream up all these things, and it grew and grew. And it became something more. And suddenly it became everything, how we got through. And..."

She trailed off, and I found my gaze rapt on her, watching the way her mouth formed words, the way her eyelashes swept down, how the flush grew and grew down her neck. I studied her again...and then again, trying to find something I didn't know I was even looking for. I frowned.

"Sorry, *Kyzaire*," she said, throwing me a smile that was both disarmingly bright and mildly desperate, as if she would do anything to disappear, to get away from me. My lips parted, having never seen a smile quite like it.

And suddenly my mind caught on Erina, this keeper under my employ, and it held. I feared when that happened because when my attention was caught on something, I didn't let it go.

"I'm almost finished cleaning the glass, but I'll come back later to—"

"No," I said quickly. "Stay." I smiled when she looked startled. "Please."

Her eyes flickered back and forth between my own before

they dropped away, as if remembering herself. "Of course, *Kyzaire*."

I remembered why I was there.

"Erina. Look at me," I asked. Slowly, her gaze rose, though it was quizzical. "I wanted to apologize to you for what happened earlier this afternoon."

Her cheeks blushed harder, redder than I thought was possible for a human. "There's no need to—"

"But there is," I said. There would be some who believed it wasn't my place to *need* to apologize to keepers. But I was my mother's son, and I believed otherwise. "I didn't know anyone was in this section of the keep. We should have been more discreet, and I'm sorry that I put you in an uncomfortable position, one you never should've been put in as one of my keepers. The…well, the proverbial fog has cleared, and I'm ashamed of how I handled that."

Erina's lips were parted as she stared at me.

"What is it?" I asked after a long moment of quiet.

"Nothing. It's just that…no one has ever apologized to me before. It's strange. I don't…I don't know what to say."

My lips quirked, but a bloom of sadness followed. "You usually decide to accept the apology or to reject it."

"Then I accept it," she said slowly. "But there is no need for an apology. I was lost in thought and didn't see anyone enter the room, so I didn't think to knock. This is your home, *Kyzaire*. You are free to, um, enjoy it however you wish."

A sweet sentiment and yet…

"That's where you're wrong. This might be my keep, but I do share it with many, including yourself. It won't happen again," I told her. My gaze went down to the floor, at the broken chunks of pottery from the green vase Lydrasa had purposefully broken. "Let me help you with this."

I crouched and began to sweep the shards into a large pile with the sides of my palms.

"No, it's all right, *Kyzaire*. I'll do it," Erina said quickly.

"I insist."

"It's just that I—I have a system," she continued, sounding nervous as she crouched opposite of me. "I'm sorting the pieces, you see."

My gaze flicked over to the small pile that was in fact grouped in a peculiar way. I leveraged her another look, brow furrowing. "You're…sorting the pieces?"

"I'm going to try to repair it," she answered, sniffling once more as she snagged a large piece away from my hand and placing it next to another piece in her collected grouping. My lips almost twitched.

"I'll have Maudoric replace it with another—it's no bother. No one even comes in here," I dismissed.

"But I do," she said quietly. "I… This was my favorite vase in the keep."

The soft confession made me pause.

"This green," she said, handing me a larger shard. "It's beautiful, don't you think? And I've never seen its likeness. It's unique. A peculiar blend of indigo blue and soft gold, maybe a dab of maroon."

My eyes observed the green, which to me looked like any other shade of green. But realization was dawning. "You want to keep the vase."

Her cheeks flooded again. She rushed to say, "Not to steal it! It would remain in the keep. Besides…even if it's a little broken, that doesn't mean it can't be beautiful again."

A *little* broken?

I laughed, a loud, booming laugh that felt like it was pulled from my core. When it tapered off, I heard her hard swallow.

"Then how would you like me to sort them?" I asked, gesturing to the pile I'd just swept with the shard she'd given me.

"I'll do it," she insisted.

"Don't trust me?"

She moved forward to sweep back some of the pile toward herself, as if that was answer enough. I realized this exchange was *enjoyable*. It was—

I froze.

My skin wasn't buzzing. That restless energy was *calmed*. Like those blissful moments after sex when my mind was quiet though alert and my body felt like my own again. *Those* were the moments I chased, and I felt it right then. In this room. With this human keeper.

Maybe her perfume has drugged my mind into a stupor, came the ridiculous thought.

If that was the case, I would smother myself in it for the rest of my life. Who needed to breathe when I would rather feel like I wasn't coming out of my own skin day and night?

I heard her sharp hiss as she was collecting the shards up. Her hand jerked back quickly out of reflex, and then she peered down at it.

"You cut yourself?" I asked, though my blood began to rush, making my words seem muted even to my own ears.

A thin red line of dark blood appeared over the surface of her palm.

The scent of it hit me before the *realization* did.

Her blood smelled like everything I'd imagined it might. Like it was the very thing I'd been searching for my entire life. The overwhelming *rightness* of it was sublime. The scent tingled over my tongue, and I nearly groaned even as dread and dismay began to rise.

Raazos's blood, I thought, my fangs elongating quickly enough that I cut my own damn lip, venom already dripping.

"*Fuck,*" I cursed, feeling the warmth of my blood bloom.

Suddenly I knew why the buzzing in me had calmed. Because of *her.*

The Kylorr discovered their blood mates—their *kyranas*—in different ways. Some were more sensitive to their mate's calling than others. Azur, my eldest brother, hadn't realized that Gemma, his wife, was his *kyrana* until he'd tasted her blood for the first time. Kythel had had his suspicions about Millie when he'd first met her in a blood-giver establishment based purely off her scent...though he hadn't known for certain until the first feeding.

But me?

This human woman—a keeper in my employ—was *mine*. My blood mate. My *kyrana*.

I only needed a whiff of her blood to know that with the utmost certainty.

And I wished I had never stepped foot in this room because of it.

CHAPTER 4
—
ERINA

"*A*re you all right?" I asked Kaldur, staring at him with quizzical concern even though *I* was the one bleeding everywhere.

Oh. Maybe it was rude to bleed in front of a Kylorr? No, that couldn't be right. I'd seen my fair share of cuts at the orphanage, and I remembered a particular incident with Syndras where I'd received a nasty gash from decorative swords I'd been dusting. She'd helped me bandage it up without once blinking her red eyes.

Maybe it was rude to bleed in front of a *Kyzaire*, then?

I didn't know. I didn't make it a habit to bleed in front of *Kyzaires*, Kaldur being the only one I'd ever interacted with.

I squeezed my hand into the fabric of my apron, the side of my enclosed fist bumping into the notebook beneath the folds.

"I'm sorry," I said quietly, quickly.

Kaldur stood abruptly. As if my gaze was pulled by magnets, I saw that his white fangs were poking into the bottom of his lip. I'd been around enough Kylorr in my life—full-blooded Kylorr— to know that he must've been exceedingly hungry for such a response to happen. Or on the verge of a berserker rage, which was uncommon among their race unless threatened. I'd never seen one myself, but I had heard stories.

The *Kyzaire* turned, giving his wings a small pump to propel him toward the door more quickly. My heart was pounding as I slowly stood. The cut over my palm felt like it throbbed with my heartbeat.

At the threshold, he turned back to look at me. The expression on his face was one I could only describe as *torment*. His brows were furrowed low over his mirror eyes. The lines of his face had deepened, especially around his mouth, though his lips were in a firm, unyielding press. One of his fangs had pierced the flesh of his bottom lip, a bead of black blood appearing before he licked it away. His body and movements were so tight and stiff that he resembled one of the gray marble statues I dusted regularly in the front atrium.

He stared at me as if…disappointed? I couldn't understand why.

And yet…*those eyes*. I felt the back of my throat burn at the intensity in that gaze, pinning me into place like I was an unfortunate specimen that was being studied. Now I knew that his eyes made me feel like shivering. I hadn't known that before because they'd only ever skimmed over me, never settling. I knew he had the smallest silver scar over his chin, shaped like a crescent moon, a detail I was itching to add to my sketch from this morning, though it felt like I shouldn't know that.

Forbidden, I thought. Everything about him felt forbidden.

Those eyes pierced me, and then a rough sound grumbled up from his chest. He turned, pushing through the doors hard enough that it made me jump.

Then he was gone.

It took long moments for my heart to calm as I stared at the empty doorway. Then I looked down at the shattered vase at my feet.

I pulled my notebook from the folds of my dress, careful not to get blood on the soft material. I flipped open to my sketch from this morning. With my charcoal pencil pinched between my pointer finger and thumb, I added a small crescent scar to Kaldur's likeness.

A drop of my blood from the small gash across my palm landed on the sketch. I hurriedly tried to wipe it away, but it smudged the lines of charcoal, leaving a red hue right over his left eye. I stared at the red. Berserker red.

I snapped the notebook closed, my eyes flickering back to the door.

What had just happened?

***

LATER THAT NIGHT, SHORTLY AFTER MY NIGHTLY BATH SO MY SKIN was still warm and my hair damp, I was tucked in the small window seat of my room, having drawn back the sheer curtain to look over Vyaan. It was a beautiful night, the moon a crescent—which I tried to ignore—and the lights of the city were shimmering. Candles in windows, the blue glow of the orb lights throughout the winding streets, the fires that glowed from within the taverns and inns.

My gaze trailed over the roads, a beautiful organic pattern that I'd drawn too many times to count from this very place. I had one of Luc's letters open in my lap, one I'd reread hundreds of times. It was the first letter I'd received from him shortly after he'd moved to Laras. He'd promised to write me, to let me know he'd arrived with his traveling caravan safely.

His handwriting was a messy scrawl, rushed most likely. He'd always hated writing, though Wrezaan had insisted that we learned, a tutor appearing every week like clockwork for our lessons. Though, now that I was older, I knew it was Vyaan law for orphanages to provide a weekly tutoring session for all children, at minimum. And Wrezaan had only decided on the minimum.

I loved writing, and so the weekly lesson had always been the highlight of the week for me. For Luc, they'd been horrendously long and infinitely boring.

Luc's letter conveyed his excitement at being in Laras, the capital city of the Kaalium. It had been a dream of his for so long. It was there he was determined to build a life, a fortune. I never knew where his obsession with Laras had begun, but Luc had consumed anything about it, whether it was stories from travelers at the merchant square he frequented or a book that he brought home from the archives for me to read to him.

Luc was a dreamer, perhaps even more than I was, and I'd always thought that a steep impossibility.

But for Luc, Laras was a glittering beacon of hope, a fresh start to acquire everything he'd ever wanted as an abandoned, poor child. He aspired to wealth, to status so he would never be overlooked or ignored again.

And he'd promised to send for me once that happened.

There was a small worry pressing more and more firmly at the back of my mind these last two years. Luc's letters had become more infrequent. The last one I'd received had been three months ago, though I had sent many since.

I worried he would forget his promise. I didn't care about wealth or status. I only cared to see my brother again, though we were not related by blood. But we shared a family name— Denoren, the name he'd come up with for the heroine of our shared story, and one we'd vowed to take together as mere children—and we were family in every sense of the word *except* in blood.

Luc was my brother, and I knew he wouldn't forget about me. He would *never*. A part of me felt intense guilt for beginning to wonder if he had, if he remembered his promise.

I folded Luc's letter carefully. I liked this one in particular. It sounded most like the Luc I remembered, all starry-eyed optimism and an unshakeable determination.

A sharp rap came at my door, but before I could answer, Velle was pushing the door inward, the hinges creaking.

"What did you do now?" she demanded quietly, peering at me from the doorway, an unhappy frown on her features.

"What do you mean?" I asked, my brow furrowing as I tucked Luc's letter away in the drawer next to the window as I stood. "Is something wrong?"

Velle was angry with me. Maudoric had apparently made her wash up the dishes from the afternoon meal after she'd given me a scolding in the starlight hallway. Velle had told her I'd been "doodling" when I'd meant to be cleaning...but Maudoric hadn't appreciated Velle's "childish tattling." I could never understand that female.

Even at this hour, Velle looked like she could go to a party. Her dark blue hair was freshly brushed and dried, with her hairband in place, the ends slightly curled. Even her nightdress was wrinkle free, with little gold bead details at the hem, something that looked like it cost a full week's wages. It was stylish, with a deep V that ended in the middle of her breasts—shorter than I would ever dare.

Whereas I had my damp hair piled and tied on top of my head and an old pale blue shift dress that Syndras had given to me years ago. It had been one of her daughter's, and I'd had to sew up the long slashes in the material at the back meant for wings. It was the nicest nightdress I owned, however, and no one ever saw the back anyway.

"Oh, nothing's wrong," Velle said, her words edged in a sharp bite. But I knew Velle well enough to know she'd eventually forgive me and we'd go back to being friends. "Only that the *Kyzaire* has requested your presence in his study. At this hour!"

My heart leapt. "Right...*now*? The *Kyzaire*?"

"Yes," she hissed. "What did you do? Maudoric looks like she's about to start spitting fire. And I swear, Erina, if I have to wash up in the kitchens again tomorrow because of you, I'll..."

But I didn't hear whatever she said next. My heart had begun to beat thunderously in my chest, remembering the intensity of those mirrored eyes and the drop of black blood at his lip.

I stood. Velle was staring at me.

"What is going on?" she demanded.

"I have no idea," I answered honestly. Excitement, wariness, and fright all mingled together inside me at the thought of speaking with him again. "But I'll go find out."

Beneath my fresh bandage, the cut over my palm gave a small throb, as if in warning.

CHAPTER 5
—
KALDUR

I stared out the arched window in my study, observing the quietness of Vyaan below.

I'd chosen this room for my office as opposed to a larger one on the opposite side of keep—which afforded a beautiful view of the gardens, the mountains, and forests that surrounded the territory.

But here, I could see the hustle and bustle of the south side of the city. Not necessarily *now*, as late as it was, but during the day I could watch the comings and goings from the market and the daily routines of my people as they went about their lives. In some small way, that lent me a sense of comfort, of rightness.

The nobles typically congregated in the south end, but there were plenty of taverns, shops, meadows, and open spaces that drew many, from all over Vyaan, to this side of the city.

I pressed my forehead against the glass, closing my eyes, trying to ignore the restlessness under my skin, which had only grown worse since my encounter with Erina this afternoon.

A fucking disaster, I thought wearily. I couldn't help but surmise that Azur and Kythel might find this quite ironic. They might even be gleeful about it, and they'd have every right to. I'd had plenty to say about their relationships with their blood mates —my regrettable attitude when I'd first met Gemma and my smug insistence to Kythel that he would *never* be able to stay away from Millie, though he'd certainly tried at the beginning of their courtship.

Now it seemed to bite me in the ass tenfold.

A keeper, I couldn't help but scoff.

I thought of my uncle. My father's third brother, Tynaar, who'd once overseen this territory. The cautionary tale—well, *one* of the cautionary tales—of our family. He'd been played for a fool, blinded by the tempting tease of a young, ambitious beauty...and he'd lost everything.

His wife, my aunt Harnan, had razed his reputation among the nobles, having come from a long established and exceedingly respected House. I'd both feared and respected that about my aunt—she could be vicious when scorned. She'd never once felt humiliation from her husband's public affair. Instead, she'd insisted that *he* should feel the burning sizzle of embarrass-ment...and she'd made him pay.

To save face, House Kaalium had stripped Tynaar of his estate and demoted him from *Kyzaire* of the territory—all to assuage the nobles, who had, at that time, had quite weighty pull in Vyaan.

My uncle had been shamed, though he had still married the keeper after ending his own marriage to my aunt, thinking himself in love. The keeper, so I'd heard, had jumped into bed with another wealthy noble shortly after, and it was widely known among Vyaan's society that she'd been paraded around as his mistress. A mistress married to a once great *Kyzaire*. The steepest plunge from grace under public scrutiny and gossip.

Bereft from heartbreak and shame...my uncle had taken his own life not even a year after he'd been stripped of his title. As for me, I'd barely been of age, but I'd been forced to ascend to the title that had always been meant for me. *Kyzaire* of Vyaan. Sooner than expected.

House Kaalium had many dark secrets hidden away. Some terrible, some violent, some shameful. Some of my ancestors had been murderers, merciless and evil.

All of the old Houses had dark pasts. It was inescapable, given the longevity of legacy.

And yet my mother had endeavored to bear at least five children—one for each territory—so that a new era of House Kaalium's rule could begin. It had been centuries since siblings had overseen *every* territory of our nation. Some *Kyzaires* had even been distant relations to the House or trusted advisors in the past.

Yet my brothers were installed at each great territory—Laras, Erzos, Salaire, Kyne, and Vyaan—presenting a united Kaalium for the first time in a long time.

But House Kaalium as it was now had made sacrifices. My mother certainly had…for *this* Kaalium to be a reality.

And now we are on the precipice of war when we are only just beginning our plans for the Kaalium, I couldn't help but think bitterly, pushing away from the cooling touch of the window glass.

And I might very well be tempted by a keeper, just like Tynaar, I thought next as a low growl rumbled up my throat.

Blood was blood, after all. And history *always* repeated itself. That was a lesson my father had instilled in us, ever since we'd been young.

But Erina being a keeper didn't change the fact that she was my blood mate.

Nor was I married, like my uncle had been.

And yet memory ran deep in the Kaalium, like roots of an ancient tree. If I went down this road, it would be a jagged mark against me. A smirk when I entered a room of nobles. Whispering that I would catch in darkened corners at parties. The look of wariness in my brother Thaine's eyes. *I hope you know what you're doing,* he would tell me.

A knock came at the door. Soft, though not hesitant.

"Enter," I called out.

I'd already made up my mind, weighing the consequences carefully. I knew this as I watched the door open and Erina step within the darkened confines of my study. There was no other choice, and I couldn't deny that curiosity ran deep. I would always wonder—

Her scent hit me. *Hard.*

A muffled groan rose before I could stop it, and I disguised it by clearing my throat. Never before had I thought that I would be *sensitive* to another's scent, much less that of my blood mate. Azur hadn't been. Kythel had been slightly more susceptible. But me? This was madness.

She wasn't wearing that awful perfume, the one her lover had gifted her. I felt a twist in my gut at the thought but then reasoned it didn't matter if she had a lover or not. I would not share. Ever.

Without the perfume, she smelled like…*mine.* I felt the possessiveness rise, my chest straightening, my heartbeat beginning to throb.

I'd never scented anything quite so lovely, so attractive to me. Her natural scent was light and fresh. Like the first rain after harvest season. That first rain bloomed the earth.

I heard her swallow even though she didn't move away from the door. "You requested me, *Kyzaire?*" she asked.

Breathing her in too deeply was perhaps not the most intelligent thing to do. I'd need my wits about me to navigate these next few moments, to make her my offer I'd been thinking long over since this afternoon. Her scent would only muddle my mind, slacken my tongue.

But that wary realization was in direct contrast to the words that slipped from my lips, "Come closer."

She moved toward my desk, which I'd kept purposefully between us—though it seemed like a laughably moot effort now.

Erina stopped about halfway into the study, nearest the burning fire in the hearth, sparkling and crackling lowly. She was nervous, I saw. But there was also something lying in wait beneath the nerves. I'd seen it enough in my lifetime to recognize it readily.

She desires me, I thought, relieved at the realization. Perhaps because I could be a selfish bastard and if she desired me already, this would make it all the easier to convince her.

Erina's pupils were dilated and a warm pink glow was flushed over the tops of her cheekbones, before the tantalizing color snaked down and bloomed across her neck. Her dark red hair was damp from a recent bath and piled into a messy bun at her crown. She was wearing a pretty blue nightdress, as if my summons had woken her, thin enough that I could see her hardened nipples puckering the material.

The picture she made was alluring and sensual. So much so that I was momentarily frozen, studying her. I envisioned placing my mouth over one nipple, teasing her through the dress. I wondered what kind of sounds she'd make in her pleasure, if she was a quiet or a passionate lover.

It's the bond, I reasoned, shaking my head to try to clear it. *It's already coursing through me.*

But with her scent in my nostrils, I realized she'd already given me a gift, and it hardened my resolve all the more. I was calm, like her mere presence was a balm on the restless and maddening energy that had plagued me for years. Tension released from my shoulders and my wings lowered. Was this how I'd felt before? Normal? It was sublime.

All this time and she'd been right under my nose, I thought.

Slowly, I walked around the desk toward her.

My gaze dropped to her hand, bandaged up, and a burn of shame speared me.

"I'm sorry for leaving so abruptly earlier," I began, catching her eyes. "I should have helped bind your wound."

Erina blinked and then dropped her gaze down to her hand, frowning. I could see what she was wondering. If I had summoned her here at this time of night merely to apologize—again—to her. Then I wondered what exactly she thought she was doing here. What had crossed her mind when I'd sent for her to meet with me? Had she been frightened? Excited?

"But I didn't ask you to come so I could apologize for that," I added. Her head lifted.

"Then why did you?" she asked, her voice low. She had a nice voice. Pleasing and warm.

I'd thought, for the better part of the last few hours, how to approach this conversation with her, and I'd settled on a portion of the truth instead of the full truth. I'd settled on directness rather than playing it coy, like noble courtships often began, all games and riddles, meant to frustrate as well as tease.

"I'm tempted by your blood, Erina," I said carefully, watching her. "Very tempted."

Her lips parted in surprise, and my eyes swept down to them, watching her pink tongue dart out to wet them. I ignored the way my cock twitched in response.

"I'm not sure what you mean," she confessed softly, uncertain.

I wondered how long she'd lived on my home planet of Krynn. Had she been born here? Or had asylum been offered to her? Did a noble House sponsor her? And what of her parents? Humans weren't *uncommon* on Krynn, not for the last few decades at least, but I did wonder how much she truly knew about my race. Humans, from my experience, tended to stick to their own people.

"I'll put it like this," I said. "Perhaps you have a favorite meal? One you could eat over and over again. Kylorr have it too, in the form of blood. And your blood? To be blunt? I've never smelled anything quite so appealing to me."

Her eyes sharpened on me. "You want to feed from me?"

Was she appalled by that? Curious? Tempted? I couldn't tell from her expression. She looked only surprised.

"Yes," I replied, my voice gruff and low as I tried to track every small new expression I could on her face. "Very much so."

"*Oh*," she breathed, her eyes dropping to my chest, flicking back and forth between the silver clasps there on my vest, unseeing. "Oh."

Allowing her time to process the confession, I waited a small moment, and it felt endlessly long. Her scent was distracting. My fangs, I realized, were elongated. I tasted the sweetness of my venom across my tongue.

"It would be an arrangement between us," I continued, keeping my tone even and smooth, as if I had these negotiations with a blood mate every day. "This would benefit us both, not just me."

Why were my feet drawing me closer? I studied her carefully, trying to read her. She was naturally expressive. She was curious, flattered, but wary. I spied the flash of excitement, felt the energy rise off her like steam.

A knotted part in me untangled. She would accept me, accept this. *Good.*

"Can I think about it?" she asked me, halting my feet, which unknowingly had drifted straight toward her. Surprise curled in my chest. "It seems like a big decision. It would be wise to take time to…to…"

I lifted a curl of her hair that had escaped from the damp bun, watching it twine around my finger like an embrace.

"…to properly think about it. Right?" she finished, stammering slightly when she realized my nearness.

"Of course," I murmured. "Take all the time you need. But you haven't heard my offer."

"Oh," Erina breathed, her wide eyes on mine. A warm brown with strands of gold amber. Lovely. "I... Yes, I should hear your offer."

My lips quirked, knowing the offer wasn't necessary. This was a dance, a game—one I'd navigated far too many times. Everything was a transaction, disguised as courting or romance.

Yet the smell of her was intoxicating. And her eyes made my office shift and sway around me, like she'd dragged me into a strange realm where time slowed. My heartbeat was languid, at ease one moment and pounding the next.

I dropped the curl of hair, watching the end of it brush the pink of her lips. I imagined sinking one of my fangs into the fullness of the bottom one, just a small cut so I could lap at the blood, a small teasing taste as I kissed it.

Madness, I thought, slightly shaken as my body tightened.

I cleared my throat. "You would be my blood giver alone. No longer will you be a keeper in my House or expected to work as one."

"But—"

Panic flashed across her face. I wondered about it only briefly before I added, "You will move into the South Wing." My private wing of the keep. "You'll have your own rooms. You'll be paid a monthly stipend." *A quite generous one,* I thought...but I needed her to say yes. "And you'll be free to spend your days and nights as you wish."

"And what's the bad part?" she asked, surprising me.

"The bad part?" I chuffed out, flashing her a small smile. "Hardly any, unless you have an aversion to being fed from. The most unpleasant thing you'll have to do is take *baanye* regularly. I've heard it's an acquired taste." When she didn't react, I asked, "You do know what *baanye* is, yes?"

"Yes, of course," she replied. "A tea to help aid blood production."

I inclined my head. There was another edge of this arrangement, one that we would both tip over. But she would need to know—I didn't see a way around it, and I needed her to understand this from the very beginning.

"And if," I said, carefully choosing the words, like I was plucking them out from a basket, "the nature of the feedings lead to sex, you will need to take marroswood as well."

CHAPTER 6
—
ERINA

There was utter silence in the *Kyzaire's* study, save for a howling gust of wind that rattled the arched window outside. Even the fire in the hearth was silent, as if waiting for my answer.

This was everything I'd wanted, wasn't it? For Kaldur to finally take notice of me. I'd imagined a gentle courtship in my more fanciful daydreams, of walks in the garden at midnight, of stolen kisses in the shadowy stairwells of his keep, of teasing grins and romantic yearning and pinching longing.

That was how I'd always imagined falling in love might be like. Maybe it felt a little like madness—but at least you would know there was a safe place to land.

Instead, this felt…slightly disappointing. Cold. Like we were negotiating a contract, which I supposed we were.

I felt this even as I tried to hide my trembling from being near him. Even as I memorized and studied every sharp angle and beautiful slope of his features, as I saw myself reflected in those mirrored eyes. They *were* like *zylarrs*—I'd been right. But instead of lost souls feeding from them during the moon winds, I felt like *I* was ravenous for them. Ravenous to keep them on me, always. When he looked away, I felt like I'd been severed in two.

I licked my dry lips, shivering a little when a droplet from my hair ran down the nape of my neck.

"You're…you're asking me to be your mistress."

I didn't know where the bold words came from, but I found them tumbling from me.

"That you feed from," I clarified.

The idea filled me with intense and eager curiosity. I could endeavor to ignore my disappointment. Perhaps this was how things like this were done with *Kyzaires*. In quiet studies, in quiet negotiations, on quiet nights.

I thought of the scene I'd walked in on earlier, with him and his *other* mistress, and I couldn't help but flinch a little. Couldn't help but feel the burn of dismay and despair.

Kaldur's tone was crisp when he said, "To be clear, I don't like that word. *Mistress.* It implies too much or too little. In my experience, there are long-term lovers or fleeting bed partners, and yet that word is meant to encompass them all. You would be more, Erina."

More?

Hope sprung in my chest, a little trickle.

"Really?" I asked.

He seemed to catch himself. He frowned. "A blood giver is a responsibility in itself. A blood giver is respected, especially one who gives to a *Kyzaire*. I do not ask this of you lightly and certainly not on a whim."

He was so certain. That caught me off guard because I wondered *why*. Before today, I hadn't even known he couldn't stand the mere smell of me. Now? After a whiff of my blood, he was offering me…*everything*. Everything a poor, unwanted orphan girl could have ever dreamed of. A home. Stability. Status.

But what about love? Marriage? Children?

Don't get too deeply in your head, I reminded myself, though the words held the teasing edge of Luc's voice. He'd always been the one to keep me more grounded in my daydreams, hadn't he? Even though he was a dreamer himself, he always said I could out-dream the entire population of Krynn.

This was a negotiation after all, not a love proposal.

But...maybe with time, he will fall in love with me too, I couldn't help but hope.

Some people would call me a naive fool. Perhaps I was. But I also knew that there were three things I wanted in this life. To fall deeply in love and make a family of my own. To see Luc again. And to finish my series of stories so that one day, I might read them to my own children.

I *wanted* to love someone. I was desperate to. I felt I had so much love to give, if only someone would give me the chance.

I'd told Velle that once. She'd laughed. I could still hear her response running in my head: *Don't be so pathetic, Erina. These nobles can smell desperation. If you want to find a wealthy husband, you have to play the game well.*

But I didn't think love was a game. I thought it was the purest form of everything good in this life. What was so wrong about wanting to share that with someone? I didn't care about money. I only cared if someone had a good heart.

Staring at Kaldur, I wondered about his heart.

"If I agree to it," I began softly, "I would still wish to work in the keep. In some capacity."

"Out of the question," Kaldur said, his tone an easy dismissal. He was used to giving orders, to being obeyed.

"The other keepers will talk," I argued. I'd often listened to gossip at the lunch table. I didn't want to be the next subject on their list, to be laughed at.

"They'll talk regardless," Kaldur said. "What they think of you should not matter anymore."

"I care about what they think. Some are my friends."

"Ah, but if they wag their tongues behind your back, are they truly your friends?" Kaldur asked, spearing me with a hardened look that had me biting my lip. "Being a blood giver is more tiring than you might think. I don't want you working in the keep. I know how hard my keepers work. You need the rest between feedings. I'm selfish, Erina, because I don't want you exhausted—I'll taste it." I jerked at the admission. "You will be well compensated, I assure you. You will have all the time you want. To mix together your different colors and admire pretty vases in the village that you can actually purchase for yourself."

Time. Time…to work on my stories? Without the fear of Maudoric lingering around corners. Velle would no longer have a reason to be angry with me.

Maybe that wouldn't be such a bad thing.

For some reason, Velle's words wouldn't stop flowing through my mind. That males like Kaldur would smell how badly I wanted them. That I might have to play a game I knew nothing about if I wanted a chance with him. Something I'd only ever dreamed about…

It was on the tip of my tongue to say yes. To agree to it right then and there. To follow my heart instead of my head. Syndras had always teased that my heart would be my ruin.

"Can I let you know my decision tomorrow, *Kyzaire*?" I asked instead.

A good night's sleep—if sleep would come after this—would make everything clear. It always did.

A subtle expression flashed over his face. I'd surprised him, I realized, feeling a small bloom of what felt like victory. Because for someone like the High Lord of Vyaan, I figured he wasn't surprised quite so often.

He took another step toward me—when he'd already been so close. He was standing at my side, and I had to turn my head to regard him. I held my breath as those eyes skimmed over me, starting at my hair, traveling down my face, down my neck.

One hand reached out. He swiped another droplet that had

gathered at the nape of my neck, just beginning to run down. I gasped, a small little sound I wished I could take back. His thumb was searingly hot, and the gentle swipe of his calloused finger created odd sensations skittering down my spine. I shivered. I wanted to sink into that touch. I felt the pound of my heart triple, and I smelled the heat of his nearness, going dizzy with it.

My hair was tumbling down from its bun after a quick slide of his hand through the ribbon. I could smell the bloom of the soap I'd used during my bath drift up. I heard the sharp inhale, the quick catch of his own breath, and it made me jerk my head over to regard him. Was he as affected by this as I was?

By *whatever* this was?

The room felt too hot, but my feet were rooted into place. Would I burn to a crisp there if I couldn't move? He was looking at me—*really* looking at me—and I was pinned in place, like a flower being catalogued and studied, every tucked, hidden petal unfurled for his perusal.

Kaldur's head moved forward, and I sucked in a small breath. His nose lowered until I could *just* feel his heated exhale over my exposed neck.

His voice was guttural and low when he said, "Never hide your true scent from me again, Erina."

My lips parted, a flood of surprising heat rising at the words, at the strange and surprisingly intimacy of this moment.

"That perfume? Get rid of it."

I didn't know what was happening. All I knew was that my heart was trying to beat its way out of its cage and I wanted to stay there all night with his voice in my ear.

"Take some time to think about my offer," he said, his voice softening. He backed away, and I felt like all the air came rushing in. My knees wobbled, but I was pleased when I managed to keep from swaying where I stood. He added, softly, "But don't take too long."

Instead of those words feeling like a threat, they sounded like a gruff plea.

"Go," he said. He turned from me, heading toward the arched window. "Before I do something I regret."

I didn't think twice. There was no mistaking the warning in his voice then. Even though every part of me wanted to stay, I heeded the words and fled.

CHAPTER 7
—
ERINA

Sleep didn't come, and my eyes felt hollowed out with tiredness when dawn eventually broke over Vyaan.

My answer was the same as it'd been the night before in Kaldur's study. Because if it had been any other answer, I knew that I would regret it for the rest of my life.

An adventure of my own, I thought. Kavelyn wouldn't flinch away from this. And while she would be exploring dangerous jungles on Noxily or attending glamorous parties to find clues for her next discovery, I knew that even she wouldn't say no to a *Kyzaire.*

Especially one as magnetic as Kaldur of House Kaalium.

I shivered, remembering his eyes and the heat of his exhale over my skin as I dressed. I might've been tired from the lack of sleep, but I felt the currents of energy beneath my skin, buzzing and alive.

I touched the nape of my neck after I tied my apron into place, wondering where Kylorr preferred to feed from. I'd always heard it was a preference. From the neck, usually, or the wrist. But for more intimate pairings, I'd heard other, more intriguing things.

A shuddered breath escaped me. A world of possibility was laid before me. Answers to questions I'd only ever wondered about. Like a Halo orb of knowledge cupped in the palm of my hand, waiting to be explored.

I was terrified. Terrified but intensely curious.

I patted the pockets of my apron, making sure my notebook and pencils were in place. In the small mirror hanging on the wall, gilded in thin chipping gold, I brushed through my unruly hair before plaiting it neatly.

Out of habit, my hands reached for the nearly empty vial of perfume sitting on my dresser. I stared down at the lingering pool of fragrance. Luc's parting gift to me. He'd told me that by the time it was gone, we would be reunited in Laras. Some days, years prior, I'd put a tad too much on, impatient to see him again, impatient for the vial to empty. Maybe, unconsciously, I'd never stopped.

Never hide your true scent from me again, Erina, Kaldur had ordered me last night.

I knew that Kylorr were more sensitive to fragrance—to all scents, truly—but I'd never imagined that I'd been *offensively* strong. I swallowed down the embarrassment as I replaced the vial, my heart giving a morose little beat because now I wondered if I would *ever* see it emptied. Leaving it behind felt like a small betrayal to Luc.

As I did any morning, I left my room after I dressed and made my way toward the kitchen. The keep was quiet at this hour, but I knew the kitchens would be alive with bustling activity.

The moment I stepped inside, I felt comforted. It was one of my favorite parts of the day, starting my mornings here. Handfuls of keepers were seated at the long table, hunched over their bowls of porridge and steaming cups of tea. Despite the earlier hour, they were chatting happily, jovial laughs sounding—especially from the weapons master, Zyn. His booming, deep laugh could shake the walls of the keep. If Zyn *wasn't* laughing in the morning, the others knew to steer clear.

"Morning," I chirped as I pulled the kitchen door shut behind me.

I got a chorus of replies as I made my way over to the stove where Saira was stirring a big pot of stew for the afternoon meal. The tantalizing scent of freshly baked bread filled my nostrils, and I tried to focus on that even as I saw a few stray looks shot my way. I heard the scratch of the table bench against stone as Velle rose.

Just as I plucked a thick, warm slice of bread off the serving tray—bread that was folded with *syaan* berries, my favorite—Velle was cornering me.

"*What happened last night?*" she demanded softly. Her eyes were alight with intrigue, sparkling with her curiosity. But I spied a sharp glint in them, in the slight downturning of her mouth. Suspicion. "I thought you'd never spoken to the *Kyzaire* before."

"I hadn't," I said. I wondered how I should maneuver this. I couldn't tell her the full truth. But she was my friend. I couldn't lie about everything. "He, um, he called me into his study to tell me to wear less perfume in the keep."

The half-truth was idiotic and unconvincing. Even I could see that realization flash over Velle's features. She raised her brow sardonically. "The *Kyzaire* of Vyaan called you into his private study, late in the evening, to complain about your perfume?"

I felt heat wind its way up my neck. "Yes. And to apologize."

"For *what?*"

"The incident yesterday with the vase."

Even though I'd yet to smother my slice of bread in sweet jam, I took a large bite, chewing slowly as Velle studied me. Why did I always feel like I was on the verge of getting scolded when she looked at me like that? Our friendship had never held the ease with which my friendship with Luc had, but Velle had taken me under her wing when I'd first arrived at the keep, and I would never forget that.

Velle waited until I swallowed the chunk and before I could take another bite—just now realizing how *quiet* it was in the kitchens—she opened her mouth and started to say, "That is the worst lie I've ever heard and—"

The kitchen door swung open, and I'd never been more relieved by an interruption.

Until I saw that it was Maudoric, the Head Keeper, and the look on her face meant she was displeased. Very, very displeased. Her eyes scanned the kitchen before landing on me and Velle in the corner by the stove.

Please not me, I thought, feeling the familiar tightness in my chest. Maudoric was nowhere near as terrible and stern as Wrezaan had been where I'd grown up...but I could never shake the terror when anyone showed their displeasure toward me. It crawled up my spine and wrapped around me like a suffocating embrace. So I did anything I could *not* to tempt anyone's ire.

"Erina," Maudoric said in her low, unreadable tone.

My tongue was glued to the roof of my mouth. And yet I pasted on a bright smile that felt too wide on my face. "Yes, Head Keeper?"

"Come with me."

Velle shot me another look, and I was certain my loud gulp echoed throughout the entire kitchen, as silent as it was save for the pot of simmering stew and crackling bread, fresh from the oven.

My legs felt wooden and hollow as I stumbled after Maudoric.

Her eyes scanned over me, starting at my worn boots before inspecting my too-big apron. When I reached her, she went through the kitchen door and I followed. Before it even closed, I heard the eruption of whispers and wanted to sink into the stone of the hallway, in a puddle at her feet.

She went far enough away until we were in a private alcove near one of the spiral stairwells that led up to a smaller library.

"The *Kyzaire* has requested your presence at his morning meal."

My heart jolted. I had wondered when I'd see him again. I'd told him I would give him an answer today, but I hadn't expected he would send for me first thing in the morning.

"He's taking it on the garden terrace," she said. "I'll bring you to him."

Though nerves began to rise, I realized what Maudoric had done for me. "Thank you."

"For what?" she asked, frowning.

"For not announcing that to everyone," I replied quietly.

Maudoric tilted her chin back slightly. I'd always thought her a beautiful female. She was a Kylorr with light gray skin and perfectly symmetrical features, though they were all a bit too severe. The lines in her face had deepened even since I'd come to work at the keep a couple years ago. I'd sketched her once in pencil, though I'd always been too nervous to show her.

"It is the *Kyzaire*'s business. And yours. Not the keepers'," she told me, her tone clipped. She'd always disproved of the gossiping, though every House I'd ever worked in had taken part in it. It was natural. I knew that better than anyone.

But I also knew that Maudoric was loyal to House Kaalium. She'd worked in this keep longer than Kaldur had been appointed *Kyzaire* to the region. Of course his privacy would be paramount to her.

I said nothing else and followed Maudoric through the quiet keep. I was surprised that Kaldur was awake so early. I'd always assumed he slept into the afternoons, hearing rumors that he stayed up until dawn, whether it was due to his work or the bed partners whose company he kept.

The East Terrace was beautiful, situated toward the back of the keep, farthest from the sprawling towns of Vyaan and overlooking the magnificence of the House's gardens. I knew that Kaldur kept a team of talented horticulturists at his disposal, to keep the grounds in perfect condition, which had always surprised me. Until I'd learned from other keepers that his mother had been quite fond of plants and flowers, had kept the gardens of Laras meticulously. I always felt warm and fluttery when I remembered that.

I liked that he was close with his family. I liked that he kept his own gardens carefully in memory of his late mother.

It's a testament to his character, I'd decided long ago. It was one of the reasons I admired him.

When I stepped foot on the East Terrace, a cool breeze swept through my hair, releasing a few wavy tendrils. I felt his gaze on me before I spotted him. He was standing at the far end of the terrace banister, made of cream-colored stone mixed with gray swirling lines, his wings resting comfortably at his sides. He'd been overlooking the gardens, watching as two horticulturists trimmed back a smattering of starwood blooms down below, readying them for the winter season. But he turned to watch me, those silver eyes shrewd as I approached the small table, set for two, after Maudoric gestured me forward.

"Thank you, Maudoric," Kaldur said, the low timber of his voice in the early morning feeling like a sin. He strode toward me slowly, never looking away, and the graceful movement felt more like a prowl. I bit my tongue, the sharp pain giving me something to focus on as I tried to calm my racing heart.

Maudoric faded from the terrace silently. Kaldur eyed my state of dress, and I was only slightly embarrassed to note that he was in a very expensive-looking vest—emerald in color with silver catches—over a light gray tunic, only a few shades darker than his skin. On a few of his fingers were silver rings, inlaid with black stones. His black pants were neatly pressed, and there wasn't a single scuff on his shining boots.

He looked refreshed, not a single hair out of place, like he'd slept the entire night without tossing or turning once.

Where I was painfully aware that I looked as tired as I felt in my drab uniform, hidden by an even uglier apron that was two sizes too big for my frame, and half of my hair had already come loose from my braid.

"Were you worried I wouldn't feed you when I asked you to join me for the morning meal?" came his question.

I blinked. I was still trying to get my bearings, still overwhelmed by the handsome portrait he made. The green was particularly eye-catching, and I couldn't help but notice that it was a green similar in color to my prized vase—which, in the end, I hadn't the courage to steal back to my rooms after I'd cleaned it up. Instead, I'd carefully placed the shards of pottery in an empty drawer until I steeled up my nerve.

"What?" I asked.

He gestured to my hand. When I looked down, much to my mortification, I saw the slice of bread I'd taken from the kitchens, one very obvious large bite taken out of it.

Despite my flaming blush, I said, "Oh, I'm quite hungry in the mornings. One can never be too careful or assume too much."

Kaldur's chuckle was low and gentle. My shoulders relaxed when I heard it, like the sound had the ability to unknot my tight muscles from my restless sleep.

"It would be rude of me not to feed my guest," he said, gesturing forward, and my feet moved, as if solely controlled by him. His hand came to the small of my back, heat blooming from his touch. I was proud when I didn't gasp, but I felt my knees shake when his head dipped low. He inhaled gently and then said, in a more intimate tone than I was prepared for, "You smell like Alara, *zendra*."

I turned my head on impulse, surprised by the soft confession. Alara was the after realm to the Kylorr, their belief of heaven, where souls were at peace and reunited with their family. It was said to be a wondrous realm.

And he'd called me *zendra*. I'd only ever heard that sweet name murmured between couples in the villages as I passed them by. It meant "bloom," and I'd always thought it romantic. And now it was directed at *me*, from Kaldur of all people, and I felt like quivering in sheer happiness.

I smiled, unable to keep it from sliding across my face. His eyes drifted over my lips, and I felt his hand slide, taking my wrist. He brought it up, and to my surprise, I watched him take a big bite from my bread, unexpected amusement bubbling up inside me.

"*Syaan* berries," he told me, his strong jaw flexing as he chewed, and I was positively mesmerized by it. When he was done, he flashed me a small smirk and added, "My favorite."

"Mine too," I informed him.

"I have them imported from my brother's territory in Erzos. Only the best of them grow in Stellara. And once you've had the best, you cannot go back to something lesser."

"Stellara?" I asked as he pulled my chair out and maneuvered me to sit down. His movements were practiced and sure, as if he guided women into chairs all day.

"Stellara Forest," he told me, taking the seat opposite of me. "I take it you haven't traveled beyond Vyaan much?"

"Not at all," I replied, feeling a little shy to admit that. To someone like him.

"Were you born in the territory?" he asked, those eyes pinned on me.

"As far I know, yes," I said. But I didn't want to talk about how I'd grown up or where. His eyes narrowed slightly at my answer. Quickly, I said, "Vyaan is home. Though I've always wanted to see Laras one day."

Kaldur studied me but let my obvious attempt to change subjects slide. I was no master conversationalist. I'd never needed to be. It made my head hurt and spin hearing some of the nobles talk, like every conversation was a careful puzzle, an intricate dance. I wondered if Kaldur expected that.

There was a steaming cup of tea in front of me. "Is this mine?" I asked.

His gaze never left mine as he inclined his head. I took the cup gently and brought it up to my lips, feeling panic begin to rise as the silence stretched. Kaldur seemed comfortable in it. In fact, it almost seemed like a test, a game.

"You want my answer," I said when I replaced the cup, seeing no use in drawing this out needlessly.

"I do," he replied without hesitation. "Though I had hoped to charm you a little more over our breakfast before I asked for it."

Oh, he was all charm already. So different from last night. There had been an urgency and wildness in his gaze then. Something untamed that had had me shivering in place. His expression struck me as careful, his small smile part of his natural mask. It might have fooled someone else, but I'd studied his expression often and I'd found him the subject of my sketches more times than I would ever admit.

Luc had always told me to be careful of nobles. He said they used people to get what they wanted and they didn't look back to see how they fared. His mother had been a mistress to a Kylorr male of a noble House, after all. And after his rejection of her, she'd withered away, becoming a shell...until Luc had been left an orphan. He'd never trusted nobles...even though he himself aspired to be wealthy like one.

I understood why. His drive and determination, which had always bordered on obsession.

What would Luc think of this situation? I couldn't help but wonder. I was doing what his mother had done, lured in by a handsome noble from *the* greatest House in all of the Kaalium. What would become of me when he was decided he was done?

I shook myself from the fearful thoughts, feeling foolish. This was different, I reasoned. Just because Luc had warned me about situations like these, it didn't mean mine would have the same outcome. It might have just the opposite one.

Kaldur wanted me. For reasons I might not have understood, but he did. My blood called to him, and I couldn't ignore that. There was *something* here, something I needed to explore. An adventure of my own.

"My answer is yes," I told him.

His pupils flared. He leaned forward slightly, the movement nearly imperceptible.

"Yes?" he asked.

With my heart beating up my throat, I affirmed, "Yes."

CHAPTER 8

KALDUR

The relief that spiraled through me was dizzying. I'd never felt anything quite like it. Because, truthfully, I didn't know what I would've done if Erina had rejected my offer.

That's not true, I thought. *I would have pursued her until she changed her mind.*

But she'd made this easy, and I was grateful for that. Tension unknotted in my shoulders. I felt like I could breathe freely again.

"When would you like to begin?" came her quiet, shy question.

My fangs elongated in a rush, and I grabbed for my tea to wash down the sweet venom that flowed from them and to hide the physical response from her. I hadn't had this loss of control over them since I'd been young.

Raazos's blood, what would it be like to feed from a blood mate? I was both wary and impatient to find out.

But reason won, in the end.

"Once a contract has been signed," I answered, replacing the tea on the saucer, retracting my fangs slightly so they wouldn't bite into my lip during the meal.

"A contract?" she repeated, seeming surprised.

"Will that be a problem?" I asked.

"No," Erina said. "I just…I don't know how these things are done."

She acted as if this was normal to me. As if I struck contracts with blood mates every day.

She doesn't know, I reminded myself. *She doesn't realize how abnormal this situation truly is.*

Which was why I needed to navigate it with the utmost care. My reputation and family name were on the line. I didn't need the tittering speculation, not when House Kaalium needed to remain an unstoppable and powerful force. We were on the cusp of change, of an impending war, and the last thing I needed was to be gossiped about among the nobles who would help fund Kaalium's victory if that war came or if the Kaazor to the north went back on their word.

To distract myself from the dark thoughts, I motioned toward Leeta, who I spied hovering discreetly along the edge of the terrace. Trays of food were perched on her arms, and she came forward quickly, depositing them before each of us and taking away the covers with a small, practiced flourish.

I noticed that Erina flashed Leeta a small smile, though it struck me as embarrassed. "Thank you, Lee," she said to her.

Leeta only nodded, her expression carefully blank as she left.

Perhaps I wasn't the only one who feared being gossiped about, I remembered, eyeing Erina. The mere thought made amusement slide into my chest, that *she* would be embarrassed to dine with me publicly.

"I have a contract already," I informed her, wanting to see how she would respond.

Erina's gaze flashed up to mine. "You do?"

"You'll just need to review and sign it."

"In my blood?" she asked.

"Naturally," I replied. All contracts of importance were signed in blood. That was how they were binding.

"After breakfast?" she asked.

I needed to speak to Maudoric first, one last pressing detail I needed to make certain of, before I signed.

"Tonight," I replied, though I knew the wait would be strenuous for me. Now that I'd found my relief in this human female, it would be difficult to wait mere hours for my next fix of her. I was using her like I would a medicine, a drug. But the thought of feeling that familiar aching restlessness build inside me once more felt unbearable, though it'd been my constant state for nearly two years. "I'll give you the contract to read over today. I'll send for you this evening."

"All right," she said, before her eyes dropped down to the breakfast before her. Marinated *laak* eggs over seasoned *rusk* grains. A variety of fresh slices of ripened fruits, from all over the Kaalium and my own orchards, and fresh *syaan*-berry bread with a little jar of red sweet jam. I watched, a little fascinated, as her gaze went to the slice of bread she'd brought, two bites taken from it—one hers and one mine—and she sighed a little, placing it down on the table next to her plate.

"Eat," I ordered her, wondering for the hundredth time if I was making a grave mistake. A familiar mistake. She was keeper, for Alaire's sake. And young, at that. She was twenty-four or twenty-five, I guessed. Around seven years my junior. She had no place in my bed. Young females tended to have foolish ideas about love, when all I wanted was a transaction. She would get something and I would get something.

It was unfortunate she was my blood mate. The one female in this universe whose blood would call to me above all others.

For the first time in my life, I didn't know what to do. This was an entirely novel situation. And while I'd navigated similar ones, no situation had ever come close to a *kyrana*. A fated mate.

Raazos was laughing at me, surely, or testing me. The god of battle had a dark sense of humor, for certainly this would end me. This wasn't Alaire's doing. The god of mercy would never give me a wide-eyed keeper as a mate.

And yet…I couldn't help but stare with fascination as she ate her breakfast. She ate heartily and quickly, making my lips quirk more than once, as if she was afraid the food would disappear.

"It's not going anywhere," I told her, taking another long drink from my tea as I leaned back in my chair. I savored the calm of my body, the peace of the morning.

She blinked, confused, wiping her mouth with the edge of her fingers in a strangely erotic gesture. I swallowed, my cock pulsing suddenly as I straightened up, especially when her tongue licked at her fingertip, catching a stray drop of fruit nectar on the delicate pad.

When she looked down at her plate to see it nearly empty, her gaze then darted to mine, which I had yet to even touch. She blushed, the pink tantalizing as want curled in my belly.

I frowned, however, not meaning to make her feel embarrassed. "Don't misunderstand me, *zendra*. An appreciation for food is an attractive quality. You wouldn't believe how many females I've witnessed not eat a single bite at a dinner in fear they might stain their dresses."

"Do you fear staining your vest, then?" she asked, the question oddly innocent. "Since you've not eaten anything?"

I laughed, leaning forward. "Fair enough. I picked this color for you. I wouldn't want to ruin it."

She blushed an even redder color, making me grin shamelessly. I *hadn't* intentionally picked the color for her, but the small lie was a happy accident since I happened to remember the vase color from yesterday. The small lie was worth her blush—I didn't even feel bad about how easily it fell from my lips.

"Keepers learn to eat quickly," she confessed. "There's always much to be done. I'm sorry for my poor manners—it's habit."

"Don't be sorry," I said gruffly. I *was* hungry but not for food. It didn't tempt me one bit at that moment, and I'd only ordered a platter so it would make her feel more at ease. "If I were feeding on your blood right now, I assure you I'd be more ravenous than you. I wouldn't care about my manners."

She gasped.

"And once the contract is signed, you won't have to worry about rushing around the keep," I added, hiding my smile.

She fell silent. That was when I noticed Maudoric, lingering by the terrace door, a bundle of parchment in her grip, rolled and tied with a red ribbon.

Perfect timing, I thought. I gestured her forward as Erina finished her meal, washing it down with a swig of her now cool tea.

Erina didn't meet Maudoric's eyes as I took the contract from her grip. "I'll meet you up in my study shortly," I told the Head Keeper. I needed to have a talk with her. Maudoric left again after her nod, and I handed the rolled-up parchment to Erina.

She took it and tucked it into her lap, suddenly shy again, as if the appearance of the contract made everything real.

I stood from the table as she blinked up at me, her brows furrowing. "I have to meet with Maudoric, and then I have business in town. But take your time finishing your tea. Afterward, I recommend going through the gardens. There are quiet places inside where you can read over the contract."

"Oh, but I have duties to—"

"Maudoric is aware of the offer I made to you," I informed her. "You're not expected to work today. Read over the contract and take the rest of the afternoon to yourself. I'll send for you later this evening, and we can sign it together if we're in agreement with the terms."

Erina peered up at me and then her gaze flashed to the garden. I wondered if she'd ever been inside, but judging from her hungry gaze, I thought that unlikely.

"It's beautiful," I told her, softening my voice. I gestured with my chin toward one of the arched stone entrances. "Go. I'll see you tonight."

With that, I left. And with every step I took away from her, I felt that irritating buzzing begin again.

Vaan, I cursed silently, clenching my jaw tight.

In my study, Maudoric was waiting.

"You have the documents I sent for?" I asked, cutting straight to the purpose of our meeting, no pleasantries. My mood was souring, but I'd always endeavored not to take it out on anyone else, especially my Head Keeper. My brothers, perhaps. But never Maudoric.

She nodded and wordlessly handed the papers over.

"Did you read it?" I questioned.

"Yes," she said.

"Anything out of the ordinary?" I asked, already skimming over the citizen's file I'd requested.

"No," Maudoric replied. "It's what I know about her, what Syndras told me when she requested I hire her on."

"She came to work here on a referral?" I asked, half-distracted. "From Syndras of…House Terasyn?"

A strong, noble bloodline, though they had fallen on financial hardship in the last couple decades after Axia's death. I'd heard they'd needed to cut their staff.

"Yes. She's an old friend of mine," Maudoric said. "I trusted her recommendation. And she was right to recommend Erina. She's been a good, reliable keeper."

On the file, I read her full name.

Erina Denoren.

She *was* twenty-five. I'd guessed correctly, then. Location of birth unknown, though the first reported record of her was at three years old in Vyaan.

An orphan, I realized, frowning, seeing the name of a familiar orphanage that had once been situated on the outskirts of my territory. One that had been shut down years prior due to neglect.

I grunted. I hadn't guessed she would be an orphan. But according to her file, she'd been there nearly her entire life, until she'd aged out and gotten work at a noble's House. Her work history was normal enough, and she had worked at House Terasyn for two years before coming to work in my keep.

A small relief threaded through me, even though the section for her past known associates was blank. I wondered about the lover who'd gifted her that awful perfume, feeling something wiggle in my chest, something that felt awfully like *possession*.

"Will that be all, *Kyzaire*?" Maudoric asked me, even though she knew I didn't like it when she called me by my proper title.

"Do you think I'm making a mistake?" I couldn't help but ask, the words clipped but clear. But Maudoric was the closest thing to family I had near me at that moment. She knew Erina. I trusted her judgment, even though it wasn't her place to give it me. Right then, I didn't care.

Maudoric studied me. Then she sighed.

"I trust that you have your reasons for this," she told me. I hadn't told her that Erina was my blood mate, but Maudoric was shrewd and intelligent. She would realize it sooner or later, if she hadn't already. "You wouldn't do this if you didn't think it was necessary. I know that."

She turned. But at the door, she paused.

I cocked my head and watched her. The expression on her face was reluctant.

"Erina is a sweet girl, Kaldur," she said quietly. "Be careful with her. I don't think she's had an easy life...but I also think she's too naive for someone like you. For this life. For *your* life."

My jaw tightened. I knew what she meant. The life of a *Kyzaire*, the life of a son of House Kaalium was not an easy thing. It wasn't for the weak. I'd been born into this, and so I'd been well prepared all my life. But to an outsider, especially one who wasn't a noble…well, there was a reason noble Houses tended to marry into other noble Houses. The transition and high expectations weren't as jarring.

"And she doesn't deserve to be broken," Maudoric finished. "You wouldn't mean to do it. But she's not hardened enough to withstand it."

"She might not have a choice," I admitted quietly.

Because this had already been set into motion. Fate was a fickle thing. And more times than not, it demanded to be obeyed.

If she hadn't guessed Erina was my blood mate yet, I had a suspicion she just did, judging by the look of pity that flashed over my Head Keeper's expression.

"Neither do you, it seems," Maudoric said.

With that, she left. And my mood soured even more.

CHAPTER 9
—
ERINA

The arched stone entrance to Kaldur's gardens was like a doorway into another realm.

I'd seen the top of the garden from the upper windows of the keep, but beyond the slight admiration I'd felt, I hadn't given much thought to it. But now? This was like something out of a dream.

The contract was still clasped in my hand, but I nearly dropped it in my haste to reach for my notebook. I forced myself to still my movement, however. *Enjoy this moment,* I thought. If Kaldur insisted I stop my work at the keep, I would have all the time in the world to enjoy this place. To sketch every hidden nook and cranny. And conjure up more adventures for Kavelyn, inspired by this exciting beauty.

The garden was both manicured and wild. Tamed and yet free. There was a cobbled path that swirled and wound its way through the different sections. Some of the pathway broke off to make circular planters around blackwood trees, their gnarled, whimsical branches a haphazard display. Whitebell flowers were planted at their base, their green roots climbing up the wide trunks like they were trying to embrace it.

As I ventured deeper, the world melted away. All I heard was a muted breeze and the sound of singing insects and the soft pad of my worn boots on the stone path. I discovered an alcove, decorated with a circular stone bench that surrounded what looked like a *zylarr*, though it was empty. Around the bench were blue shrubs I'd never seen before, peppered with pink-and-purple flowers.

A short while later, I discovered a section of plants and blooms that made a mosaic of the night sky. The white flowers dotted throughout the black leaves of the plants were like stars in the sky. I *really* had to resist the urge to sketch it, since I was eager to explore every pathway I could. With the vastness of the garden, I wondered if I'd be able to accomplish my mission by the evening.

But as the sun steadily rose in the sky and the chill in the air began to warm, I traced and tracked over every winding pathway I could find, even the ones that weren't marked by the cobble-stones. Some were dirt pathways, leading to trees hidden from view, a nice quiet, shaded place to relax.

When I reached the middle of the gardens, I saw that it was marked by another arched stone entrance. Eagerly, I hurried to it, skimming the stone with my fingertips as my lips parted at what I found inside.

It was a courtyard, surrounded by tall dark green shrubs, all perfectly trimmed and neat, and nearly twice as tall as me. In the center of the courtyard was a large garden of starwood blooms. The indigo-colored flower looked lighter in the bright sunlight, and the small white specks in the center looked like stars. I'd never seen one in person before, had only ever seen illustrations. And as I crept closer, I touched one delicate bloom, the petal like velvet.

Starwood blooms were climbing flowers, growing wild. There were trellises staked into the earth, and they were climbing up them toward the sky. A few vines had grown outward, crawling along the cobblestones and winding their way into the surrounding shrubs, like they were melting into them.

I now understood why Kaldur employed so many horticulturists. Taking care of a garden like this was no easy feat. It would take a small army.

Surrounding the starwood blooms, tucked into carved out spaces nearest the tall shrubs, were simple benches. The sun was high overhead now. I wondered how long I'd been exploring the gardens. But judging from the way my belly rumbled, it had been at least a few hours since breakfast.

It was difficult to tear my gaze away from the beauty and wildness of the starwoods, but eventually I pulled at the ribbon and broke the wax seal of the contract Kaldur had given me. With a deep breath, I began to read.

When I was done, I sat back. The shrub hedges were sturdy enough to hold my weight. I stared down at the words, printed by a Halo orb laser, judging by the neatness and the color of the deep blue ink.

It was everything we'd already spoken about. I was to be his sole blood giver. The feedings would take place at his discretion and not more than twice per day. I would regularly take *baanye*, a sludgy tea, to keep up my strength, and if a sexual relationship began from the feedings, I would need to take marroswood to prevent pregnancy.

My face flushed hot when I read that, but I supposed it was normal.

I was to be paid ten *vron* every month—ten thousand credits. That was an amount that was *unfathomable* to me. While the *Kyzaire* paid his keepers better than any other House I'd ever worked for, ten *vron* was still more than I made in three months. And to think I was to be paid every month…and all I had to do was be his blood giver. Free to spend my days as I wanted—right here in the garden if I wished, drawing, writing, dreaming.

It was almost too good to be true.

In addition to the ten *vron* every month, I would be moved to the South Wing, Kaldur's own private wing of the keep. *I* wasn't even allowed to clean in that wing of the house. Only a handful of keepers that Maudoric trusted were assigned there regularly. I would have my own private rooms there.

A straightforward agreement. No frills. To the point. I gave him what he wanted, he paid me and kept me comfortable.

I felt that familiar feeling of disappointment bloom. I'd managed to catch the attention of the male I'd been pining over for the last two years…and while it felt exciting, it also felt emptier and colder than I'd imagined.

Maybe it's just nerves, I reasoned. This was new. And a part of me couldn't help but lament that I was below Kaldur's station in life. He couldn't be happy about that. Maybe that was why he'd insisted I not work in the keep. Because if I didn't, then I wouldn't be merely his keeper any longer. I would only be his blood giver, an automatic ascent in status.

That stung to think, but I also knew it was a harsh reality of this world, of which I'd always been on the bottom rung. While I'd dreamed of it, I knew that I had no true chance with someone like Kaldur. It felt surreal that this was even happening. To *me*.

There was space for me to sign at the bottom, next to where he would sign. I rolled up the contract to prevent me from reading it over for the fifth time. Then I sat, my gaze flitting over the starwood blooms, tracing their shapes, thinking of different pencil colors I could layer to make their unique shade in my sketchbook.

Carefully, I set the contract on the bench beside me. I took out my sketchbook. And, if only to distract myself from what the night would bring, I began to draw.

THE RHYTHMIC SOUND IN THE SKY MADE ME FROWN, AND I BLINKED up into startling darkness. My shoulders felt tight, and my fingers and the sides of my palms were smeared in charcoal. My eyes felt strained, of peering down at the pages of my notebook in steadily sinking light.

But I felt *good*.

I'd realized the passing of time slowly. A stray notice before I'd dived straight back into my work. In the late afternoon, my stomach had finally protested too much, but I'd been loath to return to the keep, loath to leave this beautiful, wild place and return to Velle's demanding questions and Maudoric's assessing stare.

Much to my delight, I'd found a ripened bluestone-fruit tree, growing in what I'd classified "the Orchard." Most of the trees were out of season, but bluestones grew best when the temperature was dropping toward winter, and I'd harvested a few to keep my energy steady. The tanginess of the fruit had made my lips pucker, but the small, crunchy seeds inside were sweet and I couldn't help but think they would bake beautifully into bread. Saira had never used them in her dishes, at least none that I could remember. I hoped I'd been *allowed* to harvest them.

That rhythmic sound grew louder and louder, approaching my position on the bench I'd reclaimed in the shielded starwood bloom courtyard. I'd posted up at different places throughout the day, to draw and jot down inspirations for scenes for my stories, but when the sun had set, I'd returned here. The stamens in starwood blooms were rumored to sparkle in moonlight. I'd wanted to see if that was true, to see it for myself because I thought it must be a magical, breathtaking sight.

I spied the stretch of wings, dark and fearsome, in the sky as a Kylorr circled above. Then they were circling down. Closer and closer to me, going almost too fast.

I gasped when they landed on the cobblestone, a short

distance away but close enough that the impact sent a ripple of powerful energy outward. It whooshed back the annoying tendrils of my hair that wouldn't stay tucked away in my haphazard bun.

The Kylorr straightened to his full height.

"Oh," I breathed. "*Kyzaire.*"

"Where have you been?" Kaldur demanded, his voice low and guttural as he strode toward me. "No one could find you."

He looked…angry? But why?

"In—in here," I stammered, waving my hand in the garden.

That made him pause. "Since this morning?"

"Yes," I replied, standing uncertainly, my notebook hanging loose in my palm, and I heard something clatter to the stone. One of my pencils rolled toward Kaldur, the tip breaking off from the impact. I'd worn it down to nothing today, using a rock to keep it sharp.

Kaldur crouched and swept up the pencil. He inspected it, and then his eyes went to the notebook. I flipped it closed, quickly, wrapping the long cord around to keep it secure.

"You said I could explore the gardens," I said swiftly, relieved when his gaze finally returned to mine. The pencil was laughably small pinched between his fingers. "It's beautiful in here. I haven't left. I, um, hope you don't mind. I stole a few fruit from the Orchard for lunch."

Kaldur still said nothing. His silver eyes were pinned to me, only an arm's length of space between us. I realized I must've looked a mess, and he looked just as fresh and put together as he had this morning. I wiped at my cheeks, wondering if I had charcoal smeared there. It wouldn't be the first time.

"You just made it worse," he informed me. When my brow furrowed in confusion, he stepped forward. I stilled when his warm hand came to my cheek, as the firm swipe of his thumb wiped away what was smudged there. "There."

"Thank you," I said, giving him a shaky smile. The muscles in his jaw clenched, his eyes on my lips. Then he looked up, plucking a pencil that I had stabbed through the mess of my hair, piled at my crown, in an attempt to keep it pinned up and out of my face as I worked.

The mass fell down. I watched his eyes flare, his nostrils widen. A shuddered breath fell from him, the small exhale surprising me.

"How is it," he began, his voice low and smooth, "that you smell even better than I remember?"

I felt those words swell in my breast. My nipples tightened under my uniform and apron.

"Look at you, *zendra*," he murmured, those eyes rapt on me. "No, not a *zendra*. Like this, you're a *dallia*."

That word jolted me.

A bubble of uncertain, soft laughter escaped me. "A *walking tree?*"

"Yes. Wild and untethered, their roots always pushing above the ground. And you know why? Because they are alive and curious creatures. They will not be bound to the confines of one place."

I sobered, though his words struck a chord that thrummed within me.

"Given that you just spent the day in my gardens, I thought the comparison would be a compliment to you," Kaldur added, his lips finally quirking up in a small, amused grin. Back to his charm, smoothing over the lines of his previous anger.

"It is quite the compliment," I told him. "There was a story I loved when I was young about a *dallia* tree named Kir. And Kir made a friend in a village boy, and they went on all sorts of adventures together across the countryside and through forests."

Kaldur's grin reached his eyes, and I realized, in a sudden jolt, that his smile was hardly ever genuine. Not truly. But *this* one was, and it filled me with a sense of victory. It was a beautiful smile.

"Yes, the fable from Salaire," Kaldur said. His smile waned. "But that story has a sad ending. Not many like it. I'm surprised you do."

"I never like to read *that* ending," I confessed to him. "I always made up my own when I told it. And in mine, I like to believe that the boy grew too old to go on any more adventures. And that Kir loved him too much to leave, so he planted his wild roots deeply near the home the boy chose so they could always be close as they aged."

Kaldur had drawn closer. "That is a nicer ending. Though the point of that fable was to teach that loss and change is a natural, important part of life."

I looked down at our booted feet, close together. One pair scuffed, one pair pristine. "And they will both feel it eventually, even in my ending. The boy will die. Kir will wither with time because even trees aren't immortal. Why not enjoy their happiness while they can? I think that's a better lesson, especially for children."

"I can't argue with that," Kaldur replied, capturing my chin to tilt my face back up to his. He was peering at me carefully. I got the strange sense he was trying to *understand* me. Like I was something to be puzzled out.

"Do you have any *dallia* trees in your garden?" I wondered, feeling my heart quicken at his nearness.

Kaldur made a chuffing sound in the back of his throat. "Even if I did, do you think they would stay for long?"

"No, I suppose not. But if I were one, I would happily spend my life in this garden."

"What were you doing in here all day?"

"Drawing. Exploring," I answered, tucking my notebook into my apron pocket, a movement that didn't go unnoticed by

Kaldur. "I'd never been in here before. And now I'm lamenting that I've wasted two years never stepping foot inside."

Kaldur glanced around the courtyard, and I caught his stray expression. One that struck me as sad, though in the next moment, it had vanished.

"And did you do what I asked? Have you read over the contract?" he asked next.

Oh. Back to the pressing business at hand.

I swallowed. "Yes."

"And?"

"We're in agreement," I replied, after a deep breath. "I'm ready to sign."

Kaldur's gaze slid to the side, into the leaves of the hedge, unseeing. He took a deep breath, his lips pressing together. I noticed his left wing raised slightly. For a moment, he looked… resigned? A warning went through me again. *Tread carefully*, Luc would tell me.

I frowned, my lips parting to ask a question I didn't even know if I could voice.

But in the next moment, Kaldur pulled a silver dagger from a hidden sheath in his vest. Seeing it jolted my heart. The handle was alabaster white, and a swirling silver pattern was etched into it.

"Where's the contract?" he asked.

I stared at the dagger only a moment more before I pulled the parchment from my other apron pocket. It was slightly flattened and crushed in, but I handed it to him, the ribbon imbedded in the wax seal caressing my palm.

Kaldur walked over to the pedestal nestled inside the tangle of starwood blooms, and I followed. He carefully maneuvered over the vines, which had overtaken the stone pathway I hadn't realized was there.

Not a pedestal, I saw. A moon dial, powered by a Halo orb slotted into the base.

But the surface was flat, and Kaldur spread out the contract, the parchment heavy enough that it lay flat, like cloth.

He didn't look at me as he cut his palm, a sharp whistle of a dagger. I watched a bead of black blood rise. Then he used my pencil of all things to dip into the wound like it was an ink pot.

In a flash, he scribbled out his signature, practiced and lacking any decorative flourish. It was neat but bold. I stared.

A deep sharp exhale left his lips, and then he turned to me, rolling the tip of the pencil between the pad of his thumb and forefinger to wipe off the remaining blood. He handed it to me.

His eyes were too silver in moonlight. So much light. I frowned but then realized why. The starwood patch had grown bright, and I realized, belatedly, that the blooms *had* begun to sparkle and shimmer. My eyes caught on one, nearest me. The stamens *and* the little dots of white on the petal were sparkling slowly, a undulating wave of light that grew dim and then brightened.

Beautiful, I thought as I took the familiar pencil from his grip.

"Are you ready?" he asked, the dagger loose in his grip of his uncut hand. "I'll heal the wound after. Any discomfort will be brief."

Heal the wound?

He thought I was afraid of a little cut?

As if I was out of my own body, I watched myself hold out my nondominant hand. His touch was warm and gentle, but the hiss of his blade felt like a searing pinch.

Kaldur's lips parted, his fangs immediately elongating when the line reddened. I got the sense he was holding his breath. His chest didn't rise and fall. I stepped forward and copied his movement, dipping my pencil into my blood—the most macabre ink I'd ever used—and signed my name.

Erina Denoren.

I'd never had much need to practice my signature. It was a messy scribble against his. Though I took pride in my illustrations and sketches, my handwriting was abysmal. If anyone ever came across my notebook and flipped it open in hopes to read some of my chapters, they'd likely be unable to.

I stared at my last name. A made-up one. A fake one. I had no true last name, only the one I shared with Luc and the character we'd created. A childish fantasy that followed and lingered with me throughout my life.

It's done, I thought, staring down at the signature. Just as he said, he healed the wound on my hand, smearing a thin line of his blood across my palm. The stinging stopped.

There was a mixture of wariness and mingled excitement as I looked up at Kaldur. Moonlight speared itself over the contract, and the twinkle of the starwood blooms illuminated his face. I looked at his fangs but didn't feel fear. Only uncertainty of what would become of this.

"When…when do you want to—"

"Now," he said, his voice low and dark, bordering on unfamiliar. "I'll confess I can't wait any longer."

Now?

My heart immediately sped, my breath coming out in a shuddered gasp. This was happening *tonight*.

"Have you ever been fed from before?" he asked, his eyes pinned on me, taking my hand to draw me closer.

"N-No," I breathed. I heard something clatter at my feet. The pencil. Already forgotten.

He dragged me even closer, until our bodies were pressed together. He was so big, so much taller than me that he stooped as his head lowered.

"I'll heal the wound after," he said again. I felt his hot breath against my neck.

"I'm not afraid of that," I told him, my voice sounding like a whisper, fluttering and feathery.

"I don't know what it will be like, Erina," he said next.

I didn't know what he meant. He'd fed from countless beings

before, hadn't he? Shouldn't he know what it was like? Maybe he meant for *me*, since this was my first time.

He inhaled deeply, taking my scent deep into his lungs. The sound of it made me tingle.

"*Raazos*," he cursed, his grip on me tightening. His tone grew desperate. "I can't fight this—I can't… I need you."

The feel of his lips brushing over my neck sent a shiver racing up my spine. A shiver that raced to meet his lips. It felt more intimate than I thought it would. The feel of his warm, hard body. The way his large hands wrapped around me, one sliding into my hair to keep me steady, the other winding around my waist until it spread across my entire back.

I felt something cool drag across my neck. *His fangs*, I realized, my eyes widening.

His ragged groan vibrated across the pulsing vein there.

The sharp prick of his bite registered in the next moment. I nearly cried out at the unfamiliar sensation, a ragged sound falling from my lips.

There was pain, though it was brief and oddly not unpleasant. There was a pulling feeling, dragging. I felt a bloom of heat begin to spread from what I thought were his fangs, lodged deep into the side of my neck.

An ache began. Deep and languid at first. It felt *nice*. Comforting like an embrace.

But then it started to become more demanding. More punishing.

My eyes widened when I realized what it was, just as I heard a rough groan ripped from Kaldur's throat, strumming across his bite.

I moaned. My hands came up to grip his shoulders tight, squeezing into the material, holding on for dear life as the intensity of pleasure began to rise. I felt every sucking pull between my thighs. Heat spread like spilling ink, until I was holding my breath with it, both desperate and frightened for more.

"Kaldur," I gasped out, not realizing I'd used his name instead of his title until it was too late. And by then, I didn't care, another wave of ecstasy erasing all memory of it.

His grip on me tightened.

And I never wanted to leave the confines of his arms.

CHAPTER 10

KALDUR

My brothers were *fucking* liars.

We'd barely discussed what it was like. Feeding from a *kyrana*, a blood mate, for the first time. And when we had, both Azur and Kythel had said simply that it was *unparalleled*. Life altering. Or as Kythel had described: *a rightness slotting into place.*

What they *hadn't* told me was that it felt like I was coming out of my bones, that my mind was rearranging itself and splitting, and that the *beast* inside me, as it awakened, was a vicious, monstrously wrong thing.

There was nothing *right* about this.

There was only a sense of doom, as sublime as it was. A doom I would gladly die within. Because I'd known the moment her blood had met my tongue, that sweetness a gift of the gods, I would *never* be right again.

I could never be.

It was loud in my mind. I could hear my heartbeat and hers. I could hear the rushing of my blood like a symphony in my veins. The gentle breeze in the garden felt amplified as it threaded through my hair and over the backs of my flared wings, a touch almost too severe. My wings…I hadn't realized they'd come around her, cradling—or trapping—her against me, as if I was afraid she would flee from this.

My senses were overloaded. I heard a door of the keep closing; I heard the deep call of a *lyvin*, howling in the forest miles away; I heard the clatter of cobblestones of the South Road being laid, even this time of night.

It was almost too much, and so I focused on Erina's scent to ground me. *Divine.* My hand tightened in her hair, pulling her head to the side even more. I needed to be closer. My body was throbbing. My cock felt like steel, pushing against the tight seam of my pants. I rocked against her and heard her gentle, intoxicating mews. They only fueled my need for her more.

Growing greedy, I drank more deeply as her heart sped, a harsh pounding I could feel even through the thick material of my vest. There was a maddening hungry need to replace every drop of blood in my body with hers. I felt my strength rise, could physically *feel* my body growing, pressing against the structured material of my clothes.

Her body bucked against me, a moan tumbling from her, echoing in the confines of my wings. I felt her pleasure. I could *taste* the orgasm as it speared through her, sharp and aching. I could taste her wildness and her innocent disbelief as she came apart in my arms.

And still, I needed *more*. Never before had I been this close to a berserker rage, but the strength was addicting. I understood my ancestors' need to bring their *kyranas* to battle. This strength was dangerous and deadly. I felt drunk on it, just as much as her blood.

"Kaldur," came my name.

I latched on to that word, at the weakened and tired sound of her voice. *Fuck,* I thought. *Too much.*

With a sharp groan, I managed to tear myself away. I flung myself back, crushing starwood bloom vines beneath my feet.

No, I thought in panic, and so I launched myself into the air, hovering above them a few feet as I caught my breath, her blood dripping from my fangs. I licked them, not wanting to waste a single drop, as my eyes focused on her below.

She'd fallen to her knees and was staring up at me, her face cast in moonlight. Her cheeks were flushed, her lips parted as she panted. Her brown eyes were so glassy they appeared like mine: silver. A stream of blood ran down from her neck. Her hair fluttered around her face with every gust of my wind, keeping me hovering.

She was beautiful.

I cursed, a maelstrom of emotion swirling in my chest. Disbelief. Lust. Resignation. Ecstasy.

Guilt.

I lowered myself in front of her. I'd taken too much, and her only true meal today had been at breakfast.

I bit down into the pad of my own thumb as I kneeled in front of her. The venom mixed with my own blood, and then I smeared it over the two small wounds at her neck. In mere moments, they stopped bleeding. I licked at my thumb as she stared at me, her gaze half-lidded.

Not speaking, I gathered her into my arms. My eyes caught on the contract as I stood, and I swiped it from the moon dial, shoving it into my pocket before I launched myself into the sky.

Erina didn't react to being in midair, except for a slight tightening of her hands on my vest. I was worried. She was quiet, too quiet. How much had I taken? I couldn't be certain—I'd been too lost—but I was reassured by the pinkness of her cheeks.

Still…

The garden grew small below us, illuminated by moonlight and the trail of golden and blue orb lights I'd had installed to light the pathways. I flew toward the South Wing, toward the balcony of my own private rooms, keeping lower to the ground and going slower than I normally might, in fear that I might scare her.

When I landed on the balcony, I pushed open the door with one booted foot. A fire had been lit, likely by Maudoric, and I placed Erina carefully on the plush chair in front of the hearth.

She shivered—and I wrapped a thick throw over her shoulders, tucking it in around her—though I was relieved by the shy smile that crossed her lips when I was done.

"Thank you," she said, her voice paper thin.

My lips were pressed into a firm line. My fangs wouldn't retract, and I felt them bite into the flesh of my bottom lip. I snagged my Halo orb—a hovering ball of soft light—when it strayed too near and sent a Com message to Maudoric before releasing it.

I kneeled in front of the chair.

"Are you all right?" I asked, my jaw tight as I studied her. I didn't know what I felt, but I would dwell on that later once I saw her well.

"Yes," she replied. But I didn't know her enough to know if she was lying to me. I got the sense that she was the kind of person to please others over herself. "I..."

"You?" I prompted when she trailed off.

"I didn't expect it to be like that," she answered. Her eyes were wide. She swallowed hard at the confession, and I knew what she was referring too. The feeding had been sexual. I'd tasted her orgasm on my tongue, laced with her blood, little pinpricks of pleasure sliding down my throat.

My cock was still hard, but I was too distracted to pay much attention to it. There were no signs of it softening.

"Is it always like that?" she asked.

"Sometimes," I answered, though it was a partial lie. Yes, a feeding *was* like that...if it was with a blood mate.

Every feeding in *my* life, however? However many countless

feedings I'd taken, whether they'd been from blood givers or lovers?

Never had it been like *that*. That had been a completely new experience, one only she—this keeper, who'd barreled into my life—could give me.

And that thought dropped like a heavy stone in my belly. I wasn't happy about it. Not at all. Because it made me need her. It made her irreplaceable. I didn't know if I could go back to a normal feeding again after tasting her blood. Everyone else would taste like ash on my tongue, tasteless and repellant.

What have I done? I thought, that familiar resignation tunneling deeply, carving pathways into my bones, whittling them down.

"Oh, did I do that?" she asked next, her voice soft and weak as she reached forward. I nearly flinched away from her touch, but she traced the seam on my arm where my sleeve had ripped. My body was pressing against the material of my clothes, too tightly restricted. I felt like I was being suffocated.

That hellish restlessness I'd felt for the last two years had been assuaged. I felt relief like no other.

And yet it had been replaced by something even more devilish.

This unfathomable need was like a tether, shackling and chaining me to a female I barely knew. A keeper in my own household. A human female, who didn't bear a drop of noble blood in her veins.

I would've never noticed her if her scent, her blood hadn't called to me.

A knock at the door saved me from answering. My movements were jerky when I stood and went to answer it.

Maudoric's eyes went wide when she saw me. She would be able to see every difference in me. She'd known me since I'd been a boy. Her eyes catalogued my enlarged state, the strain against my clothes. In her hands was a silver tray, laden with food and, most importantly, a cup of steaming *baanye* tea, hot and thick.

"*Kyzaire*," she greeted, inclining her head as I took the tray from her hands. Even her instincts were telling her to tread carefully. I was sated on my *kyrana*'s blood—for now—but we'd always been warned that the beginnings of a blood bond were often…unpredictable. "Anything else you require tonight?"

She couldn't see Erina from this angle and especially not with my bulk blocking the majority of the room from view.

"That'll be all," I said, dismissing her for the night. If she thought my tone was gruff, she was wise enough not to comment on it, and I watched her disappear down the darkened hallway.

Closing the door, I returned to Erina, who watched me with her wide eyes. Now she looked worried.

"Are *you* all right?" she asked.

She was handling this much, much better than I was, and I'd taken a lot of her blood.

"Fine," I answered, setting down the tray on the small table next to her chair. "Eat. Drink the *baanye*. You need your strength."

It went quiet as Erina reached for her tea, sipping on it. I saw the look of distaste flash across her features when the thickness of the *baanye* hit her. But her next sip was more like a gulp.

She drained it before she reached for the tray. I was tracking her movements, listening to her heartbeat. There was a need in me rising again, eager for more of her taste. It *did* feel like a foreign beast had just come alive within me. I felt unfamiliar in my own skin, and that made my temper snap.

"I have to go," I told her abruptly, already heading to the balcony.

"What?"

"Finish eating. And then rest. I won't be back tonight."

I needed to get out of here. My clothes felt too constricting. The warmth in the room was too hot. Her presence both brought me relief and made me feel on edge, like I was a moment away from losing myself again. Losing myself in her taste and the way she felt against me as she came so sweetly.

Vaan, I cursed silently.

The moment I was out on the balcony, I launched myself into the cool night air.

I didn't know where I was going. I just knew it couldn't be here.

CHAPTER 11
—
ERINA

I woke from a deep sleep to someone breaking into my room.

With a sharp gasp, I flew up to a sitting position on the bed, my heart thundering in my chest. There was still the haziness of a dream pressing onto my mind, but it cleared suddenly, like fog being stabbed with sunlight, when I saw it was Kaldur.

He was wearing a loose long-sleeved shirt tucked into black pants. His clothes were pressed, not a wrinkle within the folds, but his hair was wild, as if he'd been running his hands through it, and he wasn't wearing any shoes.

"Why are you in here?" he asked, striding toward me. His massive presence made my small room seem all the tinier. Had it always been this small? Or…had Kaldur grown *larger*?

I frowned, still blinking bleariness from my eyes. His eyes dipped down, his nostrils flaring when he spied the hard points of my nipples against my sheer nightdress.

"What do you mean?" I asked, my voice husky from sleep.

"I couldn't find you when I returned," he said, his tone mildly accusing. "You were meant to stay in the South Wing."

Low light trickled in through the window. It must've only

been after dawn. "I hadn't moved my things yet…and you left, so I assumed…"

I felt surprisingly *good*, now that sleep was leaving me.

That baanye *really helps,* I couldn't help but think, impressed.

Kaldur's jaw tightened, and he looked away from me, inspecting the details of my small room in the keepers' hall. But I had the impression he wasn't truly seeing anything. Then his eyes landed on the vial of perfume on my dresser. His eyes strayed over it and then sharpened, doing a double take on the glass.

He went over to it, lifting it up to take a small sniff. He chuffed, his mood dark, before he replaced it. "From your lover?" he asked, spearing me with a unreadable look.

I nearly reared back, my lips parting though no sound came out. If I didn't know any better…it seemed as if he was *jealous*?

And why did that small realization fill me with hope and a dark feeling of glee?

"I'll have all the contents of your room moved to the South Wing today," he informed me, pinning me with his gaze. I watched it stray down to the side of my neck. Was he remembering last night?

I touched where he was looking, and he went utterly still. The wound was healed, like magic. He'd done that for me.

A rough sound came from his throat. I realized…well, he'd said twice a day in the contract, hadn't he?

"Would you…would you like to feed now?" I asked, suddenly shy but aching all the same. I remembered the wild pinch of hunger and desire last night, an unexpected gift. I found, surprisingly, that I wasn't ashamed by how I'd acted in his arms. I'd given in to the sensation and experience of the feeding. What was there to be ashamed of in the end?

It had been exciting and new, a memory I was thankful to have.

Kaldur approached, every booted step thrumming in my

chest. There was a predator-like intensity that suddenly shot through him, one that made anticipation rise in my belly.

I'd always imagined that he would look at me this way.

"Would you want that?" he asked. One knee pressed into my bed, his other coming to cup the nape of my neck as he lowered himself. "All I can think about is last night. About you. About when I can have you again."

Wonderment burst through me. A thousand fluttery caresses traced through my veins.

He pressed closer. "I shouldn't. I took too much last night."

So why were his fangs already elongating?

I tilted my neck to the side, and the low groan that escaped him felt like a small victory. He came close enough that I felt the hot exhale of his sigh across my skin. He smelled good. Clean, like new parchment. And he radiated heat like a furnace, the heat of a male's body that called to some baser instinct within me. One that I'd never known existed, one that made me open up to him, one that made me press closer, my hands sliding up the wide berth and strength of his shoulders. I felt *sensual.* I felt like an earthly creature who *wanted.*

And gods, did I want Kaldur.

It was an addicting feeling.

"Please," I whispered.

"*Vaan,*" he cursed, a thread of disbelief in his tone. I felt his lips trail across my flesh, and I had the sudden longing to feel them on mine. He'd made me come, had held me tight in his arms, and sated himself on my blood last night...and yet I'd never felt his kiss. "I thought I could resist this. I thought it would be easier."

I tried to muffle my small cry, mixed with a moan, when his fangs pierced my skin. The strength of him was unparalleled as he immediately pressed closer, trapping me against the stone wall where my bed was abutted against. The sensation of the cool wall against my back coupled with the heat of Kaldur at my front felt sublime.

And when he started to feed, my belly quivered, heat and pleasure beginning to bloom. My hands squeezed at his shoulders, holding him to me, my head lolled to the side to give him as much access as I could.

I had the impression he was trying to go slow, to be mindful of how much he was taking especially after last night…but there was a wildness to this that I hadn't expected. A spiraling of brief insanity and need on my end that just wanted to *surrender*. To submit.

I wondered if this was how blood givers felt. Now I understood the appeal.

Tighter and tighter the pleasure wound. My clit was fluttering between my legs, and I squirmed against him, pressing closer. He ground against me. I felt the unmistakable hardness of his thick cock, scorching even through his clothes. There was a sense of relief that I wasn't the only one who felt this madness.

A choked gasp sounded.

Kaldur lifted his head, whipping it to the door.

My face burned when I saw Velle standing outside in the hallway. Kaldur hadn't shut the door fully when he'd barged in, and she must've pushed it open when she'd heard the noise.

"I-I'm sorry, *Kyzaire*," Velle stammered. It was the first time I'd ever seen her *flustered* and certainly the first time she'd ever tripped over her words. "Forgive me—I didn't mean to intrude."

"Leave us," he growled, his chest heaving, his voice nearly unrecognizable.

With a small sound, my friend flew down the hallway, out of sight. Dread spread in my belly, replacing all the warmth I'd felt before. Everyone would know now. Of course, it was only a matter of time until they all did, but I had hoped to at least speak with Velle before. So she didn't find out, well…like this.

"Fuck," Kaldur cursed harshly, pushing away from me quickly.

A stray thought crossed my mind. I'd interrupted him with Lydrasa just a couple days prior. He'd told me to leave, dismissed me just as easily as he had Velle, and then he'd gone right back to fucking Lydrasa. Only with me, he shot up from the bed as if it were on fire.

Because a keeper had spotted us? Or because *I* was a keeper and not some noble female with high connections in even higher Houses?

It was an ugly thought. One I wished I could erase from my mind.

He's in a precarious position, I reasoned. Kaldur was well-known as being a male with...amorous attentions. But only outside of his own keep. He'd *never* been involved with someone who worked for his House. Or else the gossip would've spread like fire throughout the kitchens and every single soul would've known about it.

That realization softened me toward him. He just didn't want others to know about me because it blurred the line he'd always drawn between himself, as *Kyzaire,* and his staff.

My nightdress had slipped off one shoulder, and I tugged it back into place as Kaldur glowered. His ire wasn't directed at me —I knew that. But it was more than clear he hadn't wanted to be caught in the keepers' hallway at dawn.

"I'll talk to her," I offered. "She's my friend."

"With a careless mouth, from what I've heard," he returned.

I...couldn't argue with that as much as I wanted to. Velle had never been able to keep a secret, and her eyes glittered and gleamed at the very mention of gossip. And this? This was a prime secret.

There was still some of my blood on his fangs, and I couldn't help but shiver when he licked it away. Then he bit down into his thumb, approaching the bed again. He swiped his blood across the mark on my neck before backing away.

"Maudoric will show you to your quarters in the South Wing

this evening. All your possessions," he began, his eyes straying to the perfume vial, his lips downturning even more, "will be sent there today. As stated in our agreement, you're free to do whatever you wish with your time."

There was a clipped coldness to the words, but I told myself it was because of Velle. This wasn't about me.

"Will I see you today?" I asked suddenly when he turned to the door. "Maybe…maybe we can take the evening meal together?"

"If I need you, I'll find you," he rasped, pausing at the threshold. The words pinched, but I tried to ignore it. He stayed at the doorway and then added, "Remember what I said, Erina. This is an arrangement. One that benefits both of us."

His tone shifted. It became a little gentler when he turned to regard me still sitting in the bed. His eyes were watchful, careful.

"There will be no ridiculous fantasies of a courtship or of love, do you understand?" he asked. I nearly flinched. "You're young, but you're not that young. Don't romanticize this—or me. Certainly not me. I'll only disappoint you."

And before I could say anything, he turned down the hallway and disappeared. I heard the heavy thump of his stride as I stared at my open door. I still felt the heat of lingering, unsated desire threading through my body, holding me together.

I sighed and then got out of bed, his parting words like boulders sitting on my chest.

I needed to find Velle.

WHEN I POKED MY HEAD INTO THE KITCHEN, MY GUT CHURNING AT what I might encounter, I knew I was too late. The sudden hush and the weight of a dozen pairs of eyes on me was palpably tangible. Even Maudoric turned to regard me, the spoon of porridge poised just before her lips when I stepped inside.

Damn, I thought, feeling my cheeks burn as I adjusted and

plucked at my dress—not my keeper uniform, and I'd left my apron hung on the back of my door. Instead, I had an old satchel looped over my shoulder, holding my notebook and my longest pencils.

"Good morning," I greeted, trying to keep my tone upbeat, only it came out like a strangled plea. I nearly sighed in defeat, my eyes seeking out Velle. Sitting right in the middle of the table, her stare was stony. "Can I speak with you a moment?"

She took her time getting up from the table, the screech of the bench over stone jarring.

A piece of jammed bread was pressed into my hands, along with a satchel of dried nuts, marinated *laak* eggs, and crumbly cheese, which I slipped into my apron. When I looked over at Saira, she gave me a gentle smile. "Here, lovely. Baked fresh this morning."

"Thank you, Saira," I said, the small gesture of kindness against the quiet kitchens breaking the spell. People began to talk again, though lowly. Maudoric continued eating her porridge. I munched on the bread in the corner, my cheeks hot with the scrutiny, until it was gone. Only then did Velle stride toward me.

There was a small grief in realizing that I wasn't considered one of *them* anymore. I'd spent nearly two years with all these people. I'd been part of something, part of a group with similar complaints and worries and dreams of bigger things. And in the span of two days, it was clear I was being iced out.

I'd known it would happen though, hadn't I?

"You summoned me?" Velle asked.

"Velle, stop," I pleaded quietly. Sometimes I couldn't help but draw a comparison to Velle and some of the children I'd grown up with. But if there was one thing living at Wrezaan's had taught me, it was how to deal with all kinds of tantrums. "Can we talk in private?"

She sighed. "Fine."

We went out to the hallway, away from pressing ears.

"I'm sorry about what happened this morning," I told her, taking her hands in mine. She pulled them from my grip, and my shoulders dropped. "I didn't want you to find out about…about it that way."

"And what exactly is *it*?" she asked. "Are you *sleeping* with the *Kyzaire*? If I didn't know you, Erina, I might even be a little impressed."

"No!" I said quickly. "Of course not."

"Then what is going on? He's calling you to his office at late hours, you disappear *all day* yesterday and Maudoric's lips are sealed, only saying it's not our business. And then I walk in on *that*."

"The *Kyzaire* asked me to be his blood giver," I said, licking my dry lips and watching how she would react to the announcement. "I accepted. I'll no longer be working as a keeper."

"What?" Velle breathed. She was smiling, but when she realized I wasn't joking, that smile slowly died. She looked like she'd just been struck. "You're his blood giver?"

"Yes," I said. "As of last night, officially."

"What do you mean *officially*?"

"We signed a blood contract," I told her. "The terms are very clear. It's all very…um, official."

She shot me an exasperated look. "For a storyteller, you sure do have a way with words."

I frowned. "Why are you upset? I'm sorry I didn't tell you. I was going to talk to you today, but Kal—the *Kyzaire* came to my room this morning when I was still sleeping. It all happened really fast."

"Oh, it's Kaldur now, is it?" Velle asked. She smirked. "Wow. I really misjudged you."

My brow furrowed. "Velle, I don't—"

When I reached for her hands again, she pulled them away like I was a disease. "I never expected *you* of all people to open your legs to a *Kyzaire* if he so much as looked at you twice."

My jaw dropped. "That's *not* what this is!"

"Isn't it?" she asked. "Did he mention sex?"

I floundered. "Well, it's…it's complicated."

She laughed, the sound echoing in the hallway. This was a mistake—to talk to her when she was already pissed off. I could only imagine what she'd tell the other keepers after this conversation.

"Velle, please," I said quietly, taking a deep breath. "You're my friend. You know I've always…I've always admired him. For years. Are you telling me that you wouldn't say yes if he asked the same of you?"

"Oh, I would," Velle replied without hesitation. "I would get on my damn knees right there and then because unlike you, I know what an agreement like that *really* means. And I'm not so high and mighty that I'd tried to sell it as anything different than being his paid whore."

I flinched. Silence dropped between us. My temper—if it could even be called that—wasn't stoked often.

I knew what was happening. The realization hit me too late.

"I mean, I'm just assuming he's paying you. If you're not working as his keeper anymore, you have to make your credits in other ways," she continued, twisting the dagger.

This wasn't the first time Velle had lashed out at me. The last time had been four or five months ago. We'd both been assigned to a dinner party that Kaldur had been hosting. One of the guests, an older noble from a House I didn't even bother to remember, had asked about me. We'd spoken briefly, and I could tell he'd found me attractive, though it hadn't been reciprocal.

The male in question had apparently been very wealthy, from a very old House—everything my friend valued in a potential suitor—and Velle had been cold to me the rest of the night. The whole rest of the week, truthfully, until she'd bottled it up so tightly that she'd ended up exploding at me.

Shortly after, she'd apologized and we'd smoothed things over…but I couldn't say I was surprised by this reaction.

She was jealous. Pure and simple. Not about Kaldur, specifically, but about the entire situation. A wealthy *Kyzaire* was taking me away from the life she herself despised. It was what she wanted for herself, and it likely hurt her to see it happening up close.

That realization dulled my temper. And while it was in my nature to let smaller things slide for the sake of keeping the peace, I still knew when to stand up for myself. That was one of the most valuable lessons I'd taken from growing up the way I did.

I kept my voice even as I said, "I don't appreciate that. You know me, Velle. I'm no whore. I'm untouched, for Raazos's sake." Her brow quirked. Maybe she hadn't known that. "The situation is what it is. You know how I feel about him, how I've always felt about him. My answer was always going to be yes, and that's *my* choice to make. You can judge me for it if you want, but it doesn't change this."

She stared at me. I thought, maybe for a moment, she might soften. But she only gave a huff, laced in condescension.

"Sometimes you *really* need to grow up, Erina," she said. "And I'm saying this as your friend. Stop living with your head in the clouds…because males like *that* will only hurt you if you expect too much. You want a great romance—I know you do."

My lips pressed together when she laughed.

"You're way out of your element here," Velle finished, smiling. "I'll be there when you need someone to cry to when you get your heart broken. But since you're no longer a keeper and now a blood giver, I think it's best if we don't interact from now on. Not like I'll see you if you're being moved to the South Wing anyway."

And with that, she pushed past me, jostling my shoulder hard, and stalked back down the hallway, toward the kitchens, where I was certain she would tell everyone what she'd learned. At least once Maudoric left.

Tears welled up in my eyes, but I refused to let a single one fall.

Standing in that hallway, I felt alone, like when Luc had left Vyaan for Laras. I'd watched his caravan until it had disappeared into the depths of the forest road, praying to all the gods of Krynn to keep his traveling party safe.

I'd cried myself to sleep for weeks. Missing the only family I'd ever known.

This isn't as bad as that, I tried to tell myself. I took in a deep breath, drawing on the strength of that small, somewhat comforting knowledge.

I hope you're happy, Luc, I thought. A plea or a silent prayer, I couldn't be sure.

Then I tightened my satchel on my shoulder and made my way toward the gardens, eager to lose myself in Kavelyn's latest adventure, an escape I desperately needed.

CHAPTER 12

—

KALDUR

By midafternoon, the strength from my feeding had faded, my clothes loosening around me, and I felt relieved. I'd shut myself away in my study for the duration of the morning until I felt more like myself. Beyond Maudoric, I didn't want anyone to know that I'd found my *kyrana*. Especially not my brothers.

Maudoric wouldn't tell a soul. But for now…it was best I kept the discovery to myself.

My bleary gaze was looking over the expansion proposal for the South Road, which would lead further beyond Vyaan and connect to Salaire next. Orb lights were being installed next month, an off-planet order that had been pricey. But they were permanent sources of light and would ensure safer transport of exports and traveling caravans between the territories.

I had my own doubts and opinions on prioritizing the South Road's completion when there was a threat of war looming. I'd opted against the plan, arguing that we should use our funds to begin increasing *drava* extraction. Kylorr black steel. It was mined from the Three Guardians, a mountain range close to

Erzos. *Drava* weapons and structures were virtually unbreakable and were invaluable in a time of war.

But Kythel had reasoned that the road would make it easier to defend the Southern territories. Vyaan and Salaire, specifically. The transport of *drava*, of food, of much needed supplies was made a priority. He wasn't wrong. Then again, neither was I.

Kylorr *could* transport supplies by flying them, but it expended a lot of energy, and some required groups to manage the weight, all tethered together. It was dangerous if even one Kylorr succumbed to exhaustion, potential for taking down the entire grouping, especially if they were flying with something as heavy as *drava*.

My brothers had been split, but Azur, as eldest, had made the final decision, siding with Kythel. Which hadn't been a surprise.

Maudoric entered my study with a tray of food after a short rap on the door.

She eyed me as she set it down on the small table near the window that overlooked the south side of the village.

"Where is she?" I asked first, the question nearly unconscious.

"In the gardens," Maudoric replied. "I have a few horticulturists keeping an eye out for her."

I inclined my head. When I hadn't been able to find Erina yesterday, when no one had known where she'd disappeared to, I'd…panicked. A strange burst of deep fear that didn't make any logical sense. If not for one of the horticulturists' report that he'd seen her near the starwood blooms before sundown, I would've searched the keep from top to bottom.

After a similar scare this morning, a mere twelve hours later, I'd tasked Maudoric to keep tabs on her whereabouts. I wasn't going to secure my *kyrana* only to lose her so quickly, no matter how repelled I felt about the situation.

It would be unwise for me to lose her. A blood mate was a powerful weapon, especially if war came.

Maudoric cleared her throat, and I looked up. "Lydrasa of House Azola is waiting in the atrium. Would you like me to turn her away?"

A sharp annoyance pierced through me, but I reasoned it was only habit. Lydrasa came to me every couple days like clockwork. She had for the last several months. We aligned. She was more than willing, and I'd been…needful. Anything to suppress that awful sensation growing inside me.

A sensation I assumed had begun because of Erina. She'd come to work at my keep two years ago. It was no coincidence that that was when it had started. Even beneath her awful artificial scent, that beastly thing inside me had recognized her for what she truly was.

A part of me was angry. That I'd suffered so long and so needlessly, constantly driven to distraction. Nights of restless sleep, chased by bouts of fucking that had only momentarily dulled the ache.

"Send her up," I told Maudoric, hearing something in my neck snap when I rolled it. If she was surprised by my answer—now that I had a blood mate—she didn't show it. Her expression was carefully blank.

I stood from my desk, going to the window. Sunlight skimmed over my face as I heard my Head Keeper leave the room.

Now a part of me wished I'd taken the larger office in the East Wing so that I might overlook the gardens. So that I might see where Erina was spending her time.

A gruff scoff of disgust came from me.

No. I refused to be one of those males who pined over their blood bonded like a lovesick fool. There was nothing romantic about this. I intended to use Erina like a drug, to make me feel like my old self. That was the deal. She would lead an easy, pampered life from here on out. She wouldn't have to worry about *anything*. All I required was her blood…and for her not to get too attached in the process.

My attentions couldn't be diverted from Vyaan, from the entirety of the Kaalium right now. We were on the precipice of uncertain change. I didn't need to be distracted by a female of all things.

Once, I'd scorned Kythel when he'd believed he could resist the pull of his blood mate in favor of marrying a daughter of a noble House. I'd laughed at him. Maybe now fate was punishing me.

Lydrasa entered my study, a sensual smirk already poised on her lips. "Door open or closed?" she teased.

It had always turned her on…the possibility of getting caught. I'd felt the way her cunt had clenched around me tight when Erina had walked in on us the other day.

Normally I'd have her bent over the desk by now, the tension snapping in my bones, making me want to crawl out of my skin.

Now? My cock didn't give so much as a twitch.

Another thing taken from me, I thought. *The ability to fuck others.*

I had half a mind to test it. To prove that I couldn't be controlled by a blood bond.

But I had a feeling it would make me feel all the worse.

"I need to speak with you," I said, leaning against the edge of my desk, crossing my arms over my chest as I eyed her. Lydrasa's smile slowly faded. She shut the door and then sauntered over toward me, her stride graceful. She might've been eight years older than me, but she didn't look it.

"Am I in trouble?" she asked, her easy smile flitting over her features, a mixture of innocence and teasing. "Why do I feel like I'm about to get punished?"

"We both know you would enjoy that, *zendra,*" I said easily, my lips quirking up at one corner. I needed to maneuver this carefully. Lydrasa was still a friend, a powerful ally within Vyaan. I didn't need to insult her.

She studied me, her pretty eyes raking up and down my body, and though my expression was easy, I worried about what she might discover. She was intelligent and observant, and both traits had served her well flitting through the noble Houses all these years.

"Something's different about you," she commented. I spied her finger tapping along her dress. A small movement that I knew meant she was puzzling something out. "Has something happened?"

"I'll be direct with you, Lydrasa. Our arrangement needs to end."

She didn't react to the words save for a small sharpening of her gaze. She only asked, "May I ask why, *Kyzaire*? Especially when it's one that benefits both of us so well."

"I've taken a blood giver."

Her lips pressed, her chin tilting up. "That doesn't mean *we* have to stop," she pointed out. "Unless your blood giver is the jealous type."

"She is," I lied. "There is a contract in place. It's one I am honor bound not to break."

"And you did this without consulting me?"

I grinned though irritation snapped through my spine, making my wings raise. Lydrasa noted that. I went to her, tipping her chin up to meet my eyes. "I don't have to ask for your permission, *zendra*. In *anything* I do."

She stepped back, out of my reach. "You're correct, *Kyzaire*. You most certainly don't."

The noble female was smiling now, but it held all the warmth of a hungry *lyvin*. "She must be *quite* the blood giver for you to obey so willingly."

My jaw tightened. Lydrasa would have her suspicions, of course, but I would never confirm them for her.

"I'm behaving," I said easily, "for now."

"Who is she? Where did you find her?"

"At a *dyaan*," I told her. A blood-giver establishment. "I had a taste of her and knew I wanted more. And more."

She huffed.

"Keep your secrets, then," Lydrasa said, a sensual smile appearing. She approached, pressing a couple fingers to my chest, the tip of her claw a small bite. Through my shirt, I felt the heat of them as they trailed down my front. "I'll find them all out soon enough."

"I don't doubt it."

Her touch met the waistband of my pants, skimming over my still-soft cock. She traced the length of it, and I snatched her hand quickly, giving her wrist a warning squeeze as discomfort burned in my chest. I hadn't liked that. I didn't *want* her to touch me, when before her touch had always been welcomed.

"Maudoric will see you out," I told her, voice firm, leading her to the door.

I could feel the sharp pinch of her anger as it sizzled beneath the surface. She wouldn't let this lie, I knew that. But mercifully, at that very moment, she surrendered.

"Enjoy your blood giver, *Kyzaire*," she said with a sharp grin. "Let me know if you ever want to share her. I'm not the jealous type, and I'll make it worth her while."

I knew she was poking at me now. Testing the boundaries.

I'd never been the jealous type either…and yet the thought of *anyone* touching my *kyrana*, tasting her, made rage rise.

She's baiting you—don't give in, I thought, gritting my teeth.

"Goodbye, Lydrasa."

"I'll see you at the dinner party in a few days," she promised, her eyes glinting like steel. "My father is so looking forward to your visit."

Like always, she needed the last word.

Energy was building in my veins. I needed a distraction, something to soothe the grumbling, prowling, new beast within me.

Use her, I thought.

Before I knew it, I went stalking through my keep toward the gardens.

CHAPTER 13

ERINA

The cliff's edge bit into Kavelyn's palm as she struggled to find purchase among the crumbling rock. The drop below her was a darkened, yawning mouth, hungry for ~~souls~~ morsels that dared venture too close. She was swinging precariously, her arm burning and tiring, her shoulder protesting.

The glow of the green crystal (ask Syndras about this versus gem!) clenched in her other hand cast the cave in an eerie light. She realized her predicament as her heart thundered so hard it hurt.

"Give it up, Kavelyn," came the deep voice from above. Jeb's face appeared, handsome and severe. "Toss up the crystal, and I'll pull you up."

Never, Kavelyn thought.

"I'd rather drop it," she told him. She grinned up at him even as her fingers began to slide. "Then what would *you do? There goes your millions of vrons, plummeting into darkness." (Should I use vrons or another currency?)*

His lips pressed. It hurt to look at him sometimes. How foolish she'd been to believe he'd ever loved her.

"You don't understand," Jeb ~~said~~ bit out. "I'm trying to help you!"

"You were only ever thinking about yourself," Kavelyn breathed, meeting his eyes.

Her heart felt like ice as ~~her fingers slipped~~ she let go of the cliff. She heard a quick draw of his breath, his hand flashing out for her.

But she was already plummeting into the darkness below, the glow of the crystal lighting her way.

I grinned, inspiration pulsing like a vein within me. Kavelyn would discover the portal at the bottom of the cave. She would fall through it and wake on the sorceress's wild island, on the far reaches of Noxily, which could, usually, only be accessed by charter boat.

I reread the scribbled scene, my messy notes lining the margins. I'd need to write a clean draft later.

The back of my neck prickled, and I looked up, my pencil freezing over my opened notebook, perched on my drawn-up knees. There was a sensation that I was being watched, but I didn't see anyone.

That is, until he made himself known.

Kaldur appeared, ducking beneath the long tendrils of the tree vines that made my own shaded little grove of privacy. I'd missed this place on my perusal of the gardens yesterday, but the moment I'd spied the little path to the grove, I'd known that I would spend long hours—days, weeks—perched against this very tree. It was beautiful—with a thick trunk the color of moss and long vines for branches that swayed with the gentle breeze, creating a curtain all around me.

I didn't know how he found me, but I reasoned he must have tracked me down by my scent. Maybe he could find me anywhere, now that he knew the taste of my blood.

Excitement blotted out any of the lingering inspiration I felt for writing the last part of the scene, which would lead to Kavelyn's final adventure with the feared sorceress Argamin. Next, I'd planned to begin my illustration of Kavelyn falling into the pit of darkness in the mysterious cave, her hand clenched around the crystal, the flash of horror on Jeb's face that would twist my heart as I tried to capture it. Despite what Kavelyn believed, he *did* really love her.

"*Kyzaire*," I greeted, smiling. I'd been in a downcast mood before I'd started writing, remnants of my fight with Velle. But putting my mind toward something meaningful, toward something that always lifted my spirits certainly helped.

I had a dream of binding these stories one day. There was a shop in Vyaan which sold a variety of books and bound leaflets of art. The owner had machines in the back of his workshop, ones capable of printing my stories and illustrations. I'd dreamed of seeing Kavelyn's adventures displayed in his shop window since I'd been a child at Wrezaan's. Since I'd first learned to read and write. It was, perhaps, the next thing I wanted most beyond reuniting with Luc.

Kaldur's gaze dropped to the notebook in my lap. I was sitting against the tree, my knees drawn up, a plethora of different pencils on the cool ground beside me.

"I thought I might not see you until tonight," I confessed. Even though the wound was healed, I swore I felt my neck heat, the memory of his bite, of the pleasure, like a touch.

"I find myself needing to be distracted, and you, my wild

dallia, I find very distracting," he said, those mirror eyes returning to me. I'd seen one of the sketches I'd made of him as I'd been flipping to a new page in my notebook and realized that they could *never* do him justice.

I flushed.

"You enjoy the gardens?" he asked, sliding into the bench opposite me beneath the vines. I'd opted for the tree, however. It made me feel more…connected to the stories I created. It was easier to imagine myself in the wilds of Noxily when I was surrounded by nature.

I nodded. "Very much so. Did you design them?"

Kaldur took his time answering, but he finally said, "My mother did. In her own way."

"How so?"

"These," he said, gesturing behind me and all around us, "were the designs she'd made for my family's keep in Laras. But after she died, well…Azur cares not for flowers and trees. The existing gardens suited the keep just fine, he said. So I stole the plans from our vault and had them built here in Vyaan."

A laugh of disbelief emerged from my lips. "You *stole* them?"

"When you grow up with as many brothers and a clever little sister as I did," he began, "you learn to take what you want instead of asking for permission. Because someone will always have something to say about it. But I don't have to tell you that."

I jolted but tried to hide it. "Why do you say that?"

"I hear that you grew up in an orphanage. Near the farmlands. Who was the overseer again? Rizan?"

My tongue felt heavy. "His name was Wrezaan."

"That's right," Kaldur said.

"You…you asked about me?"

"All of the keepers are vetted when they come to work in my House," Kaldur said, spearing me with a curious look, as if eager to see how I'd respond to the knowledge that he'd been poking into my past. "Maudoric merely delivered your file to me. I read it before I extended the contract to you."

I didn't know how to feel about that. I wouldn't hide anything from him if he asked, but this felt discomforting.

"Are you upset by that?" he wondered, quirking a brow.

"I'm not hiding anything," I answered.

"I never suggested that you were," he said, every word careful but clipped. Direct. Then he smirked. "Though if you were, I would be most intrigued by it."

I didn't want to talk about the orphanage or Wrezaan. Not that anything especially bad had happened to me there; it was just…they were just memories that were better placed in the deep folds of my mind where I didn't have to uncover them unwillingly. There were many that I loved though. Memories of Luc, of some of the children I'd grown up with, of discovering my love for drawing and writing.

And yet…

"You don't want to tell me, and now I will not rest until I know," Kaldur said, his gaze sharpening. "All right, little *dallia*, I'll ignore it for now. Though if you want my advice…whenever you *don't* want to talk about something, act like you don't care if you do."

"I confess I'm not so experienced in hiding my emotions as I think you might be," I said, the words tumbling out.

Kaldur laughed. A short, deep chuckle that told me he was surprised, and not offended, by the quick words.

"I'm sorry. I shouldn't have—"

"You're right—it's a skill I've practiced since before I could even speak," he told me. His smile faded. "Though now that you are my blood giver, Erina, you may need to practice just that. Nobles can be vicious creatures. They'll feast if they sense weakness."

My brow furrowed. My lips parted, but no words came out.

Kaldur snorted. "You're terrible at it," he commented. "Every emotion laid out on your face for me to see. It's beautifully fascinating as much as it's a fragility in need of strengthening."

"I didn't realize I'd need to be conversing with nobles to be your blood giver," I commented. The way he was watching me made my hands tremble. It was an intense observation, one that made me feel like he could see every throb of my heart and hear every quick catch of my breath. Like he could see inside my mind and find all the things I feared and all the things I wanted.

"Oh, did I not put that in our contract?" he asked flippantly. "I'll have to make an amendment."

He was teasing me, I realized, and I relaxed.

"But you asked me about these gardens," he said, straightening, his posture at ease and relaxed. *All a mask,* I knew. He was putting on a performance, for me, when there was no reason to. "And you have your answer. I stole the plans and gave them life here, in my mother's design. She would be flattered to know that you appreciate the beauty of this place."

That sentiment pleased me. I wondered what his mother had been like. She must've been a wondrous female for Kaldur to have gone to all the trouble to make her dream a reality. He must've really loved her.

I'd never truly felt the pinch of loss and grief. Only with Luc. I'd never known my parents. On Raazos, I didn't even know if I'd been born on Krynn or brought here. And when you had never experienced a parent's love, it was a little easier not to miss it. How could you miss something you'd never known?

But oh, had I still *craved* it.

My heart was fluttering. I'd never felt this warmth before, blooming. My face felt hot. I hoped I didn't look as red as I felt. Redder than my hair. What was happening?

"What do you have there?" he asked, gesturing toward my notebook.

I closed it, trying to keep the movement slow. I thought of his advice—act like I didn't care if he asked about something I didn't want to talk about.

"My stories and drawings, remember?" I asked. His brow furrowed, and it made me realize he didn't, which gave me a small stab of disappointment. "Of Noxily. I've been writing stories since I was young. I was just…scribbling ideas down."

"Let me see them."

A jolt of panic went through me, and when he saw it reflected on my face, a wide grin spread. Leaning forward, he kept those eyes pinned on me. He was curious to see how I'd wiggle out of it, as if this was a test.

"Perhaps another time," I suggested. "My hand's beginning to cramp, and I was going to walk to stretch my legs. Was there a reason you were looking for me?"

Kaldur stood from the bench, and suddenly the space beneath the canopy of vines felt a million times smaller. I also stood so I didn't feel so overpowered, and I tried to discreetly tuck the notebook into my satchel as I gathered it up from the ground.

"Better," he complimented, coming to stand directly in front of me, keeping me pressed very close to the tree. "You learn quickly, *dallia*. That will make this all the easier."

I stared up at him in surprise, feeling his compliment bury deep. A small, warm little stone that lodged itself in my breast. I found myself grinning up at him and was sure I looked silly. But I didn't have it in me to care.

One moment stretched into two, which stretched into three. I was keenly aware that he was studying me at his leisure and that he seemed infinitely comfortable to be doing so. His hand came up to touch my cheek.

"I would give anything to know what you're thinking right now," I confessed.

It was a moment of bravery and curiosity for me.

"Anything?" he murmured. "I'll take that deal."

I realized my mistake too late. Kaldur took my hand, lifting it up, inspecting the charcoal markings across it, which made his lips quirk up. He brought my wrist to his lips, and I nearly gasped at how sensitive the flesh was there when he kissed it.

My heart went fluttering all anew, coupled with a wild symphony of sensation in my belly.

Across my inner wrist, I felt the whisper of his words as he said, "I was thinking that it's strange how suddenly this happened. How unpredictable. How thoroughly you've invaded my thoughts, my every waking moment, when you have been within my keep for years. I never even noticed."

It was everything I'd ever wanted to hear from him, wasn't it?

"You never saw me. Not truly," I said quietly.

"Ah, but tell me, my *dallia*. Did you see me?" he asked, quirking his brow.

"Of course. Always," I whispered, feeling caught in his web as the vulnerable admission tumbled from me, as if he were a sorcerer casting a spell, like Argamin from my stories. My cheeks went bright pink, but…I wasn't ashamed. I thought it was a nice sentiment, to admire someone from afar. Was there any harm in imagining them as yours in another life?

But maybe that life could be this one, I couldn't help but realize. Especially when Kaldur was looking at me like *this*, with his molten eyes and sweet words. Could he love me?

The edge of his lips quirked up. He kissed the inner side of my wrist gently.

"I see you now, Erina," he said, his lips lingering. "That's all that matters."

Elation filled me as his fangs broke my flesh.

Just this morning, he'd warned me not to romanticize this with him. That he would only disappoint me. But in this moment, it felt like the opposite. How could I *not* dream of something more with him? Especially when he made me feel like this? Seen? Desired? Protected?

That's all I want, I thought. *To be seen by him when I've been invisible for so long.*

A swirl of pleasure and happiness exploded inside me before I felt the familiar warmth begin to spread. He fed slowly. What made this one different was that he could watch me as he did... and I could watch him. Our eyes held, making the prick of desire feel all the more pinching.

On the first large pull of blood, my eyelids fluttered and I made a sound in the back of my throat. I watched his pupils flare, his needful hunger reflected there.

He pressed me back into the tree, his strength surging. My satchel dropped to the ground with a small thud. I felt the hardened outline of his cock, rigid and thick, against the middle of my belly. My hands went around him, sliding up the wide expanse of his back as he cradled my arm between us. Nothing would make him let me go, I realized.

He was just as affected by this as I was. He desired me too, and that filled me with the confidence to explore him, to touch him when before I'd been too shy.

Kaldur groaned, feeding more forcefully, which sent a dizzying wave of pleasure through me. I was close already, the edges of a quick orgasm beginning to close in. Especially when he began to rock against me, using my body as friction against his cock.

I'd never felt this *want* before. This delicious sensuality that was freed and made normal by this act. We were nearly strangers, and yet I was on the verge of coming in his arms, trapped against a tree and his enticing cock and his fangs deep in my wrist.

"Kaldur," I moaned.

I want him, came the desperate thought. *I want to feel how lovemaking would be with him.*

This was aching madness that made no logical sense. But just like Kavelyn, I would be brave and explore where it led. I would willingly let go of the cliff—my safety and sanity—and plunge into the darkness, the unknown. I only prayed that something would catch me on the way down.

The orgasm blossomed out from my core, rippling through me with waves of intense, elongated pleasure. I cried out, gripping his shoulders tight as he thrust against me.

He watched me as I came apart in his arms, his eyes going so dark that they appeared not silver but a gray so intense they were nearly black. I'd orgasmed the first time he'd fed from me, in this very garden, in the courtyard where the starwood blooms were. And yet this felt so much more intimate. I felt connection.

His body was tightening more and more. And it wasn't my imagination, I realized…he *was* growing larger, his muscles swelling beneath my palms. A result of the feeding? I knew that Kylorr got strength from blood.

His fangs released my wrist. The look in his gaze was so severe, so full of need.

"Don't stop," I pleaded, still feeling my body pulse from the pleasure. *"Please."*

His nostrils flared. Before I knew it, he was moving forward, cupping the back of my head so I didn't hit it against the tree trunk…

And then he was kissing me.

I gasped, feeling the bite of his fangs as I tried to maneuver around them during the kiss. Not my first one, but one that was actually meaningful. I tasted my own blood, mingled with something sweet that made me arch into him. He continued to thrust, harder and harder, against me.

I went dizzy with his kiss. It was both gentle yet unyielding. I never wanted it to end. It made my whole body tingle, made my eyes squeeze shut, made my teeth hurt because it was so sweet.

"Going to come," he growled against my lips before licking the seam of them with a wicked swipe of his tongue. *"Vaan, you're going to make me—"*

I bit his bottom lip. My body moved on its own, as if guided by instinct I'd never known I possessed. One hand went to the curve of his cock between us, thick and so incredibly hard, and I felt his shuddered gasp into my kiss.

He covered my hand with his, keeping my touch cupped there, and he gave two thrusts before he went still. His breath stopped even as his tongue moved against mine.

Then…I felt the flood of heat spread below my hand. I squeezed my legs together, the sensation and realization of what had just happened erotic and strangely tantalizing. Then came his deep groan, the huffs of his breath as he broke the kiss. His forehead came down to rest against the side of my head.

After a few moments, it went quiet as he took my hand away.

"Fuck," he cursed softly, though there was only tiredness in his tone.

He pulled away, and I felt the cool rush of air replace where his warmth had been, making me shiver.

"I shouldn't have done that," he said, voice gruff when he peered down at me, over an arm's length away. "I got carried away."

"I didn't mind," I said, suddenly shy. "I…I liked it."

His eyes closed briefly. I licked my lips, tasting my own blood and him. My gaze dropped to the spreading wet patch over the front of his trews, and something quivered in my belly. Satisfaction, perhaps?

But when Kaldur opened his eyes, gone was the male who'd been in my arms. The *Kyzaire* stood in front of me, managing to look as untouchable as ever, even though he'd just come in his trews.

"Enjoy the gardens, Erina," he said, as if he was trying to erase what had just happened. Frustration pricked at me. He was determined to keep me at arm's length *now*? After what we'd just done? "I'll see you tomorrow."

"You won't want to feed tonight?" I asked when he turned away.

He met my eyes. His fangs were still out, gleaming and sharp.

"Our contract stipulated two feedings a day," he pointed out. "I've taken my allotted fill already. I'm allowed no more."

The words felt like a bucket of cold water over my head. The contract. The damn contract. It made this feel so…clinical. Especially after the heat and wildness and need of that prior moment.

"I don't care about that," I argued.

"But I do," he snapped, making me jump. He took in a deep breath. His tone gentled when he said, "Two feedings a day. That's all. That's what we agreed on, and I intend to uphold my word."

I wrapped my arms around myself, smearing blood on my dress. Kaldur noticed, biting into his thumb without a moment of hesitation.

"Give me your wrist," he demanded.

I held it out wordlessly to him, and he smoothed his blood over the bite. I stared down at the black mingling with my red.

"Don't be upset with me, *dallia*," he said softly, turning my chin up so I met his eyes. "I'm only trying to keep our agreement. My word is important to me. One of the most important things. Many times it's all someone has."

"I understand," I said. But I didn't. Not really. He held my gaze for a moment more and then stepped away.

"Have a pleasant day, Erina," he said, inclining his head.

I watched him go with stinging disappointment.

Maybe he'd been telling me the truth, I thought.

Maybe all he would do was disappoint me in the end.

CHAPTER 14
KAIDUR

By nightfall, I realized how futile it was to stay away from my *kyrana*, especially during the beginnings of the blood bond—when everything felt all the more punishing.

After the gardens, I'd filled the rest of my day with endless tasks in Vyaan. I'd met with the head builder, Jydar, of the South Road, even helping to haul blocks of rocks to burn off the surge of strength from the last feeding. I couldn't go into the villages looking like this, but I knew that the builders wouldn't ask questions. If Jydar had thought it was strange for a *Kyzaire* to do physical labor, he'd said nothing, taking the help freely, especially when I'd hauled three times as much as any of his workers.

Once my body had returned to its natural state, I'd gone into the village, burning through every meeting I had scheduled for the week early, whether it had been with the archives' master or to approve a new recruiting batch of soldiers at the training grounds or with the heads of noble Houses, discussing the trade routes of the South Road or speaking about an off-planet connection to help with its expansion.

There'd been a few probing questions about trouble stirring across the seas, but I'd kept my smile quietly confident, assuring anyone who'd tried to bring up the subject that House Kaalium was handling it directly. It hadn't satisfied everyone, however, and I'd realized that rumors would only grow. We would have to address it throughout our territories and soon. If I was experiencing it in Vyaan, my brothers surely were too.

With House Azola's impending dinner party in a few days, I knew I would have to approach the conversations with even more care. Nearly every House would be in attendance.

Even after the sunset and my business in the village concluded, I had energy and frustration to burn. I flew over the forests and circled distant mountains, pumping my wings hard—anything to not return to the keep.

But I was dripping sweat by the time the moon had risen and the village had gone quiet. I finally returned to the keep, opting to take the long way, up different stairwells and down long hallways, to my wing. For the first time in a long time, I felt calm. I'd fed from my *kyrana*. I'd physically and mentally exhausted myself. It softened and assuaged the storm in me, an old friend that had been a constant companion for *years*.

So when I caught Erina's scent the moment I alighted onto the South Wing, I followed it, giving into want instead of logic, though I might curse myself for it later. For years, I'd always done whatever I'd wanted. But as I'd grown older, as more and more responsibility had piled on my shoulders in Vyaan, in the Kaalium, I'd strived to be more like Kythel or Thaine. Disciplined and not so impulsive.

With Erina, I'd failed miserably on both accounts, especially this afternoon in the garden.

I found her in my private library. The door was slightly ajar, and when I pushed it open on its silent hinges, I saw the room bathed in golden light from the lit sconces. A Halo orb hovered over Erina's shoulder, where she was sitting on the plush carpet, a variety of books spread out in front of her.

For a moment, I took advantage of her being oblivious to my

presence. I studied her, feeling a tight knot in my chest release. *The last bit of my resolve,* I thought. *At least for tonight.*

She was dressed in the nightgown I'd seen her in when she'd come to my study. Light blue in color, in a material I knew was hard to come by, it suited her complexion well. Her hair was unbound and wildly beautiful, curtaining her face as she leaned to peer down at the books. A teacup was next to her, its content half-drained, seemingly forgotten. Her feet were bare, I saw, as she leaned over her collection of books to flip the page of one. Her features were pulled into a stern look of concentration and interest, one that struck me as adorable…and I'd never thought that about a female in my entire life.

A small wistful sigh escaped her. For once, she didn't have her familiar notebook with her. A pencil wasn't tucked into her hair. It was just her, her books, and her tea.

Finally I made myself known, stepping into the library. Her head slowly rose, her warm brown eyes appearing even darker. She was so expressive. I saw surprise and excitement first. Then I watched her try to hide it as tentative wariness replaced both.

She likes me, I couldn't help but think. I couldn't imagine why when I'd treated her so coldly.

"*Kyzaire,*" she said. My chest twisted with the word as I approached. "Good evening."

"It's well past midnight," I informed her, my voice sounding as tired as I felt. "And please, there is no need for formality. Not anymore. You've called me by my true name before. I would prefer that you do when we are alone."

If she was surprised that I sat down on the floor across from her, leaning my back against the chaise lounge, for once, it didn't show.

"Are you all right?" she asked, concerned. "You look…"

She searched for the word, her voice quiet and serene. I had the urge to close my eyes, to listen to her speak, to fall asleep with the sound of her voice in my ears. That would be a restful sleep indeed.

"Tired?" I supplied.

She shook her head.

"Unguarded," she decided on, watching me carefully to see if I would be offended by it.

My own brow quirked, not having expected that. "What do you mean?"

"Never mind," she said, tucking a strand behind her ear shyly, her gaze fluttering down her books.

"No, tell me."

"It's like what we spoke about earlier," she finally said, her tone soft and careful. "About hiding your emotions. Twisting words to make them something else than what you really mean. Only I've noticed you do it *all* the time. It's a mask for you. It's necessary. But right now, I don't see it."

I was struck briefly into silence. She dragged one of her knees up, hugging it with her arms, the silky material of her dress rippling like water.

"Why are you looking at me like that?" she asked.

I shook my head, the edge of my lip quirking, looking down at the books she had out. "I'm just looking."

I dragged one of them to me and flipped it around. I made a sound in the back of my throat. A book of fables.

"The *dallia* and the boy aren't in there," she informed me. "I checked."

Nodding, I skimmed over the rest. Some were about art and drawing. One was on the history of the Kaalium, my own House, though it was written in the Kylorr language.

"Can you read this?" I asked curiously.

"Some," she said. "Not all. I learned to read in the universal language but have picked up some Kylorrian over the years."

That impressed me. Kylorrian was not easy to read in the slightest if you were not tutored in it from a young age.

Another book was on infrastructure design for an off-planet colony. But the one she was looking at currently was a book of paintings of alien places. Paintings of the Golden City of Luxiria. Of the waterfall world of Bvaro, which was mostly shrouded in mist. Of the bustling marketplaces of the Nikk colony, the brightly colored tents of the hundreds of vendor stalls.

There was even one done of the dense, lush jungles of Pe'ji... though I'd always skipped over it. Too many memories were there.

"My sister, Kalia, gave me that book as a gift," I told Erina, watching her fingertip as it rested on the thick page. "It's a very special book."

"I'm sorry," she said quickly, jerking her hand back. "I didn't know. I didn't mean to—"

"I didn't mean that I didn't want you looking at it. Here. Push over the Halo orb," I told her. "I'll show you."

With curiosity, she did as I asked, the orb whirring quietly as it spun toward me. I snagged it, swiping my thumb against the sensor panel at the side, making it vibrate in my palm. Then I held it over the page of the book she'd turned to. It scanned it, reading the codes imbedded into the ink of the paintings.

It hummed. Then, suddenly, the landscape was spread out before us, a lifelike projection of the painting—the desolate yet beautiful wild lands of Dakkar, a place not many would ever see in their lifetime.

I could feel the palpable awe radiating off Erina as she scrambled to stand. I was forgotten, I realized, as I studied her face from my place on the floor. I smiled to myself, more intrigued to watch the appreciation flit across her features than imagine I was on a universally closed planet. If beings within the Four Quadrants thought Krynn was difficult to access, Dakkar was virtually impossible.

The pinpricks of light the Halo orb projected in front of her were true colors. The real magic of it, however, she hadn't even experienced.

"Reach out and touch it," I told her. Eagerly, she stepped forward.

The moment her fingertips met the image, it enveloped her, wrapping her up in a sphere of light. I could still see her through the transparency of it, but I knew she would only see Dakkar inside. I heard her gasp.

"I can see the sand blowing! Gods, I can feel the wind," she called out loudly and excitedly. I chuckled then, her voice much too loud in the quietness of the library, but she must've felt like she *had* just been transported light years away.

She turned slowly, a complete sphere around her that would allow her to see in every direction, something the painting in the book hadn't allowed.

There were closed slits on the back of her dress, ones I'd not noticed before, but now I realized she'd sewn them over carefully. The dress hadn't always been hers—it had belonged to a Kylorr with wings. I wondered who. And why she had it.

I watched her through the projection. Watched as she turned, marveling and cataloguing every detail.

"I could stay in here forever. All the things I could draw," she said quietly. I wondered if she meant for me to hear that. It seemed more like an observation for herself. "It's beautiful."

There was a strange tightness in my chest as I watched her. Such a simple thing, a simple code in the pages of a book, but I watched her eyes glitter with happiness and excitement.

"There are more, you know," I called out. "Is there one you wanted to see?"

Her head poked through the projection, refocusing on me. "I want to see them all," she said eagerly, her face split open in a wide grin.

"Very well," I said, dragging the book closer to me and snagging the Halo orb.

The book was part of a series, and this one held only fifteen paintings. I started from the beginning—the Golden City of Luxiria, which immediately prompted, "On Raazos, it's *hot* here," from Erina. Next came one of the New Earth colonies, then a lake of fire on a planet in the Third Quadrant, then a transport hub in the Second, which she seemed to like the least. "Too industrial," she'd decided, "and the smell makes my nose burn."

"That would be cheap fuel exhaust," I'd told her. It had a particular stench, one that felt like it was drilling a hole in your brain.

We went through them all—meadows that shone with glowing, flying insects the size of soul gems, of moonlit forests covered in pulsing blue vines, and the mountainous region on Balla during a meteor shower, which made her voice sound choked with tears when she'd proclaimed, "I've never seen anything lovelier in my whole life."

When I turned to Pe'ji, I debated for a moment, but finally I had the Halo orb scan the code.

"Oh," I heard her breathe.

I stared down at the painting, feeling some of my enjoyment of the evening lessen, but it felt...not so pinching. It didn't ache as it usually did, and I found myself curious of what Erina would decide. She had fresh eyes and a fresh perspective.

"What a peaceful place," she commented. "It's so quiet."

The irony, I thought. This painting and the recording had taken place shortly before the Pe'ji War, decades earlier. *Before.* Before everything that had happened to my aunt, Aina, her murder having been a raw ache in my family for years.

Now she was at peace...but it still hurt to remember what she must have felt in her final days on Pe'ji.

Quickly, I moved to the last page, of the waterfall city of Bvaro.

A small cry emanated from the sphere, a delighted little laugh that made my somber memories ease. I stood from my place on the floor, suddenly eager to stretch my legs and my wings. When I stepped into the scene with her, she was grinning, her hands held out as she felt the mist shroud her.

The landscape was at the terrace of the capital city. Bvaro was covered in water. Their floating cities were high above the waterfalls, and yet everything was enveloped in a fine mist. It would be hellish to live there, in my opinion, but the majority of their society and civilization were within their pristine glass domes. It was one of the wealthiest places in all the Four Quadrants, attracting only the elite for how difficult it was to secure residency.

Erina was looking over the terrace, her palms upward and out in front of her as mist danced all around. It dampened her hair, clinging to her dress. It felt good, cool against my hot skin. When she turned to see me there, she said, "This is incredible. Thank you for showing me."

No one would've ever appreciated this like she has, I couldn't help but think. At least, no one that I knew. This would've been a passing amusement for a noble before it was forgotten entirely. This book was a small thing, though rare. The Halo orb was even more common. To see the radiant joy on her features, however— so pure and so candidly honest—it filled me with contentment. I was glad she'd pulled down this particular book when I had hundreds in my library. Selfishly, I craved experiencing her happiness. I consumed it, pulling it into me like I was starved, just as I did her blood.

"You're welcome," I said. We were getting wetter by the moment. "Come. Dry off by the fire."

I took her hand, and she let me pull her through the projection. I tapped the Halo orb on the way to the hearth, and the landscape disappeared, golden light appearing again as the device circled us, no evidence left behind of the mist.

I lit the fire quickly, and when it was crackling, I placed her beside it. Erina kneeled on the carpet, holding her hands up to the warmth. Not wanting to loom over her, I sat beside her.

She smiled at me as she said, "I would've never seen any of those places if you hadn't showed me."

"You don't know that," I told her. "You have long years ahead of you yet."

"I doubt I'll ever leave Krynn," she said, but she didn't sound too upset about the admission. "I suppose I prefer my adventures in stories."

"Where's the thrill in that?" I asked.

She frowned briefly. "I find stories perfectly thrilling. Whole worlds opened to you, even made-up ones. The possibilities are endless in stories. You're not bound by time or money or connections or the logistics of travel or unromantic things like paperwork and applications. Anything can be made a reality. That's why I like them. They're magic. Just like those paintings."

I'd never cared much for reading or stories, but I didn't want to tell her that.

"Is that why you write your own?" I asked, remembering our conversation in the garden. "Why you fill your notebook with your ideas? Why you change endings of long-told fables older than yourself?"

"I'll tell you a secret I learned long ago," she said. I stilled, my breath catching at the words, at the tantalizing image she made, with her soft, playful smile and luminous eyes and damp skin. "Even when you think you have nothing, you are rich in imagination and more wealthy if you're creative. That is the key to a happy, content life. At least I think so."

A nice sentiment. A naive one, perhaps. And yet…

"For some," I said gently. "Others have ambitions of more tangible wealth, of status, of power. You can't deny that. People are inherently greedy, always wanting more."

"I just wonder that if people dreamed more, maybe they wouldn't *need* so much."

The fire crackled in the hearth. "Not everyone is gifted in their creativity as you, *dallia*."

"That's not true," she said. "Creativity is a practice and an—an *interest*, not a gift."

"I don't have a creative thread in me," I argued. "You should see me try to draw. Horrendous."

"But it's not always art or stories or crafting or painting," she said, and I could see she felt strongly about this. The passion it sparked in her was what *I* found interesting. "It's also ideas. The birth of an idea, like…breaking into your family vault and stealing your mother's garden plans so that you could create something beautiful in her vision here. Or…finding ways to cut through the Vyaan Pass for the South Road without destroying the groves by the river."

"You heard about that?" I asked, surprised.

She nodded, but it was shy. "Some of the keepers talked about it."

I made a sound in the back of my throat.

"You solve problems," she said. "That's a form of creativity."

I chuckled lowly. "When you put it like that, I am a *very* creative individual, then. You've convinced me."

She laughed. The fire's light illuminated her features, making her glow.

It was true I likely wouldn't have looked at her twice if I'd seen her in passing…and yet seeing her now, unguarded in her satisfaction, her cheeks tinged with warmth, I found I couldn't look away. And it had nothing to do with what was running in her veins and how it called to me.

When her laughter died down and she saw me observing her, she surprised me by not shying away. She met my eyes and let me look. She did the same to me, as if she was studying me. For long moments, we regarded one another, but it didn't feel strange or uncomfortable. It felt like we had all the time in the world.

"Can I ask you something?" she began slowly.

Wariness pricked me, but I nodded.

"What's changed since this afternoon? Because something has."

"I'm tired," I said. "I'm tired of fighting against this."

"Against…me?"

I inclined my head, even though it wasn't something I was certain I wanted her to know.

She frowned. "But I don't want you to. If you're worried about the feedings and the contract…"

"It's not that."

She wouldn't understand. This went beyond contracts. And yet I refused to tell her the truth. The truth was powerful, and I didn't know her enough yet to trust that she wouldn't abuse her position. I couldn't afford to tell her the truth, though I wasn't certain how much longer I could hide it.

"What, then?" she asked. The only blessing was that she *wasn't* a Kylorr. If she had been, she would've known the truth already.

I didn't answer, only shaking my head. She went quiet, her brow furrowing as she regarded the fire.

"Do you regret what happened earlier?" I couldn't help but ask. "During the feeding?"

Her cheeks tinged pink. "No," she said quietly. "Do you?"

I blew out a rough breath. "I'm in a precarious position, Erina. You must see that."

"Because you're a *Kyzaire* and I'm…I was a keeper?"

"Yes," I replied. "I'm very aware of the optics of it."

"I don't care what people think," she said quietly. "*Most* people," she corrected when I shot her an expectant look. She hadn't wanted the keepers to know, after all.

"I need to be careful," I admitted. "If I'm cold to you, that's why. I got carried away this afternoon. But it won't happen again. It can't."

I thought we might've both heard the lie. Because the reality was that when I was feeding and she was in my arms, I thought we *both* lost ourselves a little. It was nearly impossible to resist.

"Even if I want it too?" came her quiet question. One that sparked desire and exquisite need.

"Especially because of that," I answered, matching her nearly whispered tone. Though even I knew it was a losing battle. A countdown had already begun, silent but present.

"Do you plan to feed off others, then?" she asked. Based off the uncertain expression on her face, she didn't know if she had the right to ask it.

But I read between the hesitation in her words.

"I ended the arrangement I had with Lydrasa of House Azola," I told her, thinking it was one truth I *could* reveal.

"You did?" she asked, eyes widening.

I inclined my head. "You'll be my sole blood giver."

"Oh," she whispered. She tucked back her hair. "I… All right."

My lips quirked. "Is that all you'll say? Most would gloat at having a *Kyzaire* caught within their grasp."

Erina cocked her head to the side, her eyes straying to the fire, a look of puzzlement on her features.

"I think it's the opposite," she told me. She smiled, meeting my eyes. They glimmered in the firelight. "Because, *Kyzaire*, I find myself caught in *yours*. And I find that I like it. Very much."

CHAPTER 15
—
ERINA

There was a balcony attached to my quarters within the South Wing. It was, officially, my first morning in my new accommodations, and I woke up practically beaming, a giddy lightness blooming in my chest. The memory of last night didn't fade, and I went out onto the balcony, still in my night-dress, and let the rising sun warm my face.

Though there was a chill in the air, I didn't mind it. I sighed happily. With a burst of inspiration, I flew back inside, collected a thick blanket to wrap around my shoulders and my notebook before dragging one of the wooden chairs out onto the spacious balcony.

The morning over Vyaan was quiet, a hushed reverence. I'd always loved mornings. Loved the possibility of them, when the day was new and anything could happen. Perhaps I'd gotten my optimism from Luc. He'd always felt the same. But for him, a new day brought with it a fierce determination and hunger. For me, it was a softer kind of excited exploration.

With my notebook in my lap, I made a rough sketch of the view. I allowed it to be messy with smears of charcoal. But a mere twenty minutes later, I had my drawing of the view south. I could just peek the edge of the walled gardens, but beyond that, there was forest and mountains in the distance. So vast and wondrous. I wondered what Laras looked like. I wondered if Kaldur had a book like last night, but only of places on Krynn. Places that I could, conceivably, see in person one day.

Something to look forward to, I thought, smiling as I placed a few finishing touches on the messy sketch. Just something to get my hand warm, capturing a moment I would never experience again: my first sunrise in Kaldur's wing. The first morning of my new reality, of my new life.

Just thinking about last night made me sigh in contentment. For the first time, I thought that might have been the true Kaldur...and he was everything I'd imagined he'd be. Kind and thoughtful. Gentle but teasing. We'd stayed in front of the fire until the embers had burned out, talking of his garden and all the different plants he'd needed to acquire for it. He'd given me a rundown of all the noble Houses within Vyaan, regaling amusing stories of their *lore* smoke–filled lavish parties. I'd been content to listen, fascinated with every aspect of his life because it was so different from mine. I'd almost been embarrassed, telling him of my own experiences working in noble Houses before I'd come to work in his keep. My stories had seemed so dull, though his gaze had never left mine throughout.

My life was not glamorous or exciting in the way his was. I was all right with that...but for the first time, I wondered if it bothered Kaldur. How different we were. He'd hinted at it when he'd told me he needed to be careful of the optics of our situation. I understood that now, but I couldn't deny that it still filled me with disappointment.

Still...it had been nice. *More* than nice, spending time together without being rushed or on guard. It had been a perfect night.

The familiar jolt of wings made me look up toward the sky with bated breath, away from my drawing.

My heart began to speed in anticipation when I saw Kaldur,

flying back toward the keep from the southeast, from the territory that stretched beyond the gardens. I wondered where he'd been so early in the morning, but when he saw me sitting out on the balcony, I watched him pause in midair…before approaching my room.

When he was close enough that I could see his eyes, he studied me, coming to a stop a few arm's lengths away from the balcony railing, hovering. The gusts from his wings stirred the pages of my notebook.

"Good morning," I greeted, feeling my belly flutter at the mere sight of him.

"Good morning, *dallia*," he murmured, his voice warm and husky. "Why are you awake so early?"

"I always wake at dawn. Mornings are my favorite time of day," I informed him with a smile.

"Why am I not surprised?" he wondered.

My gaze strayed to the massive stretch of his wings, powerful enough to make it look like he was floating. They fascinated me. I wanted to draw them, the line every vein I could see. "Why are *you* awake so early?"

"There were reports of *lyvins* encroaching on one of the outer Eastern villages," he told me. "I went to go see for myself."

Lyvins, I'd heard, were vicious creatures and extremely territorial. "Don't they tend to stay deep within the forests?"

"Typically," he replied. "I think the South Road construction has been pushing them toward us. But it's no matter—I'll handle it."

"The problem solver," I said gently.

His grin came softly. "Exactly. Show me what you're working on."

I blinked, but I remembered what he'd said in the garden yesterday. He didn't like *not* knowing something, and when he didn't, it made him want to know all the more.

I looked down at my quick drawing, but then I stood. My heart sped when I held it out for him, biting my lip as he plucked my prized notebook from my hands. For a moment, I was worried it might drop, tumbling dozens and dozens of paces below to crash in the brush.

"It's a quick sketch," I told him hurriedly. "It's not anything special. Just something I like to do in the mornings."

His smile was lightning fast, but then he looked down to inspect my work. There was something quite achingly vulnerable that wiggled in my chest as his eyes roved over the page. I'd never been shy to share my work with Luc, and the children I'd grown up with at Wrezaan's had always begged for me to read my stories. That was how Kavelyn's adventures had begun in the first place.

But with Kaldur…it felt different. I wasn't sure I liked it.

"Even your 'quick sketch' is better than what I could do in a lifetime," he complimented. He met my eyes, and his praise felt like a warm, glowing ball lodged in my chest. "You did this just now?"

"Yes," I said shyly, tucking back a curl of my hair.

Before I could protest, I saw him flip back through the notebook. I bit my lip, a jolt burning in my belly.

"You shouldn't…"

My voice trailed off, and my face nearly exploded with heat when I saw him land on *one* of the sketches of him. The one I'd started only a few days prior, the morning before everything had changed. It was a much more detailed sketch, and I could see the obvious flash of surprise on his face when he encountered it.

It was just his portrait, the hint of his wings in the background. But it was his eyes, his features, his scar running down his cheek and the smaller crescent-shaped one I'd added in later on his chin. His full lips which I now knew were soft and warm…

When his gaze came up to mine, he said nothing. Only rose

higher above the balcony railing before he gently landed beside me. When he straightened, I craned my neck back to look at him, holding the blanket around my shoulders tighter, as if it were a shield.

"Is this how you see me?" he asked curiously.

That was not the question I'd expected him to ask.

"Y-yes," I stammered. Then I frowned, cocking my head to the side. I looked from him to the sketch. "Don't you? Did I…did I get something wrong?"

He let out a chuff of air, sounding amused. His voice was warm when he said, "Would that bother you if you did? If it wasn't my perfect likeness?"

"Well…*yes*," I replied. My embarrassment was gone as I shuffled to his side, examining the sketch and then back to his face. The sketch and then his face. Kaldur watched it all with glittering, narrowed eyes. I got the impression he was amused at my expense. "It's in your likeness. Your complete likeness," I insisted.

I would know. I'd catalogued every detail of him I could whenever I'd encountered him before. Every appearance had made my heart flip in my chest, and…he'd never really noticed me, had he?

"No, it's not," he argued.

"Where?" I demanded. "How?"

"Here," he said, turning his jawline so I could see the sharp edge of it.

"What am I looking at?" I asked, though I *was* momentarily distracted when he crouched so I could be very, very close to his face. I could almost smell the heat of him, the clean musk from his long morning flight.

He tapped underneath his jaw. There I saw the slight glimmer of a scar.

A shocked chuckle escaped me. "That's not fair. How would I have ever seen that? I've never been *that* close to you."

A knowing smirk on his features. "You have been. You got this scar right," he told me, tapping his chin.

"I added that one in," I confessed. "After that afternoon in the sitting room when I was cleaning up the vase shards."

"Ah," he said quietly. When he'd smelled my blood for the first time. "Take a good look now, then."

I did. I wasn't even ashamed to say that I was greedy with his permission, especially when he was still crouching down for me. Our eyes were nearly level, and I was so close that I could hear the small exhale as it left his nostrils and I could see every minuscule twitch of his jaw.

My hands raised, uncertain, but I wanted so desperately to touch him. When my palm met his cheek, his nostrils flared. I saw something different enter his gaze, and suddenly the moment felt entirely changed. My fingertips traced the long scar over his cheek before ending at the corner of his mouth, feeling the depth of it, wondering how he'd received it. His gray skin was surprisingly smooth, suede-like, and unblemished, save for the silver scars.

When he didn't protest, I boldly traced over his face, touching his stern brow, the sharp slope of his nose, the blade of his jawline, the slash of his cheekbones. All the while, his silver eyes had lost all signs of amusement. Instead they were heated with a familiar want, which made me feel like flying.

When my pinky brushed the edge of his soft lips, he made a gruff sound and, momentarily, his eyelids fluttered closed. I pulled my hand away.

I cleared my throat, my voice nearly a whisper when I said, "I'll do better next time now that I've seen you so clearly."

Kaldur trapped my chin with his fingertips when I went to pull away. "This is very good, Erina. Your drawing. You have immense talent. I hope you know that."

I couldn't help but beam with the praise. It filled something inside me that had long been empty.

"Thank you," I said. He released me and then finally straightened to his full height. I wasn't cold anymore in the brisk morning. My body felt warm and languid like I was under the gentle heat of a summer's day.

To fill the stretch of charged silence that lapsed, both of us not quite certain what had just transpired, he flipped through the notebook more.

But then he landed on a drawing I'd done of Luc. One I'd done from memory. His familiar features stared up at Kaldur. He might've been done in charcoal, but whenever I saw sketches I'd done of him, I only ever saw him in color. Bright blue eyes, sometimes twinkling in mischief or deviance or determination. The light gray of his skin and his curling horns. He had no wings, and he carried the lean build of a human, like his mother.

It was a dirty secret of the Houses...that many of the orphans who ended up in places like Wrezaan's were bastards of nobles. Bastards they had with their keepers or females below their station in life, some of whom were human. Many of the children I'd grown up with had been hybrids. Some had been human, like me. Others had been Bartutian mixes. Some full-blooded Kylorr.

But Luc had always straddled two worlds, and I thought that was why he'd been so driven to prove himself.

"Let me guess," Kaldur drawled softly, his eyes suddenly piercing into mine. "Your purveyor of fine perfumes?"

The words reminded me of the vial that was sitting on my new dresser. But I heard a sharp edge in Kaldur's voice, one I didn't understand.

"Yes," I said hesitantly. "Luc. We grew up together. At...at Wrezaan's."

"Hmm," came the sound. He studied me, but I felt the softness of the moment change. I felt awkward, uncertain of his mood. He snapped the notebook closed and handed it back to me. "Let's go inside."

He went through the doors of my room, and I hesitantly followed after him, setting my notebook down on the small table near my bed. The room was more extravagant than I was used to. Not overly decorated, but the detail of the architecture alone, from the arched window panes and the stone-carved reliefs in the walls. The furnishings were very fine and obviously expensive, though slightly dark for my own personal tastes. I didn't like dark places. Wrezaan's orphanage had been mostly dark wood walls and gray stone.

Kaldur turned into me, and my breath hitched when he backed me into the wall, my shoulder bumping into a framed map of the Kaalium, though it looked like it was centuries old.

His eyes burned down into mine, and I saw his desire there. *Oh.*

Immediately, I felt my body respond, as if he was slowly training me. Or perhaps I just wanted him that much. Had fantasized about being with him in my foolish, silly daydreams…and now that I had him, I was eager and selfish.

His head dipped, and I felt his lips run along the side of my exposed neck. The blanket fell from my shoulders, pooling at our feet on the floor, as I tilted for him. The gentle brush of his lips made shivers run up my spine, and I clutched at his forearms when they came around my waist.

"Did you take your *baanye?*" he asked.

"Y-yes," I breathed. "Last night."

He hummed—pleased, I thought.

"I need you again," he murmured. "You don't know how difficult it was not to taste you last night."

My breath came out in small gasps when he kissed my neck, his lips lingering over the faded markings where he'd fed yesterday morning, before Velle had caught us.

"But we must behave, *dallia,*" he said harshly. "This is a feeding only. Nothing more. We can't forget ourselves. Yes?"

"Yes," I whispered, but truthfully, I would've said anything he wanted. With his hands on me, with his lips on me and the sweet promise of his bite…I would've done anything he asked.

It was a powerful, unsettling realization.

He sighed, and I felt the hot exhale of his breath. "Good."

His bite pierced into me.

And I was in ecstasy, though I fought it with everything inside me.

Just as I'd promised.

CHAPTER 16
—
KALDUR

Two nights later, I was readying for House Azola's dinner, mentally barricading myself and preparing for the barrage of questions about the rumors of impending war. I'd spoken with my brothers earlier during our weekly meeting, and we'd all agreed to try to curb the whisperings for now, at least until we finalized a war bond with the Kaazor in the North.

It would only lead to panic. From the noble Houses, the news would spread throughout the entirety of the Kaalium. If there was one thing I'd learned from Erina, it was that keepers found out everything eventually and they would talk.

I was already on edge, and I knew *exactly* who would help ease it. But in an attempt to *not* make it obvious I'd found my blood mate by showing up to the dinner of nobles in too-tight clothing, I'd decided against taking a later feeding from her today. I hadn't seen Erina since this morning, since she'd trembled against me in the hallway, fighting valiantly against her building desire as I'd taken my fill. I could still feel the prick of her nails as they'd dug into my shoulders.

I'd never been so satisfied on blood and so sexually frustrated in my life. Merely thinking about her made my cock harden. It was becoming more and more apparent that we couldn't fight this forever on willpower alone. Sooner or later, we might both go mad.

There's no reason to resist, that devious little voice in my mind whispered. *She is yours already.*

But in doing so, it would cement the bond. Forever shackled to her. Forever reliant on her blood. That was a commitment I didn't *want* to make right now.

"*Vaan,*" I cursed under my breath, buttoning the last silver clasp on my molded vest. It looked like armor tonight, plated in silver embellishments. I thought it fitting, considering I felt like I was going into a hungry den of nobles.

If all of Vyaan knew that Erina was my *kyrana,* she would be expected to be at my side tonight. The fact that she would not be was an insult to her...so it was better she didn't know about it. Still, the news that I'd taken a permanent blood giver would undoubtedly be a topic of conversation. I was hosting a dinner at the keep in another week. Erina would need to be in attendance, as was her right. It would even be expected, especially after tonight. I had no doubt that Lydrasa had already spread the news and by now knew who she was.

I headed toward my balcony door, keen to leave, to get this dinner over with so I could return, when a knock halted me. Light and a little hesitant. I knew who it was, and my fucking fangs nearly elongated right there and then.

Blowing out a sharp breath, I went to the door. Erina was there, dressed in plain light brown trousers and a soft white shirt that billowed out around her arms but nipped her in at the torso. Her hair was up in a pile on her head, a pencil tucked behind her ear, her cheeks flushed, her eyes bloodshot.

The surge of longing that went through me was alarming.

"I'm sorry—I just came in from the gardens. I lost track of time," she said quickly. There was eagerness in her gaze. "Did you want to—"

If she asked me outright, I might not have the discipline to deny her.

"Later," I rasped. "I'm heading out to a dinner tonight."

"Oh," she said, blinking her wide eyes. She had charcoal across her cheek again, and I wiped at it, frowning, rubbing at the smudge until it disappeared, wondering how she always dirtied herself there. Her skin was hot and she smelled more tempting than that morning, but I knew that was the hunger in me. "Oh, you look very handsome."

She'd finally looked down at my clothing. The compliment fell easily from her lips, as did her pleased shy smile.

"Will you draw me like this, *dallia*?" I rumbled, unable to resist the small tease. "Look your fill. I expect to see my likeness when I return to you tonight."

Her laugh released some tension that had been lining my shoulders. The last two days had been shockingly easy with her. We had a routine, one we'd fallen into. Feedings only, yes. But there was an ease of talking with her, as charged as the conversations might be. It felt like we were both holding our breath in those conversations. I found them exciting and tantalizing, even though they were innocent. And I found myself thinking of her far too much when she was absent.

The bond, I knew, further wiggling itself into me like a parasite.

"I'll see what I can do," she replied. Her gaze ran over me again. She *had* lost track of time, it seemed. She'd been on her way out to the gardens when I'd caught her in the hallway just that morning. Had she not returned since?

"Make sure you eat and take your *baanye*," I told her gruffly. She needed to take better care of herself. She couldn't survive the entire day on fruit from my orchards if she didn't want to come inside.

"I will," she promised. "See you tonight."

I inclined my head, then watched her disappear down the hallway to her quarters.

And suddenly the night seemed endless until I could see her next.

I smiled at Kyda through the silver smoke of *lore* floating throughout the dining hall of House Azola. Even the smoke couldn't dull the snap of tension in my shoulders as I counted down the moments until I could take my leave politely now that dinner had ended.

I'd been here for hours, and I knew that Lydrasa had spread the rumors already. I'd caught the lingering stares, the ways nobles tried to hide the quirk of their mouths. Every time I caught a glimpse of my former lover, irritation burned in my gut at her sly smile.

Her message was clear. No one rejected her, not even a *Kyzaire*.

But that's her mistake, I thought. She thought herself invincible against House Kaalium because she'd had one of its sons between her thighs. *Nothing* made her protected against my House unless she was bound to me in marriage or blood…and she wasn't.

I would speak with her before I left. I would give her a warning of my own because my patience had already been rubbed thin within a mere few moments of entering House Azola.

Kyda was Lydrasa's mother, who'd pulled me into conversation as a familiar keeper roamed the room with a tray of a variety of *lore* yields from different years. My eyes had narrowed on her, knowing that she was one of mine, and I wondered why she was serving House Azola tonight.

"Tell me, *Kyzaire*, if the South Road is being extended to Salaire, then perhaps it will be easier to import the Southern silks from your brother's territory. I know the shopkeeper here in Vyaan. He would be delighted if we got a steady supply in. It always sells so fast," Kyda told me. She smiled. "Of course, he always keeps some for me. He knows how much I enjoy it."

"As he should," I said, taking a sip of my brew from the silver goblet. All around me, I could feel the circling of other nobles, all waiting for a chance to steal me for a conversation. I'd already spoken to nearly half of those in attendance. "I'll see what arrangements can be made. But if you'll pardon me, Kyda…I need to speak with your daughter."

"Oh, of course," she answered, her eyes twinkling knowingly. Whatever she assumed, I would let her assume it. As long as I could leave as soon as possible. And Lydrasa was the last obstacle in my way.

I hurried through the crowded room, dodging pulls into circles and conversations with an easy smile and apologies. *A mask.* That was what Erina had called it, hadn't she? And she'd been right.

Sometimes I worried I'd *become* this mask. I worried I didn't know who I was anymore. Once, I'd never cared about the opinions of others. I'd done what I'd wanted. The luxury of youth, I supposed.

"I need to speak with you," I murmured into Lydrasa's ear when I reached her, my grip on her arm firm. She'd been speaking with a son of House Braan. Judging by his darkened cheeks, I wondered if Lydrasa was already hunting for my replacement.

"My pleasure, *Kyzaire,*" Lydrasa purred, her lips pulled into a playful smile.

"Privately."

She inclined her head, excusing herself from the conversation. We passed the familiar keeper and Lydrasa touched her arm before leading me into a quiet hallway off the main dining hall.

"Why is one of my keepers serving at your gathering?" I asked when we were alone, enclosed in a private sitting room, blissfully quiet and clear of foggy smoke and raucous laughter. My ears nearly rang in relief.

"Velle?" Lydrasa asked, quirking a brow. "She used to work for House Azola. Did you not know? She'll still visit us at times, offer to help with our parties if it's a quiet night at your keep. I didn't think to mention it because I didn't think you'd care."

"If Maudoric cleared it, then I have no reason to care."

"I wouldn't know," Lydrasa replied with a small, delicate shrug. She circled me, tracing her fingers over my shoulders. "What's wrong, Kaldur? Are you upset with me?"

"I know what you've been up to," I informed her when she came to stand in front of me. I grabbed her forearm when she tried to move away. "I don't appreciate you spreading my private business. Nor is it your place. Consider this a warning, Lydrasa. Keep me out of your mouth."

She licked her lips. Her voice dropped and she touched my arm. "Yet I remember a time when you begged me to keep you *in* my mouth, *Kyzaire*."

"Lydrasa," I growled.

"Yes, yes," she sighed, irritated. She dropped the act, like a curtain falling, and stalked away toward the shelves, which were littered in old artifacts from across the universe. Strange rocks and glittering gems. Grotesque little figurines and pots of bright colors. "I'm only watching out for you, Kaldur."

I scoffed. "How exactly are you watching out for me? I'd love to hear this."

"*Don't* make a mockery of me, *Kyzaire*," she hissed. My title felt like a jab as she glared. "I know every noble in this territory. I've dined with or fucked or been a comforting friend to nearly all of them. I know what I'm doing. I only want what's best for Vyaan. My *home*. I'm trying to make you remember that so you don't become the next *Kyzaire* of this territory to throw away his power on a *keeper*." I hid my flinch well, but she still caught it. "I believe you will do great things here. When you and your brothers slowly started coming into power, uniting the Kaalium under one House again, I almost felt hopeful. I still feel hopeful. *Why* would you compromise that?"

She wasn't…wrong.

"Go on," I said, showing her I was listening. That was the thing about Lydrasa. She might've liked to gossip and stick her nose where it didn't belong, but I knew her loyalties were tied to House Kaalium. I knew she put Vyaan above all else. Her family had been here since the territory's inception. Every ancestor in her family's shrine had their soul gem in place here. *That* was nearly as powerful as a blood bond.

I'd be lying if I said I hadn't considered her as a potential wife. She would make Vyaan stronger, one of the better choices I could make for my territory. And while it would never be a love match, we respected one another as friends…and our sexual relationship had been satisfying. Many married couples wouldn't be able to boast that.

"I don't have to tell you, Kaldur. I know who you used to be. Everyone saw you as this unserious, *lore*-smoking womanizer with a charming smile that got you everything you ever wanted," she said, approaching me. Her coy grin was gone, replaced with a serious expression, a hardened glint in her eyes. I swallowed, my nostrils flaring at her description. "But I know that's not who you are, and you proved to these Houses that you *are* a very capable leader.

"But I'm here to remind you because you seem to have lost your way. The nobles of Vyaan ripped your uncle to shreds when he married that keeper. Laughed at him behind closed doors. You think you know what was said? You have no idea. Nobles don't have to *like* you, Kaldur. But if we are heading to war—"

"We are not—"

She shot me a look. "*Please.* If we are heading to war, the noble Houses don't have to like you. But they do need to fear and respect you. The one sure way to make sure they don't? Fuck one of your keepers and elevate her position within your House. You'd be another silly fool of House Kaalium and prove them all right. You've worked hard to get here, to shake their perception of you since the beginning. Don't throw everything away for a *woman*."

"It's nothing I haven't already thought myself," I finally said. "Believe me."

"Oh, I do," Lydrasa said. She raised her voice, "Come in."

My brow furrowed, watching the door push open, a familiar face appearing. Velle. She'd been waiting.

"Don't take it from me," Lydrasa told me. She regarded the hybrid girl across the room, gesturing her forward. "Tell him what you told me, Velle."

The keeper bit her lip, as if torn. I frowned.

"Don't worry—you won't be in trouble," Lydrasa coaxed. To me, she said, "I think you should know who you have in your bed."

My eyes connected with Velle's. I knew she was a friend of Erina's. She was the one who'd walked in on us that morning.

"If you have something to say, speak," I told her, though I kept my tone even. Everything about this felt wrong, but if they knew something I didn't...I needed to know. Citizen files could only tell me so much.

I heard her swallow. Her hands fidgeted in front of her like she was scared. "Erina and I have been friends ever since she started working at your keep, *Kyzaire*. Maudoric asked me to take her under my care as she got her bearings, and we've been close ever since. But I am loyal to your House and I thought you should know that she's not who she seems. I brought it up to Lady Lydrasa because I know you are both friends and..."

"Go on," I prompted, my tone slightly rougher. My brow was furrowed, my lips pressed into a thin line.

"Erina is a very ambitious girl," Velle said. "And in our conversations she's made it clear that she intends to attach herself to a wealthy or noble family. Or to be a paid mistress of one of the Houses. Anything to gain status and wealth…but mostly for money."

"And why is that?" I asked, narrowing my eyes. My heart had sped in my chest, dread beginning to build. Yet it didn't sound like the female I'd come to know.

"Erina never had much growing up. She was an orphan…I'm not sure if she told you. She never wants to be poor again. But she also wants money because of—of Luc."

"Luc?" I asked quickly, stilling. "Do you know him?"

"I know *of* him. They send each letters all the time," Velle replied. Briefly, her eyes went to Lydrasa behind me. Her spine straightened. "Luc Denoren."

The breath felt squeezed out of my lungs. "Denoren. Are they married?"

They share a family name? I thought in disbelief, that dread tripling in my belly.

Velle shook her head, and I didn't know why I felt such relief at that.

It was short-lived, however.

"They aren't married yet, but Erina and Luc made promises to one another. They took the same name in honor of that promise. They love each other. They grew up together at the orphanage, but when Luc came of age, he traveled to Laras. To make a name there. Her plan was to get a consistent source of credits, however she could, even if that meant marrying into a wealthy family for a time. Then she would send the credits to Luc in Laras, so that he could build a nice life for them both. Once they had enough, she planned to meet him there."

The silence in the room was deafening. A swirling of anger, jealousy, and bitterness nearly consumed me, but I would keep it bottled and compressed. At least until I was alone.

"I admire you and your House, *Kyzaire*, and you've treated all of us very well," Velle finally said, her eyes holding mine. "Even though she is my friend, I've told her that I don't like what she's doing. That it's wrong. She's…she's playing you. She acts like she's innocent, but she's quite cunning. Even the stories she writes—those are the stories that she worked on with Luc. They are her love letter to him, a way to be connected to him until they are reunited."

It took everything in me to deliver my tone evenly and with a small, disarming toss of a smile. "I assure you, Erina is my blood giver only. We have an arrangement. One that benefits us both. If it suites her for her own ambitions, that's her business. I care not what she does with the money I give her."

"It's just that," Velle said quickly, stepping forward, making me cut her a look. "You're…you're a *Kyzaire*. She caught *your* attention. You're not just any noble but a son of the Kaalium! She knows that changes everything. She will want more. She may love Luc, but like I said, she is ambitious. She knows that a marriage to you would give her everything she ever wanted, not just for her but for Luc too. She will angle for a more permanent place in your keep—I promise you that. She's told me so herself."

I grinned even though it felt like a cracking stretch of ice across my features. "Then she is welcome to try. But you must really take me for a fool if you believe a calculating keeper will ascend to the position of *Kylaira* in my keep simply because she sets her mind to it."

A warning, more for the keeper in front of me than anything else. I knew Velle's kind. I was willing to bet that her and Erina's ambitions were not so different. Like attracted like. And for her to turn on her friend…well, that told me all I needed to know about *her* loyalties.

"Thank you, Velle," Lydrasa cut in. "You can go."

Velle inclined her head and then darted from the room, closing the door behind her. Quiet once again shrouded the room, but this time it felt oppressive instead of a reprieve. There was a familiar restlessness growing within me, one I hadn't felt since the blood bond had begun.

Had Erina been playing me for a fool this entire time? Was everything as calculated as Velle suggested?

Her knowledge of Luc was damning, however. Their shared name even more so. I'd have Maudoric verify it, to find record of a Luc Denoren in Laras, but still…

If there was a chance that what Velle said was true, I needed to keep even more distance from Erina. If she weren't my blood mate, I'd have enough reason to turn her away from the keep for this. But her being my *kyrana* changed everything…especially if she loved another.

The fierce rage bubbled in my chest, and I squeezed my fists tight, piercing through the flesh with my shorn claws.

"Don't speak of this to anyone else," I ordered Lydrasa. "And make sure Velle keeps quiet."

Lydrasa inclined her head. I knew I could rely on her. "She won't say a word to anyone. I'll make sure of it."

"Good," I rasped.

"What are you going to do about the girl?" Lydrasa inquired.

I tipped up her chin, making her meet my eyes. Her lips curled at whatever she saw in my gaze.

"Nothing," I purred.

Shock rippled through her. She laughed, but it sounded more like a scoff. "*Nothing?* After all of that? You have a serpent in your House, and you'll just let her slither into your bed?"

"Like I said," I murmured, shrugging one shoulder, "she is my blood giver. I like the taste of her…for now. That doesn't mean I'll marry her. On Raazos's blood, Lydrasa, I already told you. We have an arrangement, one that I made very clear from the beginning. If she thinks she can seduce me into more…well, I'm always up for some fun. She's more than welcome to try."

"Unbelievable," Lydrasa whispered, amusement dancing in

her eyes. "Very well. You know what you're doing. Just keep it under wraps. The nobles are already beginning to titter."

"I wonder why," I whispered, pressing a kiss to her cheek. Against her skin, I said, "I'm sure it's your handiwork."

"Always have to keep you on your toes, *Kyzaire*."

I scoffed and pulled away, releasing her. "I'm leaving."

"You wouldn't lie to me about this, would you?" came the question.

Her eyes burned into me when I replied, "Lie about what?"

"About what she is to you? This whole situation reeks of strangeness. It's out of your character, and I don't like it."

She suspects, I couldn't help but worry.

I smirked. "You don't have to like it."

Lydrasa harrumphed, rolling her eyes.

"I would never lie to you," I lied, purring. "Don't you believe me?"

"No," she deadpanned.

"Good."

Then I left House Azola.

CHAPTER 17
—
ERINA

*K*aldur never came to my room that night even though I waited into the early hours.

Nor did he come to me the next morning. When I went to go search for him, I ran into Maudoric inspecting one of the rooms in the South Wing. She told me she hadn't seen him, studying the dark circles under my eyes and the clothes I'd been wearing yesterday. There was a distance in her that hadn't been there before. A polite aloofness, usually reserved for Kaldur's guests when they came to the keep. I almost preferred it when she was berating me.

I went about my day even though his absence struck me as odd. Had he…had he not come back to the keep last night? And if not, where had he been?

I frowned, allowing myself to imagine it for just a moment. Kaldur with another female, perhaps even Lydrasa again. Unfortunately I had an exact image in my mind of what they would look like making love together.

"Enough," I whispered to myself, feeling a pinching ache of jealousy and hurt, abruptly deciding to distract myself in the village today.

One of my favorite pastimes was sitting in the Southern village square on my days off and watching all the people that passed. Not only nobles and their companions, but farmers, craftsmen, merchants, travelers, soldiers, keepers. It would be a perfect distraction, I decided. A rush of inspiration always hit me for my stories after afternoons like those, and I was so close to finishing the final part of Kavelyn's book.

After changing into fresh clothes and brushing through my hair, I gathered my satchel, patted my notebook into place, and made sure I had credits if I got hungry. Then I set off.

On my way out of the keep's door, I spied Velle, wiping down one section of the stair's banister in the atrium. I sucked in a small breath of surprise. She eyed me, pressing her lips together. Her hair was held back by her familiar headband, her sleeves rolled up, a bucket of sudsy water at her feet.

"Hi," I offered, a small, hesitant smile crossing my features. "I—"

She turned her back.

A sting of hurt reverberated through me, and I bit back a sigh. I'd tried to speak to her a couple days prior, and I'd gotten the cold shoulder then too. She hadn't softened toward me, and truthfully I didn't know if she ever would. Our realities were different now.

It made me sad—the potential loss of a friend. They were hard to come by as I got older.

Velle never turned back to me, her braid swaying as she scrubbed the white smooth stone, and I felt a little guilty, slinking out the door in broad daylight while she was working. I stood on the front steps, eyeing the grand entrance, the sweeping stone staircase which rippled out from me, leading to a grand circular fountain. Starwood blooms made a ring around it.

Beyond that was the path to the village down the main road, and I took off on foot.

It didn't take me long to reach the main square, though I'd

taken my time meandering down the quiet path. It was a cool day, but I'd dressed warmly. I had a craving for a spiced tea, laden with sweet cream, and a fresh steam cake, and I went to a nearby shop, knowing they sold both.

Once, I never would've purchased something so frivolous and silly for myself. After Wrezaan's, I had hoarded every credit I could. Even when I worked for Syndras, I kept a tight buckle on my credits. I've given a lot of my savings to Luc in Laras, knowing that he poured most of his into his merchant shop, which he still ran to this day.

It was only after coming to work for Kaldur, when I suddenly had a small padding of savings at my disposal, did I start to buy things for myself. A treat here and there. A new dress, but only if it was discounted at the shop because no one else would buy it. And yet to me, it seemed like a luxury.

The only thing I ever splurged on were notebooks and a steady supply of pencils. The special kind with highly pigmented charcoal that didn't crumble even with a heavy hand.

I didn't come into the village often, but now I made it a point to buy myself a small treat or a meal. I regretted the first time I'd tried the spiced tea…because I knew I wouldn't be able to live without it. The aroma alone was enough to make my mouth water.

So when I bought it today, I felt a momentary pinch of guilt but told myself it was okay. Especially with the credits coming in from Kaldur as his blood giver. It would be more money than I'd ever seen in my life at once.

I tucked myself into a secluded bench on the very edge of the square, one where I'd be able to watch everyone coming and going without being in the way or noticed. It was shaded and cool now, but in an hour, the sun would be overhead and the stone would warm beneath me, so I let the hot tea and the steam cake heat me up for now.

After I polished off my breakfast cake, I took out my notebook, flipped to an empty page, and began to list out different things I saw. It was something I liked to do not only as an exercise for my writing but because I often loved to read them back over. Little snippets of people's lives or visuals that struck me.

Thick curling ribbons of fog creeping over the Western mountains.

Two girls passing—a blonde human and a Kylorr with red eyes— giggling over a handsome Bartutian boy, who smiled at them.

The scent of cloves and sweet cream, beaconing and welcoming like a siren.

A clumsy-footed child who tripped on the cobblestones, his worried mother rushing over to calm his wails.

The harsh whip of the banner flags in the square like a thunder clap, the icy breeze on the back of my neck.

I saw Kaldur.

My breath hitched, my hand stilling over the soft parchment of my notebook.

Then I wrote *A handsome Kylorr, with eyes like mirrors and a grin like my favorite dawn.*

Even the mere sight of him made my heart race in anticipation, but for now I was content to study him as I sipped on my spiced tea. He wasn't wearing what he'd worn last night, which brought a pinch of relief. He *had* come back to the keep last night…and yet he hadn't come to me.

He was walking with a local shopkeeper, who'd apparently flagged him down. I thought the male was a clothier and owned the shop frequented by nobles. I'd never stepped foot inside—the prices were much too high for someone like me—but I had often admired the silks and sturdy linens in the window. The beautiful embellished ball gowns mixed with simple, but elegant, everyday wear made an interesting display. But there were two kinds of people: those who went inside the shop and those who admired from outside its gilded doors.

I'd always been a part of the latter group.

I watched as Kaldur smiled, placing his hand on the clothier's shoulder and listening as he spoke. Even from afar, I was transfixed. Kaldur was the type of magnetic male that consumed one's attention, the kind to draw gazes and keep them. I'd never met anyone with his pull before. My stomach fluttered because now I knew what it was like to be on the receiving end of that smile, of that rumbling voice and those mesmerizing eyes.

Another breeze swept through the square, making my hair flutter around my face, which I tried to brush back into place.

From the distance, I saw Kaldur's head lift. Then he was looking straight at me, and I felt frozen, trapped within those eyes.

I watched him frown, his expression darkening briefly, before he turned abruptly back to the shopkeeper. He murmured something, which seemed to satisfy the clothier because he said his goodbyes and turned down the road back toward his shop.

Kaldur stood alone now and slowly turned to regard me. Hesitantly, I stood from the bench, tucking my notebook into my satchel, my cooling tea still clasped in one hand. When I made a step toward him, he shook his head, casting his gaze around the square, eyeing the milling nobles and citizens of Vyaan, many of whom were looking at him.

He gestured his head toward an alley between two shops that were closed today. There was a stiff pattering in my chest when I realized…when I realized he didn't want me to approach him. Because he didn't want to be seen with me?

That hurt more than I thought it did.

Don't assume anything, I reminded myself. Maybe he had another reason for it. Slowly, I headed down the alleyway, seeing that it led to a small, private courtyard that both of the shops shared. I guessed the doors in the back were meant for delivering goods, further evidenced by the stack of empty crates piled up to one side of the deserted courtyard.

Since it was shaded, it was cold, the shop buildings blocking out the sun. To soothe my dry tongue, I took another sip of my tea while I waited, trying to ignore the hurt that was winding its way in my chest. I waited for a long time, long enough to wonder if I'd been mistaken, if he was even coming.

Just as I was about to leave, I heard a heavy stride clattering down the cobblestones.

Kaldur appeared, and he leaned against the wall of the building, regarding me after he cast an assessing view over his shoulder.

"Don't want anyone to see us together?" I asked. It was meant to be a joke, but I was mortified when I heard the small tinge of hurt color the question.

He smiled, but it didn't make me relax. There was an edge to it, one that amplified a hardened glint in his eyes.

"You would know no peace if I didn't take precautions," he finally answered. "The Vyaan people love their gossip, just like your keeper friends in my House."

I didn't know if I should feel stung or grateful by the admission.

"I didn't expect to find you in the village today. Come to spend your stipend for the month?" he asked. "I wonder what will catch your eye…a vase perhaps?"

My brow furrowed. Something was wrong.

"Have I upset you?" I asked quietly, observing his expression carefully. His words seemed slightly mocking.

"Of course not," he replied easily enough. He slid toward me, and when he placed his fingers beneath my chin, he tilted my head back. "Why would you ask that?"

"I don't know—you seem…" I trailed off. *Let it go*, I thought. "Never mind."

His other hand came to gently swipe under my eyes. "You look tired."

"I was, um, waiting for you last night. I thought you wanted to feed when you returned, so I—"

"I returned late and didn't want to disturb you," he said,

cutting off my words. He released me. His body was close to me, but something told me he'd never been further away. I didn't understand it.

"And how was your dinner?" I asked, wondering if something had happened there.

"Illuminating," he answered, never taking his eyes off me.

He said nothing else. Merely watched me as I began to squirm under his perusal. It felt barbed, like he was dissecting me under that gaze. He hadn't fed since yesterday morning…was that the reason for his strange mood?

"I waited for you this morning too," I said softly, clutching the strap of my satchel.

"I'll feed now," came his guttural response, one that made my eyes widen, realizing we were in an abandoned courtyard but not that far away from the main bustling square. I could still hear the echo of footsteps and laughter and chatter, even tucked back here.

"Now?" I choked out. "Here?"

"Unless you'd rather not," he murmured easily.

"No, it's not that. It's…"

"I have somewhere to be soon," Kaldur replied. "I'll be gone for a while."

"Oh, I see."

He smiled. "I'll come to you another time. Let's not—"

"No," I said quickly, reaching out to take his arm and bringing him back to him when he stepped away. "Now is fine."

I didn't know how to explain it, but he felt detached, like he was purposefully trying to keep me away. When all I wanted was to be close to him. And when he was feeding, that was when we always felt closest.

I was beginning to crave that feeling like a need. I felt protected, wanted, and safe in those moments. And how could I not when it was Kaldur?

He didn't resist. I tilted my neck to the side for him, leaning back against the shop building wall. But then he shook his head. Before I could blink, he flipped me around, pressing me so that my palms were against the stone wall. I frowned, my lips parted to say something, but then I felt his hand tugging at my hair, exposing my neck.

The bite of his fangs came next, followed by the warmth of his feeding.

I couldn't see him or touch him like this. Stone scraped into my palms as my nails curled. His grip on me was unyielding, keeping me easily in place. He held himself away from my back, far enough that I could feel the cold breeze between us.

This wasn't like our usual feedings. This felt...clinical. Like I was only fulfilling a need, like I could be anybody to him.

So while the usual pleasure from the feeding was present...it didn't leave me feeling warm or excited or needful.

And it was over much too soon. Kaldur retracted his fangs before healing the bite mark. When I frowned, turning to look over my shoulder at him, his nostrils flared at whatever he saw in my expression.

"I'm sorry," he said quietly, pinching his brow as he backed away. "It's not the time or place for this."

I nodded, agreeing.

"I'm not of the right mind for this now," he said before meeting my eyes. So something was wrong? I'd figured as much. "I have to leave for a few nights."

"What?" I asked quickly, turning fully on shaking legs. "But why?"

"I'm needed in Salaire," he answered. "You should know so you don't wonder. I'll be back in a few nights. I'll come find you when I return."

My lips parted. But after one last look, Kaldur was already turning away.

"Kaldur," I said quickly.

He paused down the alley.

"Be safe, all right?" I told him.

His silver eyes peered at me carefully. "It's not your place to worry about me, remember?"

The dismissive words made me draw in a sharp breath.

Then he was gone. And I felt confused and alone in that empty courtyard. The last of my tea, I saw, had spilled all over the ground.

A waste, I thought, feeling tears spring to my eyes. But they had nothing to do with the tea at all.

CHAPTER 18
—
ERINA

To help pass the time, I wrote two letters in the three days that Kaldur was gone.

One to Luc, again though I told him nothing of my new arrangement with the *Kyzaire* of Vyaan. The other letter was to Syndras, asking her if I could visit soon. She was particular about her schedule, and while I knew she would welcome me any time in her House, I didn't want to impose unnecessarily. I had a lot of time these days, and I couldn't spend it all within the gardens.

On the third night, I was eagerly awaiting Kaldur's return, overhearing Maudoric tell one of the keepers that she'd received word he was on his way back home. I was freshly bathed, made sure to take my *baanye*, and put on my nicest dress, one of light material that was open at the neck. I worried though, especially when rain began to pelt against the windows, thick drops that never seemed to cease.

And then I waited in my quarters. I took to reading to pass the time and to calm my nerves, having borrowed a few books from the library. I'd tried to use the Halo orb to project the land-scapes from the book Kaldur had showed me, but I couldn't figure out how. I mentally reminded myself to ask him when we had a spare moment.

Mostly, I was nervous about our reunion. About what mood he might be in. Our parting had felt so cold and strange. But I'd reasoned that whatever had called him away to Salaire must've been on his mind. I had no idea of the stresses and obligations that rested on a *Kyzaire's* shoulders. I couldn't even begin to fathom it, so I endeavored to put that last interaction out of my mind. To start new again, like a fresh dawn.

Peering outside my window at the bright moon, my breath hitched when I saw a familiar figure illuminated in the rainy night sky. It was late, and he'd returned. I felt relief when I saw him land on his balcony and enter his rooms.

Only, an hour or so ticked by and Kaldur never came.

Taking a deep breath, I ventured out of room. Perhaps he thought I wasn't awake. Perhaps he didn't want to disturb me, but he must've seen that I'd kept my light on.

Even though I'd never been so bold, I went slowly to his door and swallowed hard before I knocked. I thought he would be able to hear my thumping heart even though the thick wood of his door.

It didn't take long before he answered.

His expression was unreadable when he wordlessly stepped back to allow me to enter. His room was familiar—he'd brought me here after the first feeding, after all. But the male in front of me felt like a stranger.

He closed the door, and when I turned, I saw him resting his forehead briefly on the wood, as if composing himself.

"What's wrong?" I asked.

"Stop asking me that," he growled.

Bad mood, then, I thought, biting my lip.

Finally, he turned. He was freshly bathed and dressed in loose pants and a dark blue tunic that molded to his chest. His feet were bare, his wings stretched. Even comfortable, he looked perfectly refined and presentable should a noble drop by at such a late hour.

Brushing past me, he went to a glittering bottle of amber liquid resting on a lacquered black sideboard, unstoppering the cap before pouring it into a crystal tumbler. From working in wealthy Houses before, I knew it was a potent liquor, imported from some planet I didn't bother to remember, and it often flowed at parties, coupled with the silver smoke of *lore*.

As if he read my mind, he informed me, without turning, "I was about to smoke, so you shouldn't be here."

Humans were particularly sensitive to *lore* smoke. In most of my kind, unless you took a tonic called *tassa* to counter the effects, the smoke was an aphrodisiac, eliciting a physical response.

For Kylorr, *lore* was calming.

Kaldur turned to me with his brow raised, as if questioning why I still lingered. He took a sip of his liquor, watching me over the rim.

"Do you not need to feed?" I asked. "It's been days."

He smiled, opening a smooth, hidden drawer at the front of the sideboard console. "You take your position as blood giver very seriously, Erina. You must wonder how I ever survived without you all these years."

I couldn't help but bite the inside of my cheek. He was still in his strange mood, even after three days. I'd thought...maybe it had just been a bad moment for him. I'd thought that maybe he'd even started to enjoy my company, to *like* me. Every time I'd caught him looking at me with a molten gaze, it had made me shiver. Every secretive little smirk had made my heart soar because they'd been for *me*. Mine alone.

Watching as he pulled out a slim, silver pipe from the velvet-lined drawer and a metal tin, I asked, "Does that mean you took a blood giver in Salaire?"

He'd said he wouldn't. While it hadn't quite been a promise, it had been implied, hadn't it?

Kaldur released a long, sharp breath. My heart thudded, waiting to be fissured with jealousy.

But then he admitted, "No, I did not."

I heard the honesty in those words. It was almost like he'd *wanted* to lie to me but then couldn't.

Relief made my shoulders sag. Elation rose in my breast, and I approached him, eyeing the stretch of his shoulders. He must've been tired, but there was a restlessness about him. He was fidgeting with the pipe, unclasping the tin, and stuffing *lore* into it. Though…I swore his fingers were unsteady. The *lore* was crumbling beneath his touch.

He needed to relax…so then why did he not relax with me?

I touched his bare forearm, feeling the warmth and tantalizing heat of him. I was no seductress, but I thought I *could* be considering how much I desired him.

"Let me," I said quietly. I'd served at one party before, one in which I'd taken *tassa*, and I remembered how to do it.

Kaldur allowed me to pluck the pipe from his hands, and I packed it with the dried leaves carefully. He sipped his liquor, blowing out a sharp breath, the tension pouring off him in waves.

The lore *will help calm him, and then maybe we can talk,* I told myself.

But was I really planning to stay while he smoked?

In the end, I decided it didn't matter. Whether it was with *lore* smoke or through his inevitable feeding, he always sparked desire in me. I'd come apart in his arms, his fangs deep in my neck, too many times, even the times when I'd tried not to.

When I handed him the pipe and flicked on the igniter, making the leaf burn inside, he stared down at me, realizing that *that* was my answer.

"Very well, *dallia*," he said, taking the pipe and bringing the end to his lips. "Your choice."

"It is," I agreed, meeting his eyes.

The blue end of the igniter flared even brighter when Kaldur inhaled, his cheeks hollowing. A moment later, he exhaled the smoke, thick and spiced, like the tea from the village.

It curled into my nostrils and down my throat, making me gasp.

The effects didn't take long, and I figured they were even quicker to come on because Kaldur's intense gaze never left me. As if he was fascinated by my reaction, as if he wanted to see every little change in me.

Desire began to bloom. Deep in my belly, the heat winding and spiraling tight. Then it loosened and stretched itself, spreading, spreading, especially when Kaldur exhaled another draw of smoke. I'd never felt the effects personally, having always taken *tassa*, but I wondered how much more intense it would get. I'd heard stories...

The rain was loud against the glass windows, pelting down mercilessly, but my heartbeat soon drowned it out. I felt overly flushed and warm and yet my nipples tightened to hardened peaks. He was so close that his chest brushed my arm whenever he breathed, and I...I wanted him to touch me everywhere.

I placed my hand on the sideboard, feeling the smooth, cool wood beneath my palm. Kaldur took another sip of his drink, and then he handed it to me, brushing past me to sit in the plush and padded armchair by the fire. Kylorr chairs always had straight vertical backs, thin along the spine, to allow for their wings to rest comfortably behind them. I watched as Kaldur's wings relaxed, one arm rested along the leather, as he looked into the fire. His drink was as much of an invitation as any, I figured.

The tumbler was cool in my hand, and I pressed it to one cheek. This felt different tonight. It felt...certain. There was a strange energy about Kaldur, one both resigned, restless, and accepting. There was a pinching intensity to him, like he was a blade's edge away from snapping. And in me…well, I still wanted what I'd wanted in the courtyard three days ago.

To feel close to him when he felt so incredibly distant already.

I wanted that night in the library again. When his walls were down, his mask off. I wanted to see *him*. Who he truly was. I wanted *that* Kaldur.

With the *lore* pulsing through my body, I took a sip from his glass. The *burn* of the liquor nearly made me cough, but I swallowed it down. It mingled with the *lore* beautifully, allowing it to stretch even further through my body. I turned to Kaldur.

The *lore* was beginning to make me ache.

I stopped in front of him. His eyes traced over me, and I nearly shivered, as if I were naked and he could see all of me. Those eyes started at my bare feet, traced up my legs, over the curve of my hips, the dip of my waist. They settled on my breasts, eyeing my peaked nipples, and he took a drag on his pipe as he studied them, making me squeeze my thighs. Then they flicked up to my face, just in time to catch me lick my dry lips.

There was something erotic in his casual perusal. Like I was his to do with whatever he pleased, to look at at his leisure.

"I don't think you know what you're doing, Erina," he finally said, his voice dark and guttural. He'd flown all this way in a storm, and his mood reflected that.

I took another sip of his liquor in defiance, feeling a thrill go through me when I caught his gruff grunt.

"You've been in a very strange mood since you left that night for your party," I told him. I approached. Kaldur's eyes flicked from my lips to my hips.

And then I watched them *burn* when I brought a knee up, sliding it into the empty space between his outer thigh and the leather of the armchair. I sunk and then slid my other leg up.

I had the oddest impression that Kaldur was focusing on his breath. One breath into the next, slowly and deeply, when he looked between us. I was seated in his lap now, the hot strength of his body beneath me. I didn't know where I'd gotten the courage. I'd seen a female do this one—to her lover at a party Syndras had once thrown. I'd accidentally stumbled upon them when I'd gone to fetch Syndras her favorite *lore* from the study, and there they'd been.

The female's lover had certainly seemed to appreciate it, and in my limited experience, even I could see that Kaldur reacted just the same.

I pressed the rim of the tumbler to his lips, and his nostrils flared as I tipped it back. His throat bobbed with the small swallow. Then I placed the tumbler on the small circular table next to the chair. Out of the way but within easy reach.

"Are you trying to seduce me, *dallia?*" he murmured softly, the edges of his lips curling in an almost sardonic smile. "Or are you just very sensitive to the *lore?*"

Still prickly, I thought, but I let the words roll off me, not allowing them to stick.

"I wonder how much you can take before it becomes too overwhelming," he said before inhaling on his pipe.

My eyelids fluttered when he blew out another stream and it floated around us. I bit my bottom lip, my hips beginning to move of their own accord on top of him.

"Kaldur," I breathed. *"Please."*

CHAPTER 19

KAIDUR

In all the studies I'd read of human-and-Kylorr blood bonds, one thing was clear: While humans would not feel the intensity and pull of a bond as a Kylorr would, there was still a physical reaction that began to take place on the onset of their Kylorr's venom. From the very first bite.

A human might not have felt the pulsing, entrancing, maddening need as a Kylorr would. But they would certainly feel an unexplainable connection, one they themselves might not even understand.

It could've been the *lore* smoke that had Erina writhing in my lap, yes. But I had a feeling it was the bond that had brought her to me in the first place. The bond that made her gaze soften on me. The bond that ratcheted up her heartbeat at the mere sight of me.

It was the bond that made her lean close…but it might've been the *lore* that made her bold enough to press her lips to my throat.

The lashing of lust felt like a whip. The heat of her mouth and rushed exhale across my skin made my cock harden almost painfully. Through my tunic, I felt the pointed press of her nipples, and it took everything in me not to palm them, to keep my hands firmly off my mate.

It didn't stop me from tilting my neck as I dragged in another deep draw on my *lore* pipe, as I debated what to do.

The hunger in me already felt punishing. For three days, I'd longed for this wisp of a female. This treacherous little human who made it difficult to think.

The facts were this…

There *was* a Luc Denoren in Laras. I'd had it confirmed. He had grown up with Erina right here in Vyaan. According to Maudoric, who posted all letters in the village, Erina and Luc were in frequent contact, even as recently as yesterday.

And Erina Denoren was my *kyrana*.

After Lydrasa and Velle's account, which was at least partially true, based on what I'd discovered, I realized I couldn't trust Erina's intentions. Not in the slightest.

Leave it to the gods to give me a deceitful mate.

Perhaps this was my punishment for my younger years, when all I'd truly thought of was myself and my own pleasures.

I was pissed and jealous and hungry…and I still *fucking* wanted her.

That made me angriest of all. The trip to Salaire had been a much-needed distraction. The business with my brother, Thaine, had helped divert my attention away. But now that I had returned, it brought everything I'd tried to escape back tenfold.

Fuck this, I thought. If she was going to use me to create a better life with the male she actually loved, then on Raazos's blood, I was going to use her too.

"I can make you come without my fangs in your neck, *dallia*," I purred. "Is that what you want? Is that why you came to me?"

"That's…that's not why I—"

"But you knew that I'd give you what you wanted, didn't you?" I rasped. I heard the bitter twinge in the words, but I was certain she didn't. I felt her shuddered breath against my neck just before I felt her dull little teeth bite into my flesh.

I groaned, my eyes closing, and I felt the last of my will leave with the surrender.

With my free hand, I slid my touch up her thigh, delving beneath her dress, bunching the material up around her hips.

The moment my fingers registered between her thighs, she moaned against my skin. I nearly hissed at the slick heat of her. She was dripping, coating my fingers with her desire.

My fangs bit into my lip when I gnashed my teeth together. The scent of her skin mingled with the *lore* spun me up into her web.

"Let me look at you," I growled, pushing her back, away from my neck. Partly because I wanted to watch her come apart, but mostly because I thought I might feed from her if I was any closer to her neck. And if I fed from her right now…there was no coming back from it. There was no way I would have the control to resist her.

Erina's cheeks were flushed, her eyes half-lidded.

I couldn't help but rub my cock through the loose material of my pants with the base of my palm. A flood of pre-come was already wetting the front.

"What do you want from me?" I growled.

My wealth? My family name? I wondered. That was what this was all about, wasn't it? Just like the keeper my uncle had destroyed his entire life for. I wouldn't be made a fool.

"I want you to touch me," Erina mewed.

I wondered what her beloved Luc would think if he saw her like this. A possessive part of me burned with the thought. It made me even harder, imagining fucking her while he watched. I would never allow him to touch her. I would own her completely because she was *my kyrana*. Never his. I would be everything she needed so she would never have a reason to return to him.

Madness, I thought, growing angrier with the thoughts. It felt like an untamed beast was rising in me with the aggression. Coupled with my hunger, I feared it might be a dangerous path to venture down.

She wanted me to touch her? I would give her what she wanted.

Erina cried out when I drove a finger inside her tight, slick cunt. So tight I nearly frowned. But her hips snapped over my hand, pushing me deeper inside, as if she couldn't help herself. When I rubbed her sensitive clit with my thumb, her head tilted back, a soft moan falling from her throat that nearly scrambled my entire brain.

I hated that I would remember her like this. I hated that this erotic image of her would forever be imprinted on me. I hated that my venom began to drip at the mere thought of her, that her scent calmed me in a way not even *lore* could.

I wedged another finger inside her, pressing harder against her clit. Her lips were parted, and she gazed at me with something akin to disbelief.

"I want to watch you come," I told her. To center myself, I took another slow drag of the *lore* and billowed it around her like a veil. She gasped in the smoke, rocking her hips in a practiced slow rhythm that had me wondering how many times she'd done this before. With *him*. "You're close already—I can feel it."

I watched as she rode my fingers to her orgasm. And when she was there, her whole body tightened up and she froze, holding her breath, held on the precipice of the fall. Her expression was locked with drawn brows and full parted lips I wanted to bite.

Then she hurtled into her pleasure and her body came alive. Her skin flushed pink, and she rocked her hips in a wild way, chasing and prolonging the orgasm for as long as she could, the greedy little thing. The knot at the base of my cock was beginning to swell, my balls drawn tight. *Fuck.* This was not supposed to happen like this.

I managed to keep my control, even as the slick sounds against my hand rose between us and I could smell her arousal all around me. I didn't know *how* I controlled myself, truthfully.

But when it was over and Erina was gasping to catch her breath, I simply took my hand away and leaned back in the chair. I dragged in another slow inhale of my *lore*, hoping my expression was impassive as I studied her.

"Go."

Erina nearly jumped at the word. "What?"

"Leave," I ordered her, gesturing with my chin toward the door. "Go clear your head of the smoke before we both do something we'll regret."

I maneuvered her off me, shifting my legs so that she stood. She was unsteady on them. I didn't want her falling, so I rose, taking her by the arm and guiding her to the door of my quarters. I needed to get her out of here and *fast*. It took everything in me to pull the door open, to push her through.

Out in the darkened hallway, she met my eyes in confusion, blinking, as if she didn't understand how she'd ended up out there.

She was frowning. "Kaldur—"

"*Go.*"

Then I shut the door before I could second guess myself. I gritted my jaw hard enough that I thought I'd snap a fang as I returned to the fire. I snatched the half-empty tumbler off the table and drained it, feeling the fiery burn of the liquor heat its way into me.

Then I sat, resting my elbows on my knees, prodding between my brows with my thumbs. I could still smell her everywhere. My fingers were still wet with her desire, and my cock was still *fucking* throbbing like a banging drum. *Gods*, I needed to fuck. I needed to feed.

I heard the latch of the door click. One I hadn't locked. It banged closed, and I heard her footsteps, her scent sweeping toward me.

Raazos, help me, I thought.

I closed my eyes, leaning back in the chair. I didn't have the strength to resist her a second time. I'd tried to do the right thing.

When I opened my eyes, Erina was standing in front of me, backlit by the firelight. She was studying me now, her warm brown eyes sweeping over me. My sagged wings, my tented pants, and perhaps even the defeat on my features.

"Erina," I growled in warning.

She took my *lore* pipe from between my fingers, turning off the ignitor and placing it beside the empty tumbler on the circular table beside me.

Then her hands went to the straps of her dress.

"You can try to push me away, but I'll always want you," she told me. Her voice was a balm, smoothing down the ragged edges that were tearing me up inside. "I always have."

Gods, I wanted to believe her.

The dress slipped off her shoulders, skimming over her breasts, catching on her hips before she wiggled it down. The light material pooled at her feet like water, leaving her standing naked before me. The most tempting of offerings.

She had a beautiful body. Soft curves and smooth skin. Perfectly sized breasts with brownish pink–tipped nipples I wanted to tease. There were sparse, soft curls between her legs giving way to strong, shapely thighs.

"I'm not afraid," she said, though she said it as she tried to hide the way her hands trembled.

She crawled into my lap again, the same position as before. Only now, I couldn't resist cupping her exposed body, squeezing everything I could get my hands on. Her ass, her hips, her waist.

Her lips landed on mine, gasping when my palm skimmed over her nipple. The kiss was hungry and aching and desperate.

She could taste the venom on my tongue from my fangs, and she lapped at it, squirming in my lap.

"I'm yours," she breathed. A guttural sound rose from my throat, harsh and unexpected. "You can have everything."

I kissed her harder and then pulled away. "Do you mean that?" I growled.

Her eyes were unfocused, gazing at my lips. "Yes."

"Tell me you're mine," I ordered, my hand gliding up her neck to dive into her hair, holding her in place. "I need to hear you say it again."

"I'm yours," she whispered. "I've always been yours, Kaldur."

The last of my willpower shattered like glass on stone.

I felt her hands come to my horns—and I nearly went feral with need. The feel of her tight, warm grip, guiding me down to her tilted neck for the purpose of feeding…it locked a new kink into place for me.

I felt her groan vibrate into me when I bit deep. The taste of her blood made the world go hazy. Everything fell away. Nothing else mattered except *her*. Except this moment.

I began to feed from her.

And I would take everything she offered to me. I wouldn't resist anymore.

CHAPTER 20
—
ERINA

With his fangs in my body, there was only ecstasy.

When he fed from me, I felt like I *belonged* somewhere. I felt protected in his arms. Safe.

"I'm yours," I whispered. I felt his harsh exhale over my skin, and I smiled in relief and pleasure. It was like a part of him *needed* to hear that. Had that been what he'd been afraid of? What I felt for him was only growing and expanding exponentially with every passing day. Did he feel the same?

He must, I thought, and the realization brought joy unlike anything I'd experienced before. Maybe—just maybe—I would finally get everything I'd dreamed of, everything I'd ever wanted. A male I loved and who loved me in return, a family, a home that could never be taken from me.

Pleasure was rising again though my body was still tingling from his touch between my thighs. It felt like he'd unleashed an alien creature inside me, one who was ravenous and wanton. I only desired him. I only wanted him. For a brief moment, I feared something was wrong with me. Surely to feel this aching longing and madness for someone wasn't normal, was it?

His feeding grew more and more hungry. His grip on me

tightened, his hands beginning to rove as I rocked over his lap. I wanted to experience sex with him. I wanted to feel what it was like, to have him deep inside my body in a way his fangs never could be.

So when his hands began to rip at the laced waistband of his trousers, tugging the material over his cock, I craned my head down even though it shifted his bite in my skin. My eyes widened, my hand reaching immediately for the hardened, bobbing cock that was newly exposed.

He hissed when my palm wrapped around him. I didn't know what to do, not truly, but I remembered everything I'd ever heard from keepers about sex, and their giggling gossiping of their escapades, in every House I'd ever worked in. But mostly I acted on instinct, gliding my hand up and down the hot, suede-like skin, which felt as hard as metal in my grip. I wanted to explore him more than anything…but the tight, driving need inside me didn't allow for that.

Kaldur bucked up into my hands. The power of his hips lifted even me as he chased his pleasure. He released his fangs from my neck, and I caught the wild flash of his eyes when he dragged me even closer. I gasped when his head dipped, when he caught one exposed nipple between his lips and sucked, palming the other one with a possessive touch.

I gave a soft, shocked grunt when I felt the prick of his fangs in my breast.

"Oh, gods," I breathed, my fist tightening over his cock, making him thrust his hips even harder. He began to feed from me there, and it felt *incredible*, every nerve ending sizzling up to meet his fangs. One of his hands returned between my thighs, teasing me mercilessly as I writhed against him. I was dripping—I could feel it. I wasn't even embarrassed about it. I only wanted *more*. More sensation, more pleasure, more of his touch.

"It will never be enough," came Kaldur's dark rasp of a voice, releasing me. I gasped, holding on to his shoulders when he stood suddenly, sweeping up from the chair. *"Vaan,* I want you so *fucking* much, Erina. And I hate that. I hate that I need you like this."

The words filled me with a dark sense of glee even though he sounded almost angry about it. I was helpless to clutch at his shoulders as he walked us over to his bed. My body felt empty of him, and so I bit down into his neck, listening to the feral creature inside me, knowing it would spur him on.

A snarl rose from him, and when I pulled back, I eyed him with a half-lidded gaze. With my blood dripping from his fangs, he made a frighteningly erotic sight. The scar on his face made him appear almost sinister—if only he wasn't so incredibly handsome. If only he didn't make me ache with want just looking at him.

Is this what falling in love is like? I questioned. *This spiraling descent into madness and hope?*

He flipped me face down onto the bed before I could beg or demand or whimper, tugging my naked hips back and up, bringing me to my knees. I heard a dark curse reverberate from him, sounding like a plea. I felt the head of his cock kiss my slick sex, teasing me. *So hot* it felt like a brand on my sensitive flesh. Like this, he was at a perfect height for—

"I can't resist you, Erina," he whispered, lowering himself over my back. His lips met the shell of my ear. "I just want to drown in you."

A ragged cry tore from my throat when he thrust his cock into me. My body moved of its own accord, rocking away from the pain. Despite my arousal, he was still an extremely tight fit, his thickness only allowing him to enter me partially.

"Raazos, you're tight, *dallia,"* he cursed. "Did I hurt you?"

"A little," I said, biting my lip, but I didn't want him to pull away. When he tried to, I protested, "No! Just…just hold on. *Please.* Distract me."

I tilted my neck, and he took the hint. His fangs pricked into me, and the pulling draw of his hunger, the flood and warmth of his venom, made the pain slowly fade. Every moment loosened my muscles and sharp pinch I felt deep inside.

I'd thought it would feel strange. To have someone else inside your own body. But with Kaldur, it felt completely right. Normal. If only I could see him though…if only I could wrap my arms around his body and embrace him tight.

When I gave an experimental rock of my hips, he hissed against me. He'd brought his forearms down on either side of my head—they vibrated with tension. I felt the scratch of his clothing against my back, reminding me that he was still fully clothed and I was completely naked, a tantalizing contrast of sensation.

I began to move my body in time with his feeding, the pleasure winding tighter and tighter inside me. Soon, he took the hint, dragging his length out before thrusting back inside. Over and over again. Short and quick motions that made me squirm. Soon there was no pain, only a sensation of strange fullness. I was taking him, *all* of him, and a triumphant thrill raced through me.

On his next thrust, I grunted softly because there was nowhere else for him to go. I felt something hard and thick nudge against my entrance and my eyes widened with the realization of what it was. I'd nearly forgotten. Full-blooded Kylorr had a knot at the base of their cock. I'd never seen one before, only in drawings or paintings.

Curious, I reached behind me, and Kaldur let out a hoarse cry when I cupped him there.

"Squeeze hard," he growled, releasing my neck. When I did, he let out a desperate whimper that *nearly* made me come right there and then. "*Vaan*, I want that to be your cunt. How perfect that would feel."

"Yes," I gasped. "I want that."

"No," he said, sounding as if he was gritting his teeth together. "You are in no way ready for that."

Disappointment crashed into me, and I squeezed hard, making him moan and buck his hips with power that pushed me up the bed.

"No, come here. Don't you dare escape," he growled. With ease, he tugged me back, wrapping his palm around the back of my neck to keep me in place. To keep me still as his pace increased. I'd never felt more vulnerable, more at someone's mercy, and I found I *loved* it. "Oh gods, I'm losing control, *dallia*. Too much—you feel too good," he said, his voice ending on a low rasp, just as he placed his fingers over my clit, using the force of his thrusts to rub against me.

I was an endless stream of moans and desperate cries and strangled pleas. All I could do was keep my hips lifted as he fucked me, hard and fast. My eyes landed on the stitching of his bedding, seeing the threads glimmer in the shadowed firelight that flicked over our bodies. I heard the sounds we made, the sounds of our bodies coming together in a race to find *something*.

And I had a feeling that whenever we found what we were looking for, I might not ever be the same again.

"Kaldur," I breathed, my eyes widening. "I'm going to…"

"Come," he growled. That was when I felt the prick of his fangs. I closed my eyes, the world fading away.

I was lost in the high of his lovemaking and his feeding. Every beat of my heart was reflected in the pull of his fangs. He alone controlled my body. He pulled a single string, and I came apart in his arms.

My orgasm was a fearsome, almost painful thing in its intensity. It crashed over me until I was only sensation—ecstasy itself —my body forgotten. I hung on to every last breath of it, only distantly aware that Kaldur bellowed out his own pleasure, muffled into my skin. Words—Kylorr words I didn't understand —were pressed into my neck like an oath. He felt hot, so incredibly hot, even through his clothes. Our skin was slick, and I only tried to breathe, gasping for air when the orgasm slowly released me from its tight grip.

When I opened my eyes, my gaze was blurry with tears and Kaldur was groaning, accompanied by ragged, deep thrusts, each one teasing his bulging knot against my entrance. Finally, he slowed his pace until he was resting against me. He pressed his forehead to my back, and I felt the hot exhales of his breath as he tried to calm himself. He returned his hands to both sides of my head to steady himself, and then he rose.

I moaned, a desperate little mew, when I felt him ease his cock out of my body slowly. I felt every last inch, my pussy already sore now that the pleasure had passed. Something wet flooded between my thighs. His come, I realized.

Kaldur maneuvered me carefully until I was on my back, looking up at him. I felt like a loose-limbed doll, still out of control of my own body. His hand came to my cheek, and he frowned when he saw the tears.

"Did I hurt you?" he asked.

His voice was nearly unrecognizable. And I didn't think I was imagining it this time, but his body *had* definitely grown, his muscles pressing against the seams of his clothes. I'd heard it could happen for some Kylorr. Some were more sensitive to the effects of blood than others.

Or…

Or it was a physical reaction triggered by a blood bond, but those were incredibly rare.

"No," I whispered, smiling up at him. My skin was flushed. My hair must've looked a mess and I had tears tracking down my face, but I didn't care. I felt…changed. I didn't think I would ever be the same.

"Why are you crying, then?" he rumbled, concern still touching those eyes. He bit into the pad of his thumb, spreading it over his bite marks to heal the wounds, as if that was the cause for my tears.

"I'm happy," I told him.

He grunted. His silver eyes were so dark they looked like faceted onyx, blackened and hard. His fangs hadn't retracted and his clothes were askew. I reached up to press my fingers over his lips.

"I could look at you forever," I told him. There was no need for shyness anymore. Not after *that*. The vulnerable confession fell from my lips easily. I watched his brow furrow, a peculiar expression I couldn't read flashing over his face.

He seemed...

If I had to guess the word, I would say *lost*.

He looked lost.

"What's wrong?" I asked, struggling to sit up from the bed. "Did you not like it?"

He let out a dark scoff. "Did I not like it?" he repeated.

Kaldur helped me up from the bed until I was sitting, supported by his arm. Between us his cock was still semi-hard, slick with our come. He was still pulsing, and when he saw me looking, he let out a soft sound and laced back up his trews, though it was a struggle.

"Sometimes I don't know what to make of you," he said slowly.

"And I don't know what to make of that," I confessed.

It went quiet as we regarded one another. Even though I felt open and laid bare—even *physically*—with every passing moment, I felt a little sorrow return. Because I could actually *see* Kaldur rebuilding the walls I'd tried to scratch down with my dull claws, barricading his borders like I was the enemy. He was pulling away. *Again.*

"Don't," I whispered, leaning up to press my lips to the little scar on his chin. "*Please*...stay with me."

"I can't give you everything you want, Erina," Kaldur said, his voice both softened and cold. "And I'm not a fool to be manipulated—do you understand? You don't think many have tried before?"

I frowned. "What?"

Such an odd thing to say.

"What are you talking about?"

But then he smiled, a quirking of his lips. He didn't answer me. Instead, after looking between us, he said, "I got too carried away tonight. But remember our contract—you'll need to start taking marroswood now. Understood? I'll let Maudoric know to serve it with your *baanye* starting tomorrow."

I couldn't help but flinch. The mention of the contract felt intentional, especially when he slid from underneath my grasp to go retrieve his *lore* pipe from the table.

"You can rest here if you wish," he told me, inhaling a deep inhale of *lore* before releasing it into the room. "But I won't be back tonight."

"Where are you going?" I asked, watching when he turned to the door.

"I have work to do."

And when he left me there, I felt every joyous feeling fade. I hopped down from the bed, feeling a twinge between my thighs and a new soreness emerge. I stood, naked, in the quiet room, which had only felt full and exciting moments before. Now it felt empty and cold.

I went to my dress, gathering it up from the ground, slipping it back over my head.

I was proud of myself when I didn't cry...at least not until I made it safely back to my room.

Finally, my fantasies about Kaldur had become a reality.

And in the aftermath, I had never felt lonelier.

CHAPTER 21
—
KALDUR

Intentionally, I'd expanded the guest list for the dinner tonight. Before it had been a small, intimate affair with a handful of close family friends. Now I had Maudoric wringing her hands together as more and more people flowed through the doors of my keep. Nobles, shopkeepers, leaders of guilds and organizations for farmers, builders, tradesmen, and merchants.

The atrium was filled with guests already. Instead of a formal dinner, Maudoric had changed it so there were circular tables of food and drink spread out among main reception area and into the ballroom, which barely saw any use.

I would make it up to her later, I decided, but earlier I'd been brief and gruff with my orders. The whole keep knew my mood was foul these last two days, ever since I'd returned from Salaire…and ever since my night with Erina.

Who still hadn't made her appearance.

Maudoric had ensured she had something suitable to wear for the evening. By now she would be able to hear the voices and laughter echoing throughout the entire keep. There had to be well over one hundred people here tonight.

Lydrasa arrived, on the arm of the son of House Braan. Ravar,

I believed his name was, but the House of Braan had so many sons and daughters, I couldn't be certain.

"Beautiful, as always," I complimented her when the two of them reached me. I knew she hated clique remarks, and so I said it with a smile.

She quirked her brow, a flash of amusement stinging through her. Despite her companion standing stoically beside her, she leaned close to me. Into my ear, she said, "I'm here for one thing alone, *Kyzaire*. To see the little human who's got you in knots."

The sound that fell from my throat was gruff. "You'll be disappointed, then, because she hasn't come down."

"I should warn you," Lydrasa said. "Word has spread of her. Apparently you were seen with her in the village market? The news is raging through the Houses."

"I'd noticed," I said. I'd felt dozens and dozens of eyes on me already, making my skin crawl. It had been inevitable—I'd always known that—but what worried me was *what* exactly had been spread.

I didn't want my brothers or Kalia discovering I'd found my blood mate through rumor. I wanted to tell them myself when I'd had more time to figure out what to *do* about it.

A rippling, small hush went through the atrium. I felt it like a pulse of energy, brief and startling, before the noise rose again.

When I turned, I saw Erina coming down the staircase, Maudoric a few steps behind her. She'd gone to retrieve her, then, also noticing her absence.

"Ah," Lydrasa said, her voice utterly amused, and it set my teeth on edge. "And there she is."

Erina looked beautiful. The dress I'd sent for in the village was simple in its elegance. An indigo blue—which reminded me of starwood blooms—that contrasted beautifully against her skin and dark red hair. The material was from a bolt of Salairian silk, prized apparently among the nobles, and it skimmed over her figure like a stream of water. She wore no jewels. Not that I'd given her any, but she also didn't need them.

She turned everyone's head—at least those who still lingered in the atrium. And she looked miserable.

Everyone would know who she was now. Not only was she arriving from within the keep, but I heard the whispers when I went to her, to meet her at the base of the stairs when she alighted.

Her gaze flicked up to me before it lowered again. Her hair was loose around her shoulders, the top half pinned back, though a few loose tendrils framed her rounded face.

I hadn't seen her since *that* night.

I'd be lying if I said that the thought of seeing her again hadn't made me nervous. *Nervous.* I'd nearly forgotten what that emotion was like, and I hated it. The gnawing, the atrocious ache.

"*Kyzaire,*" she greeted softly.

It was abundantly clear she didn't want to be here. But the longer I kept her tucked away, the more the nobles would talk, creating stories in their heads. And I didn't need any more speculation than there was already.

I *should* tell her that she looked…magnificent. Simply beautiful and lovely. She might not have been the *most* aesthetically beautiful female in attendance tonight—yet I only wanted to keep my gaze on her.

And she couldn't even look me in the eye.

I'd felt like the worst kind of villain these last two days, but I'd needed to center myself again. That stormy night in my rooms… I'd thought of little else, when I didn't need to be distracted right now.

That night had been dismantling. I'd felt torn apart, shredded to bits, and all I'd wanted was to beg for her to do it again.

Sex with a *kyrana*?

My brothers were fucking bastards because yet again, they

hadn't prepared me for the sheer destruction of it. Destruction so I would be made new again.

Everything in me ached to steal her away. To feel everything that night again. Erina would never know how close I'd come, on a hundred occasions, to slipping into her rooms. Of taking her into my arms and begging her to make me lose myself again.

"Are you well?" I asked, the silence stretching between us. My question felt stilted and awkward, two other sensations I rarely felt. I didn't like this. This uncertain turmoil building in my chest.

"Yes, quite well," she answered. I waited for her small, shy smile or the brightening of her cheeks, but still, she avoided my eyes…and she said nothing else.

I deserve that, I thought, dread pressing against my chest hard. I'd left her that night and hadn't come to her since. Of course she would feel hurt, her ego bruised.

I had to be careful how I interacted with her tonight. With all the eyes of Vyaan watching, I'd wanted to make something clear to them: Erina Denoren was my blood giver only. That she would get the respect from me that her position demanded, but mostly I wanted to stop the loose, wagging tongues.

She would have received her first payment by now. I'd had Maudoric deposit the sum, in accordance with our contract, yesterday. I had hoped it would help dampen her ire toward me, but I might have miscalculated.

"You look very beautiful, Erina," I said, my shoulders lowering softly as defeat went through me.

The quiet, hushed words made her breath hitch. She darted a surprised look up at me, and when those brown eyes pinned to mine, I felt relief spreading through me. Like the burn of liquor, welcome and warm.

Then she cleared her throat and said, "Thank you, *Kyzaire*."

Her eyes lowered again.

"How long would you like me to stay?" she asked next.

My lips pressed. She looked like she was walking into a den of *lyvins.*

"I thought you might enjoy a gathering like this," I told her. She said nothing. "When others leave, so can you. It would look strange if you disappeared early."

"I don't think anyone would mind," she answered, "but I'll do what you say."

I couldn't stand the hollowness in her voice. "Erina," I said quietly, stepping close so others wouldn't overhear.

Her scent grew almost overwhelming, and I realized...

A lashing of anger whipped through me.

"Are you wearing that perfume?"

The one from her *lover.* Luc. Something lodged into place in my chest, a boulder that made it difficult to breathe.

"I thought I told you not to wear it again."

"It's just a little tonight," she answered, frowning. "I made sure I didn't put on too much."

The scent made my stomach roil because I knew what it *meant.* I knew who she'd been thinking of as she'd dabbed it on, and I couldn't *stand* it.

Erina didn't know how much *I* knew. She might think me a fool. She might think she could flaunt her lover's gift right in front of me. Did she find it humorous? Her own small joke?

It was on the tip of my tongue to order her to wash it off. I wouldn't be able to stand the merest whiff of it.

Then I realized it didn't matter. The purpose of this event was to have Erina here but to show my indifference. If I had her wash her skin off—if it made me crazed to want to stake my possessive claim on her in a jealous rage—it would turn my plan on its head.

"Very well," I grated. "Like I said, you can leave when others do. Until then, I expect you to be in attendance."

Maudoric was still lingering on the stairs behind her. I met her gaze, her expression impassive.

"Enjoy your evening," I told Erina.

"You won't—you won't be with me?" she asked suddenly, confusion lacing her tone.

"No," I added. "You're not my wife. You're my blood giver. I trust you can understand the difference."

I walked away, anger and seething jealousy still burning in my chest. I felt out of control. Nothing was normal anymore. I didn't recognize who I'd become. To lose my mind over a *female*? To want to rip her lover to shreds in a berserker rage so she would have no choice but to remain at my side?

It was insanity. I loathed her for it.

When I passed Lydrasa on my way into the ballroom, she smirked, her eyes straying from Erina. "What a cute little thing. Isn't she that keeper who walked in on us fucking?"

The son of House Braan cleared his throat, his wings giving a small twitch.

Lydrasa smiled. "Yes, I think it is."

"I'll find you later," I told her, my growl a promise.

Her eyes were delighted. "I'll look forward to it, *Kyzaire*."

CHAPTER 22

ERINA

"**D**on't look like you're walking to your death, Erina," Maudoric ordered, lapsing back into her role of Head Keeper. "You'll give them all something to talk about."

Good, I thought. I didn't have it in me to care anymore.

"This is important to the *Kyzaire*," she said, turning to me and gently grabbing my arm. "To introduce to you into Vyaan society. Blood givers are still important members within a noble House. He's giving you this respect."

I didn't know what he was doing, but I didn't think it had anything to do with respect.

Still, I didn't want to upset Maudoric. The party did seem lovely. It was lit with golden sconces that made the room glow and glitter. There was food aplenty, presented on a plethora of tables throughout the room, and I thought I should try every last morsel I could. It would give me something to do at least.

A thought occurred to me, hopeful. "Is Syndras here?"

I knew that she and Maudoric were friends.

My heart sank when the Head Keeper shook her head. "She's

visiting family in Kyne and won't return until next week. But I think her daughter is expected tonight."

"Right," I said. I needed to visit soon.

I wasn't used to so many people's eyes on me when I stepped into the ballroom. I felt naked and on display in this silly dress, like a trinket or a possession placed on a shelf.

But maybe that was just the hurt.

After that night in his room, I'd felt discarded. And I was trying to come to terms with that and failing miserably. That maybe I'd read it all wrong. That maybe someone like Kaldur just took what he wanted and didn't look back to see the effects he had on others.

Yet you agreed to this. You chose this. You initiated that moment in his room, that little voice of logical reason whispered in my mind.

He'd told me to leave, after all. I hadn't listened. Instead I'd felt very hollow in the aftermath of that night. Made even more so when Maudoric had informed me that she'd deposited my funds for the month from House Kaalium's accounts.

It became clear what I was. A paid whore, whether it was for my blood or my body.

And I was more than a little ashamed to admit that I'd felt sorry for myself, allowing myself to wallow a little as I tried to mend my hurt.

But this morning, I'd told myself *enough.* I'd willingly placed myself in this situation, and now I needed to navigate it.

There was still a small part that held on to hope. There was still a small part of me that thought I only needed to talk to Kaldur when his guard was down, to tell him how I felt. Because how else would he know?

I had hoped that that would be tonight. He hadn't come to me in the last two days for his feedings. I'd almost thought he'd left the territory again until I'd heard he was still in the keep from Maudoric when she'd delivered my *baanye* and, now, marroswood.

Maybe there will still be an opportunity, I thought, sighing. I caught sight of Kaldur milling around the room, looking dangerously handsome in his deep blue vest and pressed dark trews. He stole everyone's attention—even mine.

My heart ached just looking at him. Because it made me remember what it felt like to kiss him, to hear his groans in my ear, and feel the flood of his release inside me. To see him with his walls lowered and feel a pinching ache in my breast when I realized he was *sad* and maybe even a little lost. Just like me.

That was the Kaldur I wanted. Not the grinning, charming *Kyzaire* who effortlessly got everyone to do what he wanted.

"If Syndras were here," Maudoric said quietly. I nearly jumped, forgetting her presence behind me. "She would tell you that that every noble in here is looking for a weakness in you. Don't give them a reason to talk."

My breath hitched as I turned. But Maudoric was already retreating.

Taking her place was a Kylorr female before I even could think about what I should do next.

"Salairian silk?" asked the female, eyeing my dress. "I would know it anywhere. You must be very special for the *Kyzaire* to give you such a lavish gift."

I blinked, my tongue momentarily tied up in knots as I scrambled for something to say. I made things up for my stories all the time, so why couldn't I now? Why couldn't I quip back something clever like Kavelyn would do?

"I'm Kyda of House Azola," the female said. She was dressed in a flowing bright red gown that matched her eyes. Her throat was decorated with a strand of shimmering black gems.

House Azola.

Lydrasa's mother, I determined silently.

Damn.

"It was a gift I hadn't expected," I told her, trying to paste on a small smile. I had a feeling it looked as shaky as it felt on my features. "Your necklace is very lovely. Would you consider those gems or crystals?"

The question popped from my lips before I could retract it.

Kyda gave a sharp bark of a laugh. "These are *ornyx* gems from Kyne. You don't recognize them? Surely you've seen them before. I heard you used to be a keeper here. Perhaps I've seen you helping at a few of these gatherings in the past."

My smile felt frozen on my face when her tone registered. One slightly barbed and mocking. Prodding at me. I felt something lock into place inside me.

I was an orphan, one with no true family, and never once had I experienced wealth. I would never fit in with these nobles. And they would always ensure that I felt that way.

I didn't know why Kaldur insisted on me coming tonight. To make a spectacle of me? Maudoric had said it was out of respect for my new position in his House, but then he'd abandoned me to fend for myself among his friends.

"I tried to avoid gatherings like this, truthfully," I answered, my smile widening. "I always found them so suffocating in their self-importance."

Kyda's eyes widened. I'd stunned her speechless, and a thrill of guilt-laden victory went through me.

"I hope you enjoy the rest of your evening, Lady Kyda," I said, inclining my head. "And you should try the *laak* puffs. They're always my favorite when our cook, Saira, makes them."

I walked away, my spine stiff, my limbs tight. Kaldur had strayed closer than I'd realized, and I froze when I saw him. Had he heard? His gaze was on me, studying me with narrowed eyes, but I turned my head forward and went deeper, unseeing, into the ballroom.

So much for not giving them something to talk about, I lamented now that my adrenaline had faded, biting my lip in a darkened corner, picking up a small piece of a spiced meat pastry, though my stomach was in knots.

What had possessed me to say such a thing?

Even now, I could see Kyda tittering with her socialite friends, casting me long looks. Her eyes were like arrows, her sneer the bow with which to shoot them.

As for Kaldur…he was nowhere to be seen. I didn't know how long I drifted around the room, making niceties with people I didn't know or simply being ignored. If I'd been meant to make a good first impression on Vyaan society, I'd failed miserably.

"Heard you insulted a noble," came a familiar voice.

A jolt went through my belly. When I turned, I saw Velle standing there. She was dressed in one of our nicer uniforms—pressed dark gray trews and a silver embroidered tunic that ended at her thighs. Velle had made customizations to hers, taking in the pants so they hugged her shapely figure and belting the waist of the tunic with a matching belt so it was more flattering. Her hair was in a stylish updo, her neck on blatant display. A shimmering powder had even been dusted along her collarbones to catch the golden light.

She looked pretty and calm. Surely she was much more suited to navigate these kinds of parties, even though I was the one in silk. Salairian silk, evidently.

"I never liked her," Velle said, nodding discreetly at the Lady of House Azola. "When I worked for them, she always thought I was trying to get into bed with her husband."

"And were you?" I asked hesitantly.

She snorted. "No. It was her son."

Velle felt familiar in such an unfamiliar setting. And the fact that she was finally willing to talk to me brought out hope. I knew that we had our issues and differences, but she had watched over me when I'd first come to work at Kaldur's keep. It was really only in the last several months that tension between us had begun to spread, ever since that party we'd been serving at, where that noble male had taken an interest in me.

Luckily I didn't see him here tonight.

"I didn't realize you worked for their House," I said. "You never mentioned it."

"I've worked for many Houses," Velle answered, shrugging. "It didn't seem important enough to mention because my time there was brief."

I nodded. An uncomfortable silence lapsed between us, each of us aware that we hadn't spoken since that morning she'd discovered Kaldur feeding from me. It seemed so long ago now.

And I'd been…lonely. For a friend. For a companion. My old life had been separated from me the moment I'd signed the contract. Keepers I'd thought were my friends didn't speak to me anymore. They politely inclined their heads at me in the hallway as I passed before hurrying away.

"I miss you," I said quietly, casting a glance up at her. "I don't like how it went between us."

Velle regarded me. "Me neither," she finally said.

It was as much of an apology I would get from her, but we both smiled at one another, however small.

"But I must tell you, in that dress, you did your hair all wrong," Velle tsked, frowning at the wild waves that I could never force into submission. "If *I* were the *Kyzaire*'s blood giver, I would want everyone to know it. So why hide your neck?"

"I thought it too obvious," I said quietly.

She scoffed. "Nothing is too obvious for people like these. Rub their noses in it. That's what I'd do."

But I wasn't Velle and I never could be. Though I had certainly channeled her energy when I'd been speaking with Lady Kyda.

"How have you been?" I asked.

"Good," Velle replied. A sly smile crept onto her lips. "I've taken up with a noble, but you can't tell anyone. Not yet."

"What?" I asked, eyes widening. "Who?"

Velle shook her head, her smile secretive. It was like her to be dramatic, but I was surprised when she wouldn't say the name.

"A friend of a friend," Velle said. "That's all I'll say. I don't expect to be working for House Kaalium much longer."

Everything she'd wanted, then. It happened so quickly…just like my new reality.

"I'm glad for you," I said quietly, eyeing the satisfaction and ease on her features. Was that why she'd approached me tonight? Because she might be leaving soon? "Do you love him?"

She laughed. "Love? Of course not."

I frowned, even as disappointment bit into me. For a moment, I *did* judge her. How could she give herself to someone she didn't love? Commit to them?

I picked at the pastry some more, popping a little bite into my mouth. Velle studied me for a long time, making me shift on me feet in uncertainty.

"What is it?" I asked, tucking a strand of hair behind my ears.

"I'm bored," she declared. "I find these gatherings so terribly dull now."

I supposed she would, considering her new noble.

"Want to go sneak into the kitchens and make Saira give us some of her cream pudding?"

My heart gave a little leap, mingled with nostalgia perhaps. "She made some?"

"Yes, and she didn't serve it here. She's saving it for *us*. Come on."

Us. That sounded so lovely, like I was part of something again.

Maybe this was a peace offering. And it would be nice to visit the kitchen. Like I could pretend I was my old self.

I wanted that, I realized. I wanted the simplicity of being in a warm kitchen at night, listening to all the scandalous stories and gossip the keepers had learned at the gathering while we all giggled and sipped on spiced tea, munching on the snacks that Saira had saved us.

At least I didn't feel lonely in those moments.

"Let's go," I said, and she took my hand, like we were back to normal.

"Are you sure it won't get you in trouble with your *Kyzaire*?" Velle asked. I thought I caught a flash of delight in her gaze, a small smirk on her features, though she wiped it away. Perhaps she still wasn't *quite* over what had happened between us.

"I don't even see him," I admitted. "He won't mind. I've been here long enough, and I'd rather not insult another noble when I open my mouth."

Velle pulled me from the room, and I felt a small burst of relief the moment we were away from all the prying eyes. I dragged in a deep breath, looking around the blissfully empty atrium. Everyone had made their way into the ballroom over an hour ago.

When Velle tugged me up the staircase, I frowned, "Why are we going this way?"

"Maudoric wanted the main hallway blocked off to guests. We have to go around."

"Oh, all right."

We went through the West Wing to wrap around to the stairs on the opposite side. The ballroom noise still echoed through the grand walls of the keep, since the floor below was open to the upper levels, but the farther we ventured from the gathering, the more at ease I felt.

At least until we passed by the hallway that led to Kaldur's study. Velle slowed.

"We shouldn't—" I started to say.

"Shh. Someone's in there," she whispered. She crept closer to the entrance of the hallway. Kaldur's study was the first door on the right, which I knew afforded the best view of Vyaan's villages. "Isn't that…isn't that Lydrasa's voice? With the *Kyzaire*?"

I froze as jealousy pricked at me. Why was she up here with him?

Despite my better judgment, I listened. Velle crept closer to the door, which was left slightly ajar, a stream of light spilling out onto the smooth stone floor.

After a moment of deliberation, I did the same. Was this where he'd disappeared to? Sneaking away from his own gathering with his former lover?

A churning feeling began in my gut, my heart beginning to pump wildly in my chest. I tried to hold my breath to get it to slow so that I could listen to what was being said.

He'd told me that he'd dismissed her as his mistress, that I was his sole blood giver. Had that been the truth?

I didn't know anymore. But maybe I could find out.

"I'm just saying, Kaldur, it's not good," Lydrasa was saying. "She insulted my *mother*. A noble. You need to put her in her place."

Oh gods. They were talking about me.

My face flamed bright red.

"This whole situation is ridiculous. When are you going to stop playing with the human?"

"What have the nobles been saying?" came Kaldur's voice.

"You know what they've been saying," Lydrasa said. "Or did you think you could escape their notice when you disappeared down an alley with her on a busy morning in the square last week? I *told* you this."

"I tire of these games, Lydrasa," Kaldur growled. "I think the nobles have forgotten exactly who I am and—"

"Oh, they haven't forgotten anything, *Kyzaire*. They know exactly who you are. And you've had a taller mountain to climb than your brothers, yes, because of your reputation. But like I've told you before, don't make a fool of your great House. Don't let history repeat itself here. Not for a keeper."

She spat out that last word like it was poison.

I didn't dare breathe. My eyes were locked on a knot of wood in the door. One that was protruding slightly, one that hadn't been sanded smooth.

"Do you love her?" Lydrasa asked. I nearly gasped. I pressed my fingertips to my lips to keep them closed.

Kaldur laughed, and it sunk something in my chest, the derision and amusement I heard in it. "Of course not. Don't be foolish."

"Do you care about her?"

"I like the way she tastes," he growled. "Like a tumbler full of my favorite liquor. Nothing more. We've all gone a little mad for a blood giver a time or two. It doesn't mean anything."

A dismissive answer, and it felt like a dagger slipping slowly into my chest, inch by inch.

And yet I couldn't leave. I couldn't walk away. I wanted to hear *exactly* how Kaldur of House Kaalium felt about me.

"Have you fucked her yet?" Lydrasa asked next.

And it felt like a betrayal of my privacy when he admitted, "Yes."

I felt like I wanted to be swallowed up when I saw Velle cut me a sharp glance. Her brow was furrowed.

"Did you like it?" Lydrasa continued, seemingly not surprised by the confession. Even I heard the flirtatious purr in her voice. "Was it better than *our* fucking?"

"It was fine," Kaldur said. I nearly winced, feeling a sharp ache in my chest. So pinching that I looked down just to make sure nothing had imbedded itself into me. "She was... It was fine, *zendra*."

Zendra.

He'd called me that once. Perhaps it was just a pretty little name he called all the females he encountered. That knowledge felt like ice in my veins.

"*Fine,*" Lydrasa repeated, and her giggle was delighted. "And this is who you turned me away for? A '*fine*' fuck? When we'd been spectacular together?"

Leave, my mind screamed at me. This was cruel. I didn't need to listen to it.

Kaldur said nothing in reply. Were they laughing at me? Was this whole situation just a big joke to him?

Of course it is, I couldn't help but realize. He was so far above my station in life, and so was Lydrasa. So was every noble at the gathering down in the ballroom. They'd been born into wealth and privilege and bloodlines.

Me?

I had a made-up last name because I didn't even know my real one.

I was nothing like them. And in Kaldur's eyes, I would only ever be a keeper. He'd tried, desperately, to change that.

But not for my benefit.

For *his*.

"How long will you keep this charade up?" Lydrasa asked once her laugh died down. Her tone was hard, unyielding. *Serious.* "You already know what the nobles are saying. If you can't be trusted to make sound decisions within your own keep, then how can you throughout Vyaan? They're scared you'll turn out like your predecessor. It took years to stabilize this territory again. And if you marry her—"

A low warning growl grumbled from Kaldur, making even *me* freeze outside the door.

"I will tell you this one last time, Lydrasa, and then I will never speak about it again. She is my blood giver *only*. We have a contract in place. And once I decide I don't want her anymore, that contract will be ended and I will move on with my life." He said it all slowly and clipped, as if he were speaking with a child. "This changes nothing concerning the future of Vyaan. I am not my uncle. I remember how his actions—his selfish actions— changed this territory. It won't be the same with me. And you insult me by thinking I would allow a conniving little keeper to wiggle her way into my bed and try to take a title that will *never* belong to her."

Lydrasa went silent. I simply felt numb. Velle reached out a hand and squeezed it around my wrist, wanting to pull me away from the door.

But I was rooted like a *dallia* tree, who'd chosen a place of permanence, listening to two people try to cut me down.

And one of those people I'd thought myself falling in love with. Every lingering look, every sweet curl of his lips, every ragged breath against my skin…it had meant nothing.

Only now I understood. I saw the truth of what he thought of me. And I was nothing. A passing amusement. A dessert he liked to sample. Until one day when he would decide he'd had enough and then would toss me away. Forgotten.

I would—and could—never love someone like that.

How had I convinced myself otherwise? How had I been so blind to who he truly was?

"You *do* seem indifferent to her," Lydrasa admitted quietly. "You barely looked at her tonight. She's a pretty little thing, but I know she's not your type. You'd eat her alive. The irony is that she would let you."

Kaldur said, "She's young. And more than a little naive. But you're right—this life is not for someone like her. A keeper could never be a *Kylaira.*"

Finally, I pulled away, tugging my wrist from Velle's grip. And I quickly retreated from the hallway, ignoring the sound of my friend rushing after me.

"I just want to be alone," I whispered, fighting off tears. "*Please.*"

I fled.

CHAPTER 23
ERINA

I pulled my shawl around my shoulders tighter as I looked out over the quiet night of eastern Vyaan. It was in the early hours of morning, and only recently had I heard the last of the guests departing from the keep.

Sleep wouldn't come, so I'd long stopped trying. The only thing that made me feel better was the icy night air on my hot cheeks. My eyes stung from all the tears, but I didn't have any left in me.

I just felt drained. But strangely at peace.

I knew what I had to do. It was the only thing I *could* do.

And so I left the balcony, feeling oddly calm, though my movements were stiff. I felt like I was out of my body when I left my rooms and trekked to the West Wing. I hadn't heard Kaldur return to his quarters. I thought it likely he might've still been in his study.

Maybe even with Lydrasa, I couldn't help but think, feeling a twinge in my chest.

I saw a curl of light beneath the door. I stared at the spot I'd been just mere hours before. The spot where I realized I'd had it all wrong when it came to Kaldur of House Kaalium.

Now I only needed to hear it from his own mouth.

I didn't bother knocking. I pushed open the door and stepped inside.

Kaldur's gaze snapped up to mine. He was seated at his desk, his features both illuminated and shadowed by a blue projection of architecture plans from a Halo orb.

He frowned when he saw me but gestured forward.

"Is something wrong?" he asked, his eyes flicking back down to a glowing tablet of notes before him. "I need to finish this tonight—"

"I heard what you said."

Kaldur paused and looked up at me slowly. His frown deepened. "What are you talking about?"

I almost laughed. He didn't even remember? Did he talk that way about me often, then?

"With Lydrasa," I added, keeping my tone even, keeping my eyes pinned to his so he couldn't look away. "Right here, earlier tonight."

Realization went through him.

"You were listening?" he asked, his gaze pinned on mine. I had his full attention *now*. "Did you follow us?"

"No," I said simply. "I left the gathering, and on my way up, I heard your voices. You didn't close the door. I heard everything you said."

Kaldur stood. He was still wearing his clothing from earlier, as if he hadn't bothered to change. Whereas I'd slipped out of the dress immediately, as if it were a shackle around me and not Salairian silk.

"And what exactly did you hear?" he asked, stalking around the desk to approach me.

For a moment, I thought that maybe I should fear him. He was so much bigger and stronger than me.

"What you really think about me," I told him, meeting his eyes. I was proud when my voice didn't tremble, when my voice was strong. He already thought I was a weakness. I didn't want to give him any extra ammunition. "That I'm easily disposable to you. That you'll always see me as a keeper and nothing more. That you find the idea of loving me laughable. That you never intended this to be anything more."

"Which I told you," he said. "How many times have I told you not to look too closely at what this is? If you do, you might not like what you find."

How cold he was! I didn't understand him. I didn't understand how someone could be so callous.

"And then to go laugh at me behind my back with your former mistress, telling her *private* things about moments that have nothing to do with her!"

That made him close his eyes, a deep breath falling from his lips. I would've thought it was regret if I didn't know any better. Before last night, I would've thought just that.

"You made a fool out of me," I breathed. "And I'm here now because I want you to say this to me directly. I want to know how you feel about me. Or if I'm just wasting my life, hoping one day you *might* care for me. That one day you *might* love me. Hoping one day we *might* be something more."

My voice ended on a tone of a plea...and I hated that. But I couldn't help it. For two years, I'd admired him from afar. I'd entertained fantasies of him, which made me feel less alone. Because when someone like me was suddenly in the magnetic and overwhelming presence of a male like him, she savored every scrap she could—thinking they were delicacies, only to find they were rotten.

"What are you asking me?" Kaldur growled. "Ask me directly. I'll tell you what you need to know."

"Did you say those things?" I started. The most basic of questions.

"Of course I did," he replied, looming over me, a glare on his features. He didn't bother to deny it. "You heard me yourself."

"And is that what you really think of me? That I'm young and naive? That I could never be right for someone like you? That you think me beneath you, a mere keeper trying to better her station in life by slipping into your bed?"

He smirked, and it hit me like a punch in the gut. "Isn't that *exactly* what you're trying to do, Erina Denoren?"

I nearly gasped at how hard that question hit me.

"I do think you're young and naive," Kaldur said. "But I also think you're more calculating than you appear. You fooled even me…for a little while. But I see now what you're trying to accomplish. Do you think you're the first female to try to use me for my House, for my title? Every female in my acquaintance has tried. You are certainly not the first, and you will certainly not be the last."

"I haven't," I argued, narrowing my eyes on him. "You're just so—so jaded that you can't see that. That you suspect me for doing something that I haven't done!"

Kaldur laughed, bitter and dark. "You said you wanted something more with me. That would imply a lasting position within this House. And I'll tell you right now, Erina, I'd be more than happy to make you my mistress, if that's your ambition. But that's the highest you will ever ascend yourself in my keep."

My breath felt squeezed from my lungs.

"I'm surprised you would make me your mistress, considering that the sex was just *fine*," I replied hollowly.

That made his lips press together. A muscle in his jaw jumped as his nostrils flared. Did he look guilty, or was that just my imagination? I couldn't trust my perception of reality anymore because I'd been so, so wrong about Kaldur. I'd thought he'd cared about me. Every lingering look, every whispered exhalation against my skin, every meaningful touch or genuine laugh.

It had all been a lie I'd told myself.

"Can I ask you something?" I started. "Did you care when you left me in your room that night? Did you even think to check on me afterward?"

"Check on you after *what*? Sex?" he asked. "This is what I'm talking about, Erina. You expect far too much of me."

"It's basic decency," I argued quietly, shocked at the reply. I bit my lip. "I'd never...I'd never been with a male before. That had been my first time."

His eyes widened. His lips parted with a scoff. "Do you *really* expect me to believe that? Gods! How manipulative you are!"

He didn't *believe* me.

I hadn't expected that, and it made me feel like my insides were being scraped raw. The ache was excruciating.

"Manipulative," I breathed. "You made me feel so discarded, Kaldur. Like what happened didn't mean anything. I'm telling you the truth, whether you want to believe it or not."

"You got what you wanted that night," he said, dismissing my words. His expression was unreadable, but for some reason, it struck me as *stung*. "*You* made that choice. You came back into the room. So don't give me that. You got what you came for, didn't you? We both did."

He meant his feeding.

"And that's all I am to you," I said, realization crashing down on me. "*Blood.* A means to an end. That's so..."

I took a deep breath, turning from him briefly to re-center my thoughts.

"That's so tragic," I finally decided softly. "That you have everything in the world you could possibly want...and you only see people as more *things* to possess. You used me. For one thing only. I thought...I thought you were different."

"And what about you?" Kaldur replied, stepping toward me until I had to tilt my head back to look up at him again. He took my chin in his grasp. "You haven't even washed it off. I can still smell it. Your precious gift from Luc Denoren in Laras."

The name made me gasp. "How do you—"

He'd looked into him.

"I know all about your plan," Kaldur said, his eyes hardening like metal, his tone mocking. "Velle told me."

"Velle?" I breathed, shaking my head. I didn't understand. "What are you talking about?"

"She told me about how you wanted to secure credits so you could finally be reunited with him, that everything you do is only to get back to him. I know you write him letters, send him money. I know you've been in frequent contact. I know that all you want is to be with him, no matter the price. You think *I* used *you*? What do you call what you're doing?"

"That's not…that's not…" I started, my mind jumbled. I hadn't expected him to say Luc's name. It threw me, like two realities colliding that I always thought of as separate spheres. "You don't understand. I love Luc—he's *always* been there for me. *Of course* I want to see him! But it's not the same thing."

"Do you hear yourself?" Kaldur said, pinning me with a hard glare as he released my chin, as if in disgust. His fangs had elongated at the mere mention of Luc's name, and for the first time, I felt a thrill of fear sizzle within my belly. He bellowed, "You just admitted it to me! And you can try to twist it however you want, but it *is* the same thing."

I stumbled back, my heart racing. When I turned, I heard Kaldur hiss out a sharp breath, as if to calm himself.

Silence dropped between us. I stared at the wall of his study, textured in arching patterns that reminded me of depictions of wind.

I didn't know what to feel anymore. It was all too much. Too overwhelming. And I was tired.

"I'll never be enough for you," I said quietly. "I'll always be that person that the nobles whisper about at your parties. You won't defend me against them. I'll be alone. Just like tonight."

My future was so clear if I stayed.

It hit me like a stone wall, one I'd been sprinting toward. And now, dazed and hurt in the aftermath, I saw what a hopeless and naive fool I'd been. To hope that someone like Kaldur could love someone like me.

He'd been right about that at the very least.

"Your greedy ambitions leave something to be desired," Kaldur said, his voice cold. "I see what you're trying to secure for yourself—and for Luc. And I want you to know that I *know*. Your own friend, Velle, told me everything. She warned me about you. But I'll play along for now. I'll give you the credits and the status you desire. But if you've set your sights on *Kylaira*…"

I sucked in a sharp breath. Lady of the keep.

"It will never happen," Kaldur said quietly and simply. "I understand who you are now, Erina Denoren. If anything, this is a punishment for me too."

For him? What was he talking about?

"So is that what you want? To be my mistress?" he asked, coming closer. His fingers brushed over my cheek, tucking a strand of hair behind my ear. His voice was gentle, but there was only distrust in his eyes. "It would be an ascension from blood giver. Shall I have another contract drawn up? How much will you require? Will twenty *vron* a month be enough for you and your beloved Luc, or do you want more?"

I flinched back, away from his touch. I felt like curling up into myself like crushed, crumpled parchment.

"Keep your credits," I said, my voice sounding as hollow as my chest. "I don't want them."

Kaldur smirked. But when I didn't react further, that smile died. His eyes flickered back and forth between my own, as if trying to read me. "What?"

"I made all kinds of excuses for you in my head," I whispered. "For why you treated me poorly. Because I understood. I know better than anyone what I am. I know the life I was dealt by fate. I'm not a noble. I'm an orphan who became a keeper. I never lied about that. But I constantly lied to myself about *you* because I didn't want to see the truth."

"And what truth is that?"

"You're not anything like I'd hoped you'd be."

Kaldur's gaze went past me—to the textured wall of wind patterns, his eyes tracing them—as if he couldn't stand to look at me anymore. "I did tell you I'd only disappoint you. And here is the reality of it. No one can live up to ideals in your head, little *dallia*. You're foolish to believe anyone can."

The sweet name sounded mocking now, reminding me of the afternoon we'd had in the garden, under the shade of a tree, as we'd talked of fables.

"I won't make that mistake again," I said, holding his eyes.

I'd heard what I'd needed to.

I'd been a dreamer for too long. And now I was crashing back down to reality. Why was I surprised when that impact scattered me into millions of fragmented pieces?

Just like the vase I'd admired, the one Lydrasa had broken, I could try to put myself back together, but I would always be cracked and marked. Marked by this. Marked by *him*.

I couldn't stay. That much was clear.

Kaldur wouldn't care if I left. He'd made that abundantly clear tonight. Velle had, apparently, been in his ear the entire time. I didn't trust anyone. I felt utterly alone.

And there was only one person I wanted to see. One person who had always felt like home.

I thought this might be the last time that I saw Kaldur of House Kaalium.

"The first time I saw you," I started, "it was out on the terrace by the gardens. My very first day when Maudoric was showing me the keep. The moment I saw you, it was like the world swirled and everything was more beautiful."

His brows lowered. He frowned.

"*You* were beautiful to me then," I said. "But you were just a ridiculous dream. And now I know what you're really like. That makes me feel better, at the very least. It gives me peace. Closure."

I looked up at him. A face I'd drawn countless of times in pencil. Every sharp slice of shadows across his features, every tilting, curled smirk of his lips.

"Now I won't always wonder what could have been."

I turned from him, my heart both heavy and broken. I didn't expect it to *ache* so much.

As I left his study, I didn't look back once.

CHAPTER 24
—
ERINA

*B*y dawn, I had all my belongings packed in the same bag that I'd come to the keep with. One I'd purchased for mere credits at a vendor stall in the market, shortly after I'd left Wrezaan's. The handle was frayed, barely holding on by mere threads, and I worried that this was the final trip where it'd give up on me.

There was something sad about my entire life being packed into a single bag. While I didn't own much, I'd always dreamed of a home filled with lovely things. Permanent things that I'd picked up on travels or had been gifts from friends. Things that held special meaning. Things that could never be taken away from me.

In my bag, I had the clothes that I owned, my vial of perfume, my tin of pencils, and the plethora of notebooks I'd kept over the years. I'd discarded a couple dresses so that they would all fit—and I'd left my keeper uniforms, and my trusty apron, hanging in the wardrobe. I didn't have much, and it was probably a lucky thing that I didn't.

I'd done something bad as well. I'd gone to the starlight hallway, walking down it for the last time in the early hours of morning, and ventured to the sitting room where everything had changed. I went to the console drawer, where I'd hidden the vase fragments, and I stole one of the larger pieces. It really was a lovely color, and this one had the most of the delicately painted and foiled vines and flowers on it. It would be the one thing I took from House Kaalium—and I wanted it to be a reminder.

I'd wrapped it up in a spare cloth and shoved it into the side of my traveling bag. Before I left, I made sure my letters were safely tucked into my pocket.

When the sun rose over the distant mountains, I took a final look around the room and left. The keep was quiet, though I would try to avoid any keepers on my way out.

My emotions oscillated from numbness to anger to heartbreak to betrayal. On a constant loop. As I made my way through the darkened halls of the keep that had been my home for the last two years, I felt another emotion creep into my heart. *Sorrow.*

I had been content here. It had been the first time I'd felt secure. I would never forget that.

But I tightened my hand on my traveling bag and moved on. When I passed Kaldur's closed door to his quarters, I didn't even blink.

Move forward, move forward, I told myself. It was all I would allow myself to think. Move forward and start new, far from here.

Far away from *him.*

But on my way out of the keep, right when I'd made it *nearly* to the front door, I heard a familiar voice.

"Erina? Where in Raazos's name are you going at this hour?"

I blew out a breath and turned to find Velle watching me. She was dressed already, her face freshly scrubbed. She looked like was on her way to the kitchens, halting by the staircase that I'd just come down.

She was one of the last people I wanted to see. When Kaldur

had told me what Velle had said…I'd believed it. I *did* believe that she'd tried to drive a wedge between us. The ugliest part was that it was *easy* to believe.

And that should tell me everything I needed to know about someone I considered a friend. Was I so desperate to be loved by someone that I was willing to overlook anything?

That was something I needed to figure out for myself. But it wouldn't be here.

"I'm leaving," I told her.

Her eyes widened. Silence lapsed in the atrium, which just last night had been filled with a plethora of people from all over Vyaan.

"What do you mean you're *leaving*?" Velle asked carefully, her eyes narrowing on me. She looked to my bag, and she blinked, stilling. "As in leaving the keep? For good?"

"Yes," I replied.

Velle's chin tilted up. She didn't look surprised…so why did that surprise me?

I shifted the handle to my other hand. "Kaldur told me that you said I shouldn't be trusted," I said. "Is that what you really believe?"

The numbness was sliding back into my chest, spreading as I watched her. I was actually glad I'd run into her, I decided. Because I was done making excuses for people. I should start listening to them when they revealed who they truly were instead of wishing that they were different.

"I—that's not…" Velle started, but then she inhaled a sharp breath.

"Did you ever really think of me as your friend?" I asked.

"Of course I did," she replied, her tone rising in defensiveness.

"Then why would you do that?" I asked. "I'm trying to understand. Because you were jealous?"

"I wasn't," she began to say, her voice rising, her brow furrowing. Then she laughed. She shook her head. "Actually, yes. Now you know the ugly part of me, Erina. I *was* jealous. You got what *I* wanted. Guess I couldn't stand it."

Her tone was mocking, sarcastic. But didn't she realize that she was telling the truth?

Suddenly I didn't care. I was done caring. I could simply walk away. It wouldn't matter at all to Velle.

"Did you know Kaldur and Lydrasa were in his study last night?" I asked. The only thing I wanted confirmed. "Did Lydrasa put you up to it? Or was it your idea?"

When she said nothing, I knew that was answer enough. I wondered what was in it for her…

A sliver of knowing pierced me. I realized she'd told me last night.

"I hope you have a good life with your noble," I said, inclining my head at her. My tone was cool, almost chilled. "I'm sure Lydrasa picked well for you."

With that, I turned to leave. I didn't want to waste another moment more with someone who so clearly wanted to hurt me. She didn't try to stop me.

I doubted I'd ever see her again.

Good riddance, I thought, determination soaring through me when I looked over a lightening Vyaan. The morning was cold, and I wore my heaviest coat to save room in my bag. I was grateful for it, especially during the long walk into the village.

First I posted the letters. One to Luc, which should reach him tomorrow, telling him of my plans to come to Laras. The other to Syndras with an explanation and with promises to write. She likely wouldn't see it until the following week, or whenever she returned from her trip. I was only sorry I couldn't say goodbye to her in person, when she'd helped me so much, but I knew she would understand.

Next I went to the creditory to check my account, stepping up into a private booth to access my funds. Maudoric had always deposited my pay from the keep, and I'd saved up a healthy amount. I withdrew some coins for food along the journey to Laras.

I paused when I spied the ten *vron* that had come in just a couple days ago. My first payment from Kaldur. I debated only for a brief moment…but I knew if I accepted it, it would always be a lingering regret.

I rejected the amount. It would return to House Kaalium's account, where it'd come from. And while I wondered about the logic of that decision when I was about to upend my life, I didn't linger on it. What was done was done. I didn't want anything of his. After everything that had happened, I wanted to be *clean*. To be free.

But the credits I'd earned as a keeper…those were mine alone. I'd earned every last one.

When I left the creditory, I felt lighter. A weight off my shoulders. He didn't own me anymore, and I owed him nothing. Our contract was void. He'd taken and I'd given. And I vowed that I'd never let another Kylorr feed off me again.

I stocked up with food for the journey at one of the only vendor stalls open, one meant to feed the builders and merchants this early.

My final stop was the transport station. A bleary-eyed small group had already formed, humans like me or hybrid Kylorr with no wings, and I got in line.

"Do you know when the next caravan to Laras is?" I asked the older female in front of me. She was a full-blooded Kylorr but likely too advanced in her years to make a long trip by flight, especially with luggage.

"Shouldn't be long now," she replied, eyeing my bag. "Visiting the capital, are we?"

"Moving there," I corrected with a small, polite smile I didn't feel. "And finding an old friend."

Over my shoulder, I looked over Vyaan. The only home I'd ever known.

A short while later, I heard the rumbling of wheels clattering down the stone road. The caravan. A covered vehicle, larger than I'd anticipated, came into view.

Move forward, I reminded myself, even though I was scared. *Start new.*

CHAPTER 25
—
KALDUR

I woke with the beast inside me rumbling.

Judging by the light seeping through the windows, I guessed it was midday. I'd stumbled into bed in the early hours of morning, shortly before dawn. I'd barely slept since my return from Salaire, consumed with my thoughts of Erina and ignoring an odd sensation of warning in my gut.

The moment I'd hit my bed, I'd been lost to the world. I felt refreshed, the sleep much needed, but my head felt heavy. I'd become so used to regular feedings from my *kyrana* that if I went without, I felt weakened and aching. It was part of the bond, I reasoned. It made one more dependent on their mate, a biological impulse to remain close.

I got dressed slowly, remembering Erina's confrontation last night in my study.

Tread carefully, a voice warned silently. *Or you'll lose her.*

Just as I was addicted to her. Just when I'd discovered that she loved another.

Another female hell-bent on using me for my family name. For my wealth. And it stung all the more because it was my *kyrana* this time.

Even still…I'd wanted to hurt her last night.

It should fill me with *relief* to know she had someone else. All I'd wanted, after all, was to keep her at a distance until I figured out how to navigate this unfortunate pairing. Until after the completion of the South Road, perhaps, and we had a war bond in place with the Kaazor to the north. At least then, my territory would be more secure, more capable of withstanding a new scandal.

But instead, knowing she loved another filled me with rage, with jealousy that seared itself into my very bones because I knew that she would never be mine alone.

And I wanted to hurt her because of it. I wanted her to feel what I felt.

That was why I'd done what I'd done, I reasoned. If she wanted to use me for my wealth, then I would use her for her blood. But I wanted her to know that I knew about Luc Denoren —her mate of choice. My pride demanded it.

I'd misjudged her, but perhaps her friend, Velle, had been right. Perhaps she wasn't as innocent and kindhearted as I'd thought. Perhaps she'd been calculating and plotting this since the very beginning.

I needed to wrap my head around that before I saw her again. I needed to compartmentalize *this* Erina with the one that I'd spent that night in the library with—the one whose joy of the landscape projections had been infectious, the one who'd been content to simply be with me in her hand-me-down nightdress, the one who I'd been able to drop my guard around. Or, as she called it, my mask.

I would need to mourn the loss of *that* female, the one who made me want to throw caution away and disregard whatever the nobles said about her.

Because, briefly, I'd thought I could be happy with *her*.

She'd been so different from any female I'd known. Tittering, practiced females, who'd learned from a young age to be clever.

Every interaction with them had felt like a game, and I'd always been on edge anticipating their next move. I could never relax because they'd always wanted something from me.

Erina had been simple. Comforting. Genuine.

And I'd been so wrong about her.

She'd been just like all the rest.

After I dressed, I went to my study, locking myself in for hours trying to distract myself. Maudoric came in once to deliver a tray of food I wasn't hungry for. She looked worried when she glanced over at me, her brows furrowed, her lips pressed together.

"What?" I asked, the word snapping from me.

She merely shook her head and then retreated from my harsh mood. I didn't see her again until night came.

When the knock came on my door and she stepped in, I looked up blearily. My eyes felt tight in their sockets, my wings cramped. I needed to stretch or perhaps take a long flight to get my blood pumping.

"What?" I asked, gentling my tone this time though I was still in a foul mood. If not fouler.

Maudoric stepped up to my desk. No food or deliveries in her hands, which was what she usually ventured up here for.

"There's talk in the kitchens," she informed me.

My jaw gritted. I didn't need to be bothered with idle gossip, but then I realized that Maudoric wouldn't come to me unless it was serious.

"About?" I prompted, my gaze flickering back to the export approvals.

"The keepers are saying that Erina left this morning."

I froze. Then frowned.

Swiftly, my gaze flicked to Maudoric. "What do you mean 'left'?"

"She had her traveling bag with her," Maudoric said quietly, staying completely still. She was the only one in the keep who knew for certain that Erina was my *kyrana*. I'd never been able to keep anything from Maudoric. She was the only one I trusted with the knowledge. "I checked her quarters, and most of her possessions are gone. I've been searching for her for the last couple hours. I had the gardens swept and the keep searched. She's not here."

I stood from my desk, tension beginning to strum through me, that familiar rumbling that I'd woken with returning in full force.

"Then check again," I ordered. "In the village. *Everywhere.* She's here. She has to be. She wouldn't leave. Especially since..."

I didn't want to voice it out loud.

Especially since she wants what I can give her.

"Kaldur," Maudoric said, "I don't think you're going to find her in the keep. I came to you now because I just got an alert that your payment to her was rejected. It processed back into your accounts. I asked the creditory, and they said it was patched through early this morning in the village."

I paced alongside my desk.

"No, that can't be right. Check again," I said. "She needs the money. She wouldn't have given it back. That was her whole reason for agreeing to our arrangement."

"I'm telling you, she rejected it," Maudoric pressed. The look in her eyes was one of sympathy. And *worry*, especially when I saw her picking at the skin around her claws, a nervous habit she tried to hide. "I think you need to send out scouts to look for her. She's not here. I wanted to be certain before..."

Was this why she'd worried earlier?

Fuck.

Fuck, fuck, fuck.

Panic began to rise, but I pushed it down.

"All right," I said, keeping my voice even. "Have the village searched. I want to speak with whoever saw her this morning."

"Velle," Maudoric supplied.

Of course.

"Where is she?" I asked, already on my way toward my study door. I was in denial. She couldn't be gone. She wouldn't leave. Surely.

You gave her no reason to stay, a voice whispered in my head.

Last night she'd overheard me with Lydrasa. And when she'd come to confront me about it in the dead of night, I'd denied nothing because I had wanted to hurt her.

Keep your credits. I don't want them, she'd told me. I'd brushed aside the words, thinking that she was being unnecessarily dramatic to get her way.

Now? I wasn't so sure. I went over every detail of what she'd said. I remembered everything *I'd* said—and a lot of it was ugly.

"Send out scouts now," I repeated to Maudoric. "I want her found. *Tonight.*"

But that sense of foreboding warning still lingered. It had never left me today.

Now I knew why.

<hr>

FOUR HOURS LATER, I WAS DRINKING AND SMOKING *LORE* BY THE fire, nursing a tumbler even though I wanted to chug down an entire bottle of Kyne liquor. Anything to dull the restless anger that made me feel like I was on the precipice of a berserker rage.

I'd never been so close before. That fear itself kept my rooted in place, when all I wanted to do was fly over every inch of Vyaan.

Maudoric herself had shoved a *lore* pipe into my hand to keep me calm, worried I'd wreck the entire keep. I'd nearly torn it apart looking for Erina. I'd had the grounds searched three times. Every nook and cranny of the village. Every tavern and inn that offered beds. I'd even had the *dyaans*, the blood-giver establish-ments, questioned. I'd gone myself to all the old Houses Erina had been a keeper at, asking the nobles if they'd seen or heard from her.

Syndras of House Terasyn, who she'd been closest to, was out of the territory, so I knew she wouldn't have gone there…but it hadn't stopped me from journeying to Syndras's daugther's home and asking regardless.

"I know where you are," I murmured, taking another drag on my *lore* pipe, holding my breath before slowly releasing it. I'd need to be smoking constantly, or else I would go into a rage.

Because I knew she'd gone to *him*. Luc Denoren. There had been multiple caravans throughout the day that had departed for Laras, though each one had different stops along the way and arrived into the capital on separate days. It didn't stop me from sending out scouts after each one of them, to try to track them down. Short of stopping *every* caravan they came across, however, I didn't think they would find her. Even still, I'd sent them on to Laras. They would intercept the traveling parties on the other side.

You can't keep her if she doesn't want to be kept, I thought, gritting my jaw. How the nobles would gossip and whisper about me if they found out I abducted a human female in broad daylight from Laras and had her chained to my bed in the keep.

That would *actually* give them something good to talk about for the coming months.

I drained the contents of my tumbler, refilling it back up from the crystal bottle on the small table beside me.

She was gone. She'd left of her own accord. I'd misjudged her own pride.

And strangely enough, despite everything I'd thought she wanted, despite everything I could offer her…I didn't think she wanted to be found.

In the quiet of my own quarters, half-drunk on Kyne liquor, my berserker beast calmed by *lore*, I could admit that that scared me most of all.

CHAPTER 26

ERINA

Much like at my old room in Vyaan keep, my room at the inn in Laras held a small window, one that overlooked a bustling street of the market.

Laras was just like in the stories. The imposing and bustling capital city of the nation, with Azur of House Kaalium at the helm. He'd married a human woman, I'd heard, from a noble family from the New Earth colonies. Gemma, I believed her name was. I'd heard their names mentioned in passing more times than I could count as I'd searched for Luc these last two weeks.

The address where I'd been posting letters to hadn't seen him in over two months. It had been a temporary home, nothing more than a room rental.

He hadn't been receiving any of my letters.

Worry had been my constant companion ever since I'd discovered his absence. I didn't know how else to find him. The keeper of the building, whose name was Ikrin, had grumbled that he didn't enquire about his renters' personal lives. Luc had paid for the room by the week, and then one week he'd stopped paying. His things were gone, and Ikrin hadn't seen him since.

That's how it is, Ikrin had said, shrugging, seeming annoyed he'd been wasting his time speaking with me. *These workers come and go. One letter did come for him a few days ago.*

It had been mine—posted from Vyaan.

Ikrin had told me little else. All of my questions about Luc's well-being or state of mind had been met with a raised brow and an expression of amusement. Then he'd shooed me away, firmly closing the door behind me.

For a few days, I'd lingered around the building, just in case Luc returned or passed by. Finally, annoyed by my continued presence, Ikrin had told me to go to the archives if I was looking for someone. They might have record of him there, he'd said.

But after two days spent in the archives, I'd realized that was a dead end as well. Residents weren't required to submit their information to the archives upon arrival, though they were meant to. Julin, the Bartutian archivist, had tried to help me as much as he could. But he'd said it was nearly impossible to keep accurate records of those living in Laras, since so many came and went.

That struck fear in me because what if something had happened to Luc? What if he was hurt? Or what if he wasn't even here? And if he'd left, why hadn't he written? Why hadn't he *told* me?

All I knew was that he ran a shop somewhere within Laras—and I was chastising myself for not asking for the address in my letters.

My only comfort was that Kaldur, of all people, had found him. He'd told me that there was a Luc Denoren living in Laras because he'd checked, hadn't he?

But I'm not a son of the Kaalium, I thought. I didn't have the resources—or the money—to find Luc on my own. Laras was huge, the villages sprawling out from the capital's center in all directions, like rippling waves from the sea. Not to mention the bustling city center itself, where a plethora of people lived in charming little buildings and the crowds grew so large in the afternoons that it could get difficult to wade through.

Two weeks I'd searched already. And I was beginning to lose hope. I couldn't afford to. Both figuratively *and* literally.

I'd checked my creditory account and taken out all the money that was left. My room at the cozy inn I'd found—small but clean—was nearly fifty credits a night. A hefty price, but I'd quickly discovered that *everything* was more expensive in Laras than in Vyaan.

I'd already spent over 1,000 credits—one *vron*—on food and lodgings during my time here. I had a little over three *vron* left. It would last me another two or three weeks if I was careful. Four weeks if I moved into the building that Luc had rented out, and maybe then, he might return.

And that was how I found myself packing up from my little room with the window view of Laras…and moving into an even smaller room with thin walls and a sagging mattress. The same room that Luc had stayed in, according to Ikrin on my return to him. He'd only been too happy to rent it out to me, since he'd had trouble filling it.

This room had a small window that overlooked what I thought might've been docks in the distance. From here, there was a tiny sliver of the Silver Sea visible. When the sun rose, it looked like a golden crescent.

I could have stayed at the other inn if I'd kept Kaldur's payment, I couldn't help but think.

No.

I'd done my best to not think about him, though he still slipped into my mind when my guard was down. I would remember a flash of his curling, beautiful smile, and my heart would ache so fiercely. Was it possible to both detest and miss someone at the same time?

What was done was done. I'd made my choice, and Kaldur had made his…to believe terrible things about me. But even if

Velle—and possibly Lydrasa—hadn't been in his ear, he still wouldn't have wanted me. Because I would always be a keeper in his eyes, one he mistrusted, one he would always believe was trying to *take* from him.

Move forward, I ordered myself, shaking him from my thoughts, ignoring the way my heart thudded, the way it pinched and compressed in my chest.

I don't need to ask Syndras anymore what heartbreak feels like, I thought morosely.

No one had ever warned me how much it *hurt*. Or how invasive the other person was in your thoughts even when all you wanted was to forget.

I needed to find work. If I had any intention of starting a life here, I needed a consistent income. There was no shortage of noble Houses within Laras. Surely, with my references, one of them would hire me.

But I knew that might be a reach. Keepers found their work through their connections, usually on the direct recommendation of someone else, someone they knew. That was how I'd gotten work at Kaldur's keep, after all—Syndras of House Terasyn had recommended me to Maudoric.

I knew no nobles in Laras. Only Luc, and I couldn't even find him.

I thought I might have better luck at one of the inns, so the next day, I targeted the ones around the busy marketplace. There was no shortage of people gathered there in the afternoons and evenings, and I hoped it would give me a better chance of spotting Luc as I searched for work.

Three inns later and I'd been sent out from nearly every one, even the one I'd stayed at.

The fourth, however, called Kyndri's Landing, took me. The owner, a Kylorr female named Kyndri had, by chance, just let go her former keeper for stealing from her patrons' rooms.

The inn itself was farther away than I would've wanted from

the main center square and even farther from my room at Irkin's. But Kyndri had seemed pleasant enough, if a little over-worked. I didn't mention I'd worked in Kaldur's keep, because I thought it might raise her suspicions, or she might think I was lying. But I gave her a list of references, which she only waved away.

"You worked in noble Houses? That's good enough for me. If you steal from the rooms, though, I'll make sure you never find work in Laras again. Yes?" Kyndri said, waiting for my reply. Perhaps an empty threat, meant to frighten me, but I couldn't know for certain. Maybe Laras was like Vyaan, after all—and everyone talked.

"I would never," I protested, thinking about the shard of the green vase I'd stolen from Kaldur's keep. That had been different, however.

"Good," she barked, inclining her head as she served a human male, who smiled at me a little too broadly, a foaming brew in a brown jug at the bar. "Pay is fifty credits for a full day. You can find the uniforms through the door there and any cleaning supplies you need. You can do a sweep of the rooms now. Everyone should be out until evening."

And that was how I found myself working at a sleepy little inn in Laras, for virtually half the pay I'd made at Kaldur's keep. But it would keep a roof over my head. For now.

I HUFFED OUT A BREATH, TRYING TO BREATHE THROUGH MY MOUTH as I scrubbed the floor of one of the guest rooms. I'd walked in to vomit on the floor, no doubt from the drunk guest who had staggered out mere moments before.

The cleaning supplies were making me nauseous—or perhaps it was the stench of bodily fluids mixed with brew. One thing was for certain…after a week of working at Kyndri's Landing, I would *never* drink brew again. I didn't think I'd be able to stomach it after all the things I'd cleaned up.

I sat up, wiping the clean part of my arm over my forehead. Closing my eyes, I tried to fight the nausea rising, but the entire room stunk. From cleaning solutions and soap and vomit and sweaty musk. I rose, going to the window to open it, this one overlooking the main street below since it was right over the entrance of the inn.

I breathed in the fresh air, letting the cool breeze drift over my cheeks. It was warmer here in Laras, situated along the Silver Sea coast. Vyaan must've been getting its first frost by now.

A sudden pang of longing went through me. I missed Vyaan. I missed my home, the only place I'd ever known. I missed my mornings in the village, sipping on spiced tea as I watched the square come alive. I missed my small room in the keep, the quiet of the morning, warm in my bed as I sketched. I missed those brief days I'd had in Kaldur's garden, a newly discovered heaven that had filled me with so much inspiration.

I missed *Kaldur*...and I hated it. But how did one go from thinking about someone every day for two years to trying to ignore they even existed? Especially with House Kaalium's influence all over Laras?

You remember how he offered to make you his mistress because he thought you would angle to be his wife for money and status. You remember that he called you young and naive, that he said he could never love you, I thought. *That's how you get over it.*

I let out a bubble of laughter that sounded pathetic to my own ears. I watched the people passing by below. Mostly they were working people in this district, who came to lunch from the nearby docks and the fields that lay to the north. Kylorr and human and Bartutian alike. Males and females. Young and old.

When I saw Luc, it was by pure chance.

I had happened to tilt my head to look down the road, and right at that moment, I saw him crossing over to the next street.

I gasped and nearly choked.

"Luc!" I bellowed from the window.

My voice echoed around the tall buildings, funneled down the road straight to him. I saw the hybrid Kylorr freeze in place, turn his head to figure out where his name had come from.

"Wait, Luc! Stay right there!"

People were looking at me from down below, but I paid them no mind. My heart was rushing, racing in my chest, and I felt excitement and hope and relief crash over me like a wave.

He's okay. He's safe. He's here, I thought. Over and over again.

I'd found him.

I rushed down the stairs, nearly tripping.

Kyndri's gaze jerked up from behind the bar, frowning. "What are you—"

"I'll be right back!" I rushed out, the words tumbling from me, and I flew through the entrance of the inn, taking a sharp right and sprinting down the road.

He was still there, still looking around. A frown on his features.

"Luc!" I called, grinning, happy tears making my vision blurry. "Luc, I'm here!"

His gaze finally connected with mine. For a moment, he blinked, confused. Then realization slotted into place.

"Erina?" he asked, his eyes widening. "Gods, how are—"

But I cut him off, nearly knocking him off his feet when I barreled into him.

His arms came around me as I clung to him. He smelled briny, like the sea, and he was leaner than I remembered. But his embrace was most welcome even though I hadn't hugged him since he'd left Vyaan. It had been almost ten years. Ten years since I'd seen him last.

I squeezed his clothes between my fists. "I've been looking for you. I feared...I thought..."

But I descended into sobs, and Luc only tried to calm me down.

"I'm sorry—I'm sorry," I whispered.

But I couldn't stop the tears. I was just so relieved. I didn't know how long we stood in the middle of the street, in broad daylight, as dozens and dozens of people milled around us, staring.

But I didn't care.

Luc was here.

Maybe my luck had finally turned.

CHAPTER 27
ERINA

"*I* can't believe you're really here," Luc said, over a swiftly emptying jug of brew.

I'd opted for a sweet juice, given my new aversion to brew. We were at Kyndri's Landing, at one of the back tables I'd wiped down just earlier that afternoon. It was slow and quiet after the initial afternoon rush, so Kyndri had allowed me some time off when I told her I'd seen an old friend. But once the workers started coming in, she needed the table back.

"It's been…six years? Seven?" Luc asked.

"Ten," I corrected with a soft smile, gazing at him. "Almost ten."

Something flashed over his face. I was trying to match up the pieces of the Luc I'd known with the older male in front of me now.

Truthfully, I was failing. There were pieces of Luc I recognized, like the way his eyes crinkled up when he smiled. Or the way he said certain words, like how he elongated the *a* sound in Vyaan.

But much of him had changed. His gray skin looked stretched tight over him, new scars having appeared along his arms and one long one that ran beneath his tunic around his neck. His eyes were still a lovely blue, but he couldn't quite meet mine for very long. His hands were no longer smooth. They were calloused and rough, the back of his knuckles scarred.

I took his hand in mine, squeezing. "It's been a long time," I said, uncertainly. "But we found each other."

"You look the same, Erina," Luc told me. He drained the contents of his jug, raising his hand to catch Kyndri's attention for another round. He'd had two already, and when Kyndri brought the third, Luc swallowed a good mouthful before saying, "You haven't changed at all."

"You've changed," I said, smiling when I looked up from the foamy brew. "Did you get my letters? I went to the building you stayed at. I talked to Ikrin. I'm staying there now too. He said he hadn't seen you in months."

"Ah," Luc said, scratching the back of his neck. Something else that hadn't changed. He'd always done that when he was nervous. Was I making him nervous? That had never happened before. "That place was always a dump. I was glad to be rid of it."

"But you never got my letters?" I prompted.

"No," he replied. "Ikrin doesn't hold anything for past residents. I'd meant to write once I got settled again—I really did. I just…I didn't realize how long it'd been."

"It's okay," I said softly, squeezing his hand. He pulled it back, using it to take another draw on his drink.

But I was hurt he hadn't thought to tell me where to reach him. It would've saved me a lot of worry since I'd arrived in Laras. I'd thought the worst. It had kept me up at night sometimes.

"I just didn't know how to find you."

"When did you come?" he asked.

"A few weeks ago," I replied, the stench of the brew a little too overpowering. I breathed through my mouth. "I've been searching for you everywhere. It was lucky I happened to spot you today."

"And how long are you planning to stay?" came his next question.

The question caught me off guard. He'd spoken it casually, as if I was just visiting him as I passed through.

"Well, I—I left Vyaan," I stammered, cocking my head to peer at him. "I left to come find you. Just like…just like what we always talked about."

Luc looked at me. He sighed. "Erina…"

He shook his head, and I felt my stomach drop.

"All our plans," I said, my heart suddenly speeding. "Of living in Laras. You running your merchant shop and me writing our stories to get distributed one day."

"Erina—"

"No, they…they were good dreams, Luc. They were *our* dreams. What we always talked about. What we promised each other. When we were children and in our letters. We were—"

"We were *children*, Erina," Luc said quickly, a thread of irritation lacing into his tone. "Children just trying to get by, to pass another year, so that we would be one year closer to starting a life."

"You…" I trailed off, biting my lip. "You said in your letters that you were running the shop. That you had trade deals in place with merchants. You said you would send for me. Even recently, this last year, you promised…"

Luc drained his jug for a third time. I looked at him. Really looked at him. His clothes fit him well but were threadbare in some places. Salt clung to the material in the creases, but whether it was from sweat or the sea, I couldn't be certain.

"There is no shop," I said quietly. "Was there ever?"

And why had he *lied* to me?

Luc ran his hands through his hair. His eyes were more glassy than they'd been when we'd first sat down. His elbows were planted on the table as he scrubbed a hand over his face. Salt flecks dusted the table.

"Briefly," Luc said, lowering his hands. "There had been a shop."

"When?"

He laughed, but it sounded bitter. "About two years in when I first came here."

Eight years ago? I felt like my lungs were being squeezed by a vise.

"You...you always said the shop was going so well. That credits were pouring in. That's why you didn't want money I sent. I don't understand."

Luc, for his part, looked embarrassed. "I didn't want you to keep sending money, Erina. It was yours. I didn't want you to know...to see what a failure I'd become."

My brows drew together and my throat tightened. "But I would never think that of you! How can you say that?"

"Because we had all these plans!" he burst out, frustrated. "But they weren't plans, Erina. They were dreams. Dreams so unattainable for people like us. You want to know what happened to the shop?"

I nodded, frowning.

"The noble House next door didn't like that I was drawing in commoners to the area. He paid off my merchant partner, who stopped selling me goods. No one would trade with me anymore. The price for the shop went up, which was conveniently owned by one of the noble's friends, and I had no money coming in. I had to close it within a few months. All my money, everything I'd saved since we were children..." he breathed. "*Gone.* All because of one wealthy noble who'd decided my fate for me. I'd never even had a chance. To *prove* myself."

"Surely that's against Laras law," I argued. "They can't do that."

"There was no proof," Luc said. "It's my own fault. I shouldn't have opened a shop in that district, but I'd wanted…I'd wanted to be better. I'd been impatient to be better."

The confession dropped from him, and it twisted my soul.

"I'd wanted to be like *them*. To pretend that I was someone different. Laras had been a fresh start. That's what it was meant to be—a new life. One I carved out for myself. And a wealthy noble showed me how futile it was to pretend that I was anything but a poor, stupid orphan from Vyaan."

"Don't say that," I told him.

This was so unlike the Luc I'd known, the boy who'd been so full of determination and drive. Who had set his mind on one goal: succeeding in Laras. He'd seen it as his ultimate test, perhaps to prove what he was telling me right now. That he was *more* than how he'd grown up.

"You can be both," I told him. "One doesn't determine the other."

"It does here," he said, that same bitter smile crossing his lips, one I'd never seen before. "I learned that years ago."

"What…where are you working now?"

"The docks," he finally admitted.

"Fishing?" I asked.

He shook his head. "Sorting exports and imports."

I looked down at the salt flakes on the table. When he saw me looking, he wiped them away with his calloused palm. They scattered to the ground, and I'd need to sweep them up later.

"I can help you rebuild the shop," I told him, unable to stand the defeat in his voice, when I reached out to steal his hand again. "We can do it together! I'll help you this time."

"No," Luc said, pressing his lips together as he waved down Kyndri for a fourth jug. "Just leave it, Erina."

"We can do it!" I insisted. "I have some money saved up. Not a lot, but it can—"

"I said no," Luc barked, raising his voice. I reared back. He'd never yelled at me before, not once. He glared at me now. *"Leave it."*

Kyndri came by—sans the jug of brew. "Is there an issue here, Erina?"

"No," I said, looking up at the Kylorr female, who'd been kind to me. "No, everything's fine."

She gave Luc a warning raise of her brow and then went back to the bar. It was quiet at Kyndri's Landing with only a few patron tables filled, most of whom were looking over at us without trying to hide it.

"I'm sorry," Luc said, frustration still evident, "but no. I have stable work now. I'm not giving that up for anything. You don't know what it's like, Erina…to have nothing. To be hungry. To sleep wherever you can. The things you think you're not capable of until you're backed into a corner with nowhere else to go."

My brow furrowed. I couldn't stomach this—the defeat and hopelessness I saw in Luc now. It was a tragic, terrible thing.

"The universe isn't fair," Luc said, staring down at the wood grain of the table, tracing the patterns with his eyes. "I guess I just expected that *maybe* it would have pity on me after all these years. But I learned my lesson a long time ago."

I thought about what he'd said for a long time, my gut churning. Finally, I asked, "Then why did you lie to me?"

Luc sighed. "I don't know."

"Yes, you do," I insisted. "So tell me."

His shoulders sagged. He picked at a loose thread on his cuff. "Because I couldn't stand to admit to you that I'd failed."

Tears sprung into my ears, at the sorrow and mortification I heard in my dear friend's voice.

"All those years of talking, of planning…and I'd failed within mere months. I felt pathetic. You were my one string tying me back to who I used to be. And sometimes I miss him. He's not me anymore, but I like to remember him."

The way he said the words made a pang of hurt reverberate through me.

"And is that all I am?" I couldn't help but ask. "A memory to you? Someone you can write to when you want to feel better but forget about the rest of the time? Forget the promises we made?"

Luc blew out a breath. "Like I said, we were kids, Erina. It was a long time ago. Nearly a decade. I'm not that person. And if you are…you need to move on. You need to grow up and face reality."

"I love you and I always will," I argued. "You were and have always been a brother to me. Years apart don't change that. You can sit here and try to convince me otherwise. But I know you, Luc Denoren. I always have. And this isn't you."

"I can't give you what you want," Luc told me, his eyes shining. "I don't think I ever could."

"All I want is for you to be my friend," I said. "I don't care about anything else. That's all I've ever wanted. And if we have to live here in Laras and work at the docks or at inns, then all right. But at least we'll be together again. We can be in each other's lives, to some capacity. Wouldn't that make this life even a little better? To have a friend you can trust and rely on?"

"You're living in the past," Luc finally told me. "You should go back to Vyaan. Go work at a noble House. You'll be more comfortable there. Laras isn't for you. I barely think it's for me."

Luc stood.

"Wait," I said. "At least tell me how to find you."

"Don't," Luc said, his teeth gritting. He didn't meet my eyes. "Please, Erina. Looking at you…it just makes me remember Vyaan. It *hurts* to remember. I don't want to see you, all right? Just leave me be and go home. I'm begging you."

My chest squeezed tight, shock spearing through me.

Luc put down a handful of small coins on the table. "Good-bye," he said, gruffly.

"One day," I said quietly, holding his eyes as I stood from the chair, "one day when you're walking down the streets of Laras, you'll look into one of the shop windows and see Kavelyn's adventures staring back at you. *Our* Kavelyn Denoren, who we poured all our dreams and hopes and fears and triumphs into. Whose name we took for our own, so we would always be tied together. And when you do see our work, I hope you remember."

Luc closed his eyes when they watered.

"I hope you remember the boy—no, the beautiful soul I knew. Because *that* Luc Denoren saved me in so many ways, and I will always love him for it, no matter what. He protected me. He made me believe in myself. He encouraged me to always keep dreaming and, more importantly, to always keep *trying*. I hope you remember him one day too. I will never forget him."

He leveled me a quiet stare, looking struck by the words and unmoving.

I went to embrace him, breathing in the brininess and his warmth. I felt relief when his arms came around me tight.

"You know where to find me if you ever need me," I whispered into him. "You'll always be my brother, Luc. And I'll *always* be here for you. But please…don't give up."

If he did, it would break the last of my already broken heart.

Then I let him go. We stared at one another until finally, Luc inclined his head. He turned, and I tried to hold my tears back.

When he left Kyndri's Landing, I couldn't help but fear that it might be the last time I ever saw him.

The nausea churned in my gut again at the mere thought. Thankfully, this time, I made it to the washroom.

CHAPTER 28

KALDUR

"*Raazos's blood.*"

I heard the hushed curse behind me.

"What are you doing here?" I grumbled.

"I can barely see you through all the smoke," came Thaine's voice. "Don't invite a human in here. You might not escape their clutches."

He'd meant it as a jest, but when I didn't respond, only sucked down another deep lungful of *lore* smoke, he shut the door to my private quarters. Behind me, I heard him cross to the closed balcony doors. The metal shifted when he opened them, and a funnel of icy wind swept through my room, like a keeper intent on clearing away all traces of the smoke.

"Close it," I growled, feeling the icy chill on the back of my neck. I couldn't stand it. Every sensation against my skin was too much. I was overstimulated, at all times of the day. Even clothing scratched at me uncomfortably, which was why I was naked, sprawled out in the chair.

My brother came to stand in front of me, temporarily blocking out the fire flickering in the hearth behind him.

I scoffed. "Maudoric must be really worried if she sent for you."

Thaine assessed my sorry state, his brows furrowing. "What's happened, Kaldur?"

"Nothing. And I don't want to hear whatever you're going to say," I snapped.

"Yet you obviously need to," came my brother's response. His tone was careful, but even I could hear the concern lacing through the words. Thaine wasn't one to show his emotions readily. He was like Kythel in that way, whereas a lot of me ran hot like our eldest brother, Azur.

"Tell me," Thaine insisted. He dropped down onto the rug in front of me so that we were eye level.

"Don't. Get up, will you?"

"At least put some damn clothes on," Thaine grumbled. "You think I want to get an eyeful of your cock *ever*? On Raazos, what's wrong with you?"

That brought out a resigned laugh from me, one which felt foreign. I hadn't laughed in weeks.

"What, no clever retort?" Thaine questioned, his eyes flickering back and forth between mine. "Now I'm really worried."

I rose from the chair and went to my dresser. My limbs felt heavy and uncoordinated, but I managed to pull on some pants and a tunic, all while keeping the slim *lore* pipe firmly pressed between my lips.

"You shouldn't be here," I told him. "Go back to Salaire."

"Maudoric *is* worried about you," Thaine told me. "She has reason to be. I'm worried about you too, now that I see you. I've been wondering why you've been avoiding my Com calls."

When I turned back to him, even his keen observation set me on edge. I felt like I was a moment away from a berserker rage. Day or night, it didn't matter. It was hellish. I couldn't sleep, couldn't eat. Preserved blood made me want to gag now that I knew the taste of my *kyrana*'s blood.

No, don't let your thoughts wander to her, I commanded silently. *Not when Thaine is here.*

"Let's go outside to the balcony," he suggested, rising and leading me, like I was child, to the open paneled door. "You need some fresh air." A pause came. "And a fucking bath."

"You going to watch me take one of those too?" I grumbled.

"If I have to," he replied simply. "And I've already seen more of you than I care to in my lifetime."

Out on the balcony, the biting rush of the wind made me clench my teeth. Too much sensation. I almost turned to retreat, but Thaine plucked my *lore* pipe from my fingertips and leaned his forearms against the balcony banister, taking a drag. I needed that back before I could leave.

"You came here in this wind?" I asked when the silence stretched.

"Yeah, so let me smoke a little," came his reply. "It wasn't easy trying to reach you."

The longer I stayed out on the balcony, the more bearable the wind became. Soon I was even able to relax, though my head was cleared of the thick, comforting smoke inside the room. I'd been convinced that the *lore* was the only thing preventing me from a rage.

"Tell me what's going on," Thaine ordered.

Had I really thought I could hide it from my family for very long? From Thaine?

I looked out over Vyaan, at the warm yellow glow from the Halo orbs being installed along the South Road and the quiet landscape surrounding it all. The forests and mountains and fields.

Quietly, I confessed, "I found my *kyrana*."

Thaine sucked in a sharp, startled breath, and I felt him turn toward me, those brilliant green eyes hardening.

"And then I drove her away."

"*Vaan,*" Thaine whispered. "How long?"

"She left three weeks ago."

"Where is she?"

"In Laras," I replied, "to go be with the male she actually loves."

It took everything in me *not* to fly to Laras this very moment. To track her down. To chain her to my side.

"And you're just going to let that stand?" Thaine asked, after he absorbed the words. If I thought I'd get sympathy from him, I'd been sorely mistaken. "Your *kyrana*? Your one fated mate? My true brother would never have let her go. I don't know who's standing in front of me now, but it's not him."

"You don't understand," I told him, irritation making me bristle. "It was my fault."

"Then help me understand," Thaine said, handing me back the *lore*. "Help me understand so we can put this right."

We.

"There's nothing to put right," I told him, my shoulders sagging.

But in the end, I told him everything. Every ugly detail. How I'd kept Erina at arm's length, not wanting others to know she'd been my keeper. Her perfume, Luc Denoren. How I'd discovered that she'd intended to use me for my money, for my title, to better the life of her lover. How I'd thought she was different. How she'd overheard Lydrasa and me in my study. Everything she'd accused me of that I'd confirmed…how she believed I thought the worst in her. Even how I'd become aware she was my *kyrana* the day she'd walked in on me and Lydrasa.

I confessed how hellish it had been. About the day I'd found out she'd left and the scrambled, chaotic aftermath searching for her. Then the resignation had come…the anger, the fury, the longing.

It all came pouring out of me like opening a festering, pus-filled wound.

In the end, I didn't feel *clean*, but I was relieved that Thaine finally knew.

My brother had his elbows planted on the banister, and he was massaging the bones of his brows by the time I was done, his eyes closed.

"You're a fool," he finally decided. "I expected this of Kythel, trying to be all noble by sacrificing his own happiness for the betterment of our family's line. But not of you."

"Thank you very much for that insult," I snapped. "I thought you would understand it. She's a keeper, one who's made it clear she wants a higher position."

"Yeah, she's a keeper. Not a Thryki spy. Who cares? And you believe she was using you? Why? Because of the word of her supposed friend?" Thaine asked me, finally lifting his gaze. He wasn't quite glaring at me, but there was disappointment in his eyes. "Because you heard it from someone else and believed them over the sacred bond of a blood mate?"

Nothing I hadn't already agonized over in the last few weeks, but his tone made me bristle.

"She told me she loved him!" I growled, my voice echoing over the quietness of the courtyard below, which led to the garden pathway. "That night in my study. She told me she loved him."

"Who the *fuck* cares?" Thaine asked, glaring at me now. "She's your *kyrana*, Kaldur. Not some socialite you picked up at a noble's dinner. Steal her away from him like your life depends on it…oh, because it does!"

I'd never heard Thaine so willfully sarcastic. Or this fervent.

"No, this is about you," he decided, rolling his shoulders. "Did she ever admit to wanting to ascend her position within the keep?"

I gritted my jaw. "No."

She'd actually wanted to keep the blood-giver contract secret, so others wouldn't find out. So she wouldn't be the subject of idle gossip in the kitchens, of people she'd once considered friends.

And one of those same friends had sold her out.

"They share a family name," I said. "They took it together. Denoren. They grew up together at an orphanage here. Something about the way she talked about it…it just felt so permanent. How can I compete with a bond like that? Some bonds go beyond fate."

"You never even tried," Thaine accused, softening his tone. "You cared more about what the nobles would think. You're embarrassed by what our uncle did here. You're trying to save yourself the humiliation of the same thing, but you pushed away your *kyrana* to do it. You gave up. And now you look as defeated as you must feel."

I rasped, "Your comfort is really making me feel better."

"I'm not here to comfort you," he snapped. "I'm here to pull your head out of your ass and make you see *reason*—something, up until recently, I thought you understood."

I blew out a harsh breath. "I suppose I'm not as intelligent as I think I am. When I came here, Vyaan expected me to be a womanizing freeloader, benefitting off my family name. Might as well prove them right after all these years."

"You don't believe that," Thaine said, dismissing the words readily. "Stop feeling sorry for yourself, so you can help yourself. So *I* can help you."

I took another drag on the *lore*, the tip lighting up a bright blue, making the night sky appear luminous.

"What do you want?" Thaine growled.

"I want her back," came the easy words. The simple truth came tumbling out from me. Shockingly effortless.

Thaine's shoulders released their tension. He seemed pleased with the answer. Relieved.

"But she doesn't want to see me. The things I said to her…"

"She won't see you if she believes you think this of her," he finished for me. "So tell me now, right here…do you *really* believe she's just using you? Do you really believe what her friend said about her?"

"No," I said gruffly. Another simple and sudden confession, pulled from me like a prayer. "My instinct tells me otherwise."

All of my interactions with her told me the truth of what I believed—I just hadn't listened. I'd been so hell-bent on believing the worst of her, believing that she would be the end of me, that I'd trusted those I shouldn't have.

I'd met my fair share of social climbers in my lifetime. Not once had Erina ever sparked my suspicions…until that night with Velle and Lydrasa.

I thought about her simple pleasure of getting lost in the gardens all day, her notebook spread open, a pencil tucked behind her ear. She was passionate about her stories and drawings, so lit up with delight when she talked about them.

She wore hand-me-downs. She didn't seem to care overly about her appearance to others, which was so unlike all the females I'd ever known. Maudoric had only ever said good things about her, unlike some of the other keepers in my employ.

Not only that but she'd returned the credits I'd given her. If she'd been in it for the money, she never would've done that. It didn't make sense.

She was kind. She was forgiving, even when I'd been cold. She'd soothed a frayed, restless ferocity in me, made me feel like I was finally at peace in those rare moments where I'd let myself sink into her.

The only truth had been about Luc, hadn't it? She did love him. These last few weeks, I'd started to consider she might be better off with him. I'd only given her pain.

"I wanted to believe the worst about her. I'm the one who

drove her away. I did this," I confessed to Thaine quietly. "And she hates me now."

I remembered that night in the study. It seemed like a lifetime ago. I remembered her hurt, which at the time I'd thought she'd been faking.

I'd said all kinds of things about her, to her. Accused her of things I now didn't believe to be true—that she was greedy and ambitious.

You're not anything like I'd hoped you'd be, she'd told me that night with sad, defeated eyes.

Her only crime had been loving someone else, and I'd vilified her for it. Because I'd been jealous. Because it hadn't been *me.*

But if everything she'd said was the truth that night…did that mean she'd been a virgin when we'd had sex?

It didn't make any sense.

Yet I closed my eyes, knowing I'd left swiftly in the aftermath of that night. I hadn't been gentle, I'd been taking out my frustration on her, using my body like a weapon. And then I'd avoided her for days…only for her to then hear my words to Lydrasa, telling her that the sex had been merely "fine." She'd heard Lydrasa's delighted laugh over that detail.

"I think I really fucked this, Thaine," I said quietly, my gut roiling. "I really fucked this up. From the very beginning."

"Then fix it," my brother said simply.

"If only it was that easy," I said. "There's too much to make amends for, especially when she loves someone else."

"Did you ever ask her about him? About her relationship with him?" he asked.

Discomfort wiggled in my chest. "No," I admitted.

"Then you know nothing at all. Get your head on straight," Thaine told me. "Because if you go after her, you need to decide what she will be to you. Just your mistress? Or everything?"

The blood bond had made a complete fool out of me. It had brought me to my lowest point, made me realize how very mortal I was. The gods had shown me their true power. I'd spat in their face in rejecting the gift of a blood mate. Now they were punishing me for it.

And worse yet, Erina had been hurt in the process. I'd been cruel and callous to her. She hadn't deserved that.

"I'm done fighting this," I said.

"Did you try to find her?" Thaine asked.

"I sent scouts to Laras," I said. "No luck."

"And this Luc Denoren?"

I shook my head. "He changes employment so often, I haven't been able to track him down. Especially if he's not recorded in the archives. I've checked three of his last jobs and rooms where he'd been staying. He's not at any of them."

Thaine blew out a breath. "Have you told Azur? He won't stop until he tracks them down in Laras. You know that."

"No," I clipped out. "Leave him out of this. He has enough to do. This is my mess, my mistake. I'll fix it."

"He made plenty mistakes himself with Gemma," Thaine reminded me. "He would understand."

I shook my head. "I only want you to know right now. And only because you barged in here uninvited."

"Good thing I did," he replied. "Whatever you need, I'll do it."

"I know," I said. "But go back home. I don't need you here."

"I beg to differ," Thaine said. He sighed, stretching out his wings. "I'll stay in Vyaan for a few days. It'll make Maudoric feel better."

I huffed out a sharp breath. "It would."

"What's your plan when you finally find her?" Thaine asked after a long moment of silence lapsed between us.

I suddenly felt incredible tired, the last few weeks having caught up with me.

"Not be a conceited and self-serving elitist fool?"

"I'm serious," he drawled.

"So am I."

Tilting my head back to look at moon, I saw it was almost full. No wonder the winds were picking up. I'd let the world skip by since Erina had left. Since even before then. I hadn't been right since I'd discovered her, right underneath my nose.

All the time I'd wasted…

"I'll do what I should've done from the moment I knew she was my *kyrana*," I told Thaine seriously. "I'll give her every reason to stay."

Determination began to burn in me. An ember that was being stoked, carefully and purposefully.

"I need to go find her myself," I said quietly.

"Wait until after the moon winds," he advised. "They're strong. Use the time to get your head on right and clean yourself up. Your keep is in disarray, and Maudoric is trying her best to hold it together."

Logical as always.

"But after the moon winds," Thaine said, his eyes glowing green in the moonlight, "go bring your *kyrana* back home."

CHAPTER 29

—

ERINA

When three days of nausea had passed and I still wasn't improving, I knew something was wrong.

At first I thought that maybe I'd picked up a strange sickness or eaten something that didn't agree with me. But then…I wasn't so certain.

I'd lived in House Terasyn when Syndras's daughter, Willan, had been newly pregnant. I'd served her tea every morning when she hadn't been able to keep anything else down.

I'd never had to worry about it before because…well, Kaldur had been my first, whether he believed me or not.

I had to at least consider the possibility now, which was why I'd asked Kyndri for the morning off, so I could get a blood analysis done at the healer's establishment down the road.

As I waited for the healer, sitting in a small, dark room that had blue wax candles lit, the smell of which made my nose twitch, I was in denial. This was just one thing I needed to discount, one thing that would soothe my worries.

Because if I *was* pregnant…

No, I thought firmly, pushing that notion from my mind, even when I felt the familiar flooding saliva fill my mouth, felt the nausea begin to churn in my gut.

When the healer came in, a Kylorr male with wings so large they nearly didn't fit in the cramped room, he looked at his Halo tablet, glowing blue in the dark room.

"Positive result for implantation," he announced. I didn't even know his name. He hadn't introduced himself to me. He'd been no-nonsense, taking my blood with a small prick of my finger before disappearing for mere moments.

"Implantation?" I breathed, my gut churning.

"You're pregnant," he said slowly, peering up at me over the rim of the tablet. His eyes were yellow. "I'd estimate a little over a month."

The world tilted sideways, my vision going dark.

When I came to, the healer had his arms around me to hold me steady and had a cold drink pressed to my lips.

"What do you mean I'm pregnant?" I asked, my voice sounding far away.

"Just as I said. Drink," he ordered me. "It'll help."

It tasted foul, but I chugged it down because I didn't know what else to do. When the contents were drained, he said, "I'll give you some to take with you. It'll help with the nausea and fatigue. Is the father a human? Or Kylorr?" When I didn't answer, he blinked, raising a brow when he asked, "Bartutian?"

"Kylorr," I finally said, the word falling from my lips like stones as I stared, unseeing, around the room. I cleared my throat, blinking to clear my blurry vision. I realized I was crying. "The father is a Kylorr."

A son of the Kaalium.

"Hybrid pregnancies are always more difficult," the healer informed me. "It's hard to pinpoint the gestation time since it's different for everyone."

"On—on average though?" I asked.

"Four months, give or take a few weeks on either side," he told me. "So you're about a quarter through already. But I must warn you, a hybrid pregnancy is rapid. It can be dangerous. You'll need to be monitored closely and—"

I stood. The room suddenly felt too small, and I struggled to get breath.

"I have to get back to work," I told him. "Thank you."

"But I—"

I left the room, my knees wobbling. I scrambled to get outside the establishment, weaving down one long hallway until I found the entrance. When I burst through, I sucked in deep lungfuls of the morning air. I stumbled until my back was to the building, letting it support me, but then I slid down, sitting on the street as people passed by, peering at me with curious, raised brows.

I pressed my palms to my eyes when they stung.

I was pregnant with Kaldur's child.

What am I going to do? I wondered.

At the end of the long day, my feet were aching, I smelled like cleaning supplies and spilled brew, and all I wanted was to bathe in the common washroom at Ikrin's and forget this day had ever happened.

But I didn't have the luxury of doing that. Especially when I turned the corner of the alley and spotted a group gathered outside of the older building, the large, burly keeper speaking with what looked like soldiers.

"What's happened?" I asked, rushing up to the group. There was an older male who I thought lived on the floor above me, but I'd only seen him in passing. He'd only grumbled at me when I'd smiled once.

"A disgruntled renter," he said, scowling with his arms crossed. "Broke into most of the rooms. Stole."

My heart froze in my chest. My first thought was my notebooks.

I flew past and darted up the stairs of the brightly lit building. My floor was off the second-stair landing, and by the time I reached it, I was huffing from the exertion, my long day, and fear.

My room door was ajar.

"No," I breathed. I rushed inside and saw that my ordinarily neat room had been tossed. My blankets and mattress were strewn and off the frame of the bed. My traveling bag had been opened, the broken handle lying on the floor next to it, having finally given out. The contents of the bag were spilled. Mostly old notebooks, which, thankfully, hadn't been stolen.

Relief went through me when I got to my knees and rummaged through what was left. Luckily all of them were accounted for, but some pages were torn, as the thief been less than gentle.

My heart thudded when I came across an old sketch of Kaldur. One of the pages that had been ripped. It went straight down his face, hanging in two parts.

They'd been looking for—

I froze.

I pushed to my feet and raced to the little dresser in the room. The bottom drawer was loose. I'd wrapped the money in an old scarf.

The scarf was there, but as I dove my hands into the material, what I'd already feared became a reality.

The money was gone. All of my savings.

I cursed myself for taking it out of the creditory. *So stupid, so stupid,* I thought, over and over again. But it had been the account I'd used at Kaldur's keep. I feared it might be shut down when he discovered me gone, as retaliation for breaking the contract.

I sat on the floor, in my trashed room, my heart finally beginning to slow as I faced the reality of my situation.

My only saving grace was that I'd just paid Ikrin for a full week yesterday. And I had the pay from Kyndri's for today, but the wages would barely keep me here. It wouldn't cover food or expenses.

Especailly with a *baby* on the way.

"Oh gods," I whispered, tears beginning to build up in my eyes.

"You too?" came a voice at the door. The old man, huffing out breath on his way back up to his room. He was peering into my room, shaking his head.

"Have they caught them?" I asked hopefully, through watery eyes.

"Doubt it," the man said. "This happens more than you think. Word of advice? Don't keep anything you care about here. But you'll learn that if you stay long enough."

Then he hobbled up the stairs, and I stared at the open doorway in disbelief.

I didn't know how long I sat there, contemplating what to do. But I knew I only had one choice, a choice I'd already been pondering all day once the knowledge that I was pregnant began to sink in.

Kaldur deserved to know, but it would gut me to ask him for help. I didn't want to prove to him what he already believed about me...but I knew that this situation was outside of my control.

I would write the letter tonight, but I would sleep on it. If I still thought it was the right decision, I would post it in the morning. An express service wouldn't cost much more, but I did have to be careful with my credits.

Pulling myself up from the floor, I grabbed one of my notebooks, flipping to a fresh page. Luckily my pencils were still here, though they'd been scattered across the floor. I hovered the tip over the paper for what felt like ages, my gut churning.

This needs to be done, I thought silently.

My pencil touched the paper.

To Kaldur of House Kaalium, Kyzaire of Vyaan, I began.

CHAPTER 30

ERINA

Three days after I'd posted the letter to the keep, addressing it for Maudoric's attention, since I knew everything passed through her first, there was a reply.

I found it wedged beneath my door when I trudged in after another long day at Kyndri's. I'd asked to work longer hours so that I could make seventy credits instead of the usual fifty. But I only got a handful of hours of sleep because of it. Even Kyndri had started to looked concerned, and I feared that she'd decide to cut the hours back, if only for my own health.

But I needed to make another week's rent at Ikrin's. I had to pay him in two days, and it would wipe out nearly everything.

It will buy me another week while I wait for Kaldur's reply, I thought.

That had been the only thing pushing me forward.

But that evening, my heart lurched when I saw the letter and the wax seal on the backside, the familiar seal of House Kaalium, and my hands shook as I gently tore it open.

I began to read.

To Erina Denoren,

247

I cannot verify the truth of your claim, especially given your relationship with Luc Denoren. Therefore, I am of the firm belief that what you claim is false and this is another attempt on your part to obtain more credits from me.

In your creditory account, you will find the ten vron that was owed to you. No less and no more. This is the last that I will ever give you. Any other letters or attempts at communication will be ignored.

It was signed by Kaldur, written in a sure, firm, tidy script.

For a moment, I thought maybe it was a cruel joke. But the signature was familiar, from what I remembered of it on the blood-giver contract, that night in the starwood blooms when he'd fed from me for the first time.

I sat on my bed, staring down at the letter in my hands. The parchment was thick, expensive. When I saw a tear drop land on it, blurring his signature, that was when I got angry.

He wasn't anything like how I'd thought he'd be. I'd known that when I'd left Vyaan, but this letter demonstrated a new cruelty that I hadn't thought him capable of.

And I knew what it was. It was a payoff. It was a rejection. It was him washing his hands of a potential *child* that he'd sired. Maybe there were others. Maybe he did this all the time.

And it made zero sense to me, how Kaldur could be this person. Then again, perhaps I was a terrible judge of character. Perhaps I hadn't known him at all.

Perhaps what Kaldur *and* Luc had said was true. That I needed to grow up. That I was naive and foolish.

Maybe this was how I would learn. Not to trust people I thought I could.

Despair swirled in my chest. I didn't *want* that. I didn't want to become that kind of person.

But it was clear to me that I would find no help or responsibility in Kaldur. He'd sent money to pay me off, and even now, I felt like it was poisoned. I would loathe ever touching it in that cursed account…but I also knew I needed it.

Laras chewed me up and spat me out, I thought.

And I missed home, missed the familiarity of Vyaan, streets that I knew like my own handwriting. Even though being there would always remind me of Kaldur in a way.

I sat on my bed, reread the letter perhaps hundreds of times as I weighed my options.

The first of which was that I could continue scraping by in Laras. I could work myself hard at Kyndri's Landing, try to save up enough money for when the child eventually came. But in only a couple weeks, I would show more. Just this morning I'd finally noticed my belly beginning to round. *The rapid speed of a hybrid pregnancy,* I remembered the healer telling me. *Dangerous,* he'd also said.

What if something went wrong?

The second option was to return to Vyaan. Syndras would help me. Even though she could no longer afford to keep me in her employ, she was still a noble with connections to great Houses. Finding a more comfortable job, with better pay than what I would find here, would give me a better chance to get my feet firmly planted where I could actually save money for the baby.

This time I wouldn't reject Kaldur's money, but I refused to touch it unless something went wrong in the pregnancy. It would be my safety net, just in case.

"Not a lot of options," I whispered.

And Luc…

I was still grieving our conversation, still reeling. Everything I'd thought, all the hopes and dreams I had pinned on Laras were gone. Luc was gone, or at least the Luc I'd known. That hurt like a death, nearly as much as Kaldur's rejection.

Once, Luc's blue eyes had sparked with fire and determination. I had listened to him for hours talking about the grand life he would make for himself here. And he'd almost done it too. That was perhaps the most heartbreaking thing.

But I didn't know the Luc I'd met. That familiar and inspiring spark of fire had been extinguished from his eyes.

And he doesn't want me around either, I thought. He'd made that abundantly clear, even though I'd meant what I'd said.

I wouldn't give up on Luc. I would always be there if he needed me. But right now…he didn't want my help. Not that I could even help myself right now.

I need to get back on my feet, I realized. I needed to be smart about this. I had a child to think about now.

The answer became clear, even though I didn't want to do it.

I had to return to Vyaan.

Where I, at least, had connections. Where my references would mean something. I'd worked in the Vyaan keep, something I'd felt I had to lie about here. But in Vyaan, that would get me a job anywhere, especially if I had Maudoric behind me, which I thought I would.

From my pocket, I pulled the last of my credits, which I kept on me at all times.

I could either pay Ikrin for the next week…or I could spend half of it on a caravan ticket back to Vyaan.

Taking in a deep breath, I pressed my hand to my stomach. In all my panic, I'd never really given thought to what a child would mean. A little hybrid child, with budding horns and gray skin. Possibly wings.

If Luc's determination had been extinguished in him, I felt like I'd taken all of it for myself.

It burned in me.

I wouldn't let this break me. I wouldn't let Kaldur break me. I would raise my child on my own if I needed to, and I would give him or her a *good* life. A good childhood, where they knew they were loved every single day. A child I would never abandon. A child I would love with every part of me.

At least one of my dreams was coming true. To be a mother.

But like everything in life, it came when I least expected it.

———

I didn't want to leave Laras without saying goodbye to Luc. I only knew that he worked at the docks, and so I waited there whenever I could since it was a short distance from Kyndri's. But after two days, there was no sign of him and my time at Ikrin's was up.

I finished out the last evening at Kyndri's, having already looked up the timetable for the next caravan to Vyaan. I'd sent ahead a letter to Syndras, and I prayed to all the gods and goddesses I knew that she was back in the village after visiting family.

Kyndri knew I was leaving. "Sorry to see you go," she told me when the last of the patrons cleared out. I'd brought my broken traveling bag with me to work this morning because I would leave straight to the transport station from here, catching the last caravan out tonight. "You're a good worker."

"Thanks," I replied. With a heavy heart, I pushed a letter over the bar counter. The final one I'd written last night. "Will you do me a favor?"

Kyndri looked down at the letter. "For the hybrid male?"

I nodded. "I don't know how to find him. But if he ever comes looking for me here, will you give him this? It's…it's important."

"He the one who got you pregnant?" she asked next.

Surprise made me reel back. Was it obvious?

She chuffed out a soft laugh, shaking her head as she polished another jug clean. "I have three young ones myself. You think I wouldn't know what was going on? Especially when humans show sooner?"

I looked down at my belly.

"I knew a human once who delivered within two months. After that first month, she looked like she'd swallowed a *kellu* fruit."

"Two months?" I asked, hearing my audible gulp. "Well, let's hope I have more time than that."

Kyndri swept up the letter, giving me a meaningful look.

"No, it's not him," I told her. "But he's like a brother to me, and I want him know where he can find me. If he ever needs me."

She inclined her head, walking around the bar to meet me on the other side. "If he ever comes back, I'll give it to him. I promise. Don't you worry."

I'd found a kind soul in her, and I was grateful. "Thank you, Kyndri. For everything."

"Ach," she grumbled. "Get out of here before you miss the caravan. And if you're ever in Laras again, come say hello with your little one."

My throat burned. I hid my tears with a wobbly smile and collected my traveling bag from behind the bar, where I'd had it tucked away.

"Here," she said, reaching into her pocket for coins. "Your last pay. With a little extra for food. You don't eat enough. You need to keep up your strength."

I gave her an impromptu hug, one she sighed into but patted me on the back nevertheless.

"Take care of yourself, Erina."

I nodded, released her, and then gathered my bag. My eyes flitted to the letter in her hand, the only tie left I had to Luc here.

"Goodbye," I told her.

Then I left Kyndri's Landing for the last time on weary legs, navigating the darkened streets of Laras until I finally reached the transport depot.

The last caravan from Laras came on time. Behind me, Laras glittered. My heart was heavy, feeling like I was leaving Luc behind.

But for once, I needed to think about myself, what was best for me and the child I was now carrying.

Without another thought, I climbed into the caravan after the driver took my single bag and payment.

Then we set off for home.

***

FIVE DAYS LATER, I WAS STANDING ON THE STEPS OF HOUSE Terasyn. The caravan had been the lowest fare because of the ample stops along the way, and I'd only managed to bathe at a village in the middle of the country.

I was dirty and hungry and so incredibly tired.

But when Syndras opened the door to House Terasyn, when she saw me standing there, her eyes widening briefly on my rounding stomach, it felt like landing somewhere safe.

"Oh, my dear," she said quietly, ushering me in the familiar home. "Come in, come in. Get warm."

But I only embraced her, needing to feel touch and comfort. Despite my unbathed state, Syndras held me tight and stroked down my back. She'd always been kind and caring, if a little gruff, like a grandmother I'd never known. It had broken my heart to leave this House.

"You're home now," she whispered into my ear. "It will be okay."

And I'd never heard more wonderfully necessary words in my entire life.

CHAPTER 31

KALDUR

The building keeper's hands fumbled with the lock on the door when he tried to open it.

"But like I told you, *Kyzaire*," he was saying, "she left last week."

Ikrin, the Kylorr male's name was. The inhabitants of the building had all come out to peer curiously, their eyes widening when they saw me, standing on the landing of their home.

"And where did she go?" I asked, frowning.

None of this made sense.

"And was she with someone?"

"With someone?" Ikrin asked. He shook his head. "No, she was alone. I don't know where she went. She paid by the week, and when that week was up, her things were gone. That's just… how it's done here."

I leveled Ikrin a hard look, and he hurriedly pushed open the squeaking door to let me inside the small room.

Immediately, the remnants of her scent hit me hard, and I nearly gasped. With memory, with longing. I was certain I looked as hungry as a starving *lyvin* because Ikrin stayed well out of my way, though I tried to keep my temper reined. But it had been volatile lately. Unpredictable, even, without my female around to soothe it.

But her scent…her scent certainly helped. Just knowing she'd been here, recently.

Even if her accommodations made me scowl. A small room, no bigger than a washroom. An old, sagging bed and a small dresser. The rug was nearly threadbare, and there was a chill in the air, a draft funneling in from the window.

My *kyrana* had lived *here*? I lamented.

"How long was she here for?" I asked through a clenched jaw, trying to keep my anger and frustration stable.

"Three or four weeks, I think," Ikrin replied. When I peered at him carefully, he said quickly, "But I can look back at my records and find out for certain, *Kyzaire*."

I was surprised he had records for a place like this, but I supposed it was Laras law.

"Of course, if they weren't taken."

"Taken?" I asked.

"We—we had an incident nearly two weeks back," Ikrin stammered out. "Some of the rooms and my offices were robbed."

"Was hers?" I demanded, stalking toward him.

"Y-yes," Ikrin replied, making me growl. "Her money was gone, or so she told me. I don't think anything else was though!"

So she didn't have any money left? Was that why she'd left?

Fuck, I thought.

"And you don't know where she went?" I asked, alarm driving me. It had already taken me a good week to locate this place, and that had happened entirely by chance. Someone I'd asked in passing, an older male, who happened to live in the building. He'd told me a human female matching Erina's description had been renting here, and I'd decided to check it out personally. Luckily there were very few human females in Laras with red hair.

"She worked at an inn, I think," Ikrin supplied. "One off the main market square."

"What's it called?"

His eyes flickered back and forth, as if trying to recall. "A little one, with rooms on the upper floors. Down the street with the *dyaan*. Kyndri!" he said in a rush. "Kyndri's...Landing. That's the one. I'm sure of it."

"Good," I said. "Anything else you can tell me?"

When he saw me pull credits from my pockets, his eyes widened.

"She was looking for someone when she came here," he said quickly. "One of my old renters. Luc, his name was. And I know she got a letter. A real fancy letter with thick paper. She left shortly after."

A letter? I wondered, frowning.

"Thank you," I said. I pressed the credits to his palm, which he took eagerly. "That's all."

After one final deep breath, drawing her scent in deep, I left.

Finding Kyndri's Landing was easy, especially when the people of Laras kept gawking at me. When I stepped inside the inn, I saw it was quaint. A single hearth was lit, casting the room in firelight, though it was a little dark in the corners. There was a polished bar to my left, a Kylorr female dressed in trews and a tunic manning it, and to my right was a plethora of small tables and booths. Toward the back was a set of stairs, leading to what I assumed were the upper rooms.

"What can I get you?" the Kylorr female asked, running a cloth over the bar to clean up spilled foam.

When I stepped up to the old lacquered wood, I saw the female finally look up at me and her eyes widened.

"*Kyzaire,*" she breathed. She frowned. "But what are you doing *here?*"

As if she knew that her inn and tavern were a little less... savory.

"Kyndri, I presume?" I prompted.

"Yes," she said slowly. I could see her mind working, mentally conjuring up all the reasons why a son of the Kaalium would be walking into her establishment on the dockside of Laras.

"I'm looking for Erina Denoren," I said. "I was told she might work here."

But I didn't scent her, so I wondered if Ikrin had gotten it wrong. If she was here, I would know it.

"She did," Kyndri said, sparking my hopes.

"Does she still?" I asked, pressing further into the bar.

"No, she left last week," she replied. "A shame too. She was a good worker. Trustworthy. Those are hard to find these days."

"Do you know where she is?"

"Yes," Kyndri asked, "but can I ask why you're looking for her?"

My brow almost rose at the impertinence...but I thought it was good that this bar keeper was protecting Erina. It meant I could trust her.

"She's my mate," I finally said, the words dropping like stones. The first time I'd voiced the words out loud to a stranger, but I needed to find out where she'd gone. If Kyndri had loyalties to Erina, which I suspected she might've, I needed to make her understood how vital it was I find her. "It's important. To bring her home, back to Vyaan."

Kyndri studied me. I was certain she'd seen all kinds of people come through her doors, and I was equally certain she could read each and every one. If she was surprised by my admission, she didn't show it.

"As far as I know, she's already back in Vyaan," Kyndri said quietly.

"What?" I asked, freezing in place. "She told you that?"

"Last week she caught the last caravan back. I assumed she'd arrived already."

I'd already been in Laras by then, searching for her. Scouring the villages and the main holdings around the capital.

Had she...returned to the keep?

No, Maudoric would've contacted me if she had.

"Thank you," I told Kyndri, inclining my head. I turned to leave, intent to return to my territory quickly now that I knew, against all odds, Erina was *there*. "Was she…was she happy here?"

She barked out a humorless laugh. "No. She was sad. And alone. And scared, given her…circumstance."

Her circumstance? I wondered, frowning.

"But she's a strong one. She held her head up high and never complained once, no matter what she had to deal with here."

Every word felt like a jab in the chest. She never should've had to *deal* with anything. I should've protected her from this. She shouldn't have been living in a small, cramped, drafty room, paying by the week, or working in an inn for hours on end, putting up with who knew what.

I slid credits over the bar, nodding at Kyndri before departing.

Out on the street, I sucked in a deep breath, peering around the darkening market. Erina had been here. She'd looked at this view, walked this road, and been surrounded by these buildings.

But she was still out of my grasp.

My Halo orb chimed, and I fished it from my pocket.

Maudoric.

Her face was illuminated in perfect color when the projection sparked.

"Good," I said. "I found—"

"Erina's back in Vyaan," Maudoric said quickly.

Relief nearly made me sag.

"Where?" I asked quickly. "At the keep?"

"No, she's staying at House Terasyn. One of the keepers spotted her in the village. I thought you would want to know immediately."

"I'll start heading back tonight," I informed her. But the distance to Vyaan was over a day still, and that was without flying breaks. "Have my scouts keep an eye on her until I arrive."

"Be careful," Maudoric told me after nodding. "There's a storm brewing in the Southeast. You'll catch it."

I didn't care. Nothing would keep me from her.

When the Com call ended, I shot up into the air. I'd send word to Azur once I returned to Vyaan. He would understand my sudden absence when I didn't return to his keep tonight.

Once I was over Laras, I maneuvered south and began the long flight back home, back to my *kyrana*.

And once I got there, I knew it would only be the beginning.

CHAPTER 32
—
ERINA

The storm was howling outside, but Syndras's sitting room was warm and perfect. She was reading and sipping from the thimble-sized glass of sweet wine pinched between her fingers.

I was in the chair opposite her, working to mend a pair of trews that had seen better days. I knew that Syndras's wealth had been dwindling over the years after her husband's death, though I'd thought that her daughter marrying into another noble House would help her.

But she'd waved away my concerns, telling me that she was just practical and didn't like to waste credits when she had perfectly good things that just needed some love and care.

That was what I'd always admired about the elderly Kylorr female. She wasn't like any noble I'd ever worked for, who'd believed that flaunting their wealth and always buying extravagant things was the norm. Syndras lived relatively simply for a noble from a long-standing family. She only kept on one cook because she couldn't make food to save her life. But all the keepers, me included, had been let go over time, and the sitting room showed signs of it.

My nose was itching from the dust. I'd already swept out her room yesterday and wiped down the windows and surfaces. It had needed it.

"You don't have to do that, you know," she grumbled from her chair. *Still* grumbling about it, just as she'd done about all the little tasks I'd done around the home.

"I know," I said simply, conjuring up a smile for her, "but I want to. It makes me feel useful."

"You don't owe me, my dear," Syndras said for the hundredth time since I'd shown up on her doorstep a couple nights ago. "You need a soft place to land. Not days spent cleaning, especially in your condition."

I still hadn't told her who the father was. I couldn't. Not yet.

"You're kind enough to let me stay, to let me eat your food," I said softly, returning my attention to the seam I was mending. I hadn't sewn anything, hadn't patched anything in quite a long time. I'd missed it. The repetitive movements felt like a mesmerizing lull, a needed calm. "Tidying a few things is the least I can do. Besides, I would get bored otherwise."

"You?" Syndras harrumphed. "Bored," she repeated softly, smiling as she took another sip from her wine. "You're never bored, Erina. You're always galaxies away in your head."

I sobered. "That's what everyone's been telling me. They say I need to be realistic."

Out of the corner of my eye, I noticed Syndras frown.

"That's not a bad thing, little one," she said. "I think it's delightful. I think people need to be more like you. Maybe then they wouldn't be so miserable all the time."

I didn't reply. Instead I thought, *I'm just as miserable now, so what good is it, really?*

I was heartbroken after Kaldur, rejected by Luc—who I'd always thought I could rely on, pregnant, and partly still in denial about it. And I'd returned home with my proverbial tail tucked between my legs because I'd run out of money. And now I was mooching off my friend and old employer's good graces with no true plan.

So yes, I was feeling quite miserable.

"No word from your daughter yet?" I asked.

"So eager to leave me," Syndras grumbled. "But no. I'm having dinner with them tomorrow. Many nobles will be in attendance. Trust me—I'll secure you a position somewhere by the night's end."

"I don't know how to repay you," I confessed. "You've always been so kind to me."

"You keep this old female company and have always written to me," she said softly. "When you get to be my age, you realize how little else matters except those in your life who you truly care about and who care about you."

My throat burned at the sentiment in her voice.

"I do love you, Syndras," I said. Perhaps I used that word more often than most, but perhaps I felt it more often than most.

"I love you too, my dear," Syndras replied, but her voice was gruff. She didn't like to talk about these things, and I bit back a smile as I returned to my work. She added, "And you know you can tell me anything."

My smile died. "I know."

We lapsed into silence as the storm raged outside the window. When I looked out, I saw sheets of rain sliding down it and noticed that the curtains needed to be beaten, an accumulation of dust lingering in the folds.

I'd do that tomorrow, I decided. Syndras had grown much weaker these last few years, even though she'd likely take off my head if I dared to say that out loud.

There was a terrible banging at the door. *Thump, thump, thump.*

Syndras's head snapped up.

"Who in Raazos's blood…" she muttered, pushing up from her chair with some effort. "At this hour, in this storm?"

"Let me get it," I protested.

"No," she said firmly. "This is still my House, and I'm not so old that I can't greet my own guests."

I bit my lip as I watched her go from the room, slowly and with care. I sighed when she was gone but went back to my sewing. The sitting room was far enough away from the main entrance that I knew it might be a few moments. Perhaps it was her daughter or one of her keepers, come to check on Syndras in the storm.

But before I knew it, the door to the sitting room slammed opened and I was staring at a male that, for a brief moment, I didn't recognize.

Then I spied mirrored eyes, cutting through the low light of the sitting room, and I froze.

Kaldur.

He was dripping wet from the storm, his clothes plastered to his body like he'd been flying in it for hours on end. He was leaner than I remembered, the shadows of his face deeper, nearly gaunt.

He looked severe, intense, and angry. And...*relieved*. A bright relief so palpable he nearly swayed with it.

And I was nowhere remotely ready to see him again. Him being here was like a punch in the gut because even like this, he was still achingly handsome, handsome enough to make my heart sting.

Seeing him brought back all the hurt. Rushing back, as if it had never left.

Then panic flared. Luckily the sewing hid my rounding belly from view, but even a week after leaving Laras had made the rapid changes in my body all the more noticeable. Before, I could've passed the pregnancy off as a large meal. Now? No one would *ever* believe that.

"What...how did you know I was here?" came the first shocked words out of my mouth as he stalked toward me. He was dripping water all over Syndras's rugs, and I opened my mouth to tell him—

"You're coming with me," Kaldur told me. "*Now.*"

"No," I said, easily. "I'm not going anywhere with you."

Why is he here? I thought wildly.

"What do you want?" I asked.

Syndras came hobbling back into the room. "*Kyzaire*, I must protest that—"

"This is a private matter between me and my *kyrana*, Syndras," Kaldur growled.

A sound squeaked out from me just as Syndras froze, her eyes widening almost comically.

His *kyrana*? His blood mate?

"*What?*" I breathed.

My unfocused, stunned gaze went back to Syndras, hovering in the doorway. She seemed equally speechless, merely blinking her bright green eyes as she digested the words.

My eyes went back to Kaldur, who was glaring down at me. Though I had the strangest impression that this was his natural state. The lines of his face had deepened with that expression, as if they were stuck.

"You can't mean that," I murmured, suddenly scared and reeling.

No. He was doing this to manipulate me. But for what purpose? He'd made his feelings clear. Was this some ploy to get me back as his blood giver?

If it was, it was a lot of effort on his part. He looked...awful.

"For weeks, I've been searching for you," he grated, his wings sagging around him when he kneeled in front of me, his chest pressing into my knees. "Do you know what this feels like?"

The question was so ragged and aching that it nearly brought tears to my eyes. I didn't want to feel sympathy for this male. He'd hurt me on purpose, said cruel things, and made me feel so small and discarded and alone.

I want him to hurt, I thought. Then I was ashamed at the ugly thought. The only other person in this entire universe who I'd thought that of had been Wrezaan once.

"It's not true," I said quietly. "You're…you're lying. I don't understand—I don't understand why you would do this! Just let me be!"

Kaldur closed his eyes, a flash of pain scrunching up his expression.

"I'll make this right, Erina," he told me when he fastened that gaze back on me. The intensity in his eyes pulled at my heart, pulled me back in, and I couldn't afford to let that happen. I wouldn't be a blind, romantic little fool anymore. He'd taught me that. "I just need the chance to."

"It's always about what you want," I said, my voice sounding hollow. "And I don't care enough to want to please you anymore. So, *leave.* I'm not going with you. I don't want anything to do with you, especially after your last letter. You made it very clear what you wanted…and that was me, far away from you."

His brow scrunched down. "My letter? I haven't written you! I haven't even been able to *find* you!"

"Stop lying, Kaldur," I pleaded. "Just leave me alone."

"I can't do that," he growled. "I can never do that, so don't ask me to!"

I didn't understand it. It felt like he'd ripped open a wound that had just started to heal, leaving it raw and ravaged all over again. Or perhaps it had always been open and I'd just learned to live with it since that night in his study.

I was hurt and angry. Embarrassed because Syndras was watching this unfold.

"We can talk back at the keep," Kaldur finally said, standing, though he reached down to take my hand.

"I'm not going with you," I said, a little growl of my own.

His eyes shot with fire. "And I'm not leaving without you. I'll live in this *fucking* room if I must, but I will not be parted from you again. Ever."

He was mad. He must've been. Or delusional.

"You told me to never contact you again," I told him, glaring as I forcibly tried to jerk my hand from his grip. "So how dare you do this! How dare you do this to me!"

"I never said that," he clipped out. Glaring again. "What are you talking about?"

"Your letter!" I yelled out, frustrated tears beginning to drip down my cheeks, which made his tight expression pull even further.

"*What* letter?"

"*Kyzaire*," came Syndras's careful and hushed voice. I'd never heard her use that tone. "I think it's best if you come back in the morning. After you've cooled down."

"I'm not leaving without her," he replied, his mind set, her words dismissed.

Finally, he pulled me up from the chair, and the trews I'd been mending, entirely forgotten, fell to the floor.

"We can talk about this back at the—"

His words abruptly cut off when his gaze lowered to my rounding belly.

His hand was curled around the back of mine, and I felt the palpable tension shoot through him, fascinating and tangible. *Such strength,* I thought, dazed.

"What..." He trailed off, the word nothing but a stunned exhale. Then I felt tension rip through him. Apprehension shot through my belly when I saw the muscles in his shoulders begin to tremble and grow, becoming larger.

"Kaldur," I said quickly, my gaze darting to Syndras, "don't."

"Is that mine or *his*?" he growled. His voice was becoming darker, more gravelly. More unrecognizable.

I'd never seen a Kylorr go into a berserker rage. I'd only ever heard about them in stories, the trigger almost always a sense of anger or a need to protect and defend.

I knew which one Kaldur's would come from.

Two things became apparent to me.

The first being that Kaldur had no idea about the letter that had been sent to me. He'd had *no* idea that I was pregnant, nor had he written it or had knowledge of it.

He wouldn't be able to fake *this*. The sheer emotion and shock, the rage and the sorrow—which didn't make sense to me…those couldn't be faked.

And the second realization was that if I didn't get Kaldur out of Syndras's home, he might very well go into a berserker rage right here and now and destroy it entirely.

"I'll go with you," I said quietly. "Let's leave now."

Kaldur blinked, his nostrils flaring. His shoulders lowered, but his voice was unchanged.

"Is that *his*?" he asked again, the words clipped, his eyes a darkening tunnel of rage and, strangely, despair. "Is that his child? Tell me right now, Erina, or I *swear* on Raazos—"

"No," I breathed. "It's yours, Kaldur. The child is *yours*."

Out of the corner of my eye, I saw Syndras lean against the wall, as if she needed it to support her weight. My alarm grew, though Kaldur seemed to process the words.

"Mine?" he growled.

"Yes," I whispered, pressing my hand against his cheek—the side that was scarred, a scar I still didn't know how he'd received. His skin was so hot, like he had a raging fever. "Let's go. Now. I'll return to the keep with you. But let's leave now."

He pulled me against him immediately, and his clothes soaked me. But what surprised me was that he pressed his face into my neck and a tingle rushed down my spine when I felt his deep inhale.

"Missed you, missed you," he murmured, "but I found you now. I'll make this right—I promise."

My eyes stung with tears. He was trembling and his skin was so hot that steam was rising off his wet clothes. He'd been close to a rage. He hadn't known I was pregnant. Then who'd sent the letter?

It didn't matter, I decided. Not right now.

I needed to get him away from Syndras and back to the keep.

"Take me back," I ordered him, feeling the press of my belly against him. "Take me back home."

His shoulders finally relaxed at the words, and all I felt was relief. Over his shoulder, Syndras was studying me.

She inclined her head at me. A thank-you. A confirmation. A promise.

Outside, the storm mirrored the maelstrom of my thoughts.

CHAPTER 33
KAIDUR

When I alighted on the balcony leading to my room, Erina was trembling in my arms and a new sense of alarm raced through me.

I'd just wanted to get her back to the keep as swiftly as possible, but even the mere moments flying in the rain had chilled her, though I'd tried my best to keep her shielded.

I felt outside of my own body, as relief and confusion warred, when I dragged her over to the fire and began to strip her of her wet clothes. Maudoric had had it lit, knowing I was returning tonight, and I was extremely grateful the room was warm.

"Don't," Erina protested, trying to shield her body as I tugged off the clothing. "What are you doing?"

Was that fear I sensed in her voice? My muscles began to shake again, a mere trigger away from a rage, even if the threat I sensed was *myself*.

Was she afraid of me now?

"You're freezing," I grated, breathing in deeply, letting her scent calm me. *Stay focused, for her,* I ordered myself. She needed me to be present. And of a stable mind, which seemed laughable after this last month. "I need to get you warm, *dallia*."

When she was undressed—and trying to shield her sudden nudity from me unsuccessfully—I took her into the adjoining washroom. The taps ran hot and flooded into the sunken bathing tub, and I guided her down the stairs. She sat on the small ledge, shivering until the hot water reached up her calves, going higher and higher.

The restless prowling in me only released when she sighed as the water fully enveloped her. And even though it took everything in me, I stayed on the opposite side of the small pool, still fully dressed, and paced back and forth in the water.

Erina watched me. "You'll go into a rage, won't you?"

"Not with you here," I said, my voice harsher than I wanted. I didn't know who I was anymore. For the last month, I felt like a stranger in the body I'd had since birth.

All because of her. All because of the blood bond that pulsed through me like a heartbeat.

And already, I'd fucked it all up.

"Will feeding help?" came her small voice.

I froze in the water, whipping her a—very likely—hungry look before I closed my eyes.

"No, I won't do that to you," I growled.

"I'm scared, Kaldur," came her voice, and I felt a billow of rage sweep out from me. I nearly turned and put my fist into the side of the white marble pool but managed to control myself. "Come feed so you're calm. You're scaring me like this."

She held up her wrist from the warm water, and my fangs immediately elongated, my body drawn to her like a magnet.

"I don't want it like this," I rasped. "But I can't control it anymore. I...I haven't been right, Erina. Since you left me."

When I reached for her wrist, I thought I saw a flash of sympathy in her eyes.

"There have been no others. I've only wanted you," I confessed.

Her eyes widened.

But I bent over her wrist, determined only to drink enough to take the edge off of the rage, until I could feel calm again and some of the fear leeched from her gaze. My fangs dove into her giving flesh, and my first draw of her blood made my eyes roll back in my head.

I groaned, the taste of her so sublime. I'd *forgotten*. I'd forgotten the ecstasy. And I'd been so foolish, so arrogant to believe that I could live without her?

This last month had proved how wrong I'd been, and now she hated me.

I drank from her, determined not to feel any pleasure from it because I didn't deserve that. It felt too wrong even as her blood coated my tongue, a sweetness I'd dreamed of, I'd craved. She was looking away from me, a tightness in her jaw, and though it physically pained me, I pulled away.

I would never know where I'd received that strength and willpower to stop when I was starving for her. My fangs felt like they were throbbing.

It was enough blood. Enough to sate a little of the roaring, aggressive hunger coursing in my body.

And it could never be enough. I wanted more…and it made me feel like a villain.

I'd only taken from her. Taken more than I had any right to.

My gaze dipped below the surface of the water. She was sitting, hugging her arm against her breasts, but I could still see the firm roundness of her lower belly.

"Allow me," I said, reaching for her wrist when I saw the bloom of red swirling in the water. When she held out her arm, I felt a fierce surge of hunger at the overpowering scent of her blood, but I merely healed the wound before releasing her.

Words escaped me. I only wanted to be near her. I only wanted to force her to cling to me because I'd been lost without her. But if I did that, she might hate me even more than she already did.

Familiar determination began like a tiny seed in my chest before growing, rooting, *spreading*. It carved itself deep into my bones and flowed through every vein like a racing river.

I would win her back.

I'd had her love once, hadn't I? Until my ego and my anger had forced her away.

"You're with child," I said, trying to soften my rough voice. "My child."

I felt better than I had in weeks…but seeing her shoot me a wounded look made me feel worse.

"Yes," she said. "Like I told you in my letter."

The feeding, however small it had been, was giving me strength and energy like a blast of sunlight when I'd been in darkness for so long. But as such, it was making my wet clothes feel all the more constricting, and so I pulled them from me. Erina looked away, turning her head resolutely to the side, though she should not have been embarrassed by my nakedness —not with her mate.

But she didn't even know that important fact, I thought, a stab of guilt hitting me. *Because I'd hidden it from her knowingly. I'd blind-sided her tonight, and that should've never happened.*

She'd deserved to know. From the very beginning. Instead, I'd hidden my need for her into a contract of all things, meant to keep her close, tied to me like a leash without allowing her the respect of knowing the truth.

"What letter?" I asked, knowing I needed to keep calm.

"I'd rather not have this conversation naked in the bath with you," she said.

"Tell me," I said, keeping my tone gentle. "Please," I added.

She blinked at the word but then, the kind-hearted little human she was, gave in. If our positions were reversed, I would've told myself to fuck off. Vehemently.

"I wrote to you when I found out about the pregnancy," she

said, meeting my eyes. Warm brown and beautiful, I'd missed them. "I…I'd been scared. I didn't know what to do."

Why not ask Luc for help? I couldn't help but wonder. But that was another conversation for another time.

"So I wrote to you," she said, her brow furrowing in a tiny glare. "And the letter I got back was dismissive. It said that the validity of the pregnancy couldn't be proven and that if I tried to contact you again, it would be ignored. Then ten *vron* landed in my creditory account as a means of a payoff, I can only assume."

I kept the rage in check, but only barely. My nostrils flaring was the only sign of the war within me.

"You sent your letter here?" I asked slowly.

"Yes," she replied, lifting her chin. "It looked like your signature."

"Do you still have it?" I wanted to know. Though I thought that if I saw it, the mere sight might send me into a rage.

"Yes," she replied, and I could only imagine the reasons that she'd kept it. Perhaps to remember…

"I didn't get your letter," I said, my tone clipped and certain. "And I certainly never sent you that one back."

"I figured as much," she replied quietly. "You…you were surprised when you saw me like this. You can't fake that kind of surprise."

At least she believed me about that.

"Why am I here?" she asked next. "Why did you bring me here?"

I didn't want to scare her, but also…things would be very, very different from how they'd been before.

"In an effort to be entirely honest with you," I began, "I'll tell you this, even though it's against my better judgment: I intend to keep you as mine."

Her lips parted. And then she laughed, the sound hollow with a tinge of disbelief. Or perhaps bitterness. It sounded nothing like the woman I'd come to know. It echoed around the washroom, and for a moment, I lamented that it might be too late. That I'd done too much damage; that she did, in fact, love Luc Denoren and I stood no chance. That she didn't want me anymore.

But then a little bit of my arrogance reared its ugly head and I thought, *I'm Kaldur of House Kaalium, a* fucking *High Lord.*

Who would reject a *Kyzaire?*

She just might, I couldn't help but fear. Erina was different from all the rest, I was discovering. Wrongfully assuming she was like the females I'd grown up around was what had gotten me into this mess to begin with. Well, that and my own foolish pride.

"Wow, am I lucky or what?" she asked, her laugh fading. "Guess I *did* snag a son of the Kaalium. Guess I did manipulate my way into his keep and into his bed so I could better my position in life."

The words *were* ugly when they were thrown back into my face.

But what hurt me more was the vulnerability in Erina's voice. Any other female and the words might feel caustic and cutting. When she said them? They made me want to comfort her, to pull her into my arms because they were laced with so much *hurt.*

"Forgive me, but I don't believe you, *Kyzaire,*" she said simply, blinking away some of the sudden glassiness in her gaze.

"I intend to make you mine, Erina," I said again, still not quite having it in me to voice her full name. The name she shared with *him.* "You'll never want for anything again."

"Only love and happiness and true contentment," she said, her tone hollow.

"I went to Laras," I growled. "I saw where you were staying. I saw where you were working."

Her lips parted. "You were there?"

"I told you—I've been searching for you for weeks. I saw how you lived. So why reject what I can offer you so easily? You would have a grand keep for a home, some of the best food in the entire universe, and more credits than you know what to do with."

"But don't you see?" she asked. "None of that matters! It always seems to, to you nobles. But for someone like me, I could be happy with a whole lot less. I have been before. At least in Laras, I wasn't paid for."

I dug my heels in, hiding my flinch from the words. "I want you back here. In the keep, in my bed." She nearly gasped. "I want you at my side."

"Because I'm your *kyrana?*" she wondered. The way the word twisted from her lips made it clear she didn't believe me.

"Why would I lie about something so serious?" I asked, feeling an edge of my temper sharpen. I'd gone through absolute hell after she'd left. Did she think I'd faked that?

"Why?" she repeated, disbelief in her eyes. "Because you did everything you could to deny me when I was *here*, right beside you and wanting to be there. You made it clear that you would never love me. That my only place here was in your bed, but that you would never marry me. Because you thought I was angling to be *Kylaira* of your territory."

"I know that's not true now," I growled.

"*Now* being the operative word. And I don't understand it, this sudden change of heart. I don't trust it. But the damage is done," she said, that hollowness entering her voice again…and I couldn't stand it. "Let me make myself clear: I came here tonight so that you wouldn't raze Syndras's home to rubble. I don't intend to stay. And you can't make me."

"Name your price," I rasped as I moved my way toward her in the pool. Her gaze flicked over me, over my naked chest, before they returned to my eyes. Perhaps she still desired me, even though she clearly couldn't stand me.

I tipped her chin up with two fingers. Just being close to Erina, touching her skin, inhaling her scent, knowing she was within arm's reach, in my keep…it soothed me. Like a warm bed after an agonizing day.

"I cannot force you to stay. But it is within my power to give you whatever you want so that you choose to," I said.

Her lips parted. "You're mad if you think I'd ever *choose* that."

"I looked into Luc Denoren more in Laras. I discovered he had a failed business," I said, watching closely to see how she would respond. Her eyes widened. "Would you stay if I gave him back everything he lost? And Syndras? You care for her. Wouldn't you want her to be better taken care of? A House full of keepers so she wouldn't struggle so much?"

"You're bribing me to stay?"

"You won't take credits yourself," I rasped. "But you might stay if I gave them to those you love."

And there it was. The truth of it.

Erina was not who I'd thought she was. She'd rejected my money to make a point, and she'd nearly been wandering the streets in Laras because of her pride. But would she wield that same pride like a weapon when it came to those she loved?

Especially for her precious Luc?

"I'll take care of Luc and Syndras," I promised her. "All I need is for you to say you'll give this another chance."

That you'll give me *another chance* was what went unspoken.

"I don't trust you," she breathed.

Because I'd never given her reason to.

"I can't give you another chance. I can't do this again, Kaldur," she said, her tone almost pleading.

Resolve hardened in my very soul. "Then stay for the sake of our child. You don't have to trust me. Not yet, at least. Not until I can show you that I make good on my word. But you can at least trust that I will give our child the best I can. Hybrid pregnancies can be difficult. I don't want you living far. I want you close, so I can take care of the both of you."

She went silent. A torrent of emotions crossed her features. Longing, indecision, displeasure, hope.

She *was* willing to fall on her sword for those she cared about. And for our child. Even though she hated me.

"You'll take care of them?" she asked quietly. "Of Luc and Syndras?"

I tried not to sound too relieved, too eager when I said, "I swear it. I'll have one of my family's representatives meet with Luc, to go over a plan for the funds and the business. What happened before won't happen again with the backing of House Kaalium's name behind him. And I'll hire on keepers and a full staff for Syndras starting tomorrow."

Erina's shoulders sagged.

"Anyone else?" I asked, wondering if there was anyone else she loved in her life.

She shook her head.

"I suppose you'll want to draw up another contract," she said, her gaze unfocused, her words soft.

I made her meet my eyes, then pressed closer. "No more contracts," I growled. "This is just between you and me now. On our word and our intention alone."

Her eyes burned into mine. My mind was still reeling with a thousand different stabs of thoughts and realizations. But mostly what I hadn't wrapped my mind around yet was the life growing inside Erina.

The life I had helped create.

My child. The first of the next generation of House Kaalium.

"I want my own room," she added.

Though everything in me rebelled at the thought, I inclined my head. "Very well."

I would merely join her there, but she didn't need to know that quite yet.

"Are we in agreement?" I asked.

"Yes."

I hated that she looked miserable saying that word. As if she'd just sold her soul.

But I vowed that I would make this right.

I had to.

CHAPTER 34
—
ERINA

The gardens were just how I'd remembered them.

Only quieter now because it was before dawn and even the horticulturists were asleep…or taking their first meal of the day in the warm kitchen.

Me? I hadn't been able to sleep. I'd tossed and turned in my old room in Kaldur's wing of the keep all night. I'd woken briefly and thought I'd still been back in Laras. A fear of dread had struck me that I was still back there.

I hadn't been able to sleep since. I'd thought of Kaldur, of everything that had happened last night, of the child in my womb, of his offer to help Luc and Syndras, to my ever-tumultuous feelings about the *Kyzaire* of Vyaan.

I'd taken my notebook and my pencil tin…but truthfully, I hadn't drawn or written anything in weeks, besides half-desperate letters.

In Laras, I'd merely been too exhausted to even think of flipping open my notebook. My inspiration was gone, my creative soul a little battered and bruised.

I'd hoped that being back in the gardens might shake some

loose. The feeling of awe and beauty I so loved. This keep, these grounds had always inspired me.

Only I felt nothing now. That scared me.

I felt the *want* to create wiggling inside me as the soft sole of my boots met familiar cobblestones and winding paved pathways. The morning was chilled and brisk. Small, dripping icicles hung off the petals of one flower where the wall hadn't blocked the wind chill.

I studied the bloom. Beautiful, though a little wrinkled from the bitter cold. I flicked off the icicles and smoothed the petal, soft and velvety beneath my fingertip.

Maybe one day, that could be me again. But right now, I felt a little shriveled up, beaten down, and heartbroken. I'd felt that way since leaving Vyaan…but Luc's rejection had made it all the worse. Seeing his defeat had killed something in me, the perpetual glimmer of hope and optimism I'd endeavored to keep close.

I felt like I'd left a big part of me in Laras, a vital piece.

Would I find it again in Vyaan?

I didn't know.

My hands moved to my rounding belly. The firm press of it felt strange and foreign still. I'd barely given much thought to what a child would actually mean. It had been about two weeks since I'd discovered the pregnancy. Nearly halfway through it, if the healer was to be believed.

"Erina."

I closed my eyes.

Kaldur.

I turned to regard him, approaching me swiftly down the pathway. Seeing him made a pang shoot through my heart. His hair was disheveled, his clothes askew, as if he'd just woken up and thrown them on.

"I don't like you leaving the keep without telling me," he said.

My expression remained stoic. "I didn't realize I was a pris-
oner here."

Kaldur blew out a sharp breath. His hands were trembling, I
saw, when he raked them through his hair. He stepped up to me,
the spread of his warm hand coming to my cheek.

"I just got you back," he said, voice hushed. He smelled like
how I remembered. Clean and comforting. "I still fear you'll
disappear again. A part of me believes you're still just a dream,
that I'll wake up any moment and you'll be gone again."

There was a haunted hollowness in his gaze when he said the
words. I felt a flutter of sympathy, of guilt, before I forced the
emotions away.

"Besides," he said, "news of our child will spread."

Our child.

The words struck me nearly dumb as I stared up into his eyes.

"And right now," Kaldur said, looking as though he was trying
to find the words, "well, let's just say that enemies are everywhere. And House Kaalium has made many beyond our borders.
You need to understand that now. My brothers have guards
appointed to their mates as a precaution. No more wandering
until I secure one for you."

I…I was out of my element here. Guards? But why? This was
normal?

I stepped back from his hand, and it fell between us. I looked
at his chest, at the silver buttons, one not properly clasped as if
he'd hurried to get dressed, as I digested the words.

"I don't need a guard. And no one has to know I'm pregnant
yet," I said.

Kaldur made a sound of disbelief. "You know better than that.
Keepers know everything. You think the news won't spread? And
besides, you can't stay in the keep forever. You'll be expected to
attend events with me."

"I wasn't before," I said. "That doesn't have to change."

"Everything has changed, Erina," he growled, drawing my eyes. "I'm not going back. *We're* not going back."

"And just because you decided that it means I have to accept it too?" I shot back, raising a brow.

I sucked in a breath when his hand wrapped around the back of my neck. His skin was hot, and when he stepped into me, I felt even more heat pour off him. Even through my coat. I only wore my nightdress beneath it, and boots with holes in them, but I still felt that heat.

"One thing you will get used to, Erina, as the mate to *this Kyzaire*, is that when I make up my mind, I do not change it. I can be impulsive, yes. My temper sometimes gets the best of me. And I can be stubborn to a fault. But one thing I am not is an oath breaker."

My breaths were shallow as I looked up at him.

"I regret what happened between us," he continued. "I regret the way I treated you. I regret that I lied to you, that I made you feel like I didn't care about you. I regret that night in my study. I could have simply been honest and it would have saved us a lot of hurt."

My heart was beating so fast and strong in my chest that I knew Kaldur would be able to hear it. His eyes were mesmerizing, like *zylarrs*. Just as I'd remembered. With the dawn mist swirling around us, I felt like I'd been transported to an otherworldly realm. I felt the burst of beauty around us as the sun finally broke through the forest tops.

"This is my promise to you now, Erina," Kaldur said gruffly. "I promise to give you the respect you deserve as my blood mate. As the mother of my child."

I breathed in deep when I heard the catch in his voice at the words, feeling a swell of emotion rise as I fought against it.

"I know I don't deserve a second chance, but I'm selfish enough to demand it of you. I know I've given you no reason to believe me when I say that it will different from now on...but in time, I hope you will. I only ask for time. *Please, dallia.* I just need time to prove that we can be right for each other."

I cleared my throat when it went tight.

"And what about Luc?" I couldn't help but ask.

I'd thought about that one night in Kaldur's study too many times to count, replaying that night over and over in my head. I'd realized belatedly that Kaldur believed I loved Luc romantically, not because I considered him my brother. It was the only thing I wished I'd clarified that night, not that it would've mattered then.

Kaldur's lips pressed together. "What about him?"

"You believe I love him, don't you?" I asked. "You asked me last night if the child was yours or his, after all."

The *Kyzaire*'s jaw gritted so tight that a muscle popped.

"He doesn't matter to me," Kaldur grated. "Even if you do love him, I'd already made up my mind to steal your affections all for myself."

Disbelief shot through me. "What? That's ridiculous."

"Don't test me," he rasped. "I can be infinitely charming when I set my mind to it."

"But what you don't understand is I don't want the facade you give everyone else," I said. "It's not real."

Kaldur's brow furrowed.

I cleared my throat again, turning my head to dislodge his hand at the back of my neck.

"My point is…a part of you believes that Luc and I are involved. Enough for you to question the pregnancy."

"I was surprised last night, Erina," Kaldur argued. "And half-mad, starving for you, so fucking relieved I'd found you, *and* on the verge of a rage. If you tell me that the child is mine, then I believe you."

"But you believe that I would give myself to you if I loved another so deeply?" I questioned. I wanted to understand. "Is that who you think I am? You thought I was pretending to care about you? That my feelings for you weren't genuine?"

"We still don't know a lot about each other, Erina," Kaldur told me, his voice firm even though his eyes were molten in the rising sun as they pinned me in place. "I didn't know what to believe, but I'm ashamed to say I believed someone that I shouldn't have."

Velle, he meant. And Lydrasa, perhaps. I wouldn't be surprised if it had been Velle who'd written the letter with the noble female's help. Velle would have had access to the letters coming into the House. She was the one who usually collected them and brought them to Maudoric. Perhaps she'd recognized my handwriting.

"But what I can tell you is that I'm *fucking* jealous," Kaldur grated. "And for me, that is a strange and new feeling. I'm not… I'm not handling it well."

He was jealous?

I had half a mind to let him suffer some more. It would *feel* good, wouldn't it? To let him hurt the same way he'd hurt me? He deserved it, didn't he?

I turned from him, flitting away from the center of his embrace. It was hard to think when he was so close, when his scent was enveloping me.

"You should have just asked me," I told him, staring over the calm and quiet of the morning garden. "Because if you had, I would've told you that Luc Denoren is like a brother to me. And I can tell you that the mere thought of being romantically involved with him makes my stomach churn."

Kaldur's sharp, stunned breath was all I heard. When I turned around to face him, I saw his expression looked thunderously dark as he digested what I told him.

"I've never loved Luc in that way. I love him fiercely, yes. I always have, but as my *brother*. As someone who protected me and looked out for me when we were younger."

"You share a name. I thought…"

I laughed, but it was humorless. "We were children when we

took that name. You know how we came up with it? It's from my stories. *Our* stories, because Luc and I worked on them together. And we named our hero Kavelyn Denoren because Luc liked the way it sounded. He'd heard the name once, and it had stuck with him all those years. And we were orphans with no name of our own and so we took it together. Kavelyn Denoren was born. And so were Erina and Luc Denoren. Bonded forever—maybe not by blood, but by dreams. And hope that our lives would turn out like Kavelyn's."

I didn't realize I had started crying until Kaldur frowned, stepped forward to wipe the tears off my cheek.

I was embarrassed, turning my face to the side to compose myself. I shivered in my jacket, wrapping it tighter around me.

"So now you know," I finished. "The real truth. You should have just asked."

I've only ever loved you in that way, I couldn't help but think. But that had been a naive love. One sickened with ridiculous hope and childish romanticism.

I knew better now.

"I'm sorry," came his gruff words. Kaldur stood there as sunlight crept over the entirety of his body, like he was a beautiful sculpture in a gallery. "For what it's worth, Erina Denoren, I'm sorry."

It was small, but it was something.

"Am I really your *kyrana*?" I asked, my tone sounding stiff, distant. Another thing that had kept me up at night. How had I not seen the signs if I was? Was I blind?

Kaldur inclined his head. "Yes."

"How long have you known?"

"Since that afternoon. When you cut yourself on the vase shard," he told me. My eyes widened, a hitch of my breath sounding. *That long?* That was why he'd left? Why he'd called me into his office later that night? "I smelled your blood for the first time, and I knew. Right there and then."

"You knew immediately," I said softly. That was rare, or so I'd heard.

"I likely would've known sooner," he added, "if you hadn't used that perfume so much."

Was that why he'd been so grumpy about it? Oh…because he'd thought it had been a gift from Luc, from my supposed *lover*?

"Without it, you smell otherworldly to me. The sweetest of gifts from another realm, from a godly one," Kaldur continued, his voice hushed. "I knew you were mine that afternoon. And I had done everything since to try to convince myself otherwise."

Because I was a keeper from no great family, from no family at all, I knew. Below his station in life. That realization still filled me with disappointment even though it was a reality I couldn't change.

"You found me lacking," I said quietly. When he opened his mouth, I said, "It's the truth. Don't try to deny it because it sounds pretty."

"I wasn't going to deny it," Kaldur admitted. "I have a lot of flaws. Thinking highly of myself, perhaps too highly, is one of them—at the expense of everyone else. But one thing I am not ashamed about is that I *remember*. I remember history—darker moments of my family's history, to be precise—and I know how vital it is to prevent it from repeating itself. I am highly aware that my family has not always been loved or even respected within the Kaalium. How can a lineage as ancient as mine be?"

"And you didn't want to tarnish your legacy here with a keep-er," I finished for him, raising my chin.

"Do you know what happened here?" he asked. "Before I took over this territory? You might have been too young to remember."

I frowned and shook my head.

"My uncle ruled here once," Kaldur told me, beginning to pace a little, as if he couldn't keep still with the memory. "But no one ever took him seriously, even though he was a fair leader. I learned a great deal from him. But his affairs, his parties, his excess were well known throughout the Kaalium. He had affairs with his keepers, and one in particular he thought himself in love with."

A familiar tale, I thought.

"Many have always compared me to him. They think it's a compliment because he'd been well-liked once, but I never took it as one," Kaldur admitted. "I had my wild years, but when I took over Vyaan, I took my responsibility and my pledge to my people seriously. So it always cut deeply when they made their jokes about how similar we were."

"What happened to your uncle?" I couldn't help but ask, wrapping my arms around myself.

"He announced his mistress publicly, humiliating his wife, my aunt, in the process. Soon, he broke their marriage too because he wanted to wed his mistress instead. But my aunt got her revenge," he said. "She stripped him of nearly everything and dragged him over the spikes within the noble Houses, sowing discord and mistrust. Soon not even the nobles respected him. They laughed at him behind his back. The moment he fell in love with his keeper, he lost control of his territory."

Realization slowly began to bloom as I listened to the story. I realized this was one of Kaldur's greatest fears…to end up like his uncle. Bound to repeat history, especially *here*, where it had happened in recent memory.

"I had to take over the territory sooner than expected, perhaps even before I was ready to," he admitted. "And it took me a long time to gain the respect of the nobles here, especially since I was young."

"And…your uncle?"

His expression was unreadable when he told me, "When the nobles turned on him, his new wife did too. She'd only truly wanted all the luxuries that came with her position, and she received none of it. She took another lover, another noble. And my uncle…he eventually took his own life, driven mad by heartbreak and his own failing as a *Kyzaire*."

I nearly gasped. A tragic tale. A tragic *warning*, I realized. One Kaldur had apparently taken to heart.

"I'm sorry," I whispered, looking to the ground briefly, unable to meet his eyes quite yet. "I didn't know."

Not even the keepers had spoken of it. Though maybe the majority were too young to remember, like me. I hadn't heard of this, though I'd grown up on the outskirts of Vyaan, where news hardly ever reached.

"So it wasn't *you* specifically, Erina," Kaldur finally finished, frustration evident on his features. "I've just always had to be more careful in Vyaan. I've never once gone near one of my keepers—the thought only made me remember the consequences of it. But then…you cut your hand in the sitting room that day. And suddenly all my fears that I would follow in my uncle's footsteps, when everyone already expected me to, started keeping me up at night."

I felt like he was only admitting a portion of the worries he'd carried.

"It doesn't make it acceptable," Kaldur finally finished, "but it was a decision I'd knowingly made…trying to keep you in the dark and at arm's length. I thought I could fight this." He laughed, the sound bitter. "But I was wrong. I've never been more wrong in my entire life, and I've made some pretty spectacular fuckups —believe me. And I regret it. I wish I could go back to that afternoon in the sitting room because I would change everything. But I can't."

We regarded one another in the rising sunlight of the morning as the icicles dripped off flower petals and a hint of warmth began to burn off the chill from the night.

"It's not quite a truce, is it?" he asked.

"No, it's not," I said quietly.

Then again, I *understood* now. That didn't erase the hurt and anger, however. I didn't know what could.

Kaldur inclined his head.

"Come," he said, drawing my hand into his. He pulled me back toward the keep. "I have a healer on the way. And you need to eat, not stand in the chill."

"A healer?"

"Ekor," he said. "The best in Vyaan. He'll attend to you during the pregnancy and check in regularly to make sure both of you are healthy."

"Oh," I said softly. "All right."

That was…thoughtful.

"But before you see him, I want you to eat. You look like you haven't been," came his gruff grumble.

"I could say the same about you," I mumbled. He looked better this morning but not quite the Kaldur I remembered. My blood had helped last night, but…if what he'd said was true, that he hadn't fed from another, then it had been *weeks* since his last true feeding.

I knew that Kylorr could survive off food alone, but blood was still a vital part of their nutrition, particularly for full-blooded Kylorr.

Kaldur pulled up short. "It was difficult when you were gone, Erina," he admitted quietly. "But my appetite will return now that you're here. I hope yours does too."

I inclined my head and admitted, "I…I hadn't been taking the best care of myself."

There had simply been too much to do, and I'd been worried about stretching my credits.

"That ends now," he said. "For both of us. I had Saira make a batch of your favorite bread. She's prepared a full course, and I won't let you leave the table until you've had nearly all of it."

"You're extremely high-handed, do you know that?" I grumbled, simply because I didn't know what else to say. No one had ever cared if I'd taken my meals or not. The sudden attention was…odd. Nice, but odd.

Kaldur threw me a small grin over his shoulder as the keep grew closer and closer. The grin made my heart stop clean in my chest, small and secretive and meant just for me.

Stop, I ordered myself. *Never again will I risk my heart with him.*

"You have no idea how high-handed I can be. But you'll learn soon enough."

I didn't know whether to be scared or intrigued.

CHAPTER 35
—
KAIDUR

The two sharp raps sounded on my study door.

"Come in."

Maudoric appeared. She held the door open for the keeper I'd been waiting for, who appeared hesitant as she stepped into the room.

"You wished to see me, *Kyzaire*?" came Velle's voice after she cleared her throat.

"Yes," I said, though I stayed seated at my desk.

The silence stretched out as I regarded her, and eventually she approached the curved edge of my desk after casting an uncertain look at Maudoric, lingering near the door.

My gaze went to my Head Keeper, who inclined her head briefly.

So she had it, I thought, my lips pressing tight, trying to keep the anger locked away. It had been pushing itself to the surface much too easily and readily this last month. I had to relearn keeping it controlled, though I would admit Erina's presence certainly helped. Simply knowing she was in Vyaan, in my keep helped tremendously.

"You used to work for House Azola, did you not?" I asked.

Velle's lips parted and said slowly, "Yes, a long time ago."

"How long ago?" I asked, sliding my elbows across my desk, pinning her with a piercing look to keep her in place. "Humor me."

"I...I would say four years ago now."

"And how long did you work there?"

"Briefly," she said.

"How long?" I asked, my tone clipped.

"Five months, *Kyzaire*."

"So how is it that you work in House Azola for a mere five months, a handful of years ago, and yet you have more loyalty to that House than you do to mine, where you have worked for years and been treated well?"

Velle's expression looked stricken. I thought she might've finally realized what this meeting was about.

I stood from my desk then. My wings threatened to flare, but I kept them tightly tucked, though they twitched with the effort as I rounded my desk to stand in front of her.

She stumbled back a few steps. "I am loyal to your House, *Kyzaire*."

"What did Lydrasa offer you?" I asked.

Erina had had a serpent of a friend in this keeper...then again, I'd had one in Lydrasa.

"She didn't offer me anything," Velle said. "*Kyzaire*, I don't know what this is about. Please, I—"

"What's going on?" came a familiar voice from the open door. My thunderous glare flashed up, only to meet Erina's wary eyes. She must've heard the rising voices.

Erina looked from Maudoric to Velle to me. I hadn't seen her since the healer had attended to her this morning. She'd gone to her rooms to rest, saying that she'd been more fatigued than usual. It appeared she was just waking and had likely been on her way to find food in the kitchens.

"*Kyzaire*?" she prompted, and I nearly growled. I would need to speak with her about that. Even among company, my blood mate had no duty to use my title when she spoke to me.

"I'm merely asking Velle here a question," I replied. "A question that would help answer the mystery of why she helped forge a letter in my hand and sent it to my pregnant *kyrana* in Laras."

Erina didn't look surprised, but she did step into the room, her eyes sweeping over her friend. Had she already figured that out? Why hadn't she voiced her suspicions?

If Velle was surprised to see Erina returned, she didn't show it. At least until her gaze landed on my mate's growing belly. Then I saw her jerk in surprise.

"Did you do that?" Erina asked softly.

Velle's gaze swung around to me. "No, you don't understand. I—"

"I believe she asked you that question," I answered, tilting my head toward my mate.

The keeper dragged in a sharp breath and turned to look at her supposed friend. "You don't understand."

"Then help me understand," Erina said quietly. She was much too patient, I realized. More patient than I would ever be. "What happened? You saw my letter come here, and then what?"

Maudoric reached out to squeeze Erina's arm, as if in apology. She took her duties seriously here, and it was likely she felt responsible for what had happened.

Velle's shoulders sagged. "We thought you were lying."

Erina jerked. "Lying? About the baby?"

"Yes."

"You and Lydrasa?" she asked to confirm.

Velle inclined her head with a tight jaw.

"You know me, Velle," Erina said quietly, staring at her once friend. "You think I would be capable of everything you told him? You think I would lie to try to get *money*?"

"Lydrasa convinced me that you were lying," Velle said. "She said she had reports in Laras, that you were desperate for credits.

She thought it was a ploy to get the *Kyzaire's* attention again after he had already rejected you."

"But you believed her?"

"I don't know what I believed," she admitted. "It didn't sound like something you'd do but...I know how desperation feels. I know that sometimes you do things out of desperation that might not be true to who you are."

"And is that why you did this?" Erina asked. "Because you felt *desperate*? Why? Because Lydrasa was threatening to take away your noble? The one she secured for you after you helped to drive me away from this keep? Or did you do it because you're just a cruel person who wanted me to fail?"

Velle's face twisted up. She stared at Erina in silence, an uncomfortable one that reverberated around the entire room.

"I don't believe you're a cruel person, Velle," my mate said softly. "But you only care about yourself. I don't blame you. I know how you grew up. It's self-preservation, isn't it?"

I studied Erina. She was more forgiving than I could ever be too, I realized. Because if *anyone* did that to me, I'd be sure to make it hurt. I would twist the dagger as I slid it out.

Selfishly, I was glad Erina was forgiving. Because what chance did *I* have to win her back if she wasn't?

None.

"I saw the letter come in, addressed to the *Kyzaire*," Velle said quietly, her shoulders sagging. "I read it and brought it to Lydrasa. She told me that if I ever heard news of you to let her know. She fears what your presence means here."

Fears she'd already addressed with me.

"Go on," I ordered, my tone cold, making Velle jump slightly.

"It was Lydrasa's idea to forge the letter. She had different correspondences from you, *Kyzaire*. With your signature. She easily replicated it, copied your handwriting. And she did send the credits to the account."

"As a payoff," I said.

Velle nodded. "To keep Erina away. And it was my job to be on the lookout for more letters, if they came to the keep."

Which Erina never would've sent, I knew. Because she'd thought I'd denied her pregnancy and rejected her.

Gods. What a fucking disaster.

Velle and Lydrasa had nearly cost me my mate and my child.

No, I realized next, setting my jaw tight. They'd only made Erina mistrust me more than she already had.

I *would've* found Erina in Laras, or anywhere she'd gone within the Kaalium. I wouldn't have stopped until I found her again, and I would've learned the truth regardless.

But to know that Erina had been scared and in trouble, that she had reached out to me when she'd learned of the child…that made me want burn down the entirety of House Azola.

Even though I couldn't.

Lydrasa was nearly untouchable, and she knew it. But I would handle her later.

Erina met my eyes from across the room. She was still standing in line with Maudoric, looking calm. Sad but calm. Accepting.

I'd had her all wrong, hadn't I?

I thought it very likely that she might just be the kindest soul I knew. Instead I'd made her a manipulative villain in my mind.

But I was not so kind as Erina.

"I want you gone," I said, keeping my voice even as I looked at Velle. She began to cry, fat tears dripping from her eyes, but I wasn't swayed by the theatrics. "You are not welcome in my keep again."

"Please, *Kyzaire*, I will never do—"

"Enough," I growled, glaring down at her. "It's clear where your loyalties lie. To think that House Azola had their own little spy within my own keep is enough of an offense against me. But to go after my *kyrana*, my child…that is unforgivable. Go back to them. Given your devotion to their House, I'm sure they'll take you back with haste. But you have no place here in mine."

Velle looked stricken, with a stream of tears running down her face. Even I knew that a dismissal from House Kaalium would darken her reputation as a keeper. If House Azola didn't take her back, then she likely wouldn't be able to find work within a noble House again.

I wouldn't give her the satisfaction of even thinking about her again once she left this office. But Lydrasa...I would make her remember what she'd done for years.

"Erina," she whispered. Pleading with my mate now? I barely held back my growl. "Please. This is my home."

Erina looked at her old friend steadily. I knew it might've hurt, but it needed to be done. I would not have poison flowing through my house, waiting to strike again.

"Like I told you the morning I left," Erina said, "I hope you have a good life with your noble."

For Erina's sake, however, I said to Maudoric, "Get her set up at an inn in town. She can stay there until the end of the month to find work." I met Velle's eyes again. "But that's the last I'll do for you. Go."

Velle's breath hitched and she stumbled out of the room. Erina stepped aside, out of her path, and the keeper disappeared down the hallway, presumably to pack up her room.

Maudoric approached me. From her apron pocket, she pulled out a letter, written on thin paper.

"I found it in her room," she said. Evidence enough.

I inclined my head, and Maudoric left, giving Erina's arm another touch as she passed.

Then it was just me and my mate in the study. The sunlight shone brightly through the arched window, but I couldn't help but think of the night we'd last been in here together.

You're not anything like I'd hoped you be, she'd told me.

I nearly flinched, remembering the words. I'd been so cold that night to her, so detached.

"Is that it?" she asked, gesturing toward the letter held between two of my fingers.

I looked down at the script. Neat and tidy. It was addressed to me, the seal broken.

To Kaldur of House Kaalium, Kyzaire of Vyaan.

I held it out for her, but she shook her head. "You can read it if you'd like. The words were meant for you anyway."

My brow furrowed, but I slipped my finger below the paper and unfolded it.

It was short, I noticed. To the point.

Kaldur,

I went to a healer today in Laras. His blood test revealed that I'm pregnant. The child is yours. It could be no one else's, despite what you think of me. The healer estimates I'm four weeks along, but I know that I'm nearly five.

My jaw gritted tight. She knew because it had only happened once, obviously. The night we'd had sex, the night I'd left her.

The night I'd taken her virginity and hadn't even known it, I thought, regret nearly making me shred the delicate paper with my curling claws.

You deserve to know. I would never keep this from you, but I admit that I'm scared, Kaldur. I don't know what I should do.

I am staying at Ikrin's Inn in the South Dock

District of Laras. You can write to me here, and I'll wait for your reply.

She'd signed her name, a beautiful little swirl of a signature. One I imagined her practicing as a child, over and over again.

I stared down at the letter and then read it again.

I didn't know how I should feel about it, but I felt strangely angered. "You didn't ask for money," I said.

She blinked. "You're...you're angry about that?"

I blew out a rough breath, her words already committed to memory. I folded the letter carefully and placed it on my desk. I had a feeling by the end of the night, it might be destroyed by how many times I would open and close it, to read it again.

"Had your credits already been stolen when you wrote that letter?" I asked.

She sucked in a small breath as I approached her by the door. Reaching past her, I closed it, allowing us privacy. I kept my arm up, boxing her against it as I stared down at her. Closer than I should be but nowhere close enough.

"You knew about that?" she asked. "How?

"Because I told you—I was there. I went to Ikrin's. I was asking people on the damn streets if they'd seen someone like you around. An older Kylorr male said there was a human female fitting your description living in his building in the South Dock District. The fucking *Dock District*, Erina."

"It...it was cheap," she protested, her cheeks heating.

"Gods," I rasped. "If anything had happened to you..."

I might never have known, I thought, and that realization was a sobering thought.

I breathed in deeply, trying to focus on her scent to keep the anger at bay. It calmed me down and I reached forward to clasp a small section of her dark red hair, rubbing the wild strands of it between my fingers.

"I found Ikrin's. He told me you'd been there. He told me about the theft. So I knew you had very little money," I said. "But you wrote to me without communicating the position you'd found yourself in. With very little credits to your name, working at a small inn, and sleeping in a drafty room in the Dock District."

"I'd had money until it was stolen," she argued, frowning up at me. "I was doing *fine* until that night. Getting a room at Ikrin's was only temporary, until I found a better job."

Hearing her speak about this didn't help my temper. Hearing her plans to try to make a better life for herself in Laras didn't help my temper.

And I'd put her in that position. I'd driven her to Laras. She'd been angry and proud enough to reject the money I'd given her.

"You should've asked for money," I growled.

"Why?" she said, glaring. "So it could cement who you thought I was in your mind?"

"You are pregnant with *my* fucking child, Erina," I hissed, my chest heaving.

We stared at one another. I could almost scent the rush of her blood beneath her skin, and venom flooded over my tongue. I hadn't meant to escalate this, but to think that she'd been in danger and that I could have helped her ate at me.

Her eyes dropped to my lips, and I felt the heat rise between us. I could hear her heartbeat. She might've hated me but she still desired me.

This wasn't about her not asking me for money. This was about *me* failing her so completely, and that dissipated any lust I felt in that charged moment.

It was another reminder of how I'd fucked everything up. And I was taking it out on her.

"This is my fault," I told her. Surprise flashed in her eyes when she moved them away from my lips. "I'm sorry. I'm getting angry over a hypothetical. I never would've gotten the letter anyway, even if you had asked for help."

"I did ask you for help," she said. "Just not the kind you're used to giving. I wanted to *talk* to you."

I flinched. She was right. When you were wealthy, you thought you could throw money at every problem and it would be fixed. In most cases, it was. Because people were inherently greedy.

I'd done it to Erina, even. That last night in my study. I'd smirked as I'd offered to make her my mistress, told her to name her price for her place in my bed.

I'd thought she would take it. In my arrogance, I'd thought everyone could be bought.

But not my *kyrana*.

My shoulders dropped. My head lowered too until I was bent forward, my forehead pressed into the crook of her neck—a comforting position because I could smell her so strongly. She floated in my head like *lore* smoke.

"Kaldur," she whispered.

I was careful of my horns, however. I didn't want to accidentally cut her.

"I only feel the need to protect you," I murmured. "I failed before. That's what I'm angry about. I failed so spectacularly that it's astonishing, and I can only blame myself."

I raised my head. Her expression was guarded, but I knew she was *listening*. Listening carefully to what I was saying.

"I want you to rely on me," I told her. "To lean on me if you need anything at all."

"Because you feel…guilty?"

I huffed out a breath. "Because I *need* to. I never understood what it meant to have a *kyrana*. A part of me, truthfully, detests it."

Her brow furrowed.

"Because suddenly, instantly, there's someone else in existence that can be your complete downfall," I told her. "I know you've been on your own for a long time, Erina. I just want you to know that you're not anymore."

Her expression morphed until it looked like I'd struck her. I saw the words sink in, as if she was just realizing it for herself, despite what our relationship currently was: one of mistrust and lingering bitterness.

"I know you don't trust me," I said. "But I'm not going anywhere, Erina. And I'll prove that to you every day until you believe me."

She looked unsure. And that was when I saw it.

I saw how desperately she *wanted* to believe me. That wonderment and hope in her eyes that had never quite left. There was a part of her that still had feelings for me, feelings I'd done my best to ignore or deny when she'd offered them to me once so willingly.

That was when I knew I had a chance with her still. Erina Denoren, with her open heart, was still there, as she had been before. Only now she was more guarded, a wall built up around her, one just like mine.

I only needed to break it down.

And then she might be mine again.

CHAPTER 36
—
ERINA

I couldn't sleep that night, tossing and turning long past midnight.

A hint of nausea crept up on me a few hours before dawn. When I'd thrown up the contents of my stomach, I decided to go make tea in the kitchens. Normally a keeper would be woken for such things, but I would never do that.

Kaldur's keep was quiet, everyone likely in their beds. I took one of the glowing Halo orbs from my room, and it followed me, lighting the way to the darkened kitchens, casting a golden glow on the looming walls.

When I pushed open the door, I was greeted by a familiar sight. A large yet cozy room, the stone floor having been freshly scrubbed, the stone hearth and oven on one side, neatly arranged with everything Saira would need come morning, and a long wooden table stretching down the center. Dark wood beams were overhead, hung with drying herbs and flowers and little ribbons that Saira's daughter tied whenever she came to visit.

On the far side of the kitchen lay another hearth, though it was rarely lit except in winter. It was usually more than warm enough in the kitchens from the oven. Next to it was a door that led out toward the North Terrace, where supplies where usually delivered.

I went to the stove and put on a small kettle for water, shoving fire fuel into the open door below before locking it closed. Soon, the griddle turned hot, starting to heat the water, and I went in search of the tea in Saira's stores. She'd made it for me yesterday, and I found it just where I'd remembered her putting it. A little blue tin that the healer, Ekor, had pushed over to me after my first visit with him.

I listened to the quiet of the kitchen, having not heard a peaceful quiet in a long time. Even in Laras, though I'd been alone most of the time, the noise from the city had always funneled its way past door and windows. And the city had always seemed to be alive, awake at all hours.

I'd missed the quiet, and so I savored it. After I poured my tea, I took it over to the table, trying to ignore the nausea rising. I blew on the surface of the water and took a sip, though it burned my tongue.

When I was half-finished with the mug, I felt my stomach begin to settle. I eyed yesterday's loaf of bread, still sitting in a basket along the range, and I got that too, digging out Saira's preserves from the small cellar, hoping she wouldn't mind.

With my loot, I returned to the table and happily munched on jam and sweet bread. It wasn't half bad even with the bitterness of my tea.

The door to the kitchens creaked open.

I shouldn't have been surprised when I saw it was Kaldur. We regarded one another from a distance. I wondered why he was up so late.

He seemed to be wondering the same thing until his gaze dropped to my haul on the table and I saw a small quirk of his lips. Stepping inside, he closed the door behind him.

I studied him as he gazed around the emptiness of the

kitchens, as if he'd never seen it before, though of course he had been here many times.

As if hearing my thoughts, he said quietly, "It's different without people. At night."

Moonlight filtered in from one of the windows along the North Terrace, next to the dark hearth. He slid onto the bench opposite me, leaning his forearms on the wide expanse of the table.

He knocked on it. "This has been here for centuries."

My brow raised, peering down at the table with new eyes. "Really?"

"It was a gift from the Kaazor, if you can believe it."

I nearly jolted. The Kaazor were our enemies to the north of the continent. Once, I knew, there had been peace between us. Now? That was an entirely different story.

What other surprises were riddled throughout this keep? I wondered, smoothing my hand over the black wood. Even that old, it was in incredible shape.

Far too many secrets and mysteries were hidden within these walls, I decided. The age of House Kaalium truly was awe-inspiring. And I felt out of my element, a stranger who was never supposed to belong.

"Why are you awake?" I asked, meeting his eyes. With the table between us, I felt myself relax. When he was too close, when I felt his touch…that was when the turmoil and confusion and longing began.

Yes, it was much better if he was out of arm's reach.

"I was in my study," he answered, "and caught scent of you."

I huffed out a small disbelieving laugh. "You tracked me? Like a *lyvin* in the woods?"

"I wanted to make sure you were okay," he answered. He dropped his gaze to my tea. "Were you not feeling well?"

"I couldn't sleep," I answered, sighing. "And then I started feeling nauseous, so…"

"You should have woken a keeper," he said. I shook my head, sighing. "Then find me instead if you're not feeling well."

"I wanted to come down here," I answered, looking around the kitchen. "It's rare to be here when no one else is. This place is the heart of your keep, you know."

Kaldur reached for a slice of my bread, already laden with jam. He popped it into his mouth, and I swallowed when some dribbled onto his lip, when his tongue flashed out and he licked it away. My belly tightened. But I breathed in slowly. Even after everything that had happened, I would always think he was the most handsome male I'd ever seen…and I hated that.

"It is quiet," he agreed. "It's nice."

I nodded. "Strangely, I kept thinking about this place when I was in Laras."

"Why?"

"I just remember it being so full of life. I think Saira goes mad with it sometimes, the poor thing. But I've spent nearly as much time at this table than anywhere else in the keep. It feels strange to realize that…especially since during daylight hours now, I don't feel so welcome here anymore."

"You're welcome to go anywhere you please," Kaldur answered, frowning. "No one can tell you otherwise. I've made that clear to the keepers."

My gaze flashed up to his. He'd told the keepers already?

"It's different though. You wouldn't understand. There's an unspoken rule among keepers, and I am no longer one. This is *their* place, as it has always been. But it's nice to sit in here and remember. I…I think I was quite lonely in Laras. Because I kept thinking about this kitchen."

Kaldur was looking at me. I had his full attention, I realized. I'd felt the same way once, that night with him in the library. A nice night, one I remembered fondly.

Though I wondered what he'd thought about me then. Had he

already been listening to Lydrasa? Had he already thought those terrible things about me?

And if he had, why had that night been so different?

Maybe…maybe he'd allowed himself to forget everything else, I thought, regarding him across the table. Maybe he'd been himself that night.

"What about Luc?" he wondered. I smoothed my finger over my teacup, over a dulled chip. "Weren't you with him in Laras?"

I shook my head. Thinking about the afternoon with Luc in Kyndri's Landing…it still stung. It still made my heart throb dully, remembering how different he'd been.

The Luc I'd known was gone.

But maybe…with Kaldur's offer to replace what had been taken from him, maybe some of the old Luc could come back. Maybe not all, but some.

"I didn't know how to find Luc," I said. "I saw him out of a window one day, and it was by pure chance."

"How long had it been since you saw him last?"

A small scoff of a laugh tumbled out of me. "Nearly ten years."

Kaldur made a sound. "That long?"

"I hadn't seen him since he left Wrezaan's," I said quietly, remembering that day at the transport depot. I'd been excited for Luc…but I'd also been inconsolable with despair. I'd tried to keep a brave face, but I knew it had hurt Luc to leave me behind, almost as much as it hurt me to go back to Wrezaan's, knowing he wouldn't be there.

"We wrote to each other a lot," I said. "He gave me that perfume bottle when he left. He told me by the time it was empty, we would be in Laras together."

Understanding flashed over Kaldur's face.

"So, yeah, maybe I used too much," I said quietly, shrugging a shoulder. "Because I wanted to see him again. It was stupid."

"It wasn't," Kaldur said. "It's never stupid to want to see someone again because you miss them. There are some people I wish I could see again, and I'd have bathed in that perfume if it meant I could."

"Like who?"

"My mother," he answered, the words a deep timber that melded beautifully with the quiet of the kitchen. "My aunt, Aina."

I was aware his mother had passed on into the next realm. Judging by the expression on his features regarding his aunt, I could only assume the same thing.

Not his father? I knew the head of House Kaalium hadn't been back to Krynn in years.

"But the beauty of it is that Luc is still in this realm," Kaldur finished. "Laras is not so far away."

"Yes, but the Luc I knew is gone," I confessed, lulled by the quiet. "He had once been so ambitious, so driven. Laras…that place beat him down. He told me he'd lied in his letters because he hadn't wanted me to know he'd failed. He didn't *want* to see me."

Kaldur's silver gaze was luminous in Halo orb's softened light. "He…turned you away?"

"I only saw him once when I was there. He wouldn't tell me where he lived. I couldn't find him again."

"I have people searching for him," Kaldur told me. "They'll find him eventually to make him the offer."

The one I'd bargained for.

"I just know he works at the docks," I said, nodding. "I went a couple times, but…they were a lot bigger than I thought."

"That's still helpful to know," he said. "I'll pass it along. And as for Syndras…she fought a little when a swarm of keepers showed up at her doorstep this afternoon."

I bit my lip, imagining the scene with the stubborn female. "I should've warned her."

"They explained. She told them that she expects your visit soon. To explain further."

"But she accepted them?" I asked.

Kaldur's gaze went to my finger, still smoothing over the teacup's edge, before he looked back to me.

"Eventually," he replied.

"Thank you," I said.

"No thank-yous," he said firmly.

I didn't argue. I didn't have it in me to argue. The change in Kaldur was still confusing to me. A part of me still didn't trust it. I didn't know if I ever could.

"I'm sorry about Luc," he finally said when a stretch of silence came. "That couldn't have been an easy thing to face, for someone you held out hope for as long as you did."

The words made my throat tighten.

"But after he has accepted the offer, I'll take you see him again," Kaldur added.

A sharp inhale whistled through me. "Really?"

"Once he's settled, he might be more like himself," he said. "Like I said, Laras isn't far away."

"I would like that," I admitted, trying to keep back my tears. "Very much."

That seemed to satisfy him. He leaned forward, taking more bread, slathering on more preserves. There was something almost boyish about the action, and I felt my guard slipping as a smile appeared.

"Hungry?" I asked, watching him take a large bite.

Then I stiffened a little at the flash in his eyes. His irises actually gleamed at the word.

I hadn't realized how *hungry* he truly was. But I should've known better.

It brought a flush swarming to my cheeks, remembering just how much I'd enjoyed his feedings. Luckily the darkness of the kitchen hid most of it, but he would likely still hear the quickening of my heartbeat.

Kaldur finished the bread. He had mercy on me and said, "I

forget time when I'm working. Sometimes I look up and realize it's nightfall and I hadn't eaten all day."

But I didn't want to skirt around the topic, I realized, listening to him. The old me might've. Because it was easier, because I'd been shy.

"How are your feedings going to work?" I asked. "If…if I'm your *kyrana*."

"Not 'if,'" he corrected. "You are."

"*Since* I'm your *kyrana*," I amended, holding his eyes.

That seemed to please him. He leaned in even further, his wide chest pressing into the solid wood of the table's edge. He slid his hand over the tabletop, toward my hand that was resting there.

I nearly shivered when his thumb brushed my inner wrist. Sparks prickled up my spine, like little fireworks that lit up the sky during the season of Gaara, the season of rebirth, of fertility, of spring.

"That's for you to decide," he finally said.

My brow furrowed, trying not to be distracted by his touch. But he was making small little sweeps of his thumb…and it felt nice to be touched.

"I meant…I meant in our contract," I said. "How many times a day should—"

A growl cut off the words. Soft, more of a warning than anything aggressive.

"No more contracts—I told you," he said.

I blinked.

"I told you it would be different this time," he added. "I meant it. Blood mates don't have contracts between them. I was the biggest fool in the Kaalium to even try."

"Then…when?" I asked.

He blew out a sharp breath. There was a tightness in his gaze that hadn't been there before.

"A feeding between mates should be like…sex," he answered. I stiffened, but his thumb never stopped in the slow, steady motion over my skin. "The feedings should come naturally."

There was a thread of panic in my voice when I said, "I—I don't want sex. That's not…"

Something flashed over his expression. Something I thought looked like guilt. Or dismay.

"I know," he said quietly, his voice soothing away the sudden rush of panic. I pulled my wrist away, and he leaned back, dragging his arms back toward himself, giving me space. "I feel like, lately, I have a lifetime of things to be sorry for when it comes to you."

I remembered that night in his quarters, when he'd been drinking and smoking *lore*. I remembered the burn of the amber liquor down my throat…and then the burn of desire from the spicy scent of the *lore* smoke, funneling and winding its way down my throat.

I remembered how much I'd wanted him that night. The ache, the need, the desperation curling down my spine. Because, perhaps even then, I'd both recognized that he'd needed a distraction from whatever had been bothering him—likely about me, I realized now—and also because I'd felt him pulling away. And I'd been desperate to keep him close. Because I'd thought I'd been falling in love with him.

I remembered the way he'd made me come with his touch between my legs, his kiss on my breasts.

He'd tried to send me away, and I'd come back to him. And when I had…

To me, our lovemaking had been frenzied, full of need and desire, and I'd felt like I couldn't get enough of him. I'd wanted his touch everywhere. I'd wanted his kiss everywhere. I'd wanted him to feed from me while he drove between my thighs, making me his.

To him, the sex had been "fine."

Remembering that word, remembering the conversation I'd

overheard between him and Lydrasa, made me want to shrivel up inside all over again.

On top of that, he hadn't believed me when I'd told him I'd been untouched, that I'd been a virgin that night.

That was what he'd thought of me. That I would lie about something like that. To try to manipulate him?

I felt myself retreating again, my walls building up around me, trying desperately to shut him away. Because if I let him in again, he would destroy me from the inside out.

I had to think about my child now. A rocky friendship with the father was better than hatred. I wanted to have a good relationship with him for the sake of our child, and especially since we would be in one another's lives *forever*…but I couldn't allow myself to fall in love with him.

Not again, not ever. I wouldn't survive it this time.

Kaldur stood, gracefully guiding himself over the bench. "Let me take you back to your room."

"No," I said quickly, not meeting his eyes. "I'd like to stay a little longer."

Kaldur lingered, looking like he was on the verge of saying something. Only the words never came.

"Good night, Erina."

He went to the door but paused at the threshold. I watched when his forehead pressed into the carved wood, and I heard him take in a deep breath.

Then he spun, striding back toward me.

"What you overheard that night in my study, with Lydrasa… that was a lie. Perhaps one of the worst I've ever told."

My heart skipped. I stared up at him. He splayed his hands on the table, leaning toward me so that I had no choice but to meet his gaze. It was nearly a glare, but I knew that anger wasn't directed at me.

"What a fucking laughable word for what we had that night.

Fine," he growled, no humor in his voice. "*Fine.* That word will haunt me, and it should."

"Kaldur—"

"The truth is that I fucking *burned* for you," he told me, his voice quiet and low and deathly serious. Every word in that sentence was clipped, as if he wanted me to understand each and every one. To make his meaning clear. "I have never desired someone as much I desired you that night, Erina. And I hated it. I *hated* that you could have that much control over me."

My heart was beating so fast in my chest that it felt like a caged animal.

"So no, it was not *fine*, Erina," he continued. "It was soul crushing because at that time, I thought you were just using me, that you loved someone else. I gave into you because I had never wanted you more. It was *fucking* sexy—the way you opened up for me, the way you felt around me. All your sounds and moans… I wanted to bottle them up all for me. That night will always be burned in my memory because of it. *Raazos's blood,* I get hard just thinking about it," he growled.

I nearly gasped, his words feeling like they were drowning me, pulling me deeper and deeper.

"So you need to know that because I can see it in your eyes. Right now. You believe that I don't desire you, and you couldn't be more wrong about that. You are the *only* woman I desire now. Just as I know these are just more words to you. But in time, you'll see how serious I am about this."

"You…you really haven't been with anyone else?" I whispered. He'd told me he hadn't fed from anyone else, but I'd just assumed…

"No," he rasped. "My body has been fucking *dead* since you left. I don't want anyone else."

How many times had I dreamed of Kaldur saying this to me? Only in my wildest of imaginings.

Of course, in my mind they'd been a soft confession, a romantic one, and not quite so harsh, rough.

But I thought that this felt *real*. Raw and vulnerable. I realized…I wouldn't want it any other way.

"I wish I could open up my mind to you, so that you would know I was telling the truth," he confessed. "So that you would know I'm not a lying bastard, just trying to get you into my bed again."

I couldn't take my eyes off him. I felt a strange sensation in my belly, a fluttering. Like my body was waking to him.

"Which, just to be clear, I fully intend to do," he admitted. I nearly laughed, but I didn't think I could utter a single sound right then. "I might not be a lying bastard, but I am a selfish one. So fair warning, Erina…I do intend for you to be in my bed—*our* bed—again, and then I'll do everything in my power to keep you there for good. Do you understand?"

His expression was thunderous, the intensity in his eyes magnetic. He was waiting for my answer, and I tried to make my tongue remember how to form words.

"Yes," I finally whispered, "I understand."

He exhaled a long slow breath, finally standing to his full height, not looming over the end of the table. I would be lying if I said I wasn't affected by his words, by his promise.

I wondered if it was possible to give into someone sexually while keeping one's heart safe.

I didn't know if that possible, especially for someone like me.

That fluttering returned to my belly, and I gasped.

"*Dallia?*" Kaldur asked quickly, rounding the table to stand near me. He crouched until we were eye level. "What's wrong?"

"I felt it move," I whispered, looking down at my rounding belly. "Right here. Ekor said I might feel it soon, but I—"

I pressed just below by belly button, a surge of emotion welling up in me.

It was silly, but it *finally* hit me that I was pregnant. Logically,

I knew that. But I'd been so emotionally drained in Laras, and upon my return to Vyaan, that I hadn't really *felt* it for myself.

"Oh gods," I whispered, a rush of tears falling my eyes. "I'm pregnant. I felt the baby."

Kaldur pulled me into him as I began to sob, the strong wave of realization, of fright, of relief, of awe drowning me beneath it. I'd bottled up my tears for so long that they just came pouring out of me so forcefully it was jarring. This was more than the acceptance that I was pregnant, however. It was also Kaldur's confession. It was all the emotions I'd kept wrapped around me like armor.

"I'm sorry," I whispered against him, my face pressed into his chest.

"Don't," he said, his hand coming to hold the back of my neck, his other going around my waist. I felt it rest on my side, his fingertips skimming over the bump. The warmth of his hand felt comforting, even through my nightdress. "It's all right. I'm here."

A part of me hated that he was like this. That one moment he could make me burn and the next he was a strong column of support to lean on.

Maybe I wasn't wrong about him, I thought. And that thought only made me cry harder.

"It's okay, *dallia,*" he whispered, his hand resting on our growing child. "I'll take care of you both. I promise."

CHAPTER 37
—
ERINA

The week that followed was a blur of activity, and it passed by more quickly than I realized.

Ekor came to visit me a couple more times at Kaldur's insistence, the Bartutian a quiet male with sharpish features and an imposing bulk. He rarely said anything, but when he spoke, I *really* listened, mesmerized by his soft voice. He had a patience about him that put me at ease.

Kaldur was always standing nearby during those visits, his arms crossed over his chest, watching Ekor and me closely. On his second visit of the week, when Ekor had lifted my top to reveal my growing belly, Kaldur had seemed struck for a moment. I'd caught him studying where our child was growing inside me, a peculiar expression on his face. One that I thought might be awed or frightened or determined—I couldn't be certain.

I *was* growing at an alarming rate. My joints ached though the nausea was finally beginning to wane, especially if I took my tea preemptively every morning as I got dressed. Maudoric showed up with a tray and a steaming cup every morning at my door.

Ekor assured Kaldur and me that the growth rate was to be

expected for a hybrid pregnancy. And it relieved *both* of us to know that the child was strong and healthy with no complications. Yet.

The morning after our night in the kitchens, a guard had been assigned to me. A Kylorr female, whose name was Braanelle, a soldier at the very top of the ranks within Vyaan's army, or so I'd been told upon introduction. I couldn't tell if she was pleased with her new position as my personal guard or not. Her expression was always the same: neutral but stern.

Her black hair was always pulled back in a tight braid, making her ears appear even sharper, her horns ramrod straight from her head, like twin daggers.

I'd commented on her horns during a stroll in the garden once, telling her I'd never quite seen horns like hers, that they were beautifully unique.

Her response?

"Makes it easier to kill," she'd replied, running a hand over one in what I thought was appreciation.

I couldn't tell if she was joking or not...but that was the last I'd mentioned her horns.

But Braanelle took her job very seriously, her eyes constantly sweeping the areas I'd walked into, whether it was the quiet gardens or the village square. Her hand was perpetually resting on the hilt of a blade, tucked into the sheath at her hip.

As for Kaldur, he seemed utterly overjoyed with his choice of a guard, even though I had my reservations, considering I didn't know what harm could fall on me in the gardens, which was where I spent most of my time. But for her part, Braanelle gave me my privacy, keeping a far enough distance away. As the week dragged on, I started to forget she was there.

So, I was healthy and protected, just as Kaldur had wanted. But even though I took my notebook and my pencils with me everywhere I went—more of a habit now than anything—I still hadn't worked on my stories or drawings once. Not for over a month now, and the lull was beginning to worry me.

When I wasn't in the garden, I was usually in the village, though I made sure to wear my bulkiest dress and apron, overlaid with a sturdy coat. It wouldn't be much longer until I wouldn't be able to hide the pregnancy, but for now, I did what I could. Kaldur hadn't said anything about announcing it yet, and I didn't want to be the subject of whispers and gossip.

For the most part, I only caught a few interested stares—from nobles—who had perhaps recognized me from the party that Kaldur had thrown.

Those days, I would bring spiced tea and steam cakes to Syndras and spend the afternoons in her sitting room, as Braanelle stood stock-still by the door, even declining the comforts of a steam cake.

Syndras, for her part, looked delightfully put out by the entirety of her new staff. The sitting room, I noticed, looked much changed since that night Kaldur had found me here. All the dust was gone, the air felt cleaner, and everything gleamed. I knew that if I explored the rest of her ancestral House, I would find much of the same thing. During our visits, one of the keepers often came into the sitting room with a tray laden with food for us. All of Syndras's favorites, I noticed, like marinated *laak* eggs and pillowy sandwiches spread with riverberry jam.

Syndras grumbled about it because of her pride. She'd accused me of giving into the *Kyzaire* for her sake, and I had to assure her that it hadn't been the case…mostly. We barely spoke about Kaldur during these visits. I thought she sensed that I didn't know what to say regardless, how to explain everything that had transpired between us or even the strange relationship that had sprung up lately.

The truth was that Kaldur and I were friendly. If he came to my balcony at night or found me in the gardens in the afternoon or came looking for me in the keep, we were always civil.

I didn't know if I was relieved or disappointed with our newfound relationship. It was easy to keep my walls up when we were just friendly. There wasn't a threat of anything more. But after that night in the kitchens, after everything he'd confessed to me and after he'd held me as I'd sobbed my heart out...it *had* felt different even though I'd done my best to ignore it.

Sometimes during our *friendly* moments, I would catch him studying me. Staring. *Really* looking at me as if it was the first time he was seeing me.

His leisurely studies always struck me as patient, as if he had all the time in the world to admire me. And he wouldn't seem to be in a huge rush to fill the silence that followed, except I felt every half second like a throb of my heart. I always grew shy, tucking my hair behind my ear, asking why he was looking at me like that.

He always said, *I'm just looking.*

But it felt like something more. It felt like he was committing me to memory, every strand of my hair, every pore on my face. To be studied so closely, it was a delightfully uncomfortable thing.

I'll stop, he would declare when he saw me shift. His eyes would gleam in amusement, his full lips twitching, and then he'd switch topics so expertly that it left me feeling a little dazed.

But as the week dragged on, I noticed more changes in Kaldur. His movements seemed slower, his face growing more shadowed, his cheekbones standing sharper.

I knew it was because he hadn't been feeding. He'd eaten, of course. He demanded that we have our morning meal together, and I watched him eat enough for a small army with my own two eyes.

But I hadn't realized how much a Kylorr *needed* blood. Some Kylorr, I knew, abstained from it completely. But that was easier if you were a hybrid or hadn't fed on a lot of blood throughout your life, like Luc.

For Kaldur? I imagined he felt the lack of feeding quite acutely, and I could actually see the physical toll it was taking on him.

He hadn't fed from me since that night he'd brought me to his bath, and even then it had only been briefly—a mere drop in comparison to what he usually took from me—to take the edge off his rage.

He had some strength from that feeding, but I'd watched it wane again. And I wondered…how had he gone nearly a month without my blood?

No wonder he'd nearly gone into a rage that night, I couldn't help but think.

That evening, I was sitting on a bench in the garden, the air growing chillier by the moment. But I'd returned from Syndras's an hour ago and hadn't wanted to return to the keep quite yet. I wanted to watch the sunset, and I took up post at one of the higher elevations, surrounded by beautiful blooms that smelled lightly floral but spicy. It was one scent, I found, that didn't turn my stomach, oddly.

When I felt a familiar flutter inside me, I pressed my hand to my lower belly.

"You've been quite active today, little darling," I said softly, a smile crossing my face just as I heard heavy footsteps approaching me on the path to my right.

"So have you," came Kaldur's voice.

I glanced over at him, not surprised to see him here. If I was in the garden past sundown, he usually came out to retrieve me before it got too cold. Him fussing over me…I couldn't lie and say I was indifferent to it. It felt nice to be fussed over.

Kaldur looked over at Braanelle, hidden partially behind a shrub. He nodded at her, and she inclined her head, dismissed from her duties for the evening.

"Good night, Braanelle," I called out.

"Rest well," she called back. I smiled at how it sounded like a threat. Everything she said sounded like a threat, truthfully, but I'd learned that it was just how she talked.

Kaldur stepped more fully into my view, standing before the bench to peer down at me.

"How are you?" he asked with the utmost seriousness. He dropped down, crouching until he was eye level. His hands reached for me. Well, not quite for *me* but rather for the baby.

His hands smoothed over the rounding bump, and I ignored the little quiver inside me. Kaldur, I'd discovered, was a lover of touching. He'd often brush his fingers across my cheek or tuck back strands of my hair or place his palm on the small of my back or loosely at my hip when we were walking together.

And with the baby…he was even more so.

It had taken me a few days, but now I was used to it. Before, when I'd been merely his blood giver, I'd had the impression he'd done everything he could to *not* touch me, to keep himself apart.

I couldn't help but wonder how often he'd been in his head whenever we'd been together. *All the time,* I'd finally decided. He'd gone against his natural instinct to be close to me.

Now? There was no reason to, except when it came to my own comfort.

His hand skimmed over my belly. "I wish I could feel what you do."

"Soon I think you'll be able to feel her," I said.

Kaldur stilled. He looked up at me, those mirrored eyes watchful. "Her?"

I felt my cheeks heat a little at his sudden scrutiny. "Just a feeling."

His grin started slow, those eyes never leaving mine. I always felt like I was holding my breath when he looked at me like that.

"How…how would you feel about that?" I wanted to know.

In many ways, females were more valuable to the Kylorr than males. There weren't as many of them within the population, their births rarer. Compared to Kaldur's four other brothers, he only had one sister.

Kaldur finally said, "Kalia was born last, and so by then, she had all of us to protect her. We were a bit of a terror, truthfully. Overprotective. It drove her mad."

A small smirk from memory came. Then his expression went serious.

"It scares me…for a daughter to come first." Seeing my frown, he quickly said, "Don't misunderstand me. A daughter is a great blessing, one not many Kylorr get to experience. Would I prefer at least one or two males to come before her, so that they could watch over her as we did with Kalia? Yes."

Oh. I understood now.

He continued, his palm skimming higher on my belly, "But if a daughter comes first, then I will be more protective until her brothers come later."

I nearly gasped at what went unspoken. With those eyes burning into me, he was implying that…that…

I hadn't given much thought to what would happen *after* the birth. What our relationship would be like.

But Kaldur obviously had.

He was presumptuous and charmingly determined—I would give him that. One side effect of being pregnant, I'd learned, was that I was distractingly and annoyingly aroused at nearly every opportunity. Kaldur being in such close proximity and always around was becoming an issue.

So I would be lying if I said the thought of bearing him sons *didn't* send a tantalizing zing of want through me.

I'd always wanted a large family. A home filled with children and a husband, who I loved dearly.

Once, it had been easy to imagine with Kaldur. I'd had daydreams of children running through these gardens as Kaldur chased them overhead, his laugh echoing across the sky.

But that was what it'd been…a daydream. And I was trying

not to have as many of those because I'd learned that they could be more hurtful than helpful.

Then again, it was perhaps why I hadn't been inspired about *anything*. I felt like I'd closed off a vital part of myself...or it had been lost somewhere.

"You do know that I'll take care of you, don't you?" Kaldur asked. He frowned. "I know I didn't before...but you never have to worry again. Or worry for our daughter."

I knew he meant it. My heartbeat was going too fast. He was getting too close, making me feel like I used to. I couldn't afford that.

Panic rose. I said, "Guess I *did* choose the right male to get me with child."

But the moment it left my lips, I regretted it. Especially when I saw him flinch, his jaw tightening, a flash of guilt stab into his eyes.

I supposed I did still harbor resentment. A lot of it.

"Erina—"

I was ashamed enough to blurt out, "I'm sorry. I shouldn't have—"

"No," he rasped, his gaze dropping to the shadowed notch of my throat, gaze unfocused, as if he was remembering his ugly words, as if they echoed in his head on a loop. "I deserved that."

I'd thought it would make me feel better...to *see* his guilt and regret.

But it didn't.

My shoulders sagged, tears welling up in my eyes. His hands left my stomach, and I felt a rush of cold air flood in to replace them. I felt the loss. I felt him pull back, pull away, and I cursed that small part of me that had *wanted* to hurt him.

"You're healing," he said finally. "It's only natural that these wounds rise to the surface. Truthfully, I deserve a lot more of your anger and you've been more gracious than anyone I know."

It spliced my heart in two to realize he was *willing* to take any malice that I could give him, as if that was part of his punishment, his penance. That he expected it.

But he was wrong. It didn't fill me with any satisfaction. Just the opposite in fact.

This can't happen again, I thought. No, I *decided.*

Why continue to punish him, to make little digs to try to hurt him as much as he hurt me, when it was *my* choice that I was here?

After all, my future was still *mine* to decide. I would share our child, of course, but just because I was pregnant didn't mean I had to share my *life* with Kaldur.

Once, I would've given anything for that reality to come true.

Now? I didn't know what I wanted.

But just knowing that I was in control made me feel more at peace.

"It won't happen again," I told him firmly. "I'm sorry."

The resentment would eat away at me. I wasn't going to let that happen.

Kaldur's blew out a sharp breath. He shook his head, looking at me like I was a stranger he was trying to understand, to piece together. "You really are a pure soul, aren't you? I don't understand it sometimes. Then again, I'm a worse person than you."

"I don't want..." I trailed off when my throat tightened. "Growing up, I lived in a place where all I saw was resentment. And bitterness. I understood it too, because what child would *choose* to be parentless? What child wouldn't be angry at sharing a room with dozens of other children, who all had stories and secrets and tragedies of their own? And when children are hurt, they like to hurt others. Because it *feels good* to make others suffer like you, so you're not alone anymore. And at Wrezaan's, we all felt alone.

"And I...I was lucky because I had Luc, who wasn't like any of the others there. He helped me understand that I could choose to be like the others *or* I could a different life. A better one. And I chose differently. I've seen what resentment can do to people. A lot of those children just turned out to be miserable beings. Some didn't, but a lot did."

Kaldur's gaze was knowing. "That's why seeing Luc in Laras hurt you."

"Yes," I said, my shoulders lowering. "Because he'd turned out just like many others had. And it broke my heart. A part of me wondered if there was any point, if I should give up like him too."

Panic flared through Kaldur's gaze, his wings lifting.

"But I didn't," I said. And I was proud of that. "I still want to be who I'd *chosen* to be, all those years ago."

Kaldur's expression nearly broke my heart all over again. It was an intense thing, one that made me hold my breath, the world sliding to a stop around us.

And it became clear to me that I still cared about him, deeply. That wasn't a terrible thing, to care for someone.

But it still made me feel a little heartbroken. My heart felt like a jagged thing, trying to stitch itself back up.

"How did your stories play into this?" he wanted to know.

That dragged a soft smile from me, despite my other musings. "I thought that maybe I could help give the children something nice, a distraction, an escape. We were taught how to read and write, but I was one of the only ones who enjoyed the lessons," I said. "So I started practicing by writing down stories. Luc helped me come up with them too when I was stuck. Together, we created Kavelyn's adventures, and I read a portion of what I'd worked on every night to the others. Well, the ones who wanted to hear. Those were nice moments."

"It made the children happy?"

"Some of them," I said. "As for the drawings…Wrezaan had this landscape painting on the wall of our room. And I *loved* that painting. I would stare at it all night, and it was the first thing I'd see in the morning. My bed was right across from it."

"What was it of?"

"A meadow," I told him. "The sky was so big and pink. The hills were rolling with wildflowers. I wanted to create places like that in my mind. So I copied that painting…*hundreds* of times. Then I practiced and practiced more. I began to draw Kavelyn, of alien places she would go to in the stories. Of people she met. The children loved the drawings more than the stories sometimes."

"I haven't seen you with your notebook in a while," Kaldur commented.

I tried not to let my worry show when I said, "I've, um, been feeling a little lost lately. I don't feel like creating anymore. Or, at least, not right now."

I saw the brief flit of dismay over his face.

Then…

Kaldur leaned forward, his hand cupping my cheek. It happened quickly yet slowly. The soft press of his lips against mine.

It wasn't meant to be sexual. It felt more like an embrace, a comfort, and I sighed into his lips. He kissed me again, brushing his bottom lip against my top one, and then again, this time across my cheek. His next kiss was on my nose, the next on my forehead, and then he *was* embracing me.

"I know you'll find it again," he told me, soft determination in his voice.

I allowed myself to sink into it, to enjoy his warmth even as my heart fluttered wildly. I didn't have it in me to fight, and I remembered what I'd realized. Everything was *my* choice, whatever I chose to give to him.

And right then? He gave me his comfort, and I gave him mine right back.

There was another comfort I could give him too.

"I'm worried about you," I confessed softly, feeling his steady heart thump against my breast.

"Me? Why?" he rasped.

"You need to feed," I said. "I can see what it's doing to you."

Kaldur pulled back. His eyes flitted back and forth between mine. "This moment isn't about that."

"So you don't deny it?" I asked. "You've been growing weaker because you won't come to me to feed. Don't think I haven't noticed."

"I didn't think you wanted it," he said.

I held up my wrist between us. "I think you need to. It's been too long."

Kaldur's gaze went down my wrist, his expression exploding with want and hunger. He breathed in deeply.

"Please," I whispered.

"Do you pity me, *dallia?*" he asked, his voice guttural. He forced his eyes away from my wrist, and I saw his eyes were darker—a deep gray that was almost black. He shook his head, a brief smile flitting across his features. "No, I'm not to be pitied. And that's what this would be."

"It's not—" I started to argue, frowning, but then he stood.

He turned from me briefly, and I stared at his back. When he faced me again, the hunger had faded from his expression, though the lines around his mouth seemed tight.

"Let's return to the keep," he suggested. "It's getting cold."

He helped me stand, as if I was a day away from giving birth. But our interaction still bothered me, and I couldn't put my finger on why.

A pity feeding? That had nothing to do with this.

"You said you won't feed from anyone else. That leaves just me, Kaldur. I don't pity you. I just don't want you to suffer needlessly. You're *hungry*—I can see it. Despite what happened between us…it doesn't mean I don't care about you," I told him.

"Care?" he repeated gently, tipping my chin up, his thumb brushing underneath my jaw. Then he leaned forward, pressing his lips there in another small kiss, as if to say he wasn't stung by the interaction. That it was okay. "I think I had your entire heart once, didn't I?"

That same heart thudded in my chest as my lips parted. I felt those whispered words against my skin and nearly closed my eyes as the answer flitted through my mind.

Yes, I thought. *You did.*

"And I was clumsy with it," he concluded. "Careless. I had it once, and I didn't even know it until it was too late."

"You had the heart of a girl who didn't know better," I told him, keeping my voice light when he pulled back to look at me. "It was an innocent love. It didn't mean much."

"And still, I want it back," Kaldur replied simply, his eyes gleaming. "Because then I could nurture it. Care for it and grow that love as I should have."

I didn't know what to say. My tongue felt like heavy *drava* metal in my mouth.

Kaldur's smile was knowing, a little sad, even.

"Thank you for offering your blood, my *dallia,*" he said. "But I think feeding right now would mean something different to me than it would to you. You're not ready—you might never be. I understand. But this is my choice."

My shoulders sagged. Too many words were jamming up into my throat that they were getting stuck. I didn't know *how* to explain what I felt to him.

"Let's go back. You need to eat," he said.

So do you, I thought.

But I followed him regardless.

CHAPTER 38

KALDUR

That night, after I'd made sure that Erina ate a hearty dinner, I received word of a potential *lyvin* pack—again—along the outer villages. And so I left to meet with the soldiers I'd dispatched.

The village, ironically enough, was where Erina had grown up. Wrezaan's abandoned orphanage lay on the outskirts, and I flew over it on my way to the edge of the forest.

It was mostly farmers in these outer villages, taking advantage of the sprawling fields and land that rippled outward. As such, they abutted the forests. *Lyvins* weren't common in this area, but I feared that the construction of the South Road was pushing them inward toward the main towns instead of farther away. I'd received more and more reports of them in the last two months, encroaching on new territories and becoming aggressive when a villager strayed too close.

Luckily no one had been hurt yet, but I feared it was only a matter of time. And the villagers didn't want protective fences along the forest's edge—they thought it clashed too much with the natural beauty of their land.

That night, the *lyvins* were long gone by the time I reached the village, though I could still hear their hair-raising howls echo in the forest. I spoke with the soldiers briefly and ordered three of them to keep posted there through the night as a precaution.

Then I left. But as I flew over the orphanage, curiosity got the best of me, and I circled overhead before landing at the front entrance. It was an old manor-style house, dark in color with gray tinted windows.

I frowned, unable to imagine Erina here. When I went inside, the wood floors creaked under my weight. The choking layers of dust made my lungs squeeze tight, but I explored the old house, peering into the different rooms. It was smaller than I'd thought it'd be.

Stricter laws had been passed within the Kaalium for orphanages a decade before. Wrezaan's hadn't passed inspections and had been shut down, the remaining children sent to a newer one on the opposite side of Vyaan, one more closely regulated by the council.

I went upstairs, though some of the wood steps had disintegrated. They'd likely been old already when Erina *had* lived here, and knowing that only made that restlessness prowl in my body again.

In one of the back rooms, the largest of them, I saw dusty old cots lining both sides. A single window was at the far end of the room, one that would overlook the front of the house. The entirety of the room was cleared out except for the cots and a few mounds of what I thought might've been old, disintegrating clothes.

That was when I saw it.

A dirty painting, hanging precariously by a single nail in the wall, tilted haphazardly as if it used to hang by two.

The glass was covered in a thick smearing of dust, but I wiped it away with the back of my sleeve. Through the thin clearing I'd made, I saw a landscape. Of a pink sky and hills.

My heart twisted in my chest. I looked behind me, at the cot that lay across from it, and I went there. The quilt was thick, though coated with dust. The pillow was thin, and I imagined my *kyrana* lying here, her young eyes pinned on the painting across the way as she drifted to sleep.

I sat on the cot, my hands coming to my face, and rubbed at my eyes. Life had disappointed her. Over and over again. She'd remained hopeful and optimistic throughout it all...by *her* choice, I'd learned today. Knowingly.

It made her stronger than I'd ever realized.

Except...I might've been the one to have finally broken her.

No, I decided, my bleary gaze going back to the painting on the opposite wall. *Not broken, just tilted.*

I wanted to help put her right again. I wanted to help put the light back into her eyes because it had been dim since she'd returned from Laras. Did she even realize?

I didn't know how long I stayed in the room, but eventually I stood, my bones aching. I *was* hungry—she'd been right. Weaker. I didn't feel like myself.

Crossing to the opposite wall, I took the painting off the remaining nail. The wood frame nearly broke apart in my hands, but a plan formed. A gift I wanted to give Erina. Maybe it would spark her again. And I wanted nothing more than to ignite her, to bring her to life again.

With the painting firmly tucked against me, I left the decaying orphanage. It would rot here, consumed by the land. Perhaps I'd have it destroyed. Perhaps I'd build something new here in its stead. An art house. A creative retreat. A museum. She would like that. Perhaps I'd dedicate it in Erina's name.

When I returned to the keep, I still felt restless and aching. It was a new kind of hellish punishment to have my mate so near and feel like I *shouldn't* go to her.

I tucked the painting safely in a corner of my quarters. I would get it reframed and begin work on Erina's gift in the morning. Even if it made her even a little delighted, it would be well worth it.

I bathed to try to calm my racing heart, but even in the warm pool I couldn't relax.

I paced my quarters. I smoked some *lore* out on the balcony, hoping the icy chill would dull my wanting. Nothing did, however, and I should've known that by now.

She was so close I could practically scent her through the walls.

Eventually I gave in, wondering if she would turn me away. I strode from my room and went down one set of doors to her quarters. For a moment, I leaned my forehead against the door, listening to my ragged heart.

When I pushed it open, the room was dark. I went to her bedroom, and immediately her scent swarmed my senses. All around me, like an embrace. My shoulders relaxed. It was like the best *lore* I could buy.

Erina was sleeping. When I walked to the opposite side of the bed, I studied her, her expression softened in dreams, and beneath the heavy blankets, I saw the roundness of her belly.

Safe, I thought. My throat went tight as tears threatened to prick my eyes.

I slid into bed beside her. I didn't want to wake her, but I wanted her in my arms, so it was inevitable.

She was startled awake though her eyelids were heavy. The only source of light was the silvery moon outside the balcony doors, and it crept over the blankets like crawling vines.

"Kaldur?" she asked, tone groggy.

She was warm and soft and smelled divine. My arm went beneath her head as I pulled her toward me. We'd never shared a bed together. We'd only *used* mine the night I'd gotten her pregnant—another sharp regret that panged through me. Not regret for our growing child, but merely the way it had happened.

Another strike against me, another mistake I needed to make up for.

"What are you doing?" she whispered.

I thought of the orphanage and a little human girl with brown eyes and red hair, who'd stared at a painting and dreamed of *everything*.

Determination swelled.

"I told you I'm a selfish bastard," I murmured, trying to fight back the damn tears that threatened to spill. So many regrets. How could I ever make amends? "Because this is how it'll be between us, Erina. I know I don't deserve you, not yet at least, but I *can't* be without you anymore. You're my *kyrana*. I will be in this bed when you fall asleep, and I will be here when you wake. I can't stand to be parted any more than we already are."

A shuddered breath fell from her lips as her dark eyes speared straight through me. They glittered in the moonlight. She was so damn warm and felt so *right* against me that I was convinced I could die happy right here.

"But if you tell me to leave, I'll go. I swear to you," I said. "And I won't return to your bed until you invite me to it."

Erina stared at me quietly, absorbing my words. And I waited for her verdict with bated breath, though my heart was pumping my blood furiously.

Her answer came when she turned into me. Hesitantly. Slowly, as if one small movement from me would sending her fleeing. She laid her head just below the crook of my arm, her face close to my side. Her hand came over my heart, and I know she felt the wildness of it, enveloped beneath the power of her palm.

As if she was a sorceress, she whispered, "Sleep."

Relief made my eyes shut…only they never opened again. I felt our child between us, pressed against my hip, as my hand tangled in her hair, holding her close.

I did as she told me.
I slept that night.
It was the best damn sleep of my entire life.

333

CHAPTER 39

ERINA

*I*t had been two nights since Kaldur had begun sleeping in my bed.

Two days and nights of being more aware of him in a way I'd never been before. I'd never slept beside a male before. Not once. There had been a young human girl at Wrezaan's who'd some-times gotten nightmares. And I would let her crawl in beside me and soothe her back to sleep.

But that was a far cry from sleeping next to Kaldur—whose solid bulk, whose scent, whose touch made me feel *too* much.

I'd never felt safer. I'd never felt so out of control. I'd never felt so needful. I'd never felt this shredding divide between what I *wanted* and what was logically best to keep my heart safe.

Two nights of Kaldur of House Kaalium. Two nights of lying in his arms, of feeling his palm gently rest on my belly, as if he wanted to keep our child safe in sleep too. Two nights of imag-ining that hand sliding to very different places of my body, of gleaming silver eyes that could tear me apart and wicked words coupled with a curled smirk that could make me do anything he pleased.

I imagined it all, squirming beside him even as he slept

soundly. He slept hot, I'd learned, and he only made me burn even hotter.

Last night, however, he'd smelled my arousal, a frustrating effect of his better-than-human senses. I heard him drag in a deep breath, a low groaning grumble tumbling back out. "Erina," he'd murmured, his hot exhale on the back of my neck. His arms had tightened around me as he'd pleaded, "Have mercy on me, *dallia*."

My face had flamed hot. "I can't help it."

Recently my body didn't feel like my own. Or maybe it was, it was just like a different part of me had been unlocked. We'd had sex once. A single time. My only time.

Yet…I craved it. I craved him. Especially after his confession that night in the kitchen. About what he'd truly thought about our lovemaking that fateful night.

Kaldur had behaved last night, however. Much to my…disappointment? I thought it'd been for the best, but I couldn't help but wish that he *would've* touched me. He'd been strumming his fingers across my hip, and I'd nearly shifted over to make them caress between my thighs. Maybe then he would give me what I actually wanted.

I was frustrated and turned on and missing him and hating it. Sometimes at night I just wanted to scream—or beg.

Two nights of exquisite torture beside him.

But on the third night, he didn't return.

I'd seen him at dinner since we'd taken it together. But then Maudoric had interrupted us toward the end, leaning down to inform Kaldur, in a quiet voice, "Trouble along the borders."

I'd frowned, sudden concern rising, but Kaldur hadn't seemed worried. He'd left, however, and I hadn't seen him since.

It was nearing midnight, and I'd been wandering the keep, the feeling of anxiousness not leaving me.

I'd ended up in the North Wing, to the starlight hallway I

loved so dearly and into the sitting room where everything had changed.

Through the large arched window, I saw that the rounding moon was bright enough to illuminate the darkened landscape of Vyaan. The mountain range to the east, the golden lights of the villages to the west and north.

There was no sign of Kaldur's familiar wings flaring against the night sky, however. And to the north, there *did* seem to be an accumulation of lights. Very near to where I'd grown up at Wrezaan's. But from this distance, I couldn't see much of anything except the cluster of the glow.

Wrapping my arms tighter around my body, I drifted away from the window, turning to inspect the quiet, abandoned sitting room.

There was a sensation at the back of my neck, like an icy ribbon of a touch that danced there. It was nearly the moon winds again, and the lost souls were always more active. They were completely harmless, however, though their exploration could be jarring. When I walked forward into the room, I even felt the sensation across my belly.

My gaze ventured around the room, noticing that it had been cleaned recently. Once, this room had been my responsibility.

I remembered discovering Kaldur here. With Lydrasa. Just the mere thought brought a sharp stab of jealousy, especially when my eyes went to the couch where she'd been bent over.

I squeezed my eyes shut. I hated that she knew his body better than I did. I hadn't even been able to *watch* him when we'd had sex. He'd pressed my front into his bed, taking me from behind.

"Stop," I told myself, my whisper shockingly loud in the quiet room.

To distract myself, I ventured to the cabinet where I'd shoved the vase pieces into, wondering if they were still there. When I pulled open the drawer, a sigh of dismay escaped me, my hand touching the cleaned-out wood, not a speck left behind.

I didn't know how long I stayed in the room. But after another worried glance outside the window, only to find no wings in the sky and that the cluster of lights to the north had only grown, though appeared more scattered, my concern amplified.

Something was wrong. I could feel it.

I left the room and went in search of Maudoric. But as I strayed farther from the North Wing, heading toward the heart of the house, I heard voices and activity down below.

My feet quickened, my heart beginning to beat in a worried panic. When I reached the atrium, I saw that a group had been gathered there, Maudoric at the helm.

I scurried down the stairs, catching the attention of a few keepers, many of whom I knew personally, though they'd kept out of my way since I'd become Kaldur's blood giver.

A couple were guards or soldiers, dressed in the same uniform that Braanelle wore—dark, tight-fitting trews with overlapping silver mesh that acted like armor and a thick leather vest over top a long-sleeved, tucked in tunic. Braanelle's vest was always a dark blue. These soldiers were dressed in burgundy.

"Maudoric," I murmured. "What's happened? Where's the *Kyzaire?*"

The soldiers straightened, inclining their heads at me when I alighted onto the main floor. The doors to the keep were open, a chilly breeze whistling through them. As for the keepers, they stood back. They'd been roused from sleep, it appeared, though I got the impression they were merely *waiting*.

Maudoric turned to me, her back to the soldiers, and took my arm.

"Don't worry," she said lowly, her voice calm—which only made my panic spike. "The *Kyzaire* has been injured, but he will be fine."

"Injured?" I breathed, eyes wide. *"How?"*

"A *lyvin* attack," Maudoric told me, squeezing my arm in

apparent comfort as I placed my hand on my belly. "He specifically didn't want you to worry."

Her eyes had strayed to my stomach when she said that. My breath hitched in hope. "So you've talked to him?"

"No, these soldiers relayed his message," she said. "He's on his way here but by carriage."

So he was injured enough not to fly, I thought, biting my lip.

"A *lyvin* attack?" I asked, brow furrowed, shaking my head. "Since when do—"

"There have been a few reports since the South Road construction. They are pushing into Northern villages," Maudoric told me. "Kaldur's been keeping close watch there, but I think that maybe…he's been distracted. Weak."

My cheeks heated, my nostrils flaring. *Stubborn male*, I thought.

"He won't feed from me," I whispered, catching her eyes.

Maudoric's lips pressed together in understanding. She leaned close. "He needs to feed tonight. Do whatever it takes to ensure he does."

When she pulled back, we held each other's eyes. I inclined my head, understanding and determination swarming in my veins.

I was the only one who could help Kaldur heal, wasn't I? The only one.

"The injury…is it bad?" I asked before my eyes went to the soldiers behind her.

Though one of them shook their head, a full-blooded Kylorr male with piercing maroon eyes, he still said, "But he's lost a lot of blood. The pack was larger than we anticipated. They caught the soldiers stationed there off guard."

And Kaldur had been thrown into the mix of it all.

They must've been tracking the pack, I thought. Because he'd been gone for hours. This injury was recent.

I heard the clattering of a carriage along the cobblestones

outside. And my chest squeezed. I had just begun to start for the open door when I heard a commotion outside, a shout of "*Kyzaire*, wait!" Perhaps from the driver.

When I raced to the door and stood on the threshold, peering down the stairs and into the darkness, I could only see the carriage, not even halfway up the road.

Maudoric came up beside me with a frown. She called out to the driver of the carriage, "Where is he?"

"He flew up to the keep!" the hidden driver called back.

Gone to the South Wing, I knew. I shared one single look with Maudoric, and she inclined her head in knowing.

"He'll be okay," I promised her, though it sounded more like comfort for myself. "I'll make sure of it."

I turned from the doorway and ran past the soldiers and the keepers, whispering in a corner. I could only imagine the talk at the kitchen table in the morning.

I had to believe Kaldur would be okay. Ordinarily, I wouldn't worry. But he'd been so weakened lately. I didn't know how much blood a Kylorr could lose before it became a mortal wound.

My worries made me run as fast as I could through the keep, back to the South Wing, taking every shortcut I knew.

When I reached our corridor, I saw the light underneath the door of *his* room. Not mine.

My brow furrowed. He'd thought to hide this from me?

I didn't knock. I barged through his door, just as I'd done the night we'd made our child.

His balcony door was open. Even I could smell the sharp metallic tang of blood, and it only made my fear rise.

"Kaldur!" I called, slamming the door behind me.

The fire wasn't lit, but there was a single Halo orb humming in the center of the room, casting out a glow of golden light. It deepened and sharpened the shadows across the room.

"Where are—"

"I'm here," came his voice, from a darkened corner of his

sitting room. There was a chair there, and I saw the gleam in his silver eyes when the Halo light turned and a golden ray hit him.

"So stubborn," I breathed, tears of relief pushing into my eyes when he stood.

I heard his pained wince when he did as I flew over to him, already sweeping my hair over my shoulder.

Kaldur eyed me, his breathing labored. I scanned his body, finding a wet bloom of black blood along his side, around his hip and appearing to curve around his back, the material of his tunic completely shredded.

It felt like there was a lump of fear lodged in my throat, one I couldn't swallow down. It *was* a lot of blood…and already he'd been weak.

I looked into his already scarred face, my hands reaching for him.

"No tears," he grumbled, seeing them make little rivulets down my cheeks. "*Please, dallia,* I can't stand to see you cry."

I unclasped his tunic with trembling fingers, ignoring him, my heart beating fast. Kaldur grunted when I helped him out of his shirt, peeling it away from the flesh wound along his side. I reached out for the Halo orb, bringing it around so that I could see the entirety of the wound.

The smooth flesh was torn in one jagged slice. *Lyvins* had a singular sharp claw on their fore limbs. Their back claws had more.

"It'll heal," he grunted.

Determination rose in me when I saw the wound, covered in his blood. *Still* bleeding. He'd been sitting in the chair because he'd been exhausted. From the short flight up to his balcony?

Enough.

"You're right," I said. "It will heal."

I came back around to Kaldur's front, and his eyes met mine. His bloodied hand started to come to my cheek, before he remembered the state of it.

"I'm all right, *dallia*," he murmured. His voice was pained, and suddenly I was so angry at him. I was angry, frightened, worried, and wanting him.

He drove me to madness. He was equally wonderful and horribly frustrating.

I pushed at his chest, walking forward until he took a step back. The backs of his knees met the chair, and my hand on his chest made a fist. I beat it against the hard flesh to push him down.

His brow furrowed as he sprawled into the chair, grunting when the movement jostled the wound.

"What are you—"

I slid into his lap, pressing him back into the armchair. His wings were cramped but rose around us, like a cocoon. I couldn't help but realize how similar this position was to *that* night. Except Kaldur had been in a strange mood, a challenging one, like he'd wanted to test what I'd dare to do.

Now Kaldur looked up at me, his nostrils flaring, his gaze running between us.

"You want this now?" he murmured, his words on the edge of quiet amusement. Trying to make light of the situation when he likely saw I was *pissed*. And scared. "I must admit, *dallia*, I find it frightening to want you this much. I could be on the edge of death and still want you. How humbling that is."

His voice was a deep purr, laced with his pain, and he'd only meant it as a distraction.

"Stop talking," I murmured, leaning forward, keeping his eyes. "You're going to feed."

CHAPTER 40

ERINA

"**Y**ou're going to feed. And you're going to heal," I added.

I saw the physical reaction to the words, the aching hunger he couldn't quite deny.

And all I wanted to know was *why?* Why was he doing this to himself?

Was it…was it a form of punishment? Was he punishing himself for what had happened between us? If that was the case, it only made my determination burn all the brighter.

"Enough of this," I told him, a little growl in my own voice. The swell of my stomach was pressed into his abdomen, and I felt the heat of his blood seep against my nightdress. "*Feed.* Now."

When I lowered my head, beginning to turn my neck, his hand whistled up and caught my chin. He turned my face, and then his lips were on mine.

It wasn't a gentle kiss. It was hard and rough and demanding. And for a brief, selfish moment, I poured all of my fear, hurt, and frustration into that kiss.

It felt like he took it into himself. He lapped at my tongue, a deep groan—both pained and pleasured—rumbling between us as he deepened it.

"Growl at me like that again, *dallia*, and I'll show you that even in this state, I can fuck you until dawn breaks."

Was it wrong to be turned on when he was bleeding and hurt between my thighs?

And yet even bleeding and hurt, I still felt the unmistakable and unyielding hardness of his cock, which had stiffened against me.

"And I'll let you," I said, matching the tone from before, pulling back to meet his eyes. They narrowed, his pupils so large his eyes appeared nearly black. "As long as you feed first. You'll need your strength."

He would need to be enticed, and I was out of patience. I took his hand from beneath my chin and used the tip of his claw to slice a thin line against my neck.

A ragged growl tore from his throat as I pressed into him, turning my head so that all he had to do was latch his fangs into me.

"Let me take care of you," I whispered into his ear. "Please, Kaldur."

"What are you doing to me?" he breathed, the words whispered against my neck, his lips brushing the small wound. He groaned when I rolled my hips over him—an anguished sound, one that made him sound even more in pain than the wince when he'd stood.

My eyes latched on to the wildly beating pulse in his neck. I couldn't look away; I was mesmerized by it. Relieved that he was all right, that he would be fully recovered soon. If only he wasn't so stubborn.

On impulse, I bit into his neck with my dull little teeth, and he let out a hoarse cry, one of desire and surprise, and I nearly sighed in relief when I finally felt what I'd been waiting for.

The prick of his fangs. Spurred on, perhaps instinctively, by my own bite.

"Yes," I whispered. "That's it, Kaldur. *Please.*"

The familiar sensations of his feeding felt like a victory. I bit at his neck again, squeezing my teeth into the flesh, making a rush of hot breath from his nostrils flare against my skin, making his hips buck up into mine, even though he really should've kept still.

I pressed a hand to his bare, hot chest, feeling the throbbing steady beat of his heart as I tried to hold him still.

But then my hand was trailing down his chest, across his firm abdomen, to rest on the waistband of his laced trews.

Familiar pleasure was rising, and I moaned with it. Kaldur fed and fed, and I never wanted him to stop. Not until he had taken his fill.

It didn't have to mean much, I decided. My body had become this animal, with animal needs and desires, from the very first moment he'd touched me two months ago. I'd missed that touch. All I wanted was to feel it again, to let it soothe this pinching ache inside me.

The pleasure from his feeding registered, and I moaned with abandon.

"I want you," I confessed, "*so* much. I hate it."

A low rumble built in his chest when I pressed my hand against his hard cock. He was hot and pulsing, even through his trews, and desperation rose, matching the pinching pleasure. Between my thighs, my clit fluttered and throbbed, my pussy squeezing around where he should've been filling me.

I'd forgotten the wildness. The madness. The *need.*

Only this time, it felt so much worse. It was ratcheting up, building, building. Amplified by the wasted time when we'd been apart.

"Take everything from me," Kaldur rasped against my throat.

And I shivered when I felt his hot tongue lick at the spilling blood from my neck. "Take it all, my love."

My breath whistled at the endearment, but I tried to ignore it. No, this didn't mean anything. This was for Kaldur and for me. But it didn't have to be anything more than a feeding and the satisfaction, pleasure, and release from sex. We both needed that.

Kaldur's fangs returned, the sweet rush of his venom making my back arch, my belly pressing into him. With shaking hands, I ripped at the laces of his pants, knowing there was no need for shyness when it came to this. I knew what I wanted from him.

When his cock sprung forth and my hands wrapped around him, another rough groan tumbled from deep in his throat, his hips bucking, twitching beneath me. Hot and hard, like suede-wrapped steel.

The swollen tip of his cock was slick with his need, and for a brief moment, the urge to lick him there was nearly overpowering. But I didn't want to stop him feeding, so I ran my thumb over the wet slippery mess, hearing his breath hitch. A rough whimper left him, and I'd never heard a more arousing sound as more pre-come replaced what I'd teased away.

His feeding grew even more ravenous, and his hand came up to slide into my hair, holding me in place when my head threatened to loll backward.

"More," I whispered, my eyes focused on the trimming of the balcony door next to us. "More, Kaldur."

His other hand came to my nightdress, pushing it up my thighs. That hand squeezed at my flesh, at every inch he uncovered, until I felt the cool rush of air across my hot, slick pussy.

I pressed the searing head of his cock against where I needed him most, tearing another ragged groan from his throat. He unlatched his fangs, pulling back to look down at us. His hand came to my pussy, his fingers teasing over the sensitive flesh.

"No," I whispered, meeting his eyes. I took his head, pressed it back to my neck. "More."

I could actually *feel* his strength returning. It was beginning to vibrate through every sinew of his body, energy flooding into him like he'd been struck by lightning.

It made me realize just how much he'd been denying himself. I'd forgotten what this strength had felt like. The firm press of his hands, the way his muscles swelled beneath me. He was ravenous, and I could help sate him.

He began to feed again as waves of pleasure rolled through me. And I moved with it, swirling my hips, seeking his length.

With parted lips, I tilted my head to look between us without dislodging his fangs, pressing my forehead against his bare shoulder. I licked at his skin, tasting the saltiness of his sweat and natural musk. And it drove me *wild*.

I lifted my hips, pressing his cock head at my entrance...and then I wiggled around, swirling my hips in time with his deep draws, until his cock began to sink in.

A strangled sound reverberated against my neck. My nipples even tingled with the sensation of his fullness, a full body shiver going through me as I guided him inside.

A nearly constant rough purr was rising from him now. As if his mind had finally turned off and he was only sensation.

There was a brief pinching tightness when I sank down deep. I'd only had sex with him once, after all. He was *big* and thick, but I was determined. I moved over him, tiny little pulses that felt good until I was able to slide down more and more. It helped that I was incredibly slick, the arousal from his touch and his venom practically making me mew with need.

I slid my hand down the rest of his length, feeling a large swelling at his very base. I knew it was his knot. A full-blooded Kylorr male's knot. I'd felt it last time but thought there was no possible way to fit inside me.

When my entrance met the ring that my fingers made around him, I nearly grunted with the sensation of fullness.

"Fuck me," came his rough growl, bordering on a plea. "Fuck your mate, *kyrana*, while I make you come with my bite."

I nearly gasped, and my hips gave a short pump, lodging him even deeper, making him hiss in pleasure.

It was the first time he'd ever called me *kyrana* like that. I found that I liked it entirely too much. Especially when he referred to himself as *my* mate. There was an animalistic part of me that preened with that knowledge.

It was the first moment where I realized I might have claim to him. Where he could be *mine* as much as I could be his.

That was a dangerous thought, however, so to distract myself, I rose up, releasing his cock and bringing my hands up around his shoulders for leverage.

I was still getting used to my pregnant body and the changes in it. My breasts, which had already grown larger, more sensitive. The imbalance of my weight. But it didn't stop me from swiveling my hips over him, trying to get as much inside me as I could before it felt like he was lodged in my throat.

The pleasure of his feeding was coming to a cusp, surging me higher and higher. My movements over him might've been clumsy, but every thrust and bounce over his cock made him huff out a sharp exhale from his nostrils. His cock seemed to grow larger inside me, every inch sliding across places that made me tingle from the inside out, from head to toe.

His hips began to move, thrusting upward to meet my downward strokes until we were in perfect sync. Until every movement together made me see stars, as my heartbeat throbbed in time with the perceivable hungry pulls at my neck.

"Kaldur," I gasped.

My orgasm crashed into me with just a little bit of warning. Then I was crying out my pleasure, which sounded nearly like a sob. My hips slammed down, chasing that ecstasy with abandon as Kaldur seemed to hold his breath, stilling beneath me.

Then he was bellowing against my skin, releasing his fangs

suddenly, and I felt the surge of heat, of his come as it lashed against my innermost walls as I squeezed around him.

"Raazos's blood," he cursed with gritted teeth and harsh breath. "Gods, you feel so fucking good, *dallia*. I wish you could feel how good this is."

I do, I couldn't help but think desperately as my wide eyes sought him out.

"I'm so mad for you," he growled. "All I want is more."

"Take it all," I breathed, finally getting the strength of my voice back when the orgasm began to fade. My limbs felt like jelly, and the whole world seemed soft and hazy, like I was high off *lore*. Or perhaps off the venom of his bite.

When I squirmed over him, he hissed. Thinking I'd hurt him, I gasped and tried to get off, but he held me fast, his fingers tight on my hips.

"Don't you dare move," he growled, meeting my eyes. Eyes so dark they were molten silver. "I told you...until dawn. And *dallia*?"

"Yes?" I whispered.

"I'm still ravenous for you," he warned.

CHAPTER 41
— KAIDUR

I opened the door to Maudoric, who held a tray of food, fresh bandages, and a steaming pot of what I knew was *baanye*. I'd wrapped a blanket around my hips for Maudoric's sake. Even still, I spied the relief in her eyes when she eyed my side, the wound already looking much better than it'd been an hour ago.

There was a jerkiness to my movements as I took the tray, as if I'd forgotten my strength and the stretch and pull of my muscles. I felt like my old self, and yet everything had changed.

Maudoric knew better than to speak to me when I was in this state. She merely inclined her head, relieved that I'd fed from my *kyrana*, and then left. She would sleep easier tonight.

I shut the door behind her, loosening the blanket around my hips, and it fell to the floor as I continued into the bedroom.

I nearly purred in contentment when I saw my mate, sprawled across the bed the wrong way. It looked like she'd dozed off in the brief moment I'd left, and I memorized her like this as I poured her some *baanye* from the pot.

Her body was naked, her nightdress long tossed clear across the room. She was lucky I hadn't shredded it. Her skin was flushed, her lips reddened from my kiss, my bite adorning her neck.

My heart twisted looking at her. Beautiful. I knew I wouldn't ever get tired of this view, and so I committed it to memory. Every soft curve of her body, including the one of my child, every wild wavy strand of her dark red hair.

The clinking of the cup against the pot woke her. She made a sound in the back of her throat, disoriented, as she peered at me.

"How long was I asleep?" she murmured, voice hoarse from her screams.

"Not long," I replied.

Her eyes dragged over me, and I felt my cock—still hard—twitch with her perusal. Her observation felt as erotic as her touch. It skimmed over my body, the muscles swollen, surging after the feeding. Every sharp, cut line caught her attention, and I wondered if she was imagining drawing me like this. I saw her hand twitch, as if wanting her pencil, and nearly grinned.

I brought over the teacup, and she went onto her elbow to take it.

"*Baanye*," I told her gruffly. "I've taken a lot of your blood."

Maybe even too much. I had to learn to be less greedy when it came to her.

"You needed it," she answered, peering at me over the rim with those warm eyes, framed by dark, curling lashes. She took a sip of her *baanye*, pulling a small face at the bitter taste. "And Ekor said it was all right, remember?"

Ekor told us that pregnant women naturally had more blood in their bodies. He thought the *baanye* wasn't necessary while Erina was pregnant...but I wasn't taking any chances.

"Keep drinking it," I told her, dropping to my knees beside the bed, catching her startled cry when I tugged on her legs, dragging her toward me. "I want it all gone by the time I make you come on my tongue."

A shuddered gasp escaped her when I draped her legs over my

shoulders, when I licked at the seam of her cunt, still hot and slick from the three times I'd taken her tonight.

She nearly spilled the tea, managing to keep it balanced at the last moment. But then she struggled to get away, and I growled, latching my arms around her hips to keep her place.

"I haven't washed and—"

I growled again, the sound vibrating through her, her eyelids fluttering shut for a brief moment. "You think I *fucking* care?"

"N-No," she whispered.

"Drink," I ordered her. When she took a small sip immediately, I rewarded her with a gentle suckle at the sensitive little bud of her clit, making her gasp, nearly choking on the tea, her thighs giving a tremble around me. "Mmm, the things I'm going to do to you, *kyrana*. All the wicked things I've only dreamed of."

Her eyes burned into mine, the *baanye* sloshing in the cup when she shifted on the bed. I slid my hand over her growing belly, up to her breasts, tweaking and teasing one of her nipples, which I'd learned she'd liked. She groaned, her hips twitching, and I smelled a fresh flood of her arousal.

My mouth watered for her, and I lapped at her pussy, nearly smirking when she took another dutiful sip of her tea. She was so expressive, every flash of pleasure, every new sensation that flooded her right there for me to see.

She'd been untouched before me. This was all new to her. Every slow, lingering stroke of my tongue. Every gentle suckle of her lips, of her clit. Every teasing thrust as I fucked her with my fingers.

I felt her toes curl against my wings. I didn't need to look down between my legs to know that my cock was dripping pre-come all over the rug. It bobbed and twitched with every sound she made, her pleasure becoming my own.

I feasted on her until she was squirming, a steady tumble of "Oh, gods" and moans of "Yes, Kaldur" from her throat.

She was getting close. I could feel it. She nearly went flying over the edge when I got a little too greedy, momentarily losing myself in her taste and sounds. But I managed to pull back at the last moment, her frustrated cry my reward.

"You want to come, my love?" I asked.

"Yes!"

Gods, didn't she know what that little growl did to me? My normally sweet and even-tempered mate, growling at me to make her come. Demanding little thing. I would show her just how greedy she could be with me. I'd give her anything she wanted.

"Finish the *baanye*," I purred, unable to help myself as I wrapped my fist around my cock, giving it a rough, teasing pump that sent tingles zipping down my spine, right between my wings. My eyes nearly rolled back. I grunted, "Then I'll let you come."

She tipped back the cup, a couple big swallows left and it was likely unpleasant by now, cooled down.

But I teased her clit, flicking it back and forth with my tongue, just enough pressure to keep her on the edge without actually letting her tip over it.

She groaned and squirmed, her thighs tightening around my head, but she swallowed down the rest of the tea and even showed me her empty cup.

"Happy now?" she asked, voice guttural, a hint of a glare on her expression that made my cock twitch.

"Extremely," I said, taking the cup from her and placing it safely to the floor.

She fell back onto the bed with a soft huff, likely thinking I would tease her again.

But I didn't. The moment she fell back, I was ravenous and determined, focused on one thing and one thing only.

A strangled sound escaped her when I lapped and suckled at her clit like I was fucking starved. She jerked as I teased the entrance of her pussy with the knuckle of my index finger, just enough pressure to keep her aware. I would stretch her there... when she took my knot.

"You're going to make me come again," she breathed, voice ragged, trying to catch her breath as her body began to tense up. Her hips twitched, but I kept her pinned down, pressing on her pelvis to keep her still. "*Kaldur!*"

She inhaled a sharp breath. I felt a single flutter around my finger, and then she was arching up from the bed, a silent scream on her lips.

There you go, I thought. *Come for me.*

I never changed my pace between her thighs, alternating between sucking and lapping at her fluttering little clit. And I continued to do that until I knew her orgasm was over, even when she reached down to push at me.

I finally released her and stood, wiping at my mouth and jaw with a shaking hand. My movements were jerky, stilted when I stepped up to the bed, tugging her bodily down again until her bottom was just over the edge.

"Good," I murmured.

I took her ankles in my grip, pulling them wide so I could slide between them.

"Need you again," I told her, my gaze zeroing in on her, the rest of the room fading away. "Gods, I've never felt anything like this before. It drives me crazy, how much I need you, *dallia.*"

A gasp left her when I thrust into her pussy, hard and deep, and a low, extremely satisfied rumbling vibrated through my entire body. Even my wings shuddered with it.

But I needed deeper. She would take my knot, the entrance of her tight pussy *just* teasing the swelling of it.

I pushed forward, and she made a sound like a soft mew, a desperate one. I pulled back, nearly leaving the warmth of her body, before I thrust back in.

Then a haze of need shrouded me. I pressed over her, using

the weight of my body to keep her legs spread open wide, leaning down to capture her lips in a deep, hard kiss.

Was it possible to want someone *so* much? I just wanted to consume her, to keep her close so nothing would ever hurt her again. Even me.

My need for her was great, but I forced myself to go slow. To make love to her instead of mindlessly fuck, though I thought maybe that would be how this ended. Every deep, long stroke of my cock into her body made her gasp. She breathed into my kiss, like she was breathing life into me again.

Every thrust teased my knot, making fire burn in my veins. I pulled back from her kiss, already on the edge of coming.

I placed my hands on both sides of her head, capturing her beneath me like prey, my wings coming around us until it was like we were blanketed in them. I held her eyes as we shared the same breath, as I saw my own need and pleasure mirrored in her eyes.

Looking down at her, I thought that there were very few moments in my life I wanted to capture forever, to be able to relive over and over again. But that this was certainly one of them.

But just as I thought that, her eyes flickered back and forth between my own as I continued to push my body into hers, claiming her, making love to her. There was a flash of uncertainty…and then a moment of fear.

Suddenly her expression, which was usually so readable, closed off.

"This," she whispered, her voice catching in her throat with the ferocity of my thrusts. I stilled, breathing hard, trepidation curling in my gut. "This doesn't have to mean anything," she said. "Right?"

My brow furrowed, not understanding.

"It's just sex," she said. "We both want this. It doesn't have to mean anything."

I growled, understanding finally flooding into me.

"No," I rasped, cupping the side of her face so she wouldn't turn away. I gave another deep thrust, watching her bite her lip at the sensation. Each word was punctuated with a teeth-clattering thrust when I said, "*This. Means. Everything.*"

"It can't," she cried out, voice strained, torn between her rising panic, her quiet determination, and her pleasure. "It can't."

"Yes," I said, desperation now driving me. It made a fissure run through my heart—but perhaps I deserved it—merely thinking she was *trying* to keep distance between us. It was what I'd done to her, after all. "It can."

But saying it didn't hold any meaning. Erina had decided that she was open to *this*, to sex, to the feedings again. That didn't mean this intimacy meant what it had *once* meant to her. I'd ruined any chance of that.

Yet I was determined to break down every last block she'd stacked between us, the wall I'd caused her to build to keep herself safe. It ate at me, that knowledge. Knowing I'd been the cause. But I wouldn't rest until I had earned her forgiveness. Her trust. Her love.

Her fear stemmed from her uncertainty. But she needed to understand…I had never been more certain of anything in my life.

What I feared was losing her.

I thanked all the gods and goddesses I knew that I'd gotten her pregnant that night. A blessing. Because if I hadn't, she wouldn't be here right now. Would she have even given me another chance?

"Look at me," I growled, cupping her face. I leaned down, pressing my lips against hers. The words slipped over her tongue when I said, "This means everything, Erina."

She stared up at me, and I saw the raw emotion cut open on her face. I saw that she *wanted* to believe me, that little piece of her that perhaps still held hope, and that nearly broke my heart all over again. Because I knew she wouldn't fully allow herself to give in. To have faith.

Not yet.

So, I didn't pressure her. Not right then. Instead, I said, "We will make this our own. Whatever it becomes, whatever we need it to become, it will be. All right?"

Finally she nodded, and I caught her gasp with my lips, beginning to move my hips again, sinking deeply into her. There was a new determination pounding at me, beating at my very soul.

I felt the orgasm rise as she began to clench around me. I threaded our hands together, shoving my face into the crook of her neck, licking at the bite wound that I'd already healed.

"Erina," I groaned into her skin.

She made a choked, ragged sound when she felt my knot seat inside her, swelling with my pleasure. The tightness around it—gods, the *heat* and pulse of her body—I couldn't withstand it. I thought it surprised her when she began to come again—a shocked little gasp was my only warning before I felt the *squeeze*.

And that was it for me. I felt my come sizzle up my cock, my vision momentarily blackening, stars dotting the darkness.

When I surfaced again, I was bellowing with the intensity, the flood of my pleasure unleashing into her body over and over. I could only move slightly, my knot like a seal at her entrance. But every minuscule amount of friction prolonged my orgasm.

I hadn't knotted a female in well over a decade—only when I'd been young, and it had been more hassle than it'd been worth—but it certainly hadn't felt like *this*. This electricity zapping up my spine. All I could do was fuck my way through it, trying to catch my breath.

When it was over, I nearly collapsed onto her. I felt like all my renewed strength had been stolen again. At the last moment, I rolled to the side, the seal of my knot taking her with me. She groaned, her eyes holding an edge of her tiredness.

"Come here," I said quietly, my voice raw. I hitched her leg over my hip, tucking back a strand of hair away from her glistening forehead. "It'll be a while. I'll hold you until it eases."

Thankfully Erina didn't protest. She sighed, her body melting against me. It couldn't be a terribly comfortable position, but her eyes were already sliding shut, her cheek coming to rest on my pectoral.

We probably looked worse for wear. We still hadn't washed, and the blankets of the bed were a haphazard tangle of a bloodied mess from my previous wound. But I didn't find it in me to care.

All that mattered was Erina in my arms, our child safe between us.

I pressed my lips to the top of her head, already feeling the exhale of her even breaths drift over my skin. Passed out. I was still trying to catch my breath, folding my arms over my blood mate tight, my cock still throbbing between her legs.

"Everything, Erina," I whispered, more comforted by the feel of her warm, bare skin against mine than anything in my memory. "I'll give you everything."

CHAPTER 42
—
ERINA

*T*he beginnings of dawn light were filtering in through the window when I opened my eyes. At first, I couldn't place where I was, groggy with bleary eyes.

Kaldur.

There were arms wrapped around me, his familiar scent on my skin, his heat along my back, his palm cupping my swollen belly.

Last night returned like a lightning bolt, striking straight into me. For a long moment, I sank into those memories, of the strong surge of him inside me, the ferocity and passion which he'd taken me with, the relief that had bloomed with his feeding. The panic. The panic at knowing that if he continued to hammer at my defenses like he'd done last night, I was as good as doomed.

My body felt like a stranger's, I realized as I shifted slightly in his arms to peer over at him. There was a heavy soreness between my thighs—not unpleasant, but it still grabbed my attention. I thought maybe I would discover a few bruises too. Though he had been careful, especially because of the baby, there had been moments last night where we'd seemed to both abandon reason, to give in to the startling sensations of the pleasure.

There had been a wild little animal in me last night, one that had demanded him, one that had been selfish in her need and desire. And I *liked* that. It didn't feel like me, and yet it had felt right. Like unlocking a new adventure, a new part of me that I would like to explore.

The small movement woke Kaldur. But unlike me, he knew exactly where he was, and his eyes, already alert, fastened on mine. He tugged me more firmly against him, as if we weren't completely pressed against each other.

I realized another thing. We were clean. And so was the bed. I didn't remember anything after…after his *knot*.

"What a beautiful dawn," he murmured, voice gravelly from sleep, as his hand came to thread through my hair. He only looked at me, and a pleased smile threatened to steal over my face, a part of me preening at his compliment.

"What happened last night?" I whispered.

His brow rose. Mock hurt crossed his face. "You mean to tell me you don't remember? Maybe I'm losing my touch."

A huff of a laugh escaped me. "I meant…did we bathe?"

"I brought us to the bath," he said. "You were dead to the world, enough that I began to worry. But you woke briefly, gave me a kiss, told me I'm the best lover in the universe, and that you love me."

For a brief moment, I feared I might've. But then I noticed the gleam in his gaze as he watched a brief flit of panic across my face.

"I did not," I protested, struggling to sit up in indignation.

He smirked, effortlessly keeping me against his side with a small flex of his arm underneath my shoulders. "No, but I can dream."

"That's what you dream about?" I asked, huffing, trying to calm my thundering heart.

"Yes," he said. "That's what I dream about, *dallia*."

I swallowed hard, which he heard. And I knew he wasn't

referring to the "best lover" nonsense—since he knew I had nothing to compare him to anyway.

He was talking about that last bit. The last bit that made my tongue stick to the roof of my mouth.

But Kaldur was at ease with the confession, and then, true to form, he put me at ease when he changed the subject back to my original question. "I bathed us until the knot released."

Just thinking about that wonderfully burning sense of fullness made a fresh pulse of desire throb between my legs.

"Did it hurt you?" he wanted to know.

"No," I said. It had been uncomfortable at first, but then it had tingled into something else entirely. A pricking kind of pleasure that had immediately set off bombs through my nerve endings. "I…I liked it."

A low, sinful little rumble vibrated through him. His other hand skimmed up the naked roundness of my hip, before dipping into the growing curve of my waist.

He *liked* that I liked it. Obviously.

"Gods, I want you again," came his gruff words of, almost, disbelief. "I woke up in the middle of the night hard as fucking *drava* steel. You know what I was dreaming of? You. Not even dreams—memories."

Oh.

He pressed the tip of his sharp nose into my hair, just above my ear, as tingles made me shiver. "Mmm, and then I woke up and your scent was all around me. I was so close to waking you. Remembering all your sounds, the way you sighed when I was teasing your sweet little clit, the way your neck flushes as you come."

My breathing went a little ragged, lulled by the erotic memories he was conjuring with his words, his perfect voice in my ear.

"Why didn't you?" I found the courage to ask.

He huffed, a small sensual laugh following. This was still so new between us. *This* aspect of our strange relationship.

"You needed the rest," he said. "I was greedy last night. With your blood and your body."

"I liked it," I admitted, feeling that flush he was talking about wind its way around my neck like a collar. "Very much."

That pleased him. His hand squeezed at my hip but then grew gentle. His fingers traced over the curve of my buttocks, back and forth, an intimate caress that only he had the liberty to do.

"It might be the pregnancy," I began, "but I have been feeling more…um…"

"Lustful?" he purred into my ear, a deep smooth rumble.

"Y-Yes."

Or it might just be you and not the pregnancy, I thought, but I kept that to myself.

"You can use me whenever you want, *kyrana*," Kaldur said. A jolt came at the sound of that word again. I realized it was almost like a title.

"'Use' sounds so crass," I commented.

"I'm serious," Kaldur said, pressing his lips against the shell of my ear. He nipped at it. "I'm more than happy to assuage any needs you might have."

"Even when you're working in your study?" I asked, the question meant to be a tease.

"Especially then," he rumbled. "Mmm, I'll take you over the desk. Or have you lie back on it so I can feast on your pussy. Make sure you wear a dress when you come to me."

A strangled sound tore from me at the images he'd conjured.

"Sensitive, curious little thing," he noted. "I'll show you everything—I promise."

If I'd ever had any doubts about Kaldur's opinions about sex with me…I found them completely assuaged in that moment. Of course, I *had* believed him that night in the kitchens. That he'd lied to Lydrasa when he'd said our lovemaking had been "fine." But even so, perhaps my ego had still been a little bruised, uncertainty over our sexual relationship still not feeling quite settled.

Until last night. And now, hearing the intense desire burning in Kaldur's voice, the way he couldn't stop touching me, his praise making me bloom like Gaara's spring.

"We need to stop," he murmured. He took my hand and dragged it to his cock. "You feel what you do to me?"

The shocking heat and hardness made me curl my fingers around him. He was *throbbing* in my hand. When I ran my thumb over the head, just as I'd done last night, I discovered slickness there already. He groaned and then gave a desperate laugh, snatching my hand away. There was a startling intimacy to this moment, as if I'd been given permission to touch his body whenever I wanted. As if it were mine, as mine was his.

"No, my love," he murmured. "I told you—I was too greedy with you last night. So as much as I want to, no fucking today. If you need a little relief, I'll make you come without my cock. I'll make sure you're satisfied, *dallia*."

A zipping erotic thrill went through me. He'd really meant it when he'd said I could use him if the urge ever hit.

"Maybe later," I whispered, then bit my lip so I couldn't take it back. I knew he was right—we should take it easy today. I still had less than two months left of the pregnancy. I wasn't far enough along for sex to be a concern yet, as Ekor had quietly informed me upon his last visit—which had made me squeak out a reply as Kaldur had smirked from his corner. But I still thought we should be cautious.

So much for caution last night, I couldn't help but think, remembering that I'd pleaded for more at several instances.

"Was…was Maudoric here?" I asked, not changing the subject as expertly as Kaldur.

"Last night," he said. "To bring the *baanye*, but I also had her change the bedding while we washed."

Ah. It would be hard to look her in the eye today.

"And how's your wound?" I asked next. I knew it had begun healing the moment my blood had hit him last night.

"My wound?" Kaldur asked. Even he'd forgotten. "Oh."

He peeled back the bedding to expose our bodies. I hitched in a sharp breath, unable to keep my eyes from roaming across the planes of his muscles. He looked healthier already, his skin smooth, his face not so shadowed in hunger. His body was beautiful, perfect. His cock was still hard, a small pool of pre-come in the dip of his abdomen, and that distracted me longer than it should've as I bit my lip.

Focus, I chided myself.

Along his side, I saw only a faint pinkness of a scar, one that resembled a slash of a claw.

We hadn't talked about it last night. There had been no time. When I looked up into Kaldur's eyes, I saw he wasn't even inspecting the scar, however…his attention was on *my* body.

His silver eyes were practically mercurial as they slid over my breasts.

Then a growl left him and he was dipping his head, sliding up onto one forearm to lean over me. His lips latched on to my nipple, and a desperate, surprised moan left me. The startling sensation of his kiss, of the teasing suckle on the sensitive tip left me squirming.

"I'll behave," he said, but it sounded like he said it more to himself. Like an order. He groaned, raising his head, his lips damp. Cool air drifted over where his tongue had been, puckering the flesh even tighter. "Mmm, one more."

The sound that left me was a mixture of a laugh and a gasp. His fingers reached for my other nipple, teasing it back and forth, as he laved the other gently.

"*Vaan,*" he cursed, pulling back against with a sigh. His cock pulsed forward, bobbing, and he wrapped a hand around it to keep it still. "I'll be good."

What if I don't want you to be good? I wondered.

That fire was burning in me again. I'd never considered

myself a gluttonous person when it came to my own wants, but part of me wanted to throw caution to the wind.

My mouth was watering as I gazed down at his cock. I wanted to taste him.

Kaldur blew out a deep breath, and then he shot out of bed, his cock swinging. "I can smell your need. So if we don't get out of bed right now, I'll have you bent over it."

He was right. I wanted to sigh in frustration.

Kaldur crossed to his wardrobe and pulled out fresh trews, cursing as he tried to get his cock wrestled into them as I watched him from the bed. Finally, when he got his laces done up, he saw me staring. He raised his brow. His trews were tight on him, and now, I realized, it was because I *was* his *kyrana*. Stupidly, I hadn't realized it before. But feeding from a *kyrana* made a Kylorr stronger, made them physically grow larger—a trait of their berserker nature. In ancient times, Kylorr would take their mates into battle. Wars had been won because of *kyranas*.

I'd noticed Kaldur's increase of strength before, but I'd always written it off as a natural reaction to the feeding. Then again, he'd taken to wearing larger clothes, hadn't he? To make it less noticeable.

I'd been so blind.

Kaldur approached me. Leaning over the bed, he surprised me with a gentle kiss, the light brush of his lips making my head swirl.

I closed my eyes tight, thinking that he wasn't being fair. The goal was *not* to fall hopelessly in love with him again. Already he wasn't making it easy.

"Come with me," he said against my lips. "I want to show you something."

"Now?" I asked. "I don't have any clothes."

"Ah, never doubt Maudoric," Kaldur said. He retreated back to the wardrobe and then brought over a stunning dress, one I didn't recognize.

"That's not mine," I murmured, blinking as I frowned.

"It is," Kaldur said. "I had it made for you."

I struggled to sit up again, pressing the top blanket to my breasts as I regarded him. He helped me, his warm hand on the middle of my back as I righted myself.

"There are others. They were delivered a couple days ago, and Maudoric has been unpacking them and getting them ready for you."

My fingers reached out to touch the dress. It was white with embroidered flowers, sewn with dozens of different-colored threads. Hundreds of tiny blooms were scattered across the soft material. The bodice would be fitted, but it was cinched just above the waist, though the bottom of the dress was loose, perfect for my body considering the baby. It wasn't practical in the slightest, but it was the prettiest thing I'd ever seen, my heart squeezing with want.

"Do you like it?" he asked, suddenly frowning with my silence. "There are dozens more you can choose from if—"

"I love it," I breathed. "It's beautiful."

It must have cost him a small fortune. And there were *dozens* of others?

I didn't know how to feel about that, but it seemed to please him, the praise. His shoulders loosened and he gave me a beautiful smile.

"Are we going outside?" I asked, rising from the bed when he gestured me out of it.

"No," he replied, unclasping the dress backing before handing it to me. I slipped it over my head, my hands trembling from not wanting to damage it. I'd never worn anything with clasps in the back, something only nobles would need because they had keepers to help them do them up.

But I supposed I had a *Kyzaire* to do that for me, I realized.

Because after I smoothed out the material, finding that it settled around me perfectly, he did up the fastenings, brushing my hair out of the way to finish the top.

Then he pressed a kiss to the back of my neck. "Beautiful," he murmured.

"You haven't even seen it yet," I couldn't help but point out with a nervous laugh.

"I have excellent taste," he replied simply.

The sleeves on the dress were long, which would keep me warm enough if we weren't venturing outside.

I turned in his arms, and his gaze trailed down and up. His lips curled, and he tugged me over to the mirror by the dresser.

In it, I saw us both. And for a moment, I was stunned because it looked like we were *happy* together, like we belonged. I didn't even focus on the dress, only on Kaldur. And he was only focused on me.

My heart gave a warning throb, but I sighed, choosing to ignore it this time.

"See?" he murmured, wrapping his arms around me in the mirror. "Beautiful."

And I felt like it. The dress was flattering on my growing body. It was like I was wearing a garden of tiny flowers. I felt like a heroine in one of my own stories.

As I stared into the mirror, a sudden whispering of inspiration came. Of Kavelyn, walking through a field of wildflowers under the light of two full moons. She was looking for someone, her heart yearning. I saw the scene so clearly, the want on her face. She'd be looking for Jeb, naturally. The only person she'd ever loved. The one she'd given her heart to, even knowing that they could never be together. He'd told her to meet him there, that maybe they could have the one night where their rivalries, their worlds could fall away.

It was my first flash of inspiration in long weeks, and

suddenly I was hanging on to it with every piece of me, worried it might float away.

"I need my notebook," I breathed.

Kaldur's smile was soft—knowing, perhaps.

"I'll show you where you can find it," he told me, his words cryptic. And as he led me from the room, only stopping to tug on a black tunic, I couldn't help but feel relief so bright it nearly brought tears to my eyes.

I had dreamed of *something* again.

And that was a beautiful thing.

CHAPTER 43

KALDUR

"Where are we going?"

"You'll see," I replied to Erina, guiding her through the keep.

The East Wing afforded the best views of the gardens and the mountains beyond Vyaan. I thought that she would enjoy it there the most, even though it was farther from my own study. Selfishly, I had wanted to keep her close. But she was so attached to the garden, to the beauty of it, that I wanted her to be able to look at the window and see it when she was not there.

When we reached the door, she looked at me curiously. I merely grinned at her, feeling better than I had in a long time. Part of that reason was because I was excited to show her what was inside.

"Will you tell me why we're here now?" she asked, a quizzical look on her face.

"I have a gift for you."

"Another one?" she asked, blinking. I could see that the prospect pleased her, however. Erina Denoren hadn't been given enough gifts in her life, I realized, but I intended to spoil her with them.

368

She looked childlike in her sudden curiosity, waiting for me to reveal it.

"Go inside," I murmured, brushing my fingers across her cheek.

I *was* eager to see her reaction but also worried I might've gotten something wrong. I'd consulted with an artist in the village a couple days ago, who owned a shop along the row of the square, the one where Maudoric had informed me Erina visited often. The shopkeeper had only been too eager to help me.

Erina pressed down on the door handle before she swung it inward. She stepped inside while I hovered on the threshold.

Her back was turned to me so I couldn't quite see her expression, except through a gilded mirror I'd had hung alongside the opposite wall, next to the wide window. And even in the mirror, I could only see half of her face.

I watched as slow realization dawned, her eyes slowly taking in the room as she deliberated over its purpose.

"Oh," she breathed, astonishment crossing her face next. Her gaze began to flit around faster, her head swinging as if she didn't know what to settle on. "*Oh.*"

The studio had turned out just as I'd imagined it. A brightly lit room, filtering in golden light from the dawn on that gentle morning. A large enough room so that it didn't feel cramped in the slightest, with plenty of space to move around since I knew that Erina liked to pace when she was thinking something over for her stories. There was an unlit hearth to the right of the long room, the mantle decorated in fresh blooms. Straight ahead were three sets of windows that shot up a couple dozen feet in the cavernous room. The view beyond them was a perfect one of the gardens, every little vein of the pathways apparent. I could even see the tall hedges of the starwood courtyard from here and could *just* make out what I knew Erina had dubbed the Orchard, where she'd stolen many bluestone fruits to nibble upon during her long afternoons there.

In front of the window lay a drafting table, one that could be adjusted to different angles.

"I've never…" Erina started, going to it, reaching out to touch it though her hand only hovered. "I never thought I'd…"

My chest twisted, and I rubbed at my heart over my tunic. I knew what went unspoken. She never thought she'd have one of her own.

She turned to look at me, a startled look of confusion still on her face. "What is this?"

"Your gift," I replied, approaching her. I watched as her gaze darted over the shelves I'd had installed yesterday morning, stacked with supplies I'd purchased from the shopkeeper. Pencils, paper of different varieties—ranging from nearly transparent to thick parchment that was even difficult to tear, sketchbooks, brushes, and paints in nearly every color imaginable. I'd cleaned out most of the shop, truth be told, making the shopkeeper's eyes bulge.

And I worried that maybe it was too much, judging by the look of confusion on my mate's features…but I hadn't wanted to miss something important. Kythel would have known what supplies Erina might need. He had an interest in this, but the rest of us would've known nothing.

"My…my gift," she repeated. "The table?"

I laughed, reaching forward to cup her cheek. She craned her neck up to look at me, though she was continually distracted by the shelf, drawn in by the sheets of paper and the stack of notebooks.

"Everything," I murmured. "All of it is yours."

"*What?*"

I released her to gesture around the room. "Your studio. There is still one more thing coming. I had a desk made for you, custom to your height. So you can write there instead of on the drafting table. It's being lacquered today, but I suppose…I couldn't wait to show you."

She stared up at me as if I'd grown two heads.

"You…you made me a studio?"

"Yes," I replied, trying to read her and for the first time, failing. "I know you like to write and draw in the garden, but I thought you could use this room too. It's yours. You can do with it whatever you please."

Had I…miscalculated?

"Oh," she said, looking down between us, at the plush rug I'd had Maudoric purchase in the village, one that had curling vines and little leaves.

Erina promptly burst into tears, and I froze in dismay.

I took her into my arms when the shock passed, pressing her face into my chest. "I'm sorry," I said, my voice tight. "I shouldn't have assumed. I'll get rid of—"

"No!" she said, pulled away quickly. Looking up at me with a tear-stained face, her brown eyes glistening, she looked miserable as she cried, "I love it! Don't you dare change a thing."

Startled, I asked, "You do?"

"Yes!" she cried and then dissolved into full sobs again, leaving me standing there helplessly bewildered, mildly concerned, and somewhat relieved.

"What's wrong, then?" I asked, threading my hand into her hair, rubbing at the back of her neck as if that might calm her down.

"N-Nothing. It's perfect," she sobbed. "Too perfect. I—I didn't expect it. I'm just surprised."

My brow furrowed, continuing to rub at her neck even as my wings twitched in indecision. She continued to cry against me as I deliberated what to do.

"You like it?" I asked again after a long moment had passed.

When she looked up at me, this time she tried to give me a watery smile, laughing. "Yes."

My shoulders finally relaxed.

But then her eyes strayed to the left wall, at the painting I'd taken from the orphanage. Maudoric had had it reframed for me.

Erina held her breath as she stumbled from my arms. "Is that—"

"Yes," I replied, trailing after her. "I did something bad."

"You," she started, but then the words caught in her throat. She stopped directly in front of the painting, peering up at it with wide, glassy eyes. I stopped beside her, worried she might burst into tears again, my hand coming to the small of her back. "How did you get this?"

"I stole it," I informed her, quirking a brow. "Well, took it. Technically Vyaan, and by extension me, owns the land the orphanage stands on."

She turned to me, her expression still stunned. "You went there?"

I inclined my head. "It sounded important to you. I wanted you to have it back."

Unless I'd misjudged her again.

But I knew I hadn't, especially when she threw herself into my arms.

I embraced her tightly, pressing my lips to the top of her head. "Is it all right that it's here? Or would you rather have it moved?"

"I love that it's here," she breathed. She pulled back, beaming at me brightly, even though she'd begun crying again, fat little tears rolling down her face. "Gods, the pregnancy hormones," she laughed, wiping at them. "Kaldur, it's…"

She looked back at the painting.

"It's like a beautiful memory I'd forgotten, a bittersweet one," she said. "Seeing it again, it's surreal. It means a lot to me. Not only this painting but that…that you would do this for me."

I rubbed at the space over my heart again, feeling the muscle contract uncomfortably.

"You told me you had dreams of seeing your stories

throughout the Kaalium," I said. "I know that you would get there on your own. But I wanted to help you, if I could."

I saw the emotion burst in her eyes, a startling brief moment of disbelief and happiness, and she went up onto her tiptoes to press a kiss to my lips. As chaste as it was, I took advantage, keeping them captured until her laugh pushed her away.

"I've only received a few gifts in my life," she said, "but this one has to be my favorite."

My chest swelled with the words.

"And this," she said, waving her hand back to the painting, looking at it with fresh, disbelieving eyes, "makes it even better."

I watched her observe the painting. For long moments, she simply traced it with her eyes, as if going over every line and stroke she'd once made with her pencil. I imagined she could still draw every detail from memory.

Then she silently but happily inspected the rest of the room, and I stayed out of her way, content to simply watch from one of the armchairs I'd had placed in the corner. One meant for a Kylorr with wings. Me, specifically, so I might watch her work.

I watched as she fluttered from the shelves of supplies, as if cataloguing every last one. She went to the paper stacks, to the notebooks, running her fingers over the expertly stitched leather, sniffling.

She finally skimmed her fingers over the drafting table, sitting for a brief moment at the stool. It was a good height for her, I decided.

Finally she strayed to the bookshelf on the opposite side, near me and the painting. I'd left it mostly empty, deciding she could fill it with whatever she pleased.

Except…

"Is this your book?" she asked in disbelief, turning to me with wide eyes.

I inclined my head. "You should have it."

The book I'd shown her in the library, what felt like a lifetime ago. That quiet, peaceful night which had shown me a glimpse of what a future with her could be like. Comfortable, warm, fun. I had liked to please her, to watch her expressions light up in excitement.

"And another one?" she asked, her fingers skimming over the spine. Immediately, she flipped it open, her eyes hungry for the landscapes, of alien places she might never see.

"I found it at a collector's shop," I informed her. What I didn't tell her was that I had our off-planet ambassador searching for more. I would locate them all for her. Another gift for another time.

Next to the books was another Halo orb, with the capabilities of projecting the landscapes for her.

"You really thought of everything, didn't you?" she asked, looking at the Halo orb and then to me. "I had no idea. You've been busy. And this was all *before* you got attacked by that *lyvin* pack."

"That was my mistake," I murmured. "I got too impatient."

She strayed to where I was sitting in the chair. "And you were hungry."

I grunted. "Like I said, my own mistake."

"And mine," she said softly.

"No," I bit out.

She sighed, and I tugged her into my lap.

"It's different between us now," I said. "I won't let myself get to that state again, all right?"

A part of me had treated it like a punishment. For how I'd hurt her, I'd thought that I deserved to hurt too.

Now I saw how foolish that reasoning truly was.

"I know I *need* to be strong," I said gruffly. "For you. For our child. So that if anything happens, I can protect you to my full capabilities. I will *never* let myself get to that state again. I can't. I'm sorry."

It had been foolish. So fucking foolish. I saw that clearly now.

What would've happened if Erina had been there last night? What if the *lyvin* had gone after her? Would I have been strong enough to defend her? We'd tracked down the pack in the woods because they'd attacked a farmer last night. But what if that had been Erina? My child?

"Kaldur," she called, and I realized I was holding her too tightly.

I loosened my grip immediately as she reached up to smooth her finger down my face.

"I never asked how you got this," she said gently. My scar, she meant. "The keepers had a lot of theories over the years."

My lips quirked. " Like what?"

"A brawl gone wrong. A scorned lover. A childhood fall when you were too daring."

"All of them plausible, unfortunately," I drawled.

"The keepers certainly thought so," she informed me. I knew what she was doing. Trying to distract me when she'd sensed my reaction about the *lyvins*.

"My father made us all train with blades since we were young," I informed her. "Thaine and I were training one day. I must have been fifteen at the time. Thaine, a couple years older. Our instructor was teaching us how to spar two opponents at once. She never took it easy on us—she, or my father, didn't believe in that. The blades were always real, and we have the scars to prove it," I said. "We were in the forest that day. Thaine accidentally tripped over a root when our instructor was coming at us hard. He tried to turn to get out of the way of her blade, which was"—I made a wide arc with my hand overhead, showing her where it would land—"coming right here."

Right over the middle of my face.

"I saw it," I said, giving her a curl of a smile. "I lunged to push him out of the way. And it came right here."

Her fingers traced the scar. Old now—I didn't even notice it anymore.

"You saved him," she noted.

I gave a little scoff. "He would've been fine. Maybe lost an eye. It would've built his character better. I was the one maimed for life."

She shook her head, a laugh of disbelief falling from her. "I'm sure the females found it very dashing," she said dryly.

"They did," I admitted, lips quirking as I teased her. My smile faded. "Thaine did feel terribly about it. He still does sometimes. I use it to my full advantage too."

"You're incorrigible," she whispered, her eyes tracing the scar.

"I thought I saved him," I murmured, raising a brow. "I'm a hero, remember?"

"And very humble too."

I laughed. Then after it faded, so did my smile. "Truthfully, I didn't really think in that moment. There were no consequences except Thaine being seriously injured. It was instinct alone. And had it been reversed, he would've done the same for me. So there's nothing heroic about it. It was just me…"

"Loving your brother," she finished.

"Yes," I said, inclining my head. "You know what that's like." Referring to Luc, of course. "And even though they disappoint you, even though you sometimes don't agree with their decisions, you still love them."

Understanding had softened her gaze. "You love your family."

"Deeply," I rumbled. "Every last one of them, even when we can't stand each other."

"There were rumors a while back that you had a disagreement with your eldest brother over his choice of a wife," she hedged, cocking her head to the side.

"True, unfortunately," I rasped, feeling a twinge of regret when I thought of Gemma and our first encounter. "Azur…you'll meet him one day. You'll see. We call him the fire to Kythel's ice. The twins. Azur took his wife for revenge alone, married her to keep her close."

"I know it had something to do with your aunt."

"Were the keepers gossiping?" I asked, leveling her an inquiring, yet knowing, look.

"Always."

"My aunt, Aina, was murdered during the Pe'ji War," I told her. She should know. This was House Kaalium business, after all. "We were very close. And my own mother died not knowing what had happened to her sister."

"That's terrible," Erina whispered. " I'm sorry."

"We discovered that Gemma's father, Azur's wife," I said, nodding, "was involved in Aina's murder during the war. Gemma had no knowledge of it and was horrified when she found out. Me and her… I nearly went into a rage one night at a ball in his keep because I couldn't stand the thought of her own blood having been mixed up in Aina's death. It ate at me. I didn't agree with Azur, with what he was doing. But then…I didn't realize that she was his *kyrana*."

Her lips parted in knowing.

"Now I know what he'd gone through. I can understand him better," I added, tucking a strand of hair behind her ear. "He would've never given her up."

Her eyes burned into mine.

"But like me with my *kyrana*, Azur made his own spectacular failings with Gemma," I added.

Erina sighed. "Is that meant to soften me toward you?"

"Yes," I said shamelessly. "Because they are very happily mated now."

She struggled to keep her helpless smile from showing. She turned her face to look away from me, her eyes going to the painting on the wall overhead again.

"Wasn't Pe'ji in the book you showed me?" she asked. "That night in the library."

"You remember," I said. "Yes, it was."

"I'm sorry about your aunt. And your mother," Erina said, turning back to me.

A delicate question rose in my mind, one I'd often wondered. "Do you ever think about your own parents? Who they were?" I wondered. "If you ever want me to investigate, I will."

But Erina didn't look sad nor excited at the prospect. "Is it weird that I don't wonder about them often? I used to. When I was a child. Now...I think about my mother especially because I'm pregnant, but it's a stray, passing thought. And then it leaves me. Because, you see, with the exception of Luc, I've always been alone. I wonder, especially in your case, do you think it's better to have grieved those you lost, felt that terrible pain, or to have never known true grief to begin with?"

"Grief and loss is an important part of life," I said, thinking this conversation was familiar before I remembered. "Ah. Our *dallia* fable conversation again."

"It's funny how it comes back around," she said quietly, thinking over my words. "I...I would choose to grieve."

"Why?"

"Because it means you loved someone to grieve them," she said. "That's a beautiful thing. A special thing."

Our eyes met and held. My throat felt a little tight, hearing what went unspoken.

"Did you grieve me in Laras?" I wondered softly.

"Yes," she answered. An honest one, raw and open. Simple. "And then I tried to do everything I could to forget you."

CHAPTER 44
KALDUR

*H*er words were a gentle confession that twisted me up into knots.

I didn't like that she'd felt alone most of her life either. But for the first time, I was *glad* for Luc. Glad for their friendship, that he had treated my mate with kindness and love. That he'd given her hope and encouraged her dreams.

Without him, there would be no *her*. What she was. Or her unwavering optimism and resilience, though I had caused both to lose a little of their shine. One I was determined to polish back to its full brilliance.

"In Laras," she continued, a creeping of sadness in her tone, "I didn't feel like myself. I felt defeated, and I hated it. I felt more alone than I have in years."

"Erina," I growled, that familiar restlessness making me vibrate.

"And I don't blame you," she said quickly, as if realizing how I'd take her words. To heart. "Leaving Vyaan was my choice. It was impulsive, yes, but I thought...I thought things would be different. I *dreamed* that things would be different, that I would be reunited with Luc and everything we ever imagined would come to fruition. The two orphans against the world," she said, her lips twisting a little. In bitterness…and I hated to see it on her. "But just because I dreamed it, it didn't mean it would be true. Not in the slightest. Laras helped to pull back a veil from my eyes. I struggle with…"

She made a sound in the back of her throat, one that was frustrated, as if she didn't know how to express the words building in her throat.

"Try," I murmured. "Tell me."

"Everyone always told me to stop dreaming, to stop filling my head with silly ideas and face the reality of my existence. That I was an orphan, with no family. I wasn't born into a noble House. Wrezaan tore up a bunch of my stories once, told me that he was doing me a favor."

I growled. "He did *what?*"

She shook her head. "It doesn't matter. I worked any job I could find after I left Wrezaan's, until I was lucky enough to work for Syndras. Which led me here. And it wasn't glamorous work, but I was…I was content with it. Because it allowed me the freedom to think up different places and worlds in my mind, which kept my ambitions for my stories alive. Wrezaan couldn't take that from me. No one could. I was proud of that. But what Laras showed me was the truth, one I couldn't escape, no matter how much I could dream differently. That I'm still an orphan. With no real family. With a fake name."

"Then take mine."

The words fell from me easily, though nothing was easy about listening to her speak this way.

Erina's lips parted. "What?"

"Take *my* name, then," I rasped. "Take my name that stretches back generations, the lineage our child will be born into."

My *kyrana* stared at me in disbelief, but I'd never been more serious about anything.

"What you're saying is true. Objectively," I said gruffly. "You are an orphan because you never knew your parents. But you're not alone and you have a family. In me, in our child, in Luc. In Syndras, who took you into her own home when you felt like you had none and tried to protect you, even from me. And you don't have a fake name, Erina. You took a name that was meaningful to you, that made you feel not only connected to Luc, your chosen brother, but to your stories. And I think it's one you should carry for the rest of your life."

"Even above yours?" she asked.

"You could be Erina Denoren of House Kaalium," I suggested quietly. The burn of need at the sound of that name nearly humbled me. "You don't have to give anything up."

We regarded one another closely, both of us seeming to hold our breath. I knew she wouldn't give me an answer right now. But I would be patient.

"You don't need to decide now," I told her. I saw a burst of relief she couldn't quite hide and felt the sharpness of disappointment spear through me. "It will always be yours if you choose to take it."

Silence lapsed between us again, but it wasn't uncomfortable. It was speculative.

Then my mate's breath hitched, wonderment entering her expression, a small smile following. She took my hand, placed it on her ever-growing belly.

I felt it then. A slight fluttering that could be mistaken for a heartbeat, only it was sporadic and came and went.

"She's moving," Erina said.

My throat went tight, disbelief and awe bursting in my mind. The first time I'd felt our child in her womb, and it was…indescribable.

We grinned at one another as morning light flooded the room, golden rays stretching across the floor. A special moment that eclipsed everything else.

When she finally stopped and I couldn't feel any more movement, Erina sighed. Her brow was furrowed, and I could see her mind turning.

"I don't want you to misunderstand me...or—or think that I'm sad about how this all turned out. It's the opposite," she said. "I think I needed Laras. My time there humbled me, and I think it was a blessing. I think I needed to face the cold sting of reality, to realize that not everything will be perfect just because I want it to be. That's foolish. But...I also don't want to lose who I used to be. I...I don't think it's a bad thing to romanticize life, to wonder about the endless possibilities, to hope for something more," she finished.

And hearing that relieved me. I nearly closed my eyes with it.

"I don't want you to lose that either," I confessed. "Because I love that about you, Erina."

She went shy with the words, this maddening female, trying to hide her smile which threatened to burst. "You do?"

Among many other things, I thought.

But I didn't say that aloud. I didn't want to scare her. I was working on being patient. For her.

Her gaze went back to the painting hanging on the wall.

"I worried I'd lost my inspiration to create," she said softly. "But this morning, a scene struck me and it felt wonderful. And now *this...*"

She gestured around the room before she resettled her gaze on me.

"Thank you, Kaldur," she said. "I can't quite tell you what this means to me. But I'm not worried anymore. I can't wait to get back to my stories. So, thank you."

She leaned forward to press a kiss to my cheek. Right over my scar, which she now knew how I'd received.

"You're welcome, *dallia.*"

The door opened to the studio, Maudoric humming as she entered. When she saw us sitting in the armchair, Erina sprawled over my lap, she looked as surprised as I'd ever seen her, stuttering for a moment.

"Oh, goodness—my apologies, *Kyzaire*," she said, already backing out of the room. "I should've—"

I waved away her worries, especially when I saw what was in her hands. "I wanted to show her what we've been working on."

Maudoric smiled hesitantly, inclining her head. "This was just delivered by a boy from the village."

"Thank you," I replied as I patted Erina, who stood. I followed and crossed to Maudoric, taking the ribboned box from her hands.

"Would you like breakfast brought here? Or out on the terrace?" Maudoric asked.

I looked to Erina, who said, "Here." She beamed at the Head Keeper. "The light is beautiful in here."

It pleased Maudoric, I realized. Erina's happiness. "I'll tell Saira," Maudoric said, leaving the room swiftly, giving us privacy.

I brought the box over to the drafting table and gestured Erina over.

"Another gift?" she asked, biting her lip.

"The last one for today—I promise," I teased gently. "Open it."

Erina pulled at the silky black ribbon, and the box unfolded with dramatic flourish, the sides falling open. She gasped. Because inside was a familiar vase.

"I thought it was gone," she breathed, reaching out a hand to touch it.

"Maudoric found it in the drawer. Luckily I caught her before she disposed of it," I said. It was the vase I'd helped her clean up that day in the sitting room, the one she'd cut her hand on. The one that had been the cause of everything. She'd loved it, had wanted to repair it even though it'd been shattered.

The vase had been pieced back together and was filled with precious silver along the cracks. But otherwise the potter had been able to preserve the majority of it—the dark green that she'd so loved, the delicate vines.

"It is missing a big piece though," I informed her, turning the vase to show her the back. "It's a large shard. I couldn't find it. So he kept it open."

"I have it," she admitted.

"You do?" I asked, laughing.

"I—I took it that morning I left. I don't know…it was a silly impulse. I just wanted to take something. To remember," she confessed, her cheeks flushing a little bit.

"Little thief," I murmured softly, a burst of affection in my chest.

"It wasn't the only thing I took from House Kaalium," she joked, her hand touching her stomach, "as it turns out."

"No, it wasn't," I said, watching when her eyes strayed to the vase again. "I was going to have one made in its exact likeness for you. But then I remembered what you told me."

"Remind me."

"Even if it's a little broken, that doesn't mean it can't be beautiful again."

Her exact words. Words I'd remembered.

Her breath whistled with her inhale as she stared up at me in surprise. I saw tears well, which she tried to blink away.

"You were right, *dallia*," I murmured. "I think it's even more beautiful like this."

CHAPTER 45
—
ERINA

"*D*evelopment is on track," Ekor said softly, peering down at whatever scans he'd taken on his Halo tablet. "Another six weeks, I'd guess."

Kaldur paced a short distance. "She's been having some pain… you're certain it's not anything more serious?"

"Everything is as it should be," the healer said with the utmost patience. He'd been coming nearly every day at Kaldur's request, who seemed to get more anxious as the time to my giving birth drew nearer.

"It's okay," I said, standing and catching Kaldur's arm. "I told you—you worry too much. The pain was because…"

I trailed off, flushing when Ekor cut us a curious look as he packed up his supplies.

Kaldur rumbled out, "I know."

I'd felt a sharp pain during sex, but I knew it was because we'd gone a little overboard lately. But it was hard to stay away. I was getting *hornier* as the days dragged on, and Kaldur was getting more and more concerned that he would hurt me. Which was making for an interesting dynamic, and nothing pleased me more when he finally gave into me.

"There haven't been any complications from sex in the later stages of pregnancy," Ekor answered, understanding what went unspoken, much to my embarrassment. "Even up to a few days before birth."

"That won't happen," Kaldur grumbled.

It likely *would* though. He always griped about me getting too far along, that the last thing he wanted to do was hurt me, but truthfully when we were with each other, it was...consuming. Everything else didn't matter, the world went hazy but electric, and all we wanted was to be together.

I feared I was growing addicted to his touch. Every kiss, every spine-tingling wicked word in my ear as he was deep inside me, every ragged groan and huff that I seemed to live for.

When it came to Kaldur, I was obsessed with our lovemaking, and I thought he felt the same. It had been two weeks since the *lyvin* pack attack, and we couldn't stay away from one another.

"I'm simply saying if it does continue," Ekor said, snapping his case shut tightly and making for the door, "it has not shown any adverse effects or complications once the birth comes."

I shot Kaldur a pleased look. As if to say: *See?* His jaw twitched, and then he led the healer out of his study. I would likely see Ekor tomorrow regardless, even if I was anxious to get rid of him now.

From my place, I watched Kaldur as he spoke with the healer in low tones at the threshold of the door. Ekor clasped his shoulder, inclining his head, and then departed.

I eyed Kaldur when he turned back to me. I'd been ravenous for him all day, but he'd had an early morning meeting with his brothers, so this was the first time I was seeing him.

"I know that look," he declared.

"Why don't you close the door?" I suggested, my tone the epitome of innocence.

A low groan rose in his bobbing throat, and I tried to keep my expression neutral.

"I've created a little monster," he rasped, his words punctuated by the sound of the door thudding, the lock turning.

And that sound made me squeeze my thighs together. My buttocks met the edge of his desk when he stalked toward me. His expression looked like a glare, as brooding and intense as it was, but I still caught the fervid anticipation in his silver gaze.

"Ekor seemed to think it was fine," I told him, craning my neck back when he stopped an inch in front of me, my belly brushing his groin.

"Don't say another male's name when I'm about to bend you over my desk, my love," he purred.

A sharp ache of desire spiraled downward. "Is that how you want me?"

"One way of many," he replied, already tugging at my dress. Another one he'd bought me. I could wear a new one every day until I gave birth and still not run out. Which for me, considering I'd fit my entire wardrobe in a single travel bag once, seemed excessive, but I was learning which battles I needed to pick with Kaldur. He liked to give gifts, and I wouldn't refuse them. He got moody if I did.

"Wait," I said, flitting away from his hands when he was intent on getting me naked. "You promised, remember?"

"Fuck," he whispered, briefly closing his eyes. When they opened, they were practically black with want. "*Dallia*, you'll have me on your tongue for mere moments and then I'll need to come."

"I want that," I informed him, my voice going husky with the image it conjured in my mind. I'd tried to pleasure him, as he often pleasured me, but he'd always stopped me, saying he didn't have the control he needed in that particular moment.

"Darling, the moment I feel that pink little tongue anywhere near my cock," he rasped, "or see you looking up at me with those pretty eyes with your mouth stuffed full, I will *fucking lose it*."

"I want that," I repeated again, my eyelids going half-lidded. I didn't know how many times I thought about sex with Kaldur a day, but it was obsessive. And truthfully I didn't *know* if it was the pregnancy hormones or…simply because it was Kaldur.

I was willing to bet on the latter, however, more so than the former, though that certainly played a role.

I was already reaching for the laces of his trews, and he looked skyward, saying something that sounded like a rough, hushed prayer. *Dramatic male,* I thought, eagerness making my hands shake.

When I got them undone, I began to sink to the ground in front of him, though he helped me down, ever worried. The rug bit into my knees, but I didn't mind.

My mouth watered as I wrapped my fist around his familiar thickness, giving a slow pump up the shaft. He grunted, and I watched as pre-come pooled at his tip. The bulbous head was a dark gray, swollen and throbbing already with his need. Truthfully I'd never seen what his cock looked like *soft,* so I had nothing to compare it to.

"Erina," came his ragged whisper from above me. My gaze went from his cock to his face as I lowered my head. His expression looked struck, those eyes rapt on me when my lips brushed the tip. It was *sexy,* the way he looked at me, and I could very easily grow addicted just to those hooded eyes alone.

His cock gave a throb that made him growl, a low rumbling that vibrated through his entire body as I slowly wrapped my lips around his head.

I dragged my tongue over the underside of him, his hips giving an unsteady jerk, a hiss of pleasure escaping him. I pulled back. My voice sounded throaty when I asked, "Like this?"

"Raazos, *yes,*" he rasped. "That's so good, my love. Again. *Please.*"

His praise turned me on even more. When I took his cock between my lips again, I repeated what he'd liked, earning me another roughened groan.

"Look at me," he ordered. When my eyes flicked up, he hardened even further in my mouth, which I hadn't thought would possible. I moved down his shaft, testing how much I could take, and I tasted the earthiness of his pre-come bloom across my tongue.

He sucked in a sharp breath, his hand flashing down to squeeze around the very base of his shaft, above his swelling knot.

"Mmm," I hummed.

"Suck me, *kyrana*," he ordered. Immediately my cheeks hollowed over the tip of his cock, and Kaldur bucked, a gruff cry on his lips. With gritted teeth, he growled, "More."

I sucked harder, moving up and down, and the sound that left him made my thighs squeeze.

"Fuck," he breathed, shaking his head, an edge of panic in his expression. "Gods, I get so wild for you. I told you—I'm not going to last like this."

I released him with a pop. "A little longer?"

His eyes slid shut, breathing steadily through his nostrils in deep huffs, and I grinned a little before taking him back inside. As if he would *suffer* through it, for me.

One of my hands was on the shaft of his exposed cock, but the other was trailing to my inner thighs, desperately needing some relief. I hadn't expected this to turn me on so much. But I felt like I was on the verge of coming just because of *his* pleasure, as if ours were connected.

I felt his body begin to tremble. I knew I wouldn't have much longer, and so I sucked on his cock harder, moving my fist up the rest of his exposed shaft. Up and down, but then when my palm met the swelling of his knot, I squeezed.

A ragged cry tore from him. I was up before I knew what was happening, a low warning of a rumble my only indication that I'd teased him beyond his control. I was flipped over, my breasts pressed down into his desk, allowing my growing belly room below. My dress was shoved up with rough, impatient hands as my legs widened for him. He took my hips, roughly pulling me back, and then—

Kaldur slid deep, swift and hard.

My gasp was followed by a satisfied moan, unable to keep the smile from curling over my features. One of his palms was squeezing one cheek of my backside in appreciation as he continued to thrust hard.

"My little mate," he purred, though a hardened edge clipped through his tone. "Trying to test your boundaries? Trying to make your male lose control?" He laughed, which was punctuated by a particular deep thrust that made my breath squeeze from my lungs. "Oh, *kyrana*, you can do whatever you want to me. Then again, I can do whatever I want to you, yes?"

"Yes," I moaned.

"Tell me you're mine," he growled.

I stared across his neat desk, which we were steadily making a mess of. Out the window overlooking Vyaan, it was a chilled but beautiful day. The first snowfall might come today, and I wanted to watch it out on the balcony with Kaldur, warm in his arms.

"I'm yours," I whispered, my heart squeezing with the words.

"I know, my love," he murmured, his front coming down on top of me so I could feel the length of him, though he was mindful of the pressure because of the baby. His lips pressed a sweet kiss to my temple, completely at odds with the hard, claiming strokes between my thighs. "*Always. So. Fucking. Good.*"

"Going to come," I breathed, feeling the familiar tightening in my abdomen.

The prick of Kaldur's fangs came, the familiar dizzying pull of his feeding as his venom flowed into me. I cried out, the orgasm ripping through me immediately. I heard his bellow, muffled against my skin, his hips jerking, his rhythm going choppy.

When it was over, I let out a tired, delighted laugh. He caught his breath quickly, his recovery much more swift than mine, pressing a kiss to his bite on my neck.

"Mine," he said quietly. The word drifted over my skin before it settled comfortably.

Tears welled in my gaze, but they weren't unhappy tears.

"Yours," I whispered.

THE FIRST SNOWFALL DID COME THAT NIGHT, AND I WAS, IN FACT, bundled in Kaldur's arms out on the balcony. Pure white, fluffy flakes were falling beyond the covered balcony, and Kaldur was watching me quietly as I sketched the scene. Or tried to. I would never quite capture its quiet serenity or the way I felt in that singular moment: protected, warm, and encouraged.

Kaldur had been absent since our afternoon in his study, his attention having been pulled away toward the South Road. Specifically about the *lyvins*. He'd hired a team to draw the pack away, deeper into the forest, into another habitable location *not* near a populated village.

The South Road was currently being built toward his brother's territory of Salaire. Thaine. The brother he'd told me he was closest to, the brother he'd taken his scar for, the brother he said I would be meeting quite soon.

"I like watching you draw," came his sweet, soft words. "Even the scratching of your pencil is soothing to me. Your movements are so certain. I don't know how you do it. I could never be still as a child, and yet I could sit here forever watching you."

I bit back my smile, turning a little to regard him. Our faces were close. I was sitting sideways across his lap, his arm bracing around my back as support, and he'd brought out two blankets. One to drape over my shoulders but allowed my hands to be free, and the other was carefully tucked around my lap. I was warm enough with the blankets, but coupled with Kaldur's heat and it felt like a summer day. The baby was moving again, Kaldur's hand resting on the swell.

I looked back to my drawing, trying to see it from his perspective. I thought it was simple, if a little messy. I shaded in the moon a bit more, adding charcoal to the left side, rubbing at it with the pad of my fingertip to blend a harsh line.

"Another week and the moon winds will be here," I commented.

Almost a month I'd been back in Vyaan. How fast it had gone by. This time last month I'd still been in Laras…and yet everything had changed.

Well, not everything. Luc was still being a little stubborn about accepting Kaldur's assistance. But Kaldur assured me that whoever he had in correspondence with my brother would make him see reason.

Give him time, Kaldur had told me, just a few days ago, when I'd wanted to write a letter to Luc myself. *If he's anything like how I imagine, he needs time.*

Luc didn't trust it. I knew that. A stranger appearing out of nowhere and offering to give him his dream back? Everything he'd lost? At no cost, with no strings? Of course he would be wary.

If he didn't accept after the moon winds, Kaldur told me he'd personally travel to Laras. Or have Azur speak with him if Ekor didn't think it was a good idea for him to be gone.

I'd agreed in the end, knowing that Kaldur was right. I was learning that he had a very diplomatic and almost patient way of dealing with most issues, especially when it came to matters concerning Vyaan or the Kaalium. I understood now why he made such a good leader, why nearly all the nobles I'd ever come across seemed to respect his position there. He worked incredibly hard—sometimes too hard and at his own expense, like with the *lyvin* attack.

"I would like to have a gathering here on the moon winds,"

Kaldur told me, capturing my attention again. "What do you think?"

He was asking me?

"Then you should," I replied.

"You could invite Syndras," he suggested. "I believe that Thaine will come. He wants to meet you. All my siblings do."

That made another jolt of nerves go through me, even though I would be both equally excited and trepidatious of meeting them.

"What's wrong?" he asked, no doubt sensing the way my body went a little tight. When I hesitated, he pressed with, "Tell me. I want to know, even if you think I won't like it. I want us to be honest. In all things. Are you worried he won't like you?"

"Yes," I said.

Kaldur actually laughed, but it wasn't unkind. "*Dallia*, I don't know a single soul who doesn't like you."

"Velle," I said. "Lydrasa. To name a couple."

"They don't count," he grumbled, the mere mention of them souring his mood. He sighed. "You have nothing to worry about. Besides, this is Thaine. He's the most sane perhaps out of any of us, next to Kythel. What is it, really?"

I put down my pencil in the seam of my notebook. I bit my lip, judging how to express what I felt. Finally I settled on, "Sometimes I still feel like an imposter in your life."

Kaldur scowled.

"Someone who doesn't quite belong, though circumstance— and a child, on Raazos's blood—brought us back into each other's lives. We're so different, you and me. We couldn't be more different."

"And that's a good thing," he said. "You think I want someone like me? I would go mad. As for you, I think you need someone to fill your life with inspirations for your stories. And I'll take that responsibility very seriously."

"I'm being serious," I said.

"So am I," he said simply, turning my cheek so I looked him in the eye. "You belong in my life like you're my family. All right? I don't want to hear this because it's simply not true."

My heart fluttered. "You don't think your brothers or Kalia will take issue with the fact that I used to be a keeper in your House? Or that I have no legacy, no ancestry of my own?"

"Of course not," he rasped. "But I realize you can't know this for yourself until you meet them. I was the bastard who gave you these fears anyway. And my brothers' mates? Gemma was the daughter of a disgraced war hero who turned out to be a murderer and gambled away his entire fortune. Millie was found abandoned on a transport colony and then later worked at a *dyaan* as a server. That's where Kythel met her."

"She was?" I asked. Millie had been abandoned too? And she'd worked at a blood-giver establishment? I hadn't known that. I'd known Gemma had come from a noble House from the New Earth colonies but not that her father had nearly lost them everything.

Kaldur blew out a sharp breath. "I'm not saying Kythel rejoiced in the fact that Millie wasn't connected to a noble family. He had planned to marry the daughter of the family who owned the Three Guardians in Erzos. He thought it was his duty, the fucking martyr, to marry for a *purpose*, for the betterment of his people. As for Azur, well, I've told you my feelings on what he did before."

"You're not making me feel any better," I couldn't help but point out.

His shoulders shook with the dryness in my tone. "My point is that none of that mattered. It's simple. They love their mates, even though that love didn't come easily. Mistakes were made. Very terrible mistakes. But in the end, they chose each other, regardless of circumstance or class or old wounds. Because they knew that they couldn't live without each other, nor did they want to."

My throat went tight again. Kaldur was looking at me with that familiar look I'd become accustomed to: one of softness, of ease. And whenever he looked at me like that…all I wanted was to throw caution to the wind and fall into him.

The silence that lapsed between us made me hold my breath. His lips parted, and he pressed a kiss to the corner of my mouth. Then when a snowflake fell on my cheek, a brief burn of icy cold, he trailed his lips to where it'd fallen, warming me again.

When he pulled back to look in my eyes, my heartbeat spiked.

"Just like I can't live without you," he said quietly. "I love you, Erina."

My tongue felt like it was stuck to the roof of my mouth as I stared at him. Below his wide, firm palm, I felt our daughter move again.

"I know that you know that," he continued, tilting his chin down slightly so that our foreheads touched. "I also know that you're not there with me yet, and so I don't want you to say anything right now. But I just wanted to tell you…I'm not going anywhere. You're all I want."

I breathed out, my gaze going to his lips as they formed these beautiful little words that I wanted so desperately to claim as mine.

"I can't promise that I'll never hurt you again. I think we both know I can be a stubborn, hardheaded bastard, and I intend to live a long life with you. In terms of time, the odds are against me there. But I *can* promise that I will always choose you. I won't ever turn my back on you. Never again. Because I see you now, Erina Denoren. And I never want to look away."

I couldn't help the tears when they started. They came on softly but then began to stream as I absorbed his words. He told me not to say anything, and so I didn't. I only pressed my face into his chest as I cried.

The last barrier between us was only my refusal to give him

my heart again. That last small decision. One that would be so easy and effortless because he'd made it easy to love him. Again.

These last two weeks, I'd been *happy*. Except for this one small thing that I couldn't allow myself to give.

"The moon winds are always a time for rebirth. A fresh start," he murmured into my ear, wrapping his arms around me.

Maybe it will be ours, I thought.

CHAPTER 46

ERINA

"You've sighed enough to fill my entire House with your worries," came Syndras's wry observation, her bright eyes peering over the rim of her cup as she took a sip of wine.

"I'm sorry," I said. Then sighed again. Then laughed, the sound sheepish. "I'm sorry."

"Is it the child?" Syndras asked, her voice knowing. Her lips curled. "Or the father?"

My eyes went to Braanelle, who was standing stock-still by the door of the sitting room. I'd decided to visit Syndras this afternoon after she'd written to me yesterday.

Braanelle met my eyes, inclining her head briefly, before she stepped from the room, closing the door behind her until it was just me and Syndras.

"The father," I answered. "Not that anything has been bad between us. It's the opposite actually. Everything has been perfect. But that's the problem."

"Ah," Syndras said. "I understand."

"You do?" I asked, a little hopefully.

397

"My dear girl, I'm older than some of the trees in Vyaan," she said softly, setting down her teacup on the small table next to her. One of her keepers, Finly, had brought in a small tray earlier, laden with special treats. "Tell me what's been troubling you."

Relief threaded through me as I looked at Syndras, who was, perhaps, my only friend outside of Kaldur. Maudoric held affection for me, yes, but I felt like I could tell Syndras whatever I needed. With Maudoric, it was difficult because her loyalties would always lie with House Kaalium, as did Braanelle's. I didn't want to put them in a difficult position.

I stared down at my belly, running a hand over where our daughter grew.

"I've been happy," I confessed.

Syndras laughed. "That is terrible news indeed."

"These last few weeks have been...they've been everything that I always imagined they could be," I added. "With Kaldur."

She sobered. "And you don't trust it."

"Exactly," I breathed, my shoulders sagging. "I keep waiting for the bad."

Syndras rose from her chair, reaching for her cane. Her wings were weathered, the membranes slightly wrinkled. I knew it had been years since she'd last flown. I frowned when I watched her walk over to me.

"Hush—you're pregnant," she said when I began to fuss. "I'm merely old."

I sighed but waited as she took the seat beside me on the chaise. She took my hand, her palm cool to the touch. She turned it over, inspecting the flattened surface, running one finger down my middle one.

She met my eyes, and in her patient way, she said, "Tell me, my dear. And I'll give you what advice I can."

Advice was what I desperately needed.

Syndras saw my struggle, however, to form the words of everything that was jumbled in my mind.

Instead, she asked, "Tell me one thing. Do you love him?"

The answer seemed to ring through my entire body. Syndras probably saw it plastered over my face because her expression was almost sympathetic, though understanding.

"I think that," I began, "the heart is such a stupid, foolish thing, with no sense of self-preservation at all."

"That has been my experience, yes," she said, her eyes twinkling with mischief. "And isn't it marvelous?"

Syndras's hand was as soft as silk when I gave it a gentle squeeze.

"I do love him," I said quietly, the confession easy, "but it's hard to trust *myself* with that love."

"It's not about him, then?" she asked, trying to puzzle it out in her careful way.

"It's both—me and him. I don't trust myself because I've been so wrong about him before. But I'm also afraid. I'm afraid to *give in* to that love because if I do and he breaks my heart again, it will shatter me completely. Into trillions of little pieces with no hope of piecing myself back together this time."

Understanding dawned on her face.

"I know what I *want* to do," I added. "I want to just…sink into him. I feel so shackled by this fear, and I just want to be free of it. I want to be free to love him."

"There's no stopping you from doing that."

"It's this barrier I keep encountering. In me," I admitted. "And I don't know how to get over it. I don't know what to do. We've been so happy that it feels strange. So it breaks my heart a little because I know he *feels* this wall I'm still keeping between us. It hurts him too, but he's been so patient. And even with the baby, *gods*, he'll make an incredible father, and that alone just makes me want to—to launch myself at him and never let go."

I was crying again. I didn't realize it until Syndras reached forward to wipe the tears away from my cheeks. I cried so often these days, wild emotion pumping through me like a factory.

Yesterday I'd cried over how perfectly a pattern had been stitched onto the shirt I'd been wearing, much to Kaldur's bewildered concern.

"Breathe," Syndras told me, her voice calm, the stable rock I desperately needed right now. "And, in my opinion, it's perfectly normal to feel this way, Erina."

"You think so?" I asked, relieved.

"Naturally," she said. "You didn't tell me everything about what happened between you two, and I don't want you to. Some things are between couples, and no one else should know. But you told me enough for me to fill in the gaps. He hurt you. He broke your heart. He was your first love, and that one always hurts the most. He wasn't gentle about it, was he?"

I swallowed. I shook my head.

"Of course it's natural for you to have doubts. He made a mistake. A terrible mistake. And you can spend your life punishing him for what he did," Syndras said. "A broken heart can become a terrible weapon if you're not careful, after all."

Hearing those words made my heart twist. Because I didn't want that.

"*Or*…you can make the hard choice to forgive him and *choose* to build a life with him. But in making that decision, you will need to promise to let the past go. You need to cleanse yourself of it. Him too, because I'm sure he's been punishing himself."

He had been. At first I'd thought that seeing his regret and guilt would make me feel better, that it would heal the part of me that felt broken.

In the end, however, it had just made me feel worse.

"He told me he loved me a few nights ago," I confessed.

"Do you believe him?"

"Yes," I said. "But even still, there's this tiny voice in my head that sows doubt. How can I trust that he loves me? How can I trust that what he feels is for *me* and not because of our blood bond or because of the baby?"

"You can't ever know for certain," Syndras said simply, shrugging. "That's where faith comes in. You can choose to have faith, or you can always be uncertain in wonder. I, for one, know which one I'd choose."

Her eyes strayed to the painting over the lit hearth. It was snowing outside, a cold and dark afternoon, but it was cozy and warm in her sitting room. It was my favorite place in this House. Even when I'd worked for Syndras, we would spend time in here together.

"My Axia reminds me of your Kaldur," Syndras said. Her eyes roved over the painting of the handsome Kylorr male. Her husband, who'd long passed. His soul gem was enshrined in Vyaan, and every moon winds, Syndras still visited with him. "He was stubborn and high-handed. Oh so charming. You should have seen him at parties. He had everyone there enveloped within his wings. The most handsome male in the room. It was so hard staying mad at him. But *gods*, he made me so mad sometimes."

I smiled, my nose stinging a bit at the raw emotion I *still* heard in her voice. To love someone for so long, even when they drove you mad, it must've been a soul-binding love.

"There were times in our relationship where I wanted to leave," she said. "Times where he was struggling or I was too cynical. But you know when I fell even more in love with him? When I *chose* him and he chose me. Over everything. It would've been easier to walk away, but we fought for our love and it grew even stronger."

I hadn't known that, but I supposed in her long marriage, they would've struggled.

"I do still love him terribly. Even in the next realm, when we meet one another again, we'll still give each other hell. And I'll be happy."

I started to tear up again. "You've lived a full life, Syndras."

"Don't act like I'm on my death bed yet," she grumbled,

though she patted my hand. "My Axia will have to wait at least two decades more before I join him in Alara."

I bit back my watery smile, thinking over her words.

"Forgiveness is hard," Syndras said. "But luckily for the *Kyzaire*, you are more forgiving than anyone I've ever met. It's not a weakness; it's a strength. It means you have an open heart. It would be a shame to close it because of fear."

After Braanelle led me back to the keep that night and saw me safely inside, I was still thinking over Syndras's words.

I didn't want to live a fearful life. That much I was certain of.

Kaldur was likely still in his study at this hour, but I made a short detour to my studio first.

Inside, I couldn't help but be hit by a sense of disbelief and awe, still not used to the realization that this place was *mine*. It was everything I'd ever dreamed of, every perfect little piece, and I'd already spent hours upon hours in here. Now that the weather was growing colder, spending all day in the garden wasn't practical.

On my drafting table, I had sheets of sketches I was working on. Old sketches from my already finished stories of Kavelyn's adventures. For binding purposes, they couldn't be hidden away in my notebooks any longer. If I wanted them printed, I needed the final versions. I already had the written stories uploaded to my Halo. All I needed was the drawings that would accompany them.

That was what I planned to work on until the baby came. And every moment that I wasn't with Kaldur or visiting Syndras in the village or in the wintry garden, I was in here, sometimes late enough into the night that Kaldur had to come collect me for sleep—with charcoal smeared across my cheek and pencils jabbed into my disheveled bun.

But I wasn't here tonight to draw, though I neatened the pile, adjusting my pencils.

My gaze turned to the vase. Another of Kaldur's gifts, beautiful in its brokenness. The lines of silver added character. They looked like roots of trees, winding around the vase, or a silver river that wrapped around the painted vines.

I went to it, picking it up in my hands, admiring it as I often did. I remembered that afternoon, picking up the pieces, cutting my hand on a shard of it. Because of this vase…everything had changed.

I spun it until I could see the gaping hole in the back. The shard that I'd stolen.

Going to the drawer of my drafting table, I pulled it open and plucked out the missing shard. Every time I thought of replacing it, of fully repairing the vase, something stopped me. I stared at the gaping hole at its back and thought of all the times I'd smoothed my fingers over the sharpened edge of the shard in Laras. Turning it this way and that way in my hands, remembering Kaldur.

I had tucked it in the drawer for another day, unable to face the restlessness in my heart. But I wasn't afraid anymore.

The shard was familiar in my hand. I would need to send it to the potter to get the last piece soldered in with silver, but for now this would do.

Carefully, I placed the piece back into the vase. Its edges had crumbled away with time in my traveling bag and my repeated admiration—and even a talisman of my heartbreak and grief—so it wasn't a perfect fit. Not anymore. But that was all right. It wasn't the same as it'd been before, after all.

I stared down at the vase, stepping back to see it restored. In the morning, I'd send it to the potter, I decided.

Then I smiled. I backed out of the room and then went to go collect Kaldur from his study, feeling more at peace with myself than I had in a long time.

In a few days, the moon winds would come.
A time of rebirth.
I was finally ready.

CHAPTER 47
—
ERINA

The last time there'd been a dinner party at the keep of Vyaan, I'd had my heart broken.

But that wasn't why I was standing out on the East Terrace balcony, overlooking the garden as the chill of the wintry moon winds cut through my dress. Braanelle was in close proximity, standing near the door, looking as anxious as I'd ever seen her.

"My Lady," she kept saying, "it's much too cold and—"

"Just a moment longer," I'd said, smiling.

I felt the chill in the air, yes, but there was a wildness to the night, one that I wanted to savor. The moon winds were strong, and I closed my eyes, nearly grinning at the way they tangled my hair up, like hundreds of fingers wrapping around the waves. One gust came so strongly that I gave a cry of delight, one that nearly made Braanelle run out to save me.

The winds came and went. I'd always loved the moon winds. They were exciting to me, the fierceness of nature always humbling. I'd often stand outside in them and let them guide me, swaying or dancing. I would just let myself fall into them, a release, a submission.

I hadn't done it in quite a long time, but tonight felt like a perfect time to revisit my fond memories.

Though I would likely be a rumpled mess for dinner. I'd chosen a beautifully simple dress for the occasion, deep green in color that reminded me of the vase. The material was light as silk. Perfect for the warmth of a dinner party, especially when clothes had begun to feel more and more restrictive on me as the pregnancy progressed, but not so ideal for a winter night during a storm.

The lightness of the material made me feel exposed, vulnerable, naked. It wasn't unwelcome. In a way, it made me feel like my younger self, who would stand outside in the rain just so she could describe it perfectly for her stories.

A voice came, my eyes shooting open.

"So you're the female who has finally enthralled my brother."

I knew exactly who the Kylorr male was. I eyed him, my heart suddenly picking up with nerves as he approached me along the terrace.

Thaine of House Kaalium was dressed perfectly, just as any member of the noble family would be. His burgundy-colored vest with gold catches led to finely supple leather pants. He was more leanly defined than Kaldur, though slightly taller, coming in at nearly two heads taller than me.

And like his brother, he was distractingly handsome, though his features were edged in careful observation rather than disarming charm. He had a broad face, with a sharp nose and dagger-like cheekbones that lent him an elegance very few Kylorr possessed. His eyes, a brilliant and luminous green, of which I'd never seen a likeness to before, were hard to look away from.

Tendrils of his black hair dipped into the line of his gaze from a blowing gust of wind, but he paid it no mind.

"You're not at all what I imagined," Thaine said, "though seeing you now makes perfect sense."

My smile was uncertain, but I held his eyes as the wind whipped at me. "Thaine."

He gave me a slow grin, inclining his head. "Sister."

The title startled me enough to make me gasp.

His eyes slid down to my rounding belly, his gaze flickering with an unreadable emotion. "And my niece, or so I've heard from my brother."

I placed a hand there, unable to stop the smile from spreading. "I believe so, yes."

"The first child of a new generation," he commented. "None of my siblings would have believed it would be Kaldur. But I think I understand now."

He was observing me in a way that made me feel like a painting on a wall. Was this how Kaldur felt whenever I studied him?

"I've come to escort you back," he said. "Your mate has been searching for you. And as much as I would like to skip the entirety of the dinner, I'm afraid it's about to start."

That earned a laugh from me, his lips quirking in response as he held out his arm for me. I took it. I must've looked a mess from my time out on the balcony.

"I've never seen Kaldur like this before," came Thaine's sudden words. He stopped us halfway to the door, turning to face me, his eyes rapt on me. I felt their sudden intensity, making me swallow hard.

"Like what?" I asked softly.

"*Here,*" he said. When my brow furrowed, he explained, "Kaldur has always been ambitious. He's always been determined. He bears the weight of responsibility perhaps more seriously than any of us. But because of it he can box himself in and his frustration explodes. All of that energy needs somewhere to go. He was wild when he was younger—he'd be the first to tell you that—always testing boundaries."

"Yes," I said, uncertain, "I know."

"But he only ever got more restless as the years went by. To outsiders looking in, he was everything that everyone expected him to be. But to us, we could see what the pressure did to him. To live up to expectations that he put on himself. He could go mad with it. And so he never seemed *still*. Present. His anger could drive him, just as easily as his need for diplomacy. He was swinging between extremes, back and forth like a pendulum. And he couldn't stop himself. The last time I saw him, I believed he was at his lowest."

It twisted my heart, the Kaldur he was describing. But I could imagine him so easily because I recognized that part of Kaldur myself.

"When was that?"

"When you were in Laras and he'd barely left his keep for weeks," Thaine replied.

My heart stuttered, a breath hitching in shock. We'd never talked about what he'd done when I'd been gone. He'd only mentioned that he hadn't been well. I had seen that clearly for myself when I'd returned.

But…he'd shut himself away?

"But now?" Thaine breathed, shaking his head. "This is the best version of my brother. One I've seen only in glimpses. He feels *present*. Here. It's like you've rooted him into the earth. And I, for one, am thankful for it."

Emotion welled in me. Shock at the sweet words made tears prick my eyes, and the last thing I wanted to do was cry in front of Thaine during our first meeting.

"I wanted to tell you that, in case I didn't get the opportunity tonight," he finished, inclining his head. "I only came to meet you, but I must return to Salaire tonight."

A violent gust of wind blew over us, and Thaine moved to shield me from the worst of it, flaring his wings wide.

I was still speechless from his words, but I wanted to be honest with Kaldur's brother, whom I knew he was closest to.

"I love your brother," I said softly. Words that I wanted to tell Kaldur myself tonight. "I've loved him for a very long time. I know we don't know each other very well. But I want you to know…I'll be by his side, no matter what."

Thaine studied me, his gaze flicking back and forth between my eyes. He seemed content with whatever he found. "They're waiting for you," he finally said, guiding me from the terrace and into the keep.

When we reached the candlelit dining hall, we found everyone already seated and dozens and dozens of different pairs of eyes turned to regard us. They swung from Kaldur, who was at the head of the table, an empty chair directly next to him. Mine?

My mate was standing, looking as though we'd interrupted a speech. I realized I'd lost track of time out on the terrace, just as I'd often done in the starlight hallway, daydreaming away.

But instead of looking irritated by it, Kaldur only gave me a grin that made my heartbeat triple in speed. I thought that, perhaps, it was so loud even Thaine could hear it next to me.

I was a mess. My windswept hair and flushed cheeks. The green dress was snagged around my ankles, twisting oddly around my unmistakable bump that caused more than a few whispers to reverberate through the dinner.

But the way Kaldur was looking at me? It made me feel like the most beautiful female in the universe.

I saw Syndras smiling at me from near my empty chair. Maudoric was in attendance as well, not as a keeper but as a guest, dressed in a pretty silver frock. I recognized a few of the nobles—old friends of House Kaalium, I knew. One House I did not see, however, was House Azola. Lydrasa hadn't been invited.

It was an intimate dinner compared to the last one that had graced House Kaalium.

And compared to those in attendance, I looked perfectly out of place, and yet I only beamed at Kaldur, who made me feel like I finally belonged.

His voice raised again. "I was just thanking our guests for joining us for the moon winds," he informed me, a little twinkle in his gaze, though it was curious when it traced to Thaine at my side. "You're just in time."

Even across the room, I felt pulled by his gaze.

It flicked briefly to his guests before it returned to me. "Tonight is a special night, not only because of the moon winds. At this table are some of our closest friends, friends of my family and of House Kaalium for generations. And tonight I wanted to introduce to you all my *kyrana*, Erina Denoren."

Surprise whistled through me as more whispers erupted through the room. There were dozens of guests in attendance. Kaldur knew exactly what he was doing. By morning, all of Vyaan would know my name. They would know Kaldur had claimed a female of his own, they would know of our child.

I was glad that Thaine was holding my arm because my knees might've trembled under the weight of the stares. But I only kept Kaldur's gaze, blinking back the sudden tears.

"Erina," Kaldur said, and it was like the guests fell away. Until it was only us. "You're everything I ever wanted—a soft place to come home to, an embrace I would forever seek. Once I was too blind and proud to see that you are the only person in this universe for me. But never again."

This was a very public declaration of his love, romantic and stunning. It was a new start, with my name intertwined with his for all of Vyaan to know.

I was warm and flushed. I swore I even heard Syndras sniff at the end. This was like something out of my stories, only made real.

Then I heard a voice that cut through the warmth like an icy shard.

"That was very touching," Lydrasa of House Azola declared. "I knew you were always a romantic at heart, *Kyzaire*."

She strode into the dining hall in a beautiful red dress from the opposite door, closest to the entrance. Kaldur's expression darkened.

"Sorry I'm late," Lydrasa said. "Where should I sit?"

CHAPTER 48
—
KALDUR

"How dare you," Lydrasa hissed when I pulled her into an empty room out of earshot. "For centuries House Azola has always been at your table, Kaldur. It's the highest of insults. Everyone is already talking. And if you thought I'd lie down and—"

"You're lucky I didn't do worse," I said simply, keeping my temper in check.

But just knowing that Lydrasa's betrayal had only driven a larger wedge between my mate and me, she was lucky I hadn't made an example of her entire family. Once, House Kaalium had not been so *diplomatic*. There was a reason my ancestors had once been feared. Never had I been tempted to return to such use of power, but with Lydrasa, I was *really fucking close*.

What stopped me was the realization that I didn't want to be that kind of leader. For a socialite, her own punishment would be the expulsion of her House from noble society, of which she'd placed the highest of values. It would be a slow death. And only that would satisfy me.

If it was known that House Kaalium didn't do business with House Azola any longer, if they were no longer welcome to the keep, others would want to know why. And they would discover that Lydrasa had betrayed my trust, that she'd forged a letter in my hand with the sole purpose of sowing discord within my own family. She'd tried to keep my *pregnant* blood mate away from me, making her believe that I'd turned my own back on her.

Just remembering that made my blood boil, but I kept my temper in check. My mate was in the next room, as were dozens of other *invited* guests.

"You're making a fool of yourself," I said, glaring. "Barging into my keep and making a scene in front of my guests? That's a little shocking, especially for you, Lydrasa. But I suppose when one is desperate and backed into a corner, there's no telling what they'll do."

Lydrasa's nostrils flared. "It was one letter. What does it matter? You got her back. I was doing it to help you, Kaldur."

"To help me?" I asked, hissing as disgust burned through me. I wouldn't give her the satisfaction of my hatred. Truthfully I wished I could forget that Lydrasa even existed. I couldn't believe that once, I'd believed she was a friend.

"Krynn is on the cusp of war," she snapped. "We need to show strength right now. Not weakness. *She* is a weakness."

"She is my *kyrana*," I growled. "Weakness? I could raze down this entire territory on a drop of her blood. How it that for weakness? Standing at my side, that makes her one of the most powerful females in the Kaalium, don't you think?"

Lydrasa's jaw tightened.

"But you didn't know that. Not for certain. You suspected, but you wished it wasn't true," I finished. "Why? Because you were always jealous. It wasn't even about my affections. You knew I never cared for you in that way. But you always wanted to be *first*. You always wanted to be *seen*. That's why you did what you did. You can stand here and try to lie that you were doing it for the Kaalium. We both know you were doing it out of spite."

She glared. "That's not true."

"I won't waste my breath anymore," I said, straightening. I wanted to get back to Erina, not argue with a female I'd once believed was an ally. "But let me make one thing clear: Fuck with my House again, Lydrasa, and I will burn yours down. Go near my *kyrana* or my child again and you'd better make friends with the Thryki because no one will welcome you in the Kaalium any longer."

"You don't mean that," she said, a thread of fear *finally* lighting up in her eyes.

Kythel would be proud because my tone was controlled and ice cold when I said, "If you think I won't, then you never knew me at all. Because what's the one thing I would do anything for to protect? At all costs? My family. Don't underestimate the lengths I will go to for them."

The door swung open, and Erina stepped inside the room. Her scent seemed to envelope me as she approached, and I breathed her in deep to keep my control.

"Listening at the door again, are we?" Lydrasa rumbled, annoyed, as if she'd heard nothing of what I'd just said.

I growled in warning, but Erina touched my chest, her palm firm.

"It's best if you leave, Lydrasa," she said, voice quiet but calm. "Braanelle will see you out if you choose not to go."

Her personal guard appeared in the doorway, arms crossed, ready to intervene if necessary.

"You don't want a scene," my mate continued. "You don't want to be the talk of the village come morning. Leave now to save your family the embarrassment. Let this be."

She was much too kind, even to the female who'd thought nothing of her.

Braanelle stepped further into the room, and Lydrasa snapped, "I'm going. Don't touch me."

"Will you tell me one thing before you go?" Erina asked. She didn't wait for Lydrasa to respond. "How's Velle?"

Lydrasa scoffed. "Working in my House."

My mate had much too big of a heart. Even now, she asked about the friend who'd helped betray her. But I knew that they'd been friends once. And Erina had told me why she chose to forgive. Because it was her power, her choice to make. No one could take that from her.

"And her lover?"

"He changed his mind," Lydrasa said, sliding past. She cut me a sharp look. "That's the thing about hearts. They're always *so* fickle."

Then she swept from the room.

"Always one to have the last fucking word," I sighed, pinching the space between my brows.

Braanelle followed after Lydrasa, to make sure she left. I took Erina into my arms. "Are you all right?"

"I'm fine," she said, looking up at me, giving me a small smile. She actually *was*. The encounter didn't seem to have phased her in the slightest.

"I'll deal with her later," I promised.

"Don't," she said. "She heard you. Loud and clear. And if she knows what's best, she'd be wise to fear your warning. I don't think she'll cause any more trouble. She wouldn't risk it. I've worked for nobles like her before."

I wasn't so certain we'd seen the last of Lydrasa, but for once, I wanted to be a little optimistic like my mate.

"Besides, don't give her that power," Erina said, sliding her hand over my chest again.

"You're right."

I pressed my lips to her cheek, savoring her warmth as I tried to forget about Lydrasa. Erina had the right idea. Why give her the satisfaction of my anger? She deserved nothing from me.

"Did you like my speech tonight?" I asked, to try to take her mind from the sourness of Lydrasa's unexpected presence.

My lips were trailing to hers, and so I felt, rather than saw, her smile. "Yes. Though it took me by surprise."

"What was surprising about it?" I asked, confused.

"That you said it in front of everyone," she said, pulling back to look up into my expression. "Now they'll all talk. Aren't you worried about what they'll say? That I'm the keeper who manipulated you and trapped you with a child?"

Her tone was soft, almost teasing. She cared about what people might think of me, now that the truth was out. It was what I'd feared after all, to have history repeat itself within these walls of the keep.

And I realized I didn't care. Because this was me and Erina.

"I'll tell them the truth if they dare to ask," I said, grinning.

"And what truth is that?"

"That you didn't trap me in the slightest," I said. "I'll tell them that I wanted you so much that I briefly lost my mind with it."

"Is that what happened?" she asked, laughing a little.

"You were there that night," I grumbled. "I would say that's an accurate assessment of what happened. I could barely see straight, I wanted you so much. Looking back, I think I was a little in love with you already. And half-mad with jealousy because I thought you loved someone else."

"All right," she said, going up onto her tiptoes to press a kiss to my cheek. "That's what you can tell people."

"Good. I'm glad we're in agreement."

"Me too," she said. "Now, let's get back to the party. I'm starving."

CHAPTER 49

—

ERINA

After our guests had departed and Thaine had left to return to Salaire, I led Kaldur through the keep. He was confused when I made an impromptu detour, heading not to the South Wing but to the North one. Yet he was patient, his gaze twinkling, as he wondered where I was taking him.

I walked a few paces ahead of him, looking back over my shoulder every hallway to see if he was still following. His lips would twitch. He watched me as if I were his prey, tracking me from the darkness, playful even in his confusion and looking so handsome in his dinner attire that it made me ache.

When we reached the North Wing, I went to the starlight hallway. Through the stained glass, with the full moon shining, it looked like stars speared through the darkness. The souls were active tonight, but I wasn't afraid. They were curious, inquisitive, but harmless.

"Why come here?" he murmured, snagging me from behind when I stepped into the hallway.

"I like this place," I told him, smoothing my hand over his. "No one comes here, except the old souls, and I didn't want to be interrupted."

I looked back at him before turning in his arms. "Do you mind it?"

His smile was wry. "Truthfully I hated this hallway as a boy. I would come to Vyaan often, to learn from my uncle when he was still in power over the territory. And I always avoided it when I could. Most times, I still do."

"Why?"

"I could always feel the lost souls here. And I always hated that I felt powerless. I couldn't help them."

"Just because you can't help them doesn't mean you should ignore them," I answered. "Besides, I've always thought a *zylarr* would be helpful in this hallway. Just there."

I gestured to a place where the hall protruded outward in a decorative half circle. A small table was there now, but a *zylarr*, a feeding place for souls, would be perfect.

"You've given this a lot of thought," he commented.

"I love this hallway," I told him. "It's one of my favorite places in the keep. I get lost here sometimes, maybe just like the souls."

"And why do you like it?" he wanted to know, smoothing back a wild wave from my face.

"Because it feels like how stories do. Like you can be transported to another place," I said. "Here the world goes quiet. It's like an endless night, one filled with starlight, even on the sunniest of days. It's like magic. To me, that's what stories are. Little moments of magic…in an otherwise normal day."

His gaze was soft as he listened to me. "I do like the way your mind works, *kyrana*."

He seemed loath to look away, but he considered the hallway with new eyes, observing the stained-glass windows, no two the same, and the darkness beyond.

"A *zylarr* for the souls? Consider it done," Kaldur murmured, pressing a kiss to my temple. "Any other requests?"

Suddenly I was nervous. I'd gone over the words in my head multiple times, and still they didn't sound right. I'd even written them out, practicing them. But all my attempts now seemed silly in the face of reality.

This was Kaldur, after all. He appreciated directness and simplicity.

His lips quirked in confusion when I stared up at him. "What is it?"

"I…I lo—"

He flinched, jerking his head to the right. "A soul touched me."

"Well," I bit out, my heart racing, "a *zylarr* would certainly help. Like I was—"

He inhaled sharply again, his wing flaring as if brushing something away.

"Another one," he murmured. *"Raazos's blood."*

His other wing flared out, and I laughed out of nerves and hysterics.

"Kaldur."

"Why are there so many suddenly? It's—"

"Kaldur, I'm trying to tell you that I love you!" I rushed out in a breathless laugh.

His breath inhaled in a sharp whistle, his wings frozen and hovering after trying to bat away unseen souls, those silver eyes pinned on me.

"Only, it's not going quite how I planned. Nothing with you seems to and yet it's always just how it's meant to be," I said, smiling up at him as tears made my vision waver. "Perfect."

A long beat of silence passed. Then…

"Say it again," he growled.

I softened, relief making me dizzy. Such simple words, and yet…they'd meant everything to me.

I held his eyes. I reached up to touch his lips, feeling them part between my fingertips. "I love you," I said quietly as the moon winds howled outside the hallway. "I've loved you since I first saw you the day I came to work in your keep. I thought that it was an innocent love. But now I think a part of my soul recognized you as mine that day, and it's been captured by you ever since."

"Erina," he murmured. He processed the words before the corner of his left lip lifted. He looked pensive or perhaps nostalgic—I couldn't be certain. All I knew was that the way he was studying me made me feel like it the first time seeing him all over again. All fluttering pulses and electric excitement.

Then he sighed, a small laugh escaping him. Kaldur took my face into his palms, cupping my cheeks.

"I never told you this, but two years ago I started feeling like a stranger in my own body," he said.

"What?" I asked, smiling a little in confusion, still feeling the adrenaline rush of my confession. "What are you talking about?"

"There was this terrible restlessness, like I could never be still. This ache that made me want to crawl out of my skin. It clawed at me at all hours of the day and night, like my body was seeking something. Or someone."

A sharp realization made dismay fill me.

"It was hell. Sometimes it was difficult to sleep," he admitted, but his expression was gentle. "That's why I was so…manic. Why I…" He sighed. "Why I went through females like blood. Sex was the only thing that gave me some relief from that feeling."

I found I wasn't jealous. It was a startling realization, but I knew he was being honest. We'd promised to be honest. And I knew that those females had come before…and that none would come after me. That truth rang clear, settling the uncertainty I'd felt. But to learn that Kaldur had been trying to escape the feeling, had been trying to drown the sensation with sexual release… it made sense. What he was describing—I felt anyone would go mad with it.

"Two years, I was like that. Two years…around when you came to work in the keep," he finished. "It was because of you, Erina."

"Kaldur, I'm sorry," I breathed. "If I'd known—"

"I wouldn't change anything," he said, his tone steady and uncertain. "I would go through decades of that hell if it would eventually lead me to you."

Oh.

"Just the mere promise of it," he said. "I tell you this now because…well, you say that a part of your soul recognized mine when you first saw me? So did mine. A part of me always knew you were near. And I always think…if only I'd *looked* at you, really looked at you, I would have seen my future so clearly. We both could've saved ourselves a lot of heartache."

"You weren't ready to see," I said. "And I wasn't nearly prepared to accept. We needed that time. I realize now that everything happened as it was meant to. I, too, wouldn't change anything at all. Because we got to this place."

His smile was bright. "The place where you love me. Again."

I laughed. "Yes."

I loved him with every jagged piece of me. Every piece of me that had been heartbroken, every piece of me that had been mistrustful and lonely. Every piece of me that admired him in the careful lines of my sketches, a face I could never escape because he was always at the forefront of my mind, my constant companion. He had filled those empty places of my heart with patience and steadiness.

He was in my stories. He was in my dreams. I fell asleep beside him, and I woke to him every beautiful dawn.

And I wanted to do that for the rest of my life.

I took a deep breath, sliding my hands around his neck, curling my fingers into his black hair. His eyes were molten and watchful.

"I do have one more request, besides the *zylarr*," I said.

"Tell me."

"You offered your name to me once," I said. His eyes flared in *want,* and seeing it made me breathless. "I wasn't ready to take it then. But I am now. If the offer still stands."

"Do you know what that name means?" Kaldur asked quietly, his eyes pinned to mine. He seemed to be holding his breath. "That you'll be the *Kylaira* of Vyaan. My wife."

"Yes," I whispered, shy at the title. "I know."

A sharp sound escaped him.

Kaldur's kiss was soft, a mere brush of his lips as if he were savoring the words that had just left mine. Then it deepened as I clung to his shoulders. Between us, our child, due in a handful of short weeks, shifted. And she was safe between us. Healthy.

My family, I thought, smiling as joyous tears burned the backs of my eyes. What had I ever done to deserve this blessing?

"You'll marry me?" he asked, and I felt his heart thundering against my palm. "You'll be my wife, *dallia*?"

"Yes," I breathed. "I will."

"Erina Denoren of House Kaalium, *Kylaira* of Vyaan," he said, grinning. His silver eyes twinkled in the starlight hallway as the moon winds raged, wild and wondrous.

Then he sealed my name with his kiss.

EPILOGUE
—
ERINA

$\mathcal{S}$ ix weeks later, our daughter was born. A perfect girl with light gray skin and blue eyes, which I hoped one day might turn silver like her father's.

She had no wings, but she had budding horns that Kaldur would run the pad of his finger over in awe, ever careful with his claws.

We named her Alysara. In the Kylorr tongue, it meant *beautiful dawn*. After a full day of labor, the name was fitting, considering she'd been born just as the sun had crested over the forests of Vyaan. And that morning, when I'd held her in my arms for the first time, with tears streaming down my cheeks, as hair had clung to my damp forehead, all the pain had been forgotten and I'd never seen anything more beautiful in my entire life than our daughter.

It was the first time I'd seen Kaldur cry.

Perhaps in sheer relief, considering the delivery had been difficult. He'd stayed at my side every moment, a pillar of strength seeing me through. But there had been times when I'd caught the stray edge of fear he couldn't hide, as if confronted again with the possibility of losing his mate.

But then I'd watched my husband, my mate fall in love with our daughter, with glassy eyes and a quiet expression, his hands hovering over her like he could conjure a shield around her, to keep her forever safe.

He'd pressed his lips to her forehead as she'd wailed with life, flaring his wings over us so that Ekor and the handful of midwives he'd had at the ready couldn't see our very private moment. They'd filed out of the room, leaving us alone so that we could coo over our child, admiring every little part.

And in the days that followed, we tucked ourselves away in the keep. Mostly for me to recover my strength and for Kaldur to watch over me. He didn't let anyone disturb us, only Ekor to check on me and Maudoric, who he would never say no to. I would wake sometimes to find Kaldur holding Alysara by the window, rocking her back to sleep, the tiny bundle of blankets in his arms laughably small against the bulk of his body. I'd never known such peace, such joy and love as I did in those moments. If she was awake, however, he'd bring her to come feed. I'd feel the pinch of her latching onto my breast, contentment and relief flowing through me, as Kaldur watched.

And in the weeks that followed, once I could leave the bed and we got a better handle on our new routine and life with our daughter, we welcomed his family to meet their newest member of House Kaalium. Azur and Gemma, who had a wonderful calm about her that immediately made me feel at ease, though I'd been nervous about meeting them. Kythel and Millie, the stoic and quiet Kylorr male a complete contrast to the warm openness of his wife. Thaine and Lucen.

Kalia, Kaldur's only sister, pressed her lips to my cheeks when she met me, embracing me tightly. "Welcome, sister," she whispered so no one else could hear. And I sunk into her, a feeling of *belonging* finally hitting me with the words. They made me feel like I belonged in this family, like I wasn't out of place. For one the oldest legacies in all the Kaalium, they made an orphan girl feel like she'd finally found a permanent place to call home.

Kalia had much to say about how we'd wed without inviting the family, however. Kaldur and I hadn't wanted to wait to be married, though it was certainly out of the ordinary for a *Kyzaire*'s wedding to be so rushed. Though Azur and Gemma had married off-planet, in a quick and cold ceremony at a Nulaxy courthouse, so they came to our defense.

In the end, Kaldur merely said he couldn't wait to be married to me, and it seemed to please Kalia enough that she let it drop. With the promise, however, that she would throw us a celebration ball when we were next in Laras. Only when we agreed did she let it go.

They all doted on Alysara, naturally—especially and surprisingly Thaine.

But inevitably they needed to return to their respective territories, though Kalia lingered in Vyaan a week longer than the rest. Which I thought relieved Kaldur because he had someone he trusted to watch over me—with the exception of Braanelle—when he had to be away in the villages.

Eventually she too left, murmuring about an obligation in Laras she couldn't put off. And while the keep certainly felt quieter after her departure, having my husband and my daughter all to myself again was a relief.

The first night the keep was quiet again, Kaldur put Alysara to sleep in our bed, her little face scrunched against his bare chest, his wide palm over her back. He'd dozed on and off, his tiredness a combination of helping with her late night feedings and Vyaan business, and I found I could watch them forever. Instead of reaching for my sketchbook, one of which I always kept near, I simply enjoyed the moment, tracing over the lines of their bodies, the quietness of their expressions, the movements of Kaldur's chest which made Alysara lift and fall.

In that moment, and in many more, I knew true happiness

and love. And it was more beautiful and awe-inspiring than I could've ever dreamed up.

"There's someone here for you," Kaldur whispered into my ear after he came into my studio. He glanced over at Alysara, napping in the little bassinet we'd set up for her near my drafting table. His gaze went soft, as it always did when he looked at his daughter. He reached down to smooth his finger across her cheek, as if he couldn't help himself.

"Who?" I whispered back, feeling a swell of pride and affection fill me when I looked down at Aly. *Perfection,* I thought.

"A surprise," Kaldur said, meeting my eyes again. "Out on the garden terrace. I'll watch her. You go."

I looked down at the last of my drawings for Kavelyn's book. The final one before I could send everything to the printer to be bound and distributed. A hundred copies would go to each territory to start. I was so close, I could taste it. A dream finally coming true.

Curiosity drove me out of the room after one last lingering kiss on Alysara's cheek. I navigated the keep until I found the door of the garden terrace in the East Wing, Braanelle waiting just beyond it, always on duty. But I didn't think that was who Kaldur had meant.

Instead I spied a familiar head of dark hair through the glass door. I gasped, pulling it open, my heart thudding.

The hybrid Kylorr male turned when he heard me. Blue eyes pierced me.

"Luc," I breathed, happy, confused, hopeful, relieved. I stood, frozen on the terrace in front of him as I tried to understand how he'd come to be here.

But then...

Kaldur.

Of course.

"Erina," he said, his lips lifting in a half smile, uncertain as he studied me. There was a wash of emotion that entered his eyes, his gaze going over me, studying my still-recovering body from the birth, the slight rounding of my belly still apparent. "I— I'm so…"

I heard what went unspoken, the hurried words clogging up in his throat, as if he couldn't wait another moment to get them out.

His eyes were glassy enough that he closed them, as a pinching of ache darted through my chest.

I went to him, wrapping my arms tight around him. I was glad that he didn't feel so…*transparent*. It was an odd word, but it was the only one I could think of. Back in Laras, he'd looked like he'd been a moment away from fading away. So unlike the confident and brash Luc I'd once known.

"I'm so glad you're here," I whispered into his ear, up on my tiptoes. I didn't trust my voice. I could barely see through the blurring of my eyes.

"Are you?" he asked, his voice tight with uncertainty.

I pulled back with a frown, keeping a grip on his arms as if he'd fly away. I wiped at my cheek. "Of course I am. How can you ask that?"

Luc closed his eyes again, and I heard his rough swallow. "In Laras…I… That day haunts me. The things I said. I know I just got here, but let me say this. I've thought of nothing else."

I nodded.

He took a deep breath. "Seeing you again, it was startling. It made me feel ashamed, and I just wanted to leave. To disappear so you didn't see me anymore." His eyes fastened on me, despair in his gaze. "I'm sorry, Erina. I don't know how I thought I could turn my back on you. I guess…I thought I was doing you a favor. Or else I feared I'd drag you down too."

His explanation brought a clog of emotion into my throat, one that I struggled to loosen up. "You're my brother, Luc."

He inhaled a deep breath at the words.

"You'll always be," I said. "I have seen you at your best, and I've seen you at your worst. If you think that one day would've changed my love for you…you know me better than that."

"I do," he said quietly. "I do. I…I got your letter."

Hope burst in my chest as I led him over to the bench down the steps of the terrace. It would afford us more privacy, away from Braanelle, though still within a distance that would please her.

"You went back to Kyndri's?"

He nodded. "She told me you'd left already. And I wanted to come back to Vyaan, to speak with you, to ask you to forgive me for how I treated you. But I didn't know if you wanted to see me. Not yet."

"I always want to see you," I told him. "That's never changed."

A hesitant smile *finally* creeped over his features. He was so much older than I remembered, but I swore I could still spy the boy I'd grown up with underneath it all. I was pleased to note that his clothes looked new, clean. The shadows across his face weren't quite so deep, and there wasn't the bone-aching defeat I'd spied in his eyes in Laras.

"I was going to come see you, was saving for a ticket to Vyaan," he told me, "because I didn't think a mere letter would be sufficient. But then…House Kaalium's ambassador found me."

My lips quirked, and I hung on to his hand, squeezing. "He said you gave him quite the rough time."

"I didn't believe him. Not as first," Luc said simply. "It was hard to trust again, you know? Especially a noble House." I nodded…because I *did*. "But then the *Kyzaire* of Laras visited me himself."

Shock made me jolt. "Azur spoke with you?"

Kaldur hadn't told me that.

Luc nodded. "That's when I finally realized that it was real and not some big farce. I…I had no idea you were connected to them. That you—that you would do that for me."

A quietness dropped between us as we regarded one another.

"And now you're a mother," he said, his voice choking up again. "A wife. A *Kylaira* of the territory we grew up in. But ultimately you're still *you*, Erina. I can still see *you* even though everything has changed. The dreamer, the romantic, the forever optimist. You never lost that. And after we spoke in Laras, it gave me hope. It made me want to be the boy you once knew because I saw the disappointment on your face when you'd realized I'd lost him somewhere."

My brows scrunched down. "Luc—"

"You made me realize I'd given up, and that's not who I wanted to be. That's not who we *vowed* to be all those years ago. And I came searching for you at Kyndri's to tell you that," he said. "Then a week later, the ambassador found me. I put up a fight at first, but…then I accepted the help. And it was all because of you. I came here because I wanted to thank you, Erina. Thank you for not giving up on me. Thank you for keeping me in your heart all these long years, even when I didn't make it easy. You saved me. You really did."

The tears that dripped down my face were both happy and sad.

"It was you who saved me, Luc," I told him.

The confusion flashed over his features.

"I am who I am because of you," I said. "You were a parent, a brother, and a friend. You never had to be, but you chose to be. I never forgot that. You encouraged me to be *better*. I allowed myself my dreams because of you. You have nothing to thank me for. I'm only happy you're here."

"You'll forgive me?" he asked quietly.

"Of course," I breathed, leaning forward to wrap my arms

around his neck, embracing him. "You're here now. That's all that matters. Nothing else."

We embraced longer, a sense of relief snaking through both of us. Luc was a wound that had never quite healed since Laras. He'd always been a restless question, a worried ache in my mind. Kaldur knew that. He'd made this happen—he'd brought Luc here to make me happy.

Every day it seemed I found more reasons to love my husband a little more, and I'd already thought that an impossible feat.

"One day I want to come see the shop in Laras," I told him. "All right?"

"You're always welcome. When you get them printed, I'll stock Kavelyn's books. A big display, right in the front window, so everyone can see them. Just as you always dreamed."

Tears stung my eyes. Happy ones. I pulled back.

"I'd *love* that."

We grinned at one another.

"Come," I said, taking his hand before standing, wiping away my tears. "It's time for you to meet your niece."

"ANOTHER SURPRISE?" I ASKED, MY LAUGH A LITTLE DISBELIEVING. "I don't know if I can take much more."

Kaldur's gaze practically twinkled, and I heard his unspoken thought. A naughty twist of my words that left me blushing.

"You can, my love," he purred. Which was exactly what he'd told me the last time we'd had sex—before the birth—when I'd moaned into his ear.

While Kaldur had *finally* resumed his feedings from me, he still wanted to wait another week to be physically intimate again. Which made me impatient, considering we'd gotten the go-ahead from Ekor. But the last thing Kaldur wanted to do was hurt me, especially after a difficult labor, which I thought still haunted him a little. He was being cautious, and while it frustrated me, I also loved him for it.

His hand was curled around my hip, tucking me close to his body. The gardens were a wintry, quiet paradise this time of the year. Not a soul was around us, even though it was a beautiful sunset.

"I can't tell you enough how much seeing Luc meant to me," I said, enjoying the private moment with my mate. "Thank you."

He leaned down to press a kiss to my temple. "He was already looking for you. Finding him was easy. A small thing."

"But a wonderful thing," I said. "You make me happy. So very happy."

If I thought Kaldur could ever look *shy*, I saw the expression flit across his face at that exact moment.

"That's all I want," he said quietly, meeting my eyes. "To make you as happy as you make me."

A bloom of warmth made me take a deep breath. Sometimes I thought my heart could pound so fast and hard it might burst out of my chest.

"But what's this surprise, now?" I asked. He was leading me further into the garden, past the starwood bloom courtyard, the indigo flowers finally having gone dormant for the season, their crawling vines retracting. Very near to the Orchard, there was a new section that had recently been created. At the center was a large tear-shaped planter bed, which was the meeting point for multiple different pathways, all leading to different parts of the garden.

"This is your surprise," he told me.

In the center of the planter bed was a tree. A gnarled tree with thick ropes of bark that trailed up its dark trunk. It didn't have any leaves in winter and the trunk was rather slim, but I gasped nevertheless.

My lips parted, awe touching the edges of my mind.

"Is that…?" I breathed.

"Yes," Kaldur said, smiling as he saw my reaction. "It is."

"But…"

A *dallia* tree.

A walking tree, though it looked like it'd planted its root deep into the earth of the planter bed. It had made the alcove its home.

"It wandered off in the Orchard this morning, but it seems to like this spot," Kaldur told me. "Though I thought we lost it a couple days ago. I found it near the starwood blooms, by the moon dial."

Astonished, I approached the tree eagerly. "Hello there," I greeted softly. "Pleased to meet you."

Then I pressed my hand onto the trunk, and I felt the whole tree shiver, as if saying it was happy to make my acquaintance too.

"Where…wherever did you find one?" I asked, grinning.

"In Salaire," Kaldur told me, regarding me with a small smile a few paces away. "Thaine often wanders the forests there. He discovered it, and he knew I'd been searching for one for you. It had been quite weak from the harsh winter. I wasn't sure if it would survive the journey here, but…it pulled through. It's been very active in the gardens, which is a good sign."

"I'll take care of it," I promised. "I'll bring Aly. She'll love it, especially when she grows older."

Kaldur's lips quirked. "I thought you might say that."

The bark was rough beneath my hand, its bough swaying above me.

My husband came up beside me. I beamed up at him, feeling my love for him, for how thoughtful and kind he always was radiate through me.

I'd never been wrong about him, I thought. Once, I'd lost faith that I had been. But now I knew I could trust my instincts when it came to him.

"You're wonderful," I whispered, going up onto my tiptoes to press a kiss to his jawline. "Thank you."

"Don't thank me yet," he murmured. His gaze went back to the *dallia* tree. "Maybe it will leave. Or maybe it will choose to stay. Regardless, I like to imagine it here. Wandering the garden with you, with Aly, watching over you both like a guardian. It's young still. It'll grow with our daughter."

I smiled at the picture he painted. A wonderful one.

"I would like that," I said against his skin. When I pulled back, I said, "I'll do everything to convince our *dallia* to stay."

"Just as I did to you," he said quietly, those silver eyes capturing mine and holding them.

"Yes." I laughed. "I suppose so."

His arms came around me, and I sighed into his embrace, pressing my cheek into his chest, feeling the solid pump of his heartbeat. Forever comforting and reassuring.

"You're everything," I said, leaning back to meet his *zylarr* eyes, trapping me like a wandering soul. "You're everything I had hoped you would be and more. I love you. Each day it astonishes me how much."

Kaldur's eyes turned fierce and molten. He leaned down to capture my lips in a hard, claiming kiss. I grinned and melted into it, clutching onto his vest when my knees threatened to tremble.

"My *kyrana*," he murmured. "I'll choose to be by your side forever."

"Just like the fable of the *dallia* tree," I whispered. Then I grinned sheepishly. "At least, in *my* version."

"Yes, you're very good at rewriting endings, after all," he teased. "Thank the gods for it."

He captured my laugh with another kiss.

Beside us, the *dallia* tree swayed, its bare branches creaking like it was making music on the crisp winter evening.

And it was like magic. Just like stories. Just like our daughter. Just like a peaceful dawn.

Just like *us*.

Want to hear about new releases,
exclusive giveaways, and get access to **bonus
content,** like extended epilogues and character art?

Sign up for my newsletter:

**If you're already subscribed to my
newsletter, access all bonus content here:**

www.ZoeyDraven.com/bonus-content

ACKNOWLEDGMENTS

To Naomi, my rockstar PA and friend. Thanks for plotting out this book with me on a random October night when we were both half-dead from packing up Kickstarter orders. This book would not have been what it is without you.

To Mandi, thanks for being such a fantastic editor over all these years, even when I'm being a hot mess author when it comes to deadlines. Also, I live for your GIF reactions when I'm going through your edits!

Thank you to Jay, my wonderful cover designer for this series. To my author buddies, Juliette and Emma, who are always so supportive. Can't wait to see you both at ApollyCon!

To all my friends and family, who put up with me when I'm deep in the writing cave. <3

And of course, to all my readers, who are always so amazing. Your enthusiasm and excitement for this series keeps me going. Thank you!

CONNECT WITH ZOEY

SCAN THE QR CODE BELOW WITH YOUR PHONE TO ACCESS HER LINKS:

I'm mostly hanging out on Instagram. Come say hi!

ABOUT THE AUTHOR

Zoey Draven has been writing stories for as long as she can remember. Her love affair with the romance genre started with her grandmother's old Harlequin paperbacks and has continued ever since. As an Amazon Top 50 bestselling author, now she gets to write the happily-ever-afters—with an otherworldly twist, of course! She is the author of Sci-Fi and Fantasy Romance books, such as the *Horde Kings of Dakkar* and the *Brides of the Kylorr* series.

When she's not writing, she's probably drinking one too many cups of coffee, hiking in the redwoods, or spending time with her family.

Website: www.ZoeyDraven.com
Facebook group: Zoey's Reader Zone

facebook.com/zoeydraven
instagram.com/zoey.draven
pinterest.com/zoeydraven
threads.net/@zoey.draven